"DON'T YOU DARE LEAVE ME HERE LIKE THIS!"

Nicole grabbed for his arm, just grazing the superfine material of his jacket.

Holt swung back to face her. "Sounds *real* menacing, kid." He walked toward her until they stood only a foot apart. "You gonna pull a gun on me again?" With the toe of his boot he lifted the hem of her gown as if to peek beneath it. "Got one hidden under that tent?"

She swung at him then, but he captured her fist easily within his. He pulled her flush against him. "You know what the problem is, kid?" His lips were so close she could almost savor his breath, a seductive combination of cognac, tobacco, and the sheer sweet taste of him. Slowly, his hands relaxed their grip and he ran his callused fingers up her bare shoulders to her neck, his thumbs massaging the pulse points there. His lips grazed her cheek; he gently nuzzled her neck, sending chills down her spine to her toes. "It's frustration, pure and simple." He blew the words softly into her ear, making her tingle. His mouth brushed against her earlobe, his whispered words a caress. "It's because we both want this something fierce."

He stroked her neck with his lips, then kissed the curve of her cheek. His arms wrapped around her, and his fingers found the bare flesh of her back. Nicole arched toward him, feeling his warmth surround her.

"God, I want you." He kissed her then, a fierce coupling of their mouths. His tongue plunged deep within her, touching hidden recesses until she could feel her toes curl. "I want you, Nicky."

She tried to push him away, knowing she had played a terrible game, and lost. But when he finally released her, he did so with such gentleness, she almost wished she'd not initiated her retreat. . . .

White Tiger

OLGA BICOS

A DELL BOOK

Published by
Dell Publishing
a division of
Bantam Doubleday Dell Publishing Group, Inc.
666 Fifth Avenue
New York, New York 10103

This book is a work of fiction. Names, characters, places, and incidents are either the product of the author's imagination or are used fictitiously. Any resemblance to actual events or locales or persons, living or dead, is entirely coincidental.

ISBN: 0-440-20723-1

Printed in the United States of America

Published simultaneously in Canada

October 1991

10 9 8 7 6 5 4 3 2 1

RAD

The
Hunt

The Rajput is always at the front of a fight; the wall will give way before the Rajput falls.

A proverb

1

Kumaon District of the Northwestern Provinces, India: 1860

Katherine Nicole Marshall stared into the gold, feral eyes, captivated by their beauty. She shook her head, dispelling the enchantment, and cocked the second barrel of her rifle. Jamming the walnut stock of her gun into her shoulder, she aimed directly at the leopard.

A whisper of a breeze rippled through the elephant grass, veiling the cat for a split second. Perspiration itched down her brow as the leopard came into view once more. Big, larger than she'd ever imagined, the animal curiously mimicked her inspection. Spreading her legs wide for balance, Nicole trained her gaze down the sights of her Purdy. The cat's powerful muscles bunched.

No more hedging. It was time to shoot.

Slowly, she pulled the trigger back . . . back . . . then eased her finger off the metal.

The leopard remained crouched in the grass. Waiting. Watching.

Her heart pounded; the breath caught in her chest. What was wrong with her? She was a hunter. Why did she hesitate? She struggled to recapture the excitement she felt hunting back home in England. Her legs would be ankle deep in frigid water, the tall reeds a concealing wall around her while the servants waited to release the retrievers circling on the banks. She was a crack shot. She enjoyed pitting herself against the other hunters, always coming away with the greater prize.

Tearing her gaze away from the leopard's eyes—eyes almost the same shade of gold as her own—she flipped her thick black braid over her shoulder and focused on the animal's pelt. She studied the inky rosettes for the best target.

Pull the trigger, girl, her uncle's barked instructions echoed in her head. *Show me what you're made of! Shoot before the prize gets away.* She could almost see her uncle's smile of pride when she showed off the leopard—*a magnificent trophy.* He might even forgive her for going off into the jungle without an escort.

All she had to do was shoot. *Shoot, Nicole! Shoot!*

She licked her dry lips. She held her breath. Aiming, she stared down the sights . . . then closed her eyes with a sigh.

Nicole lowered her gun until she held it cradled in her arms. She couldn't do it. She couldn't shoot this gilded creation. She just didn't have the heart to destroy it.

Don't you mean the courage! her uncle's voice taunted.

Looking through the swaying grass at the exotic creature, she tried to silence the criticism in her head. This kill felt nothing like the hunts back home at her brother's estate. Something about the leopard, its size perhaps, so close to her own—or the eyes, flashing yellow fire, beaming with life —stopped her from shooting. The animal seemed connected to this land, an integral part of India. Like the jungle that had lured her from the campsite. India. At last, India. Where she'd come to find the truth.

As if sensing her thoughts, the leopard slumped down into the grass, panting, seemingly relaxed. Nicole smiled. Even the cat knew today was not a day for killing. *No, not today.* This wasn't the prize she sought.

"Another time, uncle," she said under her breath. The man who had taught her to use this rifle like an expert, who, like her brother, had played the part of father because she had never known her own, need never find out she had turned her back on such a trophy. Releasing the hammers into the half-cocked position, she hefted her rifle to her shoulder and turned to leave.

A growl rent the air. Nicole whipped around in time to see the leopard charge. Her mind went numb. The cat leapt. A voice inside her railed, urged her to action. The cat soared toward her, cresting its arc. The warning call within her pierced her wall of fear. Too late to aim the heavy rifle and shoot, she held the butt and barrel in front of her like a shield.

A gunshot split the early morning air.

I didn't fire!

The cat's weight slammed into her chest, knocking her backwards. Her rifle flew from her grasp. *No air.* She couldn't breathe! She tensed for the searing pain of teeth slashing through her throat.

It never came.

Nicole sucked in a breath, realizing she was still alive. She tried to sit up, but the cat's massive paws pinned her shoulders to the ground. Her eyes fluttered open and she cried out at the sight directly before her. Inches from her face, the cat's head rested between her breasts. Stamped between its black-rimmed eyes was a bullet hole smaller than a ha'penny.

Nicole swallowed a rising scream and rolled to her side, heaving the cat off her. She scrambled to her knees even as the jungle blurred around her. Her hands began to shake; they were stained with blood. Panting, she glanced at the dead animal beside her. The leopard's jaw hung slack. Four yellowed fangs accented twin rows of razor-edged teeth. Teeth that had been inches from her neck. . . .

A bitter taste filled her mouth and she swallowed back her gorge. Doubling over, she wrapped her arms around her middle and tried desperately not to retch.

A warm touch on her shoulder startled her, but the gentle pressure that followed stopped her from getting up to see who helped her. Large hands—a man's hands—cradled her head, giving her the support she needed to fight her nausea. Nicole remembered the gunshot that had killed the leopard and relaxed. For certain, her rescuer held her.

She sat back on her heels as the man behind her offered a soft piece of white linen. Taking the handkerchief, she gathered her wits to turn and give her thanks.

"Lady, are you crazy or just bat blind?"

Nicole froze. Charged with disapproval, the deep voice behind her had an American accent, sounding distinctly out of place in British India.

"I have never seen *anyone* turn their back on a leopard at twenty paces," the voice continued with growing censure. "Why didn't you shoot, for God's sake?"

Nicole pressed her eyes shut, unable to face her rescuer. The scorn she heard so clearly in his voice echoed her uncle's words: *Idiot! Incompetent!* How right that judgment seemed. The cat's exotic beauty had tricked her. She, an experienced huntress, had been lulled into inaction. What a fool her uncle would brand her if he could see her now. Just thinking of Uncle Marc and his anger made her hands shake harder. She almost dropped the handkerchief and a strangled cry escaped her lips.

"Oh, for the love of . . ." The American grabbed the linen from her fumbling hands and steadied her, holding her by the shoulders. "Leave it for now. Catch your breath."

For an instant, she thought of turning and finally meeting her rescuer face to face, but instead she found herself giving in to his touch as he rubbed her arms, granting comfort. She relished this kindness—used it to combat her growing fears of confronting her uncle with the news of the botched kill. Closing her eyes, she slowed her breathing. His grip shifted and he pulled her into his arms. The back of her head rested against a strong chest and a reassuring heartbeat thumped near her ear. Right now, anyone who walked on two legs was a friend.

She had almost died. Dead at twenty-one—hardly an impressive demise for a hunter with over twelve years' experience. She suppressed a strangled laugh as she imagined her uncle at the eulogy. Serves her right for going off on her own, damn the girl's hide, he'd say. Not for one second did she think her mentor in hunting would thaw long enough at her passing to forgo his ready temper. His motto: If you weren't the best, you were nothing. Nothing. And the best never made a mistake. Never hesitated.

She shivered. Thank God for the American.

Thinking of her rescuer, Nicole turned on her hip and huddled closer—and found her cheek resting against a very warm, very bare, chest.

Like a shot she was on her feet, facing the American. Her gaze fell to the native shirt tucked into the waistband of his dusty, doeskin trousers. A path of dark curling hair climbed up his washboard-hard stomach to T across two distinct planes of muscle. Her face heated up hotter than burning powder when she realized she was examining him with the intensity of a marksman on a target shoot. She swallowed hard and immediately looked up into the American's half-shaven face.

An angular nose. Short, rather shaggy hair, a shade shy of black. And beautiful eyes. Nicole caught her breath. His eyes were a collage of gold, jade, and brown specks mingling to create the image of a startling green. Immediately, she lowered her gaze to his full mouth where bits of soap clung to the corner of his lips. She was just making things worse by this endless scrutiny. She offered her hand, eager to get beyond the embarrassing moment.

"That was a rather nice shot." She launched into her introduction, keeping her gaze above his neck, as if standing in front of a half-naked man were something she did every day. "My name's Katherine Nicole Marshall. But please, call me Nicky; almost everyone does. I'm with the Marshall party, just arrived by stage from Naini Tal."

His lips curled into a sneer. "Nice to meet you, kid." Ignoring her outstretched hand, he grabbed the shirt hanging at his waist and used it to wipe the soap from his face.

"If I'd known you nabobs were coming, I'd have dressed for the occasion."

Nicole lowered her hand at his rebuff. Wishing she had not given in to her desire to explore the hillside alone, she picked up her rifle and watched him pull on his shirt then take out a paper cartridge and percussion caps from his pocket. When he finished loading, he grabbed her gun out of her hand.

"I better take that. A hunting party?" Shaking his head, he swung her back toward the village and pushed her forward in a manner so brusque it made a lie of his gentle touch of minutes before. "Lady, you better hope you have nine lives because you just used up one."

After two steps, Nicky dug her heels into the ground. He'd taken her rifle.

No one took her rifle away. No one.

Turning to face him, she held her hand out, palm up. "I'll have my gun back, if you please."

The gold-green eyes studied her until Nicky felt herself flush. So, he thought her incompetent with a rifle. Well, she'd given him cause, but she'd not budge a step without it. How often had her uncle drilled into her that a hunter never went on the trail without his gun? It was a truth she'd been weaned on. That Purdy was a part of her.

"The gun?" She extended her hand closer to him.

"Suit yourself. I just thought I might help you out. It wasn't doing you much good." Just as she touched the strap, he drew the gun back out of her reach. "You *do* know how to use it, don't you? Or was it just part of the jungle wardrobe you ordered?" His eyes trailed over her, as if judging the merits of her twilled cotton trousers and shooting jacket, and finding them wanting.

Nicky felt her flush deepen, familiar with the disapproving glance at her trousers. Men usually responded to her that way. She grabbed the gun out of his hand. "I know how to use it."

"Then what the hell were you doing back there? Acting

like you were strolling through blessed Saint James Park? Lady, you turned your back on a leopard!"

She balanced the Purdy's weight in the crook of her arm, swallowing back a sharp answer. He'd saved her life. She owed him the courtesy he himself withheld. After checking her rifle for damage, Nicole met the American's glare. "I'll know better next time."

"You're damn lucky there's going to be a next time," he grumbled, brushing past her through the grass and lantana in the direction of the village. When Nicky didn't follow immediately, he stopped and turned back to her. "What are you waiting for? A formal invitation to *be* dinner? Listen, lady. That cat back there was puny—maybe under a hundred pounds. There are animals out here that could carry you in their jaws like so much grass stuck between their teeth. I suggest you get back to your party before a tiger gets hungry enough for a small snack." Giving her his back once more, he started toward the village.

He thought that leopard puny? Something cold and hard settled in Nicky's throat. She followed quickly, scanning the tall grass and the forest ahead for any other predators.

"You know," she said, once she'd caught up with him. "I didn't catch your name back there." Perhaps a civil conversation could set things back on a proper footing for her and her rescuer, as well as distract her from her fears.

"The name's Atley."

"Atley something"—she smiled hesitantly—"or something Atley?"

"Atley will do just fine."

He delivered the words with the same caustic cadence as his earlier criticisms. Nicky realized immediately she'd made another mistake. The American was as hard a man as her uncle. She doubled her step, trying to keep up with his longer stride, suspecting that even his pace was meant to highlight his superiority.

Holt Atley glared down on the small woman sprinting next to him. Nothing but hair and eyes, he thought. The thick black hair she wore braided down her back swung suggestively across buttocks outlined by her cotton trousers. His eyes lingered there.

Nice, very nice.

He gave himself a mental shake. He'd been away too long on this charting expedition if he could get excited about the kid skipping next to him. Shifting his gaze up the small curves of her compact body, he felt the tingling hunger he'd just denied shoot up from his groin. Reminding himself that he preferred mature women, he thought of the small oval face, searching for signs of her youth. Instead, he recalled only her exotic eyes. The eyes of a Rajput princess. They were a deep golden shade that made him think of the jungle nights: hot, sultry—alluring in a dangerous way. Trouble. He picked up his pace.

So he was being obnoxious. Well, seeing a pretty little piece of fluff become leopard fodder sort of brought that out in a man. If he'd been a second later . . . But Holt had recognized what that thick, almost tangible silence meant in the jungle. Any *shikaree* who lived long enough to earn that title knew. The instant the langur monkeys and chital deer began their warning shrieks, he'd grabbed his gun from the river's edge where he'd been shaving and searched out the danger. Then he'd seen her, magnificently silhouetted against the backdrop of the Kumaon hills, her rifle aimed at the cat—until she'd simply lowered the barrel and turned away.

He still couldn't believe it. She handled her gun like an expert, her touch on the stock and barrel secure, knowledgeable, as if shooting was second nature. Yet she'd made the mistake of a novice with the leopard. It didn't make sense. Did she have straw for brains? Could anyone be that foolish?

Or had she acted out of courage, thinking to spare the animal, as he himself would have done?

Holt shook his head. Why attribute noble motives to such

a foolhardy act? No one turns their *back* on a leopard. Definitely straw for brains.

He'd known there would be trouble as soon as Nursoo had told him about the Marshall party. He'd expected a bunch of prim and proper Englishmen, monocled and mustached, ready to shoot anything and everything—from as far away as possible. But a woman! And a small, feminine thing at that. Even in her male attire, she looked female and fragile, barely able to lug the ten-pound rifle. Holt glanced at the bloodied collar of her shooting jacket and frowned. Other than being a little green around the gills, she'd gotten over her brush with death quickly enough. You'd think facing leopard attacks was something she did every day. No screaming, no fainting, no tears. His frown deepened. Maybe she was just too dumb to know better.

"Are you with a hunting party as well?" Nicky asked, filling in the damning silence in spite of herself.

He shot her another superior glare. "No."

"Have you been here long?"

"Long enough."

"Do you hunt?"

The slight unwelcome bend of his mouth downward answered her question first. "Look, Miss Marshall, if you want a list of how many bears, leopards, and tigers I've shot, I don't keep count."

With a sigh, Nicole gave up her attempts at conversation, having had enough of the man's surly responses. Seeking some other distraction, she surveyed the area around her with wary eyes. On the horizon, the rolling line of the Kumaon hills blurred into the clouded peaks of the Himalayas. She listened to the strange calls of the forest creatures, a cacophony of coughs, barks, and howls that both fascinated and frightened her, as she and her companion entered the tangle of pine and cypress at the edge of the glade. She estimated the path she'd used from the village was up ahead to her left. With the barrel of his gun, the American pushed aside a thick clump of jungle vines that had crept shoulder high. She jumped aside when a colorfully plumed bird, looking much like some mystical cousin of the common rooster, dashed out from behind the flowering bush. The American signaled her to proceed him.

"Nicole!" The shouted name blurred through the heavy shielding of jungle shrubbery. "Nicole!"

Nicky felt a heavy sense of dread sink to her toes. She stepped past the waiting man in the direction of the voice. "That's my uncle."

As Holt watched, a determined look shuttered the young woman's features. "Uncle Marc"—she waved a hand over her head—"I'm over here!" With a quick glance to Holt, she merged into the maze of pines ahead and disappeared.

Holt let the jungle creeper fall back into place, then hiked the leather strap of the Hall's carbine over his shoulder. He elbowed his way through the curtain of viny, purple flowers. So the cavalry had arrived. He prepared to meet the whole kit and bilin' of them, sure that the entire gang had set out in search of Miss Marshall, ready to rescue their missing maiden. Though his father had been British, Holt felt no connection to these people, having grown up in Boston with his mother before joining his father in India ten years ago. How Nursoo could put up with these Brits, their incompetence and their staged hunts, was beyond Holt. He'd given up years ago.

When Holt reached the reunion site, he found half a dozen natives, armed with stones, ancient matchlocks, and long sticks, hovering behind two men dressed in fashionable shooting jackets and trousers, gaiters to their knees, and helmet caps. Nicole's small breadth was swallowed up in the embrace of the taller of the two, a dark-haired, distinguished-looking man who, Holt thought cynically, appeared old enough to be the uncle she'd spoken of. His possessive hold and the gleam in his pale blue eyes told Holt he was not. The shorter man, gray haired and gray mustached, stood beside the hugging couple, a look of disapproval etched deeply on his heavily lined face.

With an odd sense of satisfaction, Holt watched Nicole Marshall try, very diplomatically, to extricate herself from the tall man's tight clinch. His satisfaction swelled at the sight of her flushed face and lowered eyes when she managed to step out of the grip, both indications of her embarrassed response to the public show of affection.

"Uncle Marc, Drew." She hooked elbows with both men. "This is . . . Mr. Atley." She raised her brows slightly, pausing to allow Holt to correct her introduction. "We met while I was scouting about. Mr. Atley, allow me to introduce my uncle, Marcus Elliot Marshall, and Lord Andrew Harrington." She smiled a sweet, heartfelt smile at the hovering man. "My fiancé."

The smug look of possession that crossed the noble's features at the mention of their engaged status left a surprisingly sour taste in Holt's mouth. Nicole Marshall appeared to be around seventeen years old. Harrington looked well over twice that. While marrying young virgins off to the landed geriatric gentry was standard for the Brits, Holt thought it a shame in this case. He had to admit, Harrington was indeed distinguished looking, if not out-and-out handsome, if you cared for arrogant aristocrats. But the gray in the bushy side-whiskers suggested that the man had peaked quite a few years back.

"As Nicole's intended"—Harrington stepped forward and offered a hand—"you can imagine, I was quite concerned to find her missing this morning."

"A misplaced fiancée." Holt's expression remained carefully bland. "Always a problem this far north."

Holt watched the man's pale eyes narrow as Nicole added, "I was telling Drew and Uncle Marc—"

"You were recounting some drivel," shouted her uncle, "to try and explain why you went off, half-cocked, on your own without an escort! Damn if you're not just like your father! Impetuous to the end. That's what got him killed, I tell you. Always knew better than anyone else, he did. And you! Running out of camp by yourself. That was damned ignorant, Nicole. I'll not stand for you taking needless risks like your father. I've taught you better. And what about the gunfire?" He waved a hand in front of Nicky's shirt. "And the blood? I demand an explanation, young lady."

A curiously hurt expression crossed her face as the Marshall girl bore her uncle's scolding. Holt felt it radiate through him and sink heavily in his stomach. The kid had faced a leopard with less vulnerability than she was showing now. He knew what it felt like to get a dressing-down after you'd made an ass of yourself—had experienced it himself a few times when he'd hunted with his father before the old man had died—but her reaction was more intense than that. She seemed to shrink under her uncle's poison tongue. The woman who had gotten to her feet and walked from a leopard attack rather than being carried away in a dead faint appeared strangely beaten. For some reason he refused to analyze, her look of defeat bothered Holt.

"The blood came from a leopard your niece shot." Holt's words effectively cut off the uncle's slicing monologue. He intercepted Nicole Marshall's look of surprise with a cocky smirk. "A rather nice shot," he drawled, using her own description of the kill. He watched the heavy-lashed eyes widen, and lifted one of his brows in response, challenging her to contradict his story. She remained silent. Marcus Marshall by contrast reacted immediately. His features brightened, his tirade against his niece miraculously forgotten as he patted her back in congratulations, then stretched a hand toward Holt.

"What did you say your name was?"

He shook Marshall's hand. "Atley." Watching Nicole behind her uncle, he added, *"Holt* Atley." He gave her a mocking smile.

Turning his attention back to the uncle, Holt jogged his head toward the glade. "You'll find the leopard in the middle of the clearing behind us." He could see that Marcus Marshall was already more interested in his niece's success than her failure.

With a wide grin to all, Marshall wrapped his arm around her shoulder and gave her a quick squeeze. He looked as if he were about to pronounce her a chip off the old block. "Why didn't you mention the leopard right off, Nick? A good shot was it?"

He posed the question as if he wanted to hear the praise repeated. Holt accommodated him. "A beauty. It will make a nice trophy."

"What do you think, Drew? It seems our Nick here has made the first kill of the hunt." Her uncle's bushy mustache shifted with his proud smile.

The fiancé turned Nicole roughly by her shoulders to face him. A pinched expression marred his aristocratic face and narrow blue eyes. "I don't understand why you put yourself in danger, Nicole. Couldn't you wait for a proper hunt?"

"Stop coddling the girl, Drew. If you two are going to be married, you'll have to understand Nick is a hunter, first and foremost. Come along." Her uncle headed toward the meadow; several natives trailed behind. "I'd like to get a look at the prize."

Lord Harrington frowned. Giving Nicole one more look of disapproval, he released her shoulders and followed her uncle.

A bit uncomfortable with his ruse over the kill, Holt avoided looking at the girl now that they were alone. When he finally met her gaze, the topaz color of her eyes had deepened, turning the same shade of gold as the ancient artifacts the government was constantly spiriting away.

"You didn't have to lie." She said the words softly, but Holt heard the underlying bite.

"I didn't hear you correcting me."

"That's right. I didn't, did I? Well, I suppose once offered such a tempting prize as escape from my uncle's endless scolding, I couldn't refuse. It appears I'm in your debt once more." This time, the thanks were delivered with a marked lack of enthusiasm. Holt sensed that like him, she hated admitting her weakness.

"Your fiancé, Lord Herringbone—"

"Harrington."

"Whatever—he's right about you being here. It's too dangerous. Go home, lady. We don't need a bunch of lords and ladies around here. If you're looking for a pastime, try tatting or pianoforte. Listen to your fiancé and go back to your afternoon teas before you really get hurt."

A closed, defensive look clouded her eyes. Any hint of vulnerability was notably absent. "You're wrong, Mr. Atley. Drew organized this hunt. It was his idea that I come along. He wanted this for me, just as badly as I want it for myself. He and my uncle know I can hunt. They believe in me." She brushed past him. "Excuse me. I'd like another look at *my* kill." Stopping, she wheeled around to face him once more. Her eyes were intensely bright. "Next time, it really will be mine. And it will be a tiger."

"You plan to shoot a tiger?" Holt smiled, thinking her chances of success minimal after this morning's exhibition, but he couldn't resist baiting her. "On an elephant, no doubt, in the true English manner. You're such courageous hunters, you English, letting native beaters drive the game to you while you wait with both barrels cocked and a bearer ready to hand you the next loaded rifle."

She shook her head. "No elephants. Not for this tiger. The *shikaree* said she must be hunted on foot or not at all. We're hunting the white tigress." Her youthful features hardened with the resolve threading through her voice. "It's the ultimate prize. And I mean to shoot it, Mr. Atley."

Holt Atley stared at the small figure winding her way back to the clearing. The white tigress?

My God. She was after Enchantress.

Holt hiked up the piled slate that served as the entrance steps to the stone-laid-in-mud house. He didn't bother to knock, but slammed the plank door open against the wall. A tall Hindu, dressed in a blue, long-sleeved *kurta* shirt and doeskin trousers similar to Holt's, stood in the corner of the dimly lit, single-room accommodation. He turned to greet Holt with a smile on his handsome face, but soon found himself suspended in the air as Holt picked him up by his shirt and banged him up against the whitewashed wall.

"Nursoo! You worthless piece of water buffalo dung."

A smile curved beneath the Indian's curling mustache as he adjusted the wool cap Holt had nearly knocked off his head. "Ah! You found out about the tigress?"

"You're after Enchantress. *My* tiger!"

Nursoo shrugged his shoulders at his longtime friend. "These English, what do they know about hunting tiger? They will never catch the white tigress—"

Holt banged him against the wall again, sending the unlit clay lamp next to the Hindu's face careening off its wooden perch and smashing against the floor. Two or three villagers gathered outside the door. Holt knew few could understand the argument conducted in English, a language he'd helped teach Nursoo to speak fluently, but the men remained huddled around the threshold just the same.

"Don't hold out on me, Nursoo." Holt's voice dropped to a deadly whisper. "I talked to a certain bloodthirsty lady by the name of Nicole Marshall. She says you're hunting Enchantress. On foot. That makes me believe this is a legitimate attempt to bag her. What is it, Nursoo? A bonus? A special reward if they make the kill?"

Nursoo seemed to consider his response, then his smile broadened. "We are old friends, Holt sahib—"

"Answer me, damn you! How much?"

The Indian's dark eyes narrowed. In a harsh whisper he said, "Enough to make certain my marriage to Padmini will no longer be delayed."

Holt released his hold on the shirt, and Nursoo slumped to the ground. Turning away, Holt swore under his breath. After a moment, he again faced his Indian friend. "We go way back, Nursoo. You and my father taught me how to survive here. You've saved my hide on more than one occasion. But so help me, if you go after Enchantress, you'll not call me friend again."

The Indian shook his head sadly. "You were once a fearless hunter. A true *shikaree.* Now, a worthless tigress means more to you than a friend."

Holt knelt down next to Nursoo. "You're the only other *shikaree* capable of tracking her besides myself. If you keep out of this, she's safe." His expression dark as obsidian, he asked, "Are you going after her or not?"

There was a minor skirmish at the door as villagers vied for a better view. The father of Nursoo's young bride-to-be pressed his way through to the threshold, then stopped, the calculating look in his near-black eyes trained on Nursoo.

Holt knew the young Hindu's answer before he nodded his head.

"I go after the tigress, sahib."

"You'll not get her, Nursoo." Holt stood slowly. "No one is going to kill Enchantress."

Without a look back, Holt pushed through the doorway and shouldered his way past the crowd of villagers.

Jeffrey Ratcliffe, Deputy Commissioner for the Kumaon District, stared at the piled messages on his desk, regretting the execrable task of answering them. The stack had been thinned by his secretary, but these letters required his personal attention. His concentration was not, however, at its peak.

Lord it was hot. Not even the swaying *punkah,* the fan operated by the Indian boy seated on the floor behind him pulling its cord, granted relief from the heat. Though he knew it was a good deal cooler in these hills, to Jeffrey, the heat felt as suffocating as that of the plains. Sweat beaded on his nearly nonexistent forehead and on the balding crown of his head. With short, precise pats of his handkerchief, he dabbed at the perspiration beneath the fringe of graying sorrel-colored hair. In an unconscious gesture of concentration, he smoothed the pencil-thin mustache etched above his upper lip with his index finger and thumb. It was April, well into the hot season. Now through May was the best time to hunt tiger, as the animals would have to range farther and farther away from the protection of the hills to seek out the dwindling water supply. Jeffrey permitted himself a silky smile. Yes indeed, it was a good time to bag a tiger. Even a white one.

He stared at the letter spread before him, willing his attention to focus on the missive from the Department of Communications. It was bloody difficult to think about routes and railroad ties this morning. Thoughts of Serena buzzed in and out of his consciousness like an irritating fly, draining his energies. They'd had another row last night and she had run off to her hideaway, a cottage on the ridge below Almora. Even as they'd quarreled, he'd sensed their argument was staged, her dramatic departure premeditated.

Her lover was back. Now, she was that much closer to him.

Like a tigress on the prowl, his wife of twenty-one years was restless. He could almost smell the pent-up sexual energy fueled by her lover's absence. During the past weeks of forced monogamy, she'd grown ever more vicious, searching out new grounds for complaint. The list was endless: Their social life was nil, the servants lazy and ill-mannered, their housing sparse. She'd harped and carped until he'd finally sworn he would resign from his post and take her back to England, as she'd been begging him to do for the last two years.

The news had not pleased her. She had paled, as if the coveted prize was no longer laudable. And he knew why.

She didn't want to leave her lover.

She would probably be with him this very night.

Jeffrey slammed his fist down on the letter with a curse. By God, he'd show him. He'd make the bastard pay for debauching his wife!

The walnut door opened softly and his Indian butler announced his visitor. A cruel smile threaded beneath the scrap of dusty-colored hair above Jeffrey's thin mouth. "Show the gentleman in, Ramu."

Jeffrey watched Holt Atley enter his study, walking with the same grace and authority as the big cats he studied. He examined Atley's native cotton shirt with disdain. Yet, despite the fellow's unfashionable attire, Jeffrey acknowledged the man was handsome enough. Unlike the commissioner, Atley was young, powerful and proud in his bearing. Jeffrey could see Atley's attraction to the ladies, even as he despised him for it.

"How may I help you this morning?" Jeffrey kept his voice smooth, just on the edge of smug.

Atley leaned over Jeffrey's desk, his hands planted firmly on the inlaid wood design at the border. "You can tell me why in the hell you authorized the hunting of a protected animal!"

Jeffrey settled against the cushioned back of his Bombay blackwood armchair. "You mean the white tigress?" he answered softly. "I'm afraid you misunderstood my plans for the animal. The tigress is exempt from the fifteen rupee reward offered to the natives for tiger kills. I would hardly term it 'protected.' "

With the satisfaction that his petty power permitted, Jeffrey watched the ruddy color creep up the tanned skin of the man hovering over his desk. Not so handsome now, he thought.

"The tigress is one of a kind," Atley argued. "She's to be studied, not destroyed. I've been writing London for a year now, carefully detailing her habits. She's given birth to a litter. I haven't gotten a close enough look, but there could very well be more white tigers. It could be the beginning of a new strain!"

"She's an albino. A mutant. Even I know that. A gaggle of mutants is hardly cause for celebration."

Jeffrey watched Holt shake his head. "The tigress has blue eyes—not pink. She could be an entirely new subspecies—"

Jeffrey raised his hand to stop Atley. "It's out of my hands. Andrew Harrington is a very important man. He was quite insistent on this hunt." It had given Jeffrey great pleasure to be able to satisfy the aristocrat after having denied the man's other request. But the geographical reports Lord Harrington desired were unavailable for public perusal. He'd had to deny Harrington access, despite the man's insistence. The white tigress was another matter. To pacify Harrington and at the same time thwart Atley had doubled the pleasure of signing the hunting permit.

"Why wasn't I informed about this?" Holt demanded.

"You forget yourself, Mr. Atley," Jeffrey answered coldly. "Your position as a forest officer for the Conservator gives you little say in the matter. Of course, if you weren't always on your charting expeditions, unavailable for comment, you may have discovered Lord Harrington's plans yourself. He was here for months planning the details."

The commissioner narrowed his eyes on Atley. This time, Jeffrey held all the cards. He had the power to destroy what Atley wanted above all else—just as Atley had ruined the thing that mattered most to Jeffrey.

"I don't know why you're doing this, Ratcliffe. But I'll fight you."

"You do that, Mr. Atley. You do that." Jeffrey leaned back in his chair, relishing the man's frustration as Atley turned and left the room.

He smiled. That would teach Mr. Atley to leave his Serena alone.

Holt directed the small white Arabian through Almora's cluster of buildings. Located on a bare saddle-shaped ridge, the town stood at the heart of the Kumaon district, serving as both a military and a civil station. The hot trip to Almora to confront Ratcliffe had taken its toll. Holt was in dire need of a change of clothes and a long cool bath, but he had something he must do first, before he could return to the village.

As he continued down the flagstone paved street, admiring the intricate wood carvings that covered the upper stories of the houses lining the road, he thought over his futile discussion with Ratcliffe. He'd not known of Harrington's interest in hunting Enchantress. The expedition must have been organized while Holt was off charting in the south, a trip from which he had just returned. He blamed himself for not taking better steps to protect the tigress in his absence. But he'd thought her safe. Ratcliffe damn well knew the animal's importance!

Blast that power-hungry bastard. He'd actually taken a perverse thrill in signing Enchantress's death warrant. Well, Holt would fight him. He'd fight the whole damn lot of them. No one was going to kill Enchantress.

Dismounting in front of the government building, he cursed the need to come in person rather than head back home to Baijnarn. But how could you rely on a system of communication where one villager jumped on top of the roof of the sturdiest house and yelled a message to the next village, relaying the dispatch in hopscotch fashion, from village to village, until it arrived, if it ever arrived, at its destination. Though he'd been able to conduct his business in person with that scavenger Morgan, he would have to hire a runner for this message.

Holt climbed the front steps, dismissing his qualms over hiring Morgan. It couldn't be helped. If he wanted to save Enchantress from the Brits, he needed more than one plan of action. As he entered the whitewashed building that contrasted with the mica slate houses surrounding it, he looked around. The place appeared abandoned, but an Indian man soon stepped in from the back room in answer to Holt's call.

"How may I help you, sahib?"

"I need a government runner." Taking a piece of paper out from his pants pocket, Holt held it between his second and third fingers and waved it in front of the peon's nose. "I want this delivered as soon as possible."

"Yes, sahib. Tomorrow there—"

"I want it sent today." Holt slid a few rupees across the desk.

The Indian slipped the money into his pocket. "It shall be as you say."

Holt smiled. "Thanks."

"The destination, sahib?"

Holt answered the peon's questions concerning delivery absently, thinking of the message inside the folded paper and its significance. The note he'd written to London was short and to the point. It read simply: "Yes. But it will cost you."

Once again, he'd made himself a hired hunter.

2

Nicky gave the hide cover of her portmanteau a kick. It didn't help her frustration one whit. In the morning they would break camp for the Kumaon hills and the hunt would begin. Less than twelve hours from now, she would be expected to aim her Purdy rifle and kill. Nicole Marshall was a huntress—a dead shot. Nothing had changed.

Everything had changed.

Nicky sighed. The day's exhausting activities had left her tired, too drained to battle her mental demons. She stepped back around the portmanteau, careful not to upset the bamboo poles supporting the thick country cloth of her tent, the same dingy, cramped *pal* that sheltered the natives they'd hired for the hunt. She wound her way around a cane stool to the washstand and poured water into the brass basin. After splashing her face, neck, and arms, she extinguished the candle on the folding table beside her before stumbling back to her bamboo travel bed, cursing the eight-feet-squared area that made movement so difficult. Perched on the edge of the bamboo rail of the camp bed, she pulled her loose black hair over her shoulder, so as not to sit on it, and crossed one leg over the other to tug off her boot. It fell with a soft thud to the ground.

Despite her best efforts to quell the fear that gnawed at her, her thoughts swung back to its crux with the precision of a pendulum. This morning she'd made an unpardonable error in judgment. It had almost cost her life.

What if it happened again? In front of her uncle?

He wouldn't be the least bit forgiving. The moment she panicked before shooting, he'd put her on the next ship home, branding her a hazard to herself and the other hunters.

Nicky threaded her fingers through her hair to her scalp. Coal-black curls cascaded over the net of her hands toward the floor. To be sent home now was unthinkable. She was so close, so very close. Rajputana bordered the Northwestern Provinces. She couldn't abandon her hopes with her goal so near.

Nicky sat up, whipping her hair back off her face with a sharp flick of her head. She sent the second boot to the floor and yanked off her jacket. Mumbling an unladylike assessment of her lack of courage, she finished undressing and slipped a linen night rail over her head.

She had thought herself prepared for this trip, that she'd be as successful here as she'd been in England. She'd depended on her abilities to execute some marvelous shooting feat, a trophy that would so impress her uncle, he would grant her any wish—even one he so fervently disapproved of. And why not? It was a miracle she'd gotten this far.

She'd considered her uncle's decision to travel to India a grand coup in view of their past arguments. His acceptance of Drew's invitation to hunt here had inspired great hopes in the plan she'd devised after she'd learned of the proposed trip. But she'd not anticipated her reaction to big game hunting. Ducks and pheasants—they were small specks, a blur racing to the sky that she could sight and drop better than most accomplished hunters. The sleek leopard had been so close, close enough for its soulful eyes to charm her. All that beautiful golden fur, the distinctive ebony spots, it had been breathtaking, so much a part of this beautiful and exotic country. A fairy tale animal she'd not wanted to shoot—until it had charged with a ferocity that had left her stunned. If it hadn't been for Mr. Atley . . .

"Holt." She said the name out loud, rolling the vowel in her mouth as if tasting it.

Holt. He hadn't wanted her to use his Christian name.

Nicky balled up her clothes and threw them at the open portmanteau.

"Do I know how to use a gun?" she mimicked his taunt. "Part of my jungle wardrobe, indeed! Thinks I'm a perfect idiot, does he?" she asked the canvas walls. "Just some fool woman *playing* huntress who should stay home tatting and sipping tea." Well, she'd come across that attitude before. And she'd conquered it!

Snatching back the mosquito netting, Nicky settled beneath it, onto the pallet. Despite her boast, her heart felt like a bucket of lead shot lodged behind her ribs. She was, after all, so very weary of her battles.

All her life she'd fought to change people's perceptions of her. To the men who shunned her for her masculine pursuits, she'd wanted to prove she was just as desirable as any other woman—but managed to demonstrate only that she was a better shot. To the women who whispered about her dark foreign looks, she'd bragged about her royal heritage—and alienated them further.

And her uncle. How many times had she sought to prove her courage to the man who treated her like a son? He'd devoted his life to making her the best. He'd told her so often enough. And he *was* always proud of her accomplishments as a hunter. But the struggle never ended. She was only as good as her last hunting feat. Over and over, she'd had to prove her talents to her uncle—to erase the time she'd failed so miserably.

Nicky shut her eyes, trying to bar the image of her first hunt. She burrowed further into the comforting softness of her down pillow. But as the seductive call of sleep lulled her, and her eyelids relaxed into a gentle seal, the niggling image of the leopard's attack gnawed at the back of her consciousness. Even in her dreams, she could not forget her hesitation just when her instincts as a huntress should have taken over. *Hesitation.* Slowly, as she drifted into sleep, the word echoed in her mind. *Hesitation.* So deadly a mistake. Just like the first time . . .

"Dammit, girl! Shoot now!"

Nicky stood at the center of a lighted patch, alone. The words echoed down a long tunnel of darkness. Her arms trembled from the weight of eight pounds of Damascus steel and iron twist she held parallel to the ground. She hefted the mahogany butt against the small shoulder of her eight-year-old frame and straightened her aim. A salty, lead taste seeped into her mouth where her teeth bit into her lip.

"I can't," she cried.

"By God, you'll shoot when I tell you to." Her uncle's voice flooded her senses, like a great wave ready to engulf her.

"But I don't *want* to kill it."

"What did you think you were going to do—target shoot for the rest of your life? I've spent months teaching you. Have I *wasted* my time? You've got a clear shot now. Shoot, for God's sake!"

Within the narrow pool of light, Nicole sighted her target, a small gray rabbit. Her surroundings formed into a hazy image of the woods near her brother's estate. It was just short of noon, but everything looked shrouded in darkness. One minute she could see the rabbit clearly, then it would disappear. She lowered her gun barrel, shaking her head.

"I'm terribly ashamed of you, Nicole." Her uncle towered over her. "Are you so weak willed, so cowardly?" His voice grew louder with each reproach. "Can't you shoot a simple rabbit? And I thought to make a grand huntress of you!"

"Please, don't be angry, Uncle Marc. I'll do as you say. Watch me; I can shoot. I can!"

The target at the end of her gun blurred through the tears she refused to shed. Nicky took aim as best she could, and shut her eyes as she pulled back the trigger. The gun bit into her shoulder and a familiar roar exploded around her. She dipped the gun barrel to the ground, its weight now too heavy to lift. Her eyes remained closed and a tear slipped down her cheek.

The soft crunching of twigs warned her of Uncle Marc's return before his fingers bit into her upper arm.

"I want you to see what your cowardice has yielded." He pulled her viciously forward, practically dragging her. Her legs became as leaden as the gun she carried. The ground seemed to suck her downward, making each step more difficult than the last.

"You've botched it, Nicole." With a last push forward, her uncle directed her to a small lump of fur and blood.

Nicky landed on her knees before her first kill. The rabbit lay on its back, its four paws jerking skyward, its round body shaking in spasms.

"That's what happens when you hesitate, Nicole. The poor thing is suffering because of you. If you'd shot it properly, as I've taught you, this wouldn't have happened."

Nicole watched blood gush from the rabbit's hind leg in rhythm with its still pulsing heart. The sting of cold metal filled her hand. She looked up to her uncle, then wrapped her fingers around the carved handle of the revolver he'd given her. She stumbled to her feet.

Don't hesitate . . . never hesitate.

Taking careful aim at the jerking body a few feet before her, she drove the trigger back—

Nicky sat bolt upright in the camp bed, her linen night shirt moist with sweat. She inhaled deeply, trying to calm her pounding pulse, then buried her face in her hands. The memories of her first shooting expedition had returned in the form of a vivid nightmare.

Never hesitate. For the past thirteen years she'd kept that promise. She'd learned to shoot like an expert, never balking before a kill.

Until the leopard.

That's why she'd allowed Holt Atley to lie to her uncle. She couldn't admit repeating the mistake of her childhood—a mistake that had almost ended in disaster. But the lie had been an even greater show of cowardice than her failure to shoot.

She shook her head and sunk back against her pillow. She was always trying to prove something—and losing sight of what really mattered in the process. Not this time, she vowed. The most important thing to her right now was to remain in India. If she had to shoot one tiger to stay here, then she'd find the courage to do it! She wouldn't hesitate with the tiger. She just had to remember what it was she was shooting. Tigers were a menace. They terrorized villages, ate livestock. Man-eaters. A pestilence that the government paid to be rid of—

"Oh for heaven's sake!" She fisted her feather pillow, then plumped it up again before hollowing a groove in its soft folds for her cheek. "Put it to rest and get some sleep, Nick," she ordered herself.

She flipped from her left side to her right, then, after a minute, flopped onto her back. The thin straw mattress felt scratchier than ever. The distant chanting of a Nat woman, luring men to the Gypsy camp outside the village, hummed in harmonic discord with the braying of the resident goats. Even the occasional call of a peacock, whose exotic lament had always tantalized her, grated against her nerves. The sweat pooled between her breasts.

Nicky swept back the sheet and mosquito netting, scooting off the bamboo bed, now wide awake and too impatient to wait for sleep. She maneuvered her way to the folding table, stubbing her toe on her portmanteau as she avoided colliding with the cane stool. At that moment, with the pain radiating up her leg, she almost sympathized with Drew's complaints about the paucity of their traveling arrangements. Most civilian groups toured with large pavilions, complete with elegant furnishings so that no one suffered the least hardship. But their decision to pursue some exotic creature found only in the hills, where the supplies needed for the servants, horses, and camels of a fully equipped camp would be unavailable, had cut short that idea—to

Drew's great chagrin. Nicole cared little for luxury. Her only complaint had been that the hills were a great deal north of Rajputana.

"White tiger indeed," she mumbled while digging through the contents of her trunk. Why couldn't Uncle Marc have settled for bagging normal game? Farther south, she would have been much closer to her goal. Yet, even as she posed the question, she knew an ordinary tiger would never have drawn her uncle to this forbidden country. At least the arrangement kept her companion, Mrs. Tod, ensconced in Naini Tal, clinging to the last vestiges of civilized society.

Nicky searched through the layers of clothes with one hand, plunging elbow-deep within the jumble as she sought the feel of soft silk. If her brother ever found out she'd managed to elude the older woman, he'd never again let Nicky wander beyond the gates of Eldridge, his estate in Salisbury. But as he'd often done since the birth of his first child, a daughter who marked the beginnings of an ever expanding family, for this trip he'd passed on his responsibility over Nicole to their uncle. Uncle Marc had been easily convinced. Not only had he thought it imperative that Nicky come on the hunt, he'd appeared anxious to be rid of the meddling Mrs. Tod, whose doting attentions were decidedly fixed on him. At least the woman's romantic antics had been entertaining. Still, Nicky had been glad to evade her companion's constant harping on her appearance and what Mrs. Tod had termed her "unladylike brusqueness."

Nicole smiled in triumph as she shoved aside the last of the obstructing garments and extracted the delicate bundle she'd been hunting. She lit a candle and seated herself at the table. With ceremonial care, she stood her small looking glass against her copy of Captain Shakespear's book, *Wild Sports of India,* which she'd been reading earlier, and peeled back the gold-shot silk folds of the cloth parcel, exposing the ruby encrusted locket it held at its heart. Gently, so as not to ruin the locking mechanism, she opened the gold case and stared at the miniature inside, examining it under the flickering candlelight.

The familiar image of an Indian woman, her dark tresses almost hidden by a beautiful veil the same gold color as the woman's eyes, stared back at her. Placing the locket on the table, Nicole raised the silk cloth that had protected the jewelry until the veil's shimmering length flowed off the table onto her lap. Taking the silk in both hands, she draped its rich length over her own hair and compared her image in the mirror to the woman in the miniature.

I look like her, she thought, not for the first time. *I look so much like her.*

A warm feeling suffused her, draining out the fear of her dream. Her breathing calmed, and a curious sense of belonging nudged at her. India—at last.

In that instant, Nicole felt just a little less alone.

The dark outline of a man shadowed the entrance to her tent. Nicky jumped in her seat and turned sharply toward the entryway. "Who's there?"

"Nicole? It's me, Drew."

Whipping the veil off her head, she vaulted to her feet, nearly knocking the cane stool to the floor. "Drew?" She wrapped the locket in the gold silk and stuffed it back into her trunk. "What are you doing awake?" she asked, not quite managing to keep the guilty edge from her voice as she hid the locket.

"I saw your light. Nicole, may I come in? I'd like to speak with you."

Nicky adjusted her linen night rail, then thinking better of her sparse attire, raced back to the refuge of her bed, again stubbing her toe. She bit back a curse for Drew's sake and sank onto the straw pallet. Not bothering to draw the mosquito netting around her, she tucked the coarse sheet up under her chin and whispered for him to enter. She watched as he worked loose the sturdy laces of the gable end of the *pal* and slipped through the slit opening.

"You shouldn't be here, Drew."

"I just want a few moments alone with you, darling. It's perfectly all right." Drew pulled up the cane stool to the side of the bed and settled his large frame in its fragile support. He took up her hand and began caressing the tops of her knuckles with his thumb in a way he'd never done before. "We *are* engaged."

"Engaged, but not married. Uncle Marc would spit bullets if he knew you were here." She glanced down to where the sheet met her chin. "I'm not even dressed."

"All the better."

Nicky blushed, managing a small smile. She relished the teasing. Before Drew, she'd never had a man flirt with her. Men saw her only as a source of gossip and a shooting rival. After her coming out, she'd watched girls at balls bantering with elegantly clad young men—while she sat in the shadows of some potted plant with only her brother to offer a dance. But Drew had changed all that with his proposal and his friendship. He had changed her life, helping her join the ranks that had shunned her for so long.

She sat up straighter against the camp bed, her attitude softened by her thoughts. "Well, I'm sure Uncle Marc is fast asleep. A few minutes will surely go unnoticed."

Drew leaned forward and pressed his lips against hers. Too startled to react, Nicole sat still. Slowly, she dropped the sheet and hesitantly draped her arms around his shoulders, not quite sure where to place them. At first, she felt uncomfortable with the kiss, Drew had always been so circumspect, never granting more than the chaste peck he'd placed on her hand when he'd proposed. But as she realized what this kiss communicated, that Drew loved her, truly loved her, she gave herself up to it. Her ugly-duckling fears, fed by years of rejection by men who could not stomach her competitive spirit, faded into the background of her memories. Slowly, tentatively, she pressed herself against him.

The image of Holt Atley's firm, bare chest accented by a dark V of curling chest hair infused her consciousness. Nicole felt a sharp frisson radiate up through her stomach, startling her. The foreignness of her reaction made her draw away.

She blinked. For just a second or two, she didn't see Drew's eyes of light blue illuminated by the soft candlelight. The eyes she imagined were green and crystal sharp.

Drew's lips thinned into a smile. "I'm glad to see you missed me as much as I missed you, darling." He gave her a speculative glance. "I worried. You've been somewhat distant today."

Nicole nodded, too disturbed by what she'd experienced to speak aloud, until his words registered. "Oh, Drew." She took up his hand, sweeping all thoughts of Atley from her mind. *Drew is the only man who has ever cared for me.* "I'm so sorry. I didn't mean to ignore you. It's just that with the preparations for the hunt and all . . ."

"It's not as if we've known each other so long that a fellow doesn't become concerned." He smiled hesitantly. "I am quite a bit older. I've never asked, but it doesn't bother you, does it, darling?"

"Of course not," she answered. Drew was her betrothed. When all other men had called her "unnatural" and "mannish," this titled gentleman had set those prejudices aside— had asked her to marry him.

Yet, as she looked into his eyes, almost colorless in the pale light of the tent, she couldn't help but compare his polished, bored features to the ruggedly handsome face of the American—a face that expressed more danger and passion with a slight curve of his lips and a lift of one brow than Drew had shown during their entire courtship. Out of nowhere, the thought came unbidden: What would that suggestive mouth feel like against hers, kissing her as Drew just had . . . ?

She shut out the image of Holt Atley. Good Lord, what could she be thinking of! Growing frustrated by these small betrayals of her love, Nicky threw back the covers and embraced Drew.

She kissed him with an urgency she'd never before displayed. For a moment, Drew kissed her back. But then Nicky felt him stiffen and push her away. "Nicole!"

"I . . . I'm sorry," she stuttered, confused and a bit embarrassed by his rejection.

Drew shook his head in mock disapproval, a paternal smile on his lips. "You make it hard to resist you when you're so . . . aggressive. Do you think I'm made of stone?" He patted her hand. "I think I'd better leave. Before we do something we will regret."

Nicky nodded as Drew pressed a soft kiss on her forehead and patted her head.

"Get some rest, darling. We have a long day ahead of us."

She watched Drew retie the laces of the *pal,* then pulled back the mosquito netting and sank onto the hard pallet. She remained awake for hours, but finally the soft village sounds lulled her into a deep sleep.

Her dreams were filled with dark haunting images of firm muscles and eyes as green as the Kumaon hills. In her dreams, there was nothing submissive about her reaction to the man who held her in his arms.

Serena Ratcliffe paced before the open French doors, willing the dark green forest outside her bedroom to yield its forbidden fruit. Her white-blond hair, its color enhanced by frequent douses of lemon juice and vinegar, fluttered behind her tall, lithe frame, brushing against and merging with the white folds of her dressing gown. The delicate features of her face, lined despite a strict regime of expensive creams, didn't hide her forty years as she fervently hoped. Only her frantic and expressive cerulean eyes—eyes that beguiled with the charming innocence of a child one minute, then narrowed with venom the next—made her appear a bit younger. She glanced at the enamel clock above the ironwood mantel, squinting to bring the gold hands into focus, then stomped the heel of her slipper against the clapboard floor. He must come. He'd been back for days. Tonight, he must come to see her!

Serena stared irritably at the romantic scene she'd prepared in hopes of her lover's arrival. The muted candlelight
glowed softly from beside the silk-sheeted bed; a lone, blood
rose jutted out of its crystal vase next to the candle. Incense
permeated the air with the exotic scent of jasmine. If the
evening were not so stifling, she would have had the servants
light a fire to add to the ambiance. As it was, she'd flung
open the French doors in hopes of just a prayer of a breeze
to cool the heated room. The temperature only added to the
torment of waiting.

How much longer she could fool her husband, Serena
didn't know. She sensed he already knew the purpose behind her impromptu trip down from Almora. She'd have to
be more careful in the future. Yet, caution seemed out of the
question. She wanted, no *needed,* so very much, the physical
fulfillment she found only in her lover's arms. She'd come to
the cottage every day, hoping to meet him there—only to be
disappointed. By fighting with Jeffrey, she'd made certain
she could stay the night. She'd left a light burning in the
front window, her secret way of communicating she was
alone. If her lover came, they could spend an entire night
together, a rarity considering her husband's constant presence.

Serena bit the cuticle of one long, thin finger. Oh, he must
come. He simply couldn't let such an opportunity pass.

"Serena?"

A joyous laugh flowed from her lips as she spun around
and sped onto the open porch, flinging herself into her lover's arms. "At last, you've come. It's been so long." She
dropped kisses on his face and neck. "Why did you wait—
how *could* you wait! I've been here every afternoon until I
fairly burst from wanting you."

A low chuckle and a tight hug that caused her to squeal
from its affectionate strength let her know how much her
enthusiastic reception was appreciated.

"Serena, so ill-named you are, my siren. You're about as
serene as a monsoon."

Serena reveled in the sheer masculine strength of his arms
as he picked her up and carried her to the tester bed, cradling her against his chest. She dug her nails into the thick
brown curls and nestled into the warm haven where his neck
met his broad shoulders. "I've been in agony every moment
you've been away," she whispered.

Serena felt herself fall onto the sheets. The cool silk licked
at the exposed skin of her legs in striking contrast to the
heated body that covered her like a loving comforter. Two
starved lovers, they peeled and discarded their clothes, tasting each other's bodies. Serena kissed the jagged scar—a
memento from a tiger—that proved the great courage of this
man. "Why didn't you come sooner? You shouldn't have
waited—"

His lips cut short her complaints. Without preamble he
plunged into her. Serena started at the ferocity of their mat-
ing, feeling it almost as an attack. Then she too became
swept up in the sexual release it promised. She wrapped her
long white legs around his hips, linking her ankles behind
his back, and bucked against him. Within minutes, she felt
him stiffen, then jerk forward in release. She couldn't help
her disappointment when he rolled off her onto his back, his
arm shielding his eyes from the light on the bed stand next
to him.

Serena waited, playfully running a long nail along the
ragged tiger scar on his arm. When she thought she heard a
soft snore, she gasped and sat up, staring accusingly at the
naked man beside her. "You're not sleeping now, are you?"
She pushed him awake with a shove. "You beast. That's
hardly the reception I expected after so long an absence."

For a moment, she thought he looked annoyed, but then
the expression faded into the heavy-lidded sensual gaze that
sparked a responding hunger within her.

"I do seem to be remiss in my duties." He turned onto his
side to face her. "My humblest apologies, darling." Reaching behind him, he plucked the red rose from the vase on the
bed stand and guided its dripping stem above her naked

breasts. Cold drops splashed against each tip and dripped down the small white mounds to stain the silk sheet beneath her. He brushed the velvet petals of the bud against her lips, then trailed the flower down her neck to her breasts, swabbing each nipple until it bloomed as red and lush as the rose bud. "I shall have to make it up to you."

With one hand, he ripped the bud from its stem and crushed the rose petals between his fingers, sprinkling them like some exotic spice onto the most sensitive parts of her body. Serena lay back against the down pillows and waited in heated anticipation as the cool petals landed on her lips, her breasts, her flat stomach and her thighs, and finally, where she wanted them most, on the crest of blond curls between her legs. She was still savoring the anticipation when she felt the sharp bite of thorns tearing into her tender breasts as the barbs etched twin streaks of carmine across her pale skin.

Soothing lips smothered her gasp of pain. Her lover's soft tongue twined with hers, then pulled away to lap the blood from her breasts. Her ravaged skin licked clean, he began gathering each rose petal between his lips, kissing a path to the petals mounded on the soft curls now wet with her passion.

Serena sighed with contentment. She endured the pain—it made the pleasure that much more exquisite.

Holt Atley rode through the clearing toward Baijnarn, away from the hills below Almora. As he neared the encampment outside the village, he stopped abruptly, just catching sight of the two men waiting at the edge of the walnut orchard. By the light of the full moon, he recognized the shorter of the two. The man signaled Holt furiously with his hands.

"Blast," Holt whispered under his breath. Veering left, away from the camp, horse and rider galloped toward the waiting duo.

"Evenin' gov'ner." Donald Morgan caught the horse's

reins in his gnarled hands. He twisted his pocked face into a semblance of a smile, but the scar that snaked from his mouth to his left eye turned the effort into a ghastly grimace. Holt swallowed his distaste. Dealing with Morgan always made him feel seedy—as if he could catch the Irishman's low morals, like cholera or dysentery. He frowned. Considering he'd hired him to do his dirty work, Holt admitted he barely had a boot up on Morgan's ethics.

"I been waitin' fer ye."

"Damn you, Morgan. Does anyone know you're looking for me?"

"Not a chance. I followed yer instructions; ye want the job done real private like. No one's to know I be workin' fer ye, lime-juicer."

"Next time you call me that, I'm going to ram that quaint misnomer right back down your skinny throat."

"Come now, gov'ner. Yer father were British enough, even if ye do talk like that sweet Yankee mother of yers, bless her poor departed soul. Ye ain't ashamed of ol' mother England now, are ye?"

"Mother England has nothing to do with it, Morgan. You call me anything but mister again, and I'll see you regret it."

"Take it easy, Mister Atley. It were just a bit of a joke." Morgan nodded his oversized head toward the Korku native waiting beside him. "I wanted ye to meet me friend here. Think he can help us?"

Holt looked over the Korku, instantly wary of the man's sly expression, but what could he expect of a cohort of Morgan's? "All right. Bring him along. The more the better. I don't want anyone to get a clear shot at that tigress. No one . . . whatever you have to do."

"I got ye, gov—Mister Atley." Morgan jabbed a thumb to his chest. "Ye won't regret trustin' ol' Donald Morgan."

Holt laughed harshly. "I'm not trusting you for a second. I'll be watching you every step of the way. Don't ever forget that, Morgan." He nudged the Arabian and pulled back on the reins; the horse took two nervous steps away from the duo. "Tomorrow, you and your friend go to Nursoo and join up with the hunting party. That should give you opportunity enough to arrange things."

The Irishman fidgeted for a moment, as if carefully considering his next words. "About Nursoo. That Indian and me, we don't get along, see? I'm wondering if he'll hire us on?"

Holt Atley's eyes narrowed and a grim smile deepened the shadows on his face. "Don't worry, Morgan. By tomorrow, Nursoo will be willing to hire just about anyone. Even you."

The shouting finally woke Nicky.

At first, she thought she was dreaming the heated male voices yelling in Kumauni. But as the haze of sleep faded into the thundering argument directly outside her tent, she sprang instantly awake, entangling herself in the mosquito netting and almost toppling the bamboo camp bed. Once unhitched from the mess, she pulled on her pants and jacket and put on her boots before bursting out of her *pal.* The instant she made an appearance, the group of natives arguing with Nursoo, the guide her uncle had hired, became silent. Nicky walked to the center of the group to stand directly before the *shikaree.*

"What's going on here?" she asked.

"They refuse to go after the white tigress, memsahib."

"What?" Nicky felt her stomach contract as if he'd delivered a physical blow. If the hunt were called off, she was as good as shipped home. "Why not?"

"They have heard stories, frightening stories of spirits protecting the tigress. If they kill her, they believe she will come back from the dead to attack the village."

"That's superstitious nonsense! They refuse to work because of that? I don't believe it. They want more money."

Nursoo shook his head. "Even if I were to offer more money, they would refuse to come. They believe they will be haunted; their lives ruined. To them, no money is worth this sacrifice."

The churning in her stomach increased as Nicky watched the natives disperse, heedless of Nursoo's shouted commands. When only Nursoo remained, his face flushed from yelling, she asked, "Does my uncle know of this?"

"I have just learned of their fears, memsahib. You are the first I have spoken to of the problem."

Nicky thought furiously. Finding more men before her uncle or Drew called off the hunt presented a formidable task. "Why now?" She spoke the words softly, almost to herself, then looked up to meet the native's sharp gaze. "Why were we not told of this . . . this superstition before?"

The Indian's dark complexion deepened. "A man in the village does not want the hunt. He makes up the tale to scare the men and ruin the *hankwa* for the tigress. He turns the men away with his lies."

Nicky felt the blood rise to her face with boiling intensity. "Who! Who would sabotage the hunt?"

Rather than lowering his eyes submissively, in native fashion, the guide stared at Nicky directly. His dark eyes scanned her face speculatively, as if he were the patron evaluating her for some duty rather than the other way around. He remained curiously silent until a slow smile crept across his lips beneath his mustache.

"The sahib's name is Holt Atley. He learned of the *hankwa* from you, memsahib. He told me he wishes you to fail in your quest for the white tigress. That he will do anything to thwart your efforts, including tell these lies."

Nicky's jaw worked up and down in astonishment. She remembered her hasty boast to Holt that she would bag a tiger and his insulting response. Would he go to such lengths to see her challenge unfulfilled? Could he stoop to sabotage with hocus pocus threats of spirits and hauntings?

As if she needed more prodding, the native added, "It is a personal matter, I believe." He examined the end of the sash tied across his hips, before looking up. "Perhaps a vendetta against you or one of your party? Holt sahib promises you will never succeed in bagging the white tigress."

She pressed her lips together in an uncompromising line. Apparently Mr. Atley was willing to play low to see his prediction of her incompetency hold true.

"Hire others," she commanded.

"The result will be the same, mistress. No one will go after the tigress now. Maybe a Dom desperate for a few paise, but they are menials. No one with the true skills needed will come to our aid. The hunt is doomed."

"Round up anyone you can—if they're able to walk and follow simple instructions, they have a job. Double the pay, if you must." Nicky's gaze shifted over the Indian's head to the village behind their camp. "I'll be right back."

Nicky whipped around Nursoo and marched toward the village just beyond the walnut grove where they'd camped. A few choice curses ran through her mind. She could think of only one reason Atley would sabotage the hunt. She'd met his type before. Men who couldn't abide the thought of women pursuing areas they believed the exclusive domain of males. In the past, she'd been amazed by the lengths so-called "gentlemen" would go in order to muddle her efforts at hunting, thereby supporting their own inbred feelings of superiority. One man had even "accidently" shoved her arm to ruin her aim when she'd come perilously close to beating his companion in a target shoot, unable to accept the idea that a woman might win over a man in a game of skill. If someone of supposed breeding could stoop to such tactics, nothing the American did should surprise her.

On the outskirts of the village, Nicky watched a tribe of Doms huddled around cooking fires made of cow dung their women gathered in the fields. Half starved, the near-black men, clothed only in skimpy loincloths, hardly looked fit to pursue their usual job of scavenging the refuse of the upper caste natives and the white man, much less capable of the highly physical duties required for a hunting expedition in the foothills of the Himalayas.

The Doms belonged to the lowest caste of people, the Sudra. She'd learned that much from the magazines and books her brother had smuggled to her past her mother and uncle. A Brahman could not let the shadow of a Dom fall upon his food without fearing contamination. Pariahs in a country where no one escaped the circumstances of their birth, the Dom lived as scavengers and providers of light for the funeral pyres of the second born, never acquiring any skills, barely able to find enough to feed themselves. And it was among these poor souls their guide would produce the beaters, carriers, and personal servants for the hunt?

Nicky's mouth twisted into a frown; she felt a certain affinity with the painfully thin, dark people she passed at the gate. The Dom were not the only victims of their birth. She, too, had been marked indelibly by the past. It was that heritage she needed to meet and conquer here in India. Now, the petty prejudices of one man threatened her carefully constructed plans. Holt Atley had claimed she did not belong here, and he was doing his best to cut her stay short. Nicky clenched her fists, digging her nails into the palms of her hands. Miserable lying rotter! He'd not drive her away.

Climbing the stone causeway to the top of the spur where the village rested, Nicky found Atley's house without difficulty. As the only white man living in Baijnarn, the location of his meager abode had been pointed out to the English travelers with the same pride and enthusiasm with which one might have displayed the Tower of London back home. Unlike the buildings made of bared stone piled without mortar, Holt's house was whitewashed and of a suitable size to impress his neighbors, who lived in modest one-room dwellings. As she neared, she saw the culprit sitting on the wooden bench of his porch, where guests were traditionally entertained, away from the inner courtyard used by wealthy Hindus and Muslims to seclude their women. The sight of him calmly smoking a *bidi,* a native cigarette, his legs propped up on a bamboo chair before him, only fueled her ire. She sped up the steps, coming within arms' reach of him, feeling her anger like trapped steam ready to burst out and scald him. He just sat there, not bothering to rise, taking a lazy puff of the cigarette as if she were some bothersome insect he chose to ignore.

With a good solid hit, she kicked the chair out from under his feet. His legs slammed down to the stone porch and he bounded to his feet.

Now she had his attention.

"Mr. Atley, I understand you've predicted doom and gloom for the men of my hunt." She planted both fists on her hips. "In the guru business? Or is this a special effort for my benefit?" Nicole jabbed a finger in the middle of his chest, but his lips remained set in an obnoxious smile, feeding her anger. "You dare to sabotage *my* hunt with your stories of spooks and spirits?" Nicky felt the little hold she had on her temper slip. "Who the *hell* do you think you are, mister?"

"My, my." Holt took a slow pull from the hand-rolled cigarette and exhaled a stream of smoke. "Showing a bit of brass this morning, are you?"

Nicky felt her face burn beet red at her language and his mocking response. His lips twisted in a leer as he glanced down to her trousers.

"Herringbone like that little outfit?" Dark lashes swept up to reveal amused green eyes. "Does he play dress up for you, too?"

The suggestive lift of his brows elicited a horrid picture of poor Drew dressed in a voluminous gown. Furious that Atley could conjure such an image in her mind, Nicole attacked. "What are you afraid of, Mr. Atley? That I might actually succeed and bag a tiger? Can't you accept that a woman can be just as good at this sport as a man?"

Holt Atley stared into the wide-spaced, topaz eyes—panther eyes. Looking at the sharp, exotic features and dark thick tresses that today fanned over her shoulders to her hips, he again had the image of Indian royalty. Only the mannish hunting attire recalled her British roots, breaking the fantasy and bringing home the threat she presented. She'd vowed to take her group of hunters and kill one of the most unique animals in India—just to prove that she was as good as a man.

He threw the *bidi* onto the blue slate porch, slowly grinding the cigarette beneath the heel of his boot. She was a woman who made a career of challenging men. He shook his head. It was a damned shame, really. If there weren't so much at stake, he'd actually enjoy picking up the gauntlet.

With one long lingering look at the curves of her body, he strolled to her, bringing them within a hand's span of each other. When she stepped away, he pressed forward, backing her toward the front door. She tried to veer around him off the porch, but he hooked his arm around her waist and corralled her through the threshold. Once inside his house, he slammed the wood door shut with his foot and leaned against it. His arms crossed over his chest, he watched her hasten around his jackwood table to the opposite side, almost stumbling over a chair. One of the many charcoal drawings that covered the table fluttered to the ground.

"Lady, you want to prove you're a man?" Another sweep of his eyes and a lift of his brows suggested surprise. "You got the clothes right." He inspected each item she wore, from her fine polished boots to her stylish shooting jacket, with indecent intensity. "You've even got a big gun, as I recall. Just like a man." He dropped his gaze and stepped forward while staring directly at the crotch of her trousers. "But something's missing."

She backed away. "What are you doing?"

He advanced. "Making a point."

Holding her hands before her like a barrier, she warned, "Don't come any closer."

"Lady, I'm planning to come a whole hell of a lot closer."

A spark of fear in her eyes flickered like the yellow center of a flame when her backside met the teak chest against the wall. She almost upset the glass and half-empty bottle of arrack he'd left out as she reached behind her, resting her hands on the chest for balance. He watched her glance anxiously left, then right. Holt smiled, stepping around the table. The quarry was cornered. Score one for his side.

She darted to the side, trying to bolt around him. He grabbed her easily. Wrapping his arms around her, he cupped her buttocks in both hands and gave a soft, suggestive squeeze. "Didn't your mother ever tell you there's a difference between boys and girls?" Ignoring her efforts to break free, he pulled her flush against him, making the difference between their anatomies perfectly clear. "Lady, you'll never be a man."

Nicky stopped struggling. Her magnificent gold eyes met his gaze dead on, all traces of fear gone. "Or as good as one?" she challenged.

Holt felt the soft but firm curves he held in his palms. The two luscious forms were of a perfect shape and weighed temptingly in his hands. Breasts of a surprising proportion considering her small frame were crushed against his chest. He almost laughed, but found his mouth suddenly too dry for it. "Honey, right now I'd say you look a hell of a lot better than a man."

Before she could respond, Holt lowered his lips and brushed his mouth against the soft cushion of hers. He felt her gasp of surprise against his lips. The gently expelled breath only excited him more. The beginnings of a mumbled protest rumbled deep in her throat, but he captured the response with his mouth. Pressing his lips firmly against the slant of hers, he kissed her silent.

3

With the touch of his lips against hers, Nicole remembered her dream.

She had fantasized this very scene, created in her mind the forbidden pleasure that surged through her now. The same muscular chest pressed against her; the same tempting lips molded hers that she'd imagined in those blurred visions of passion the night before. A pleasant warmth radiated from her stomach, as if she'd drunk too much of her brother's precious Bordeaux. Her arms felt heavy and she leaned closer, seeking the support of the strong arms that held her. The slightly sweet taste of his mouth contrasted with the pungent bite of tobacco as his tongue slipped beyond her lips and his mouth slanted to a more satisfying angle. Control faded, time stopped, and the visions her mind had created in her sleep merged with reality. She allowed herself to relive the dream, to revel in the passion that turned the memory of Drew's kiss lukewarm by contrast—until she felt the shame.

It came with the gentle stroke of his fingers at the curve of her breast, creeping beyond her cocoon of pleasure: a shocking sense of wrongness.

Unlike her fantasy, reality carried a price. She couldn't indulge herself as she had in her dream. Trying to recapture the self-respect she'd sacrificed by her response, she latched onto his wrists and broke free of his arms.

She stood there, silent, watching him warily. Like her, he was breathing hard, as if they'd finished a fencing match and not just a kiss. He looked puzzled, apparently just as shocked by what had happened as she. Then slowly, a very wide, very smug smile shaped his lips.

A smoldering pain blazed across her chest at the sight of that smugness, knowing exactly its genesis. Her response to his kiss, that second of indecision, had proven his point better than any argument he could have forwarded: She was just a woman, an inferior species, easily subjugated by the man before her.

With absolutely not a care to the consequences, she swung her arm back for momentum and slapped her open hand across that cocksure grin.

The resounding slap snapped his head back. The crack echoed across the near-empty room. Holt's grin vanished. In its place emerged a dark, dangerous scowl. He looked as if he wanted to hit her. For a moment, Nicole feared he actually might, then she raised her chin an inch with an expression that said, "Go ahead and try!"

He grabbed her shoulders and forced his lips against hers with punishing strength. Nicole kicked, swung her fists, wildly landing chance blows on his shins, his back, his shoulders, but she failed to deflect his bruising mouth. In the end, he stopped the kiss—pushing her away with enough force to make her stumble back against the table. Not bothering to flip back the hair that blurred her view, Nicky again swung her arm, aiming through her curtain of hair, prepared to land a fist at his jaw. He intercepted the blow with one hand. The other, he wrapped around her waist and scooped her to him. He swept the black strands from her face, and twined his fingers through them until he held her head steady at the base of her neck. His mouth slashed across her open lips. His teeth bit the tender skin just inside her mouth; his tongue slipped smoothly within.

Her knee connected with painful accuracy with his groin.

Holt felt the white-hot fires of hell shoot up his stomach from his groin, choking the breath from him. He doubled over, falling to his knees, his hands cradling his injury. A low moan escaped his lips as he crumpled to the ground beside the jackwood table.

When he looked up, Nicky stood above him, panting. To Holt, with her hair a wild mass around her, her eyes blazing like the jeweled eyes of a Kali idol, she looked like some avenging deity ready to deliver another punishing blow.

"I thought you might try just about anything to get what you want, Mr. Atley," she said, her breath labored. "But I never suspected you could stoop *this* low."

Holt could feel the cool wooden floor against his cheek. "This is about as low as any man gets," he agreed with a muffled groan.

"To attack a woman . . ."

A strangled laugh let her know who he thought attacked whom.

". . . alone in your home—"

"Cork it, lady." He pressed his eyes shut and gritted his teeth, trying to stop the waves of pain. "I've had all I can stand of the maiden-in-distress act. You wanted to be the man . . . now's a good time to start acting the part. By the way—it's considered unsporting to hit below the belt." He moaned softly.

"Are you badly hurt? I didn't mean to . . ." Concern crept into her voice. "You frightened me . . . I had to protect myself." But she sounded unsure.

"Do me a favor." Holt took in deep steadying breaths. "Protect yourself right out of here."

"Should I send someone to help you?" She remained hovering over him.

He gave a throaty laugh that ended in a groan of pain. He thought her concern a bit tardy. Taking another deep breath, he looked up. "You wanna help me, lady? Get the hell out of my province."

Her face cleared of any sympathetic softness and her features hardened into sharp planes of anger. "You're not driving me out of India, Mr. Atley. I'll get that tigress. Despite you." Stepping around him, as if he were so much rubbish littering her path, she lifted her splendid chin and headed toward the door.

"Hey, kid." Holt couldn't help his mocking grin when she stopped at the threshold and turned expectantly. "May the best *man* win."

The next thing he heard was the door slamming shut.

Holt flipped onto his back and opened his eyes, concentrating on his breathing as the waves of pain flowed and ebbed. It didn't look like he'd intimidated the kid as he'd planned. If anything, his tactics had made the little she-cat dig in her claws. He'd thought if he could scatter the manpower available for the hunt, the Brits, unable to fathom a hunt without a multitude of servants to fetch and carry, would ship back home with their tails dragging between their legs. Judging from the kid's stubborn expression, she'd make sure her party would continue to hunt the tigress. Apparently, he'd underestimated little Miss Marshall's desire to take home a trophy.

Holt pressed his lips together. *Say it straight, Atley: You underestimated the lady. Period.*

Out of the corner of his eye, Holt watched a gray blur race across the room and dive behind the woodpile next to the cooking hearth. A long tail of alternating white and black stripes extended beyond the concealing wood like a fat, fuzzy ribbon. Holt shook his head. Stupid animal figured she was hidden as long as her head was covered.

Extending his hand toward the woodpile, Holt snapped his fingers. When that got no response, he clucked his tongue and whistled softly through his teeth. The lemur's small white face peeked around the wood, its shiny nose wiggling in the air. "It's all right, Jani girl," he coaxed. "That half sister to a keg of gunpowder is gone."

The ringtail scurried to him, the stubby ears twitching, its nose wriggling right and left with each step. A few inches from Holt's hand, it stood on its fat haunches. Delicate hands hung suspended before the soft, white underside, while the large brown eyes looked on with concern.

Holt reached out and stroked the furry belly. "Don't you worry, Jani. We won't let them get Enchantress." The lemur closed its eyes in appreciation for the attention delivered to its underside, then crept closer until it tucked itself between Holt's arm and his body, plopping its head on his shoulder.

Scratching between Jani's ears absently, Holt concentrated on his latest skirmish with the impervious Miss Marshall. The kiss had been inspiration of the moment. He hadn't planned to touch her, to take her in his arms and caress the luscious curves he'd not been able to forget since he'd first seen her yesterday. The tantalizing body the baggy trousers had hinted at was real enough. What he'd stroked and explored as he'd held her in his arms had been better than even the dark fantasies he'd dreamed last night. And their kiss, it had started off as a lark, then turned to something more. Something dark, full of power, that made him forget it was merely a game he was playing. That first taste of her had made him want much more.

Holt placed his forearm under his head like a pillow, as the queasy sickness at his stomach uncoiled its tendrils and Jani snuggled closer, drifting off into a satisfied slumber. He thought about the second kiss, the one he'd meted out like punishment after she'd slapped him. He concentrated on it like a tongue exploring a sore tooth, puzzling over his use of passion as a weapon. At the time, it seemed a better response than taking her by the shoulders and shaking her silly, like he'd wanted to do. But now he wasn't so sure. He found the idea of kissing a woman in a hurtful manner repugnant. In his thirty-one years, he'd never done such a thing. He considered sex something precious to be shared.

Judging by her reaction, she'd sensed his threat. In spite of her small stature, she'd managed to put them on equal footing quickly enough. And in a way, he was glad she had. Though it disturbed him to admit, he couldn't really say what he would have done next if she hadn't.

Holt stared up at the beams of the ceiling. He knew it that

first day he'd seen her there in the grass. The lady was nothing but trouble.

So why the hell did he feel like going another round with
her rather than putting as much distance between them as
possible?

If not for Enchantress, he'd kiss her again. In a minute. If
he ever got the chance.

That surprised him.

"Blast," he whispered.

Reacting immediately to his changed mood, Jani lifted
her head off his shoulder and peered about for danger.

The soft click and creak of the door as it swung open sent
her racing back to the cover of the woodpile. Propping himself up on his elbows, Holt turned toward the entrance
where he made out Nursoo's tall figure. He was dressed like
Holt in buckskin trousers and a baggy native shirt. Holt had
given him those pants after he'd seen how much Nursoo
admired his own. They'd been friends then.

Using the table as a prop, Holt sat up, realizing Nursoo
wasn't coming in as he would have in the past. Their
changed status would take getting used to. From Nursoo's
expression, Holt doubted this was a social call. A knowing
smile graced the Hindu's generous mouth, a grin so satisfied
that not even Nursoo's impressive mustache could hide its
smugness. At that moment, the sequence of events fell into
place for Holt.

"I suppose I have you to thank for Miss Marshall's little
visit?" he asked, dusting his hands off on his trousers as he
stood. "Whatever you said to her, it worked. The lady almost put an end to a part of my anatomy I'm particularly
fond of."

Nursoo chuckled softly. "Is it not a countryman of yours
who said there is nothing so terrible as a woman's scorn?"

"Something like that," he answered, not bothering to correct the quote.

"She is a woman of spirit, sahib. A worthy rival for you. I
believe she will be a great aid in the quest for the tigress."

Holt felt his stomach sink against the back of his ribs when he imagined the intensity she'd displayed fighting him focused on finding and killing Enchantress. Despite her hesitation with the leopard, she seemed determined to shoot the white tigress. With Nursoo's help, she and her party might succeed in bagging Enchantress.

But then Holt was no mossback, either.

"We'll just see about that, Nursoo."

"Yes, sahib," the Indian answered, a wistful sadness strung through his voice. "We shall."

Nursoo shut the door behind him, and Holt heard his steps recede. He took two paces to the door to follow, then stopped. With a sigh, he leaned against the sturdy jackwood table behind him, which served every purpose from dining table to writing desk, and glanced at one of the drawings that littered its smooth surface. He began flipping through the sketches of Indian wildlife covering the table until he came across one of Enchantress. He stared at the drawing, a charcoal that didn't do justice to the majestic animal's beauty despite its accuracy.

Nursoo was serious about this hunt. Nothing would deter him from guiding the Marshalls. He had stoked the fires that had blazed within Miss Marshall's eyes. Whatever he'd told her, he'd managed to double her resolve to go after the tigress. Score one for Nursoo. But Holt wasn't worried.

He'd just begun to fight.

Padmini stared through the gap in the courtyard wall where the crumbling mortar had given way under the weight of the stones. When the tall Khasiya man she knew as Nursoo walked past her hiding place, she held her veil tight, covering her face. It was a needless gesture; she knew he would not look her way. He would stare straight ahead, careful to avoid the site of his humiliation.

Each step he took placed him farther from her. Padmini thought it symbolic of the growing distance between her future and that of her would-be husband's. Despite the heavy sadness such thoughts brought, her heart raced faster than the beat of her mother's grindstone as she admired the handsome hunter in those fleeting moments stolen from her household chores. Though from a clan of little influence, Nursoo walked with the grace and proud carriage of any hill Rajput. His immaculate tan trousers and blue shirt belted at his hips with a brilliant red sash evinced a prosperity sorely lacking in her faded and patched skirt and bodice. His years with the sahib had brought him much wealth and had increased his social stature. How could her father threaten to call off their wedding—especially now, when at eighteen she was too old to reserve another husband and her family too poor to pay the dowry Nursoo had graciously forfeited?

Gathering a basket filled with the wheat she would grind for the family's daily *roti,* she turned back toward the grindstone near the entrance to the house. She passed her two sisters-in-law, Rumbha and Deepali, who were busy spinning as their children ran across the courtyard. With an ease earned from practice, Padmini ignored the sly looks and whispers of the two women as she walked by. In a household where the wives and children of her brothers lived off the charity of her father, Padmini's status as her father's daughter should have elevated her above that of the vicious Rumbha and Deepali. But her parents' growing frustration with the family's finances, depleted by the need to marry off three daughters, had focused itself on Padmini, giving her sisters-in-law free rein to play their petty games of spite.

Suppressing a sigh of sadness, Padmini paused at the doorway leading to the three-story house she shared with ten others and reverently patted the head of their only cow. If her marriage were canceled, as Rumbha had hinted, she would soon be eating from the leavings of her nephews and nieces at the evening meal and her humiliation would be complete.

Padmini raised her hand to her neck and fingered the silver necklace she never removed. How she'd rejoiced when Nursoo had sent his sister's necklace and her father had allowed her to keep the silver jewelry in acceptance of the marriage proposal. Nursoo had been her first breath of hope since the death of the boy she had been betrothed to when she was ten. Her parents had successfully hidden her widow status from the others of the village, the deceased bridegroom being from a faraway village in Garhwal. Padmini thought it unfair that the death of a boy she had never seen, whom she had not even wed, would make her a widow—a thing of disdain—simply because they'd been betrothed. Her parents had hoped to find another bridegroom for their youngest daughter, but for years they had been unsuccessful. Only Nursoo had shown any interest in her.

Padmini thought him perfect. He was of her caste, though as her father often complained, he was of a lower clan than her sisters' influential husbands. She'd dreamed of the day he'd take her to his native village, away from the drudgery she experienced at home. Yet, two years after their *sagai* engagement ceremony, her father still refused to set the wedding date. Last month, Nursoo had come to demand that the date be set, only to be sent away with threats that the engagement would be called off for some mysterious reason she'd been unable to overhear. Was her father crazed? How could he possibly call off her wedding? The family's only assets were the bit of land her brothers worked and the decaying mansion her father had inherited but could not maintain or repair. Even her father could not dare to sink them deeper into debt by paying the groom price necessary to marry Padmini to a man of a higher sept, as he had done with his other daughters.

"Daydreaming again, oh fair one?"

Padmini started at Rumbha's malicious reference to her dark skin color, another mark against her marriageability. The slur fetched a nervous giggle from Deepali.

"Hold on tight to your silver, Mini, lest the bridegroom snatch the necklace back," Rumbha added with vicious glee.

Padmini spun around, still holding the precious jewelry

between her fingers. "It is not the bridegroom who delays my marriage, as well you know, *Bhabhi.*"

Her sister-in-law shrugged. Leaning toward Deepali, she whispered loudly, "Poor Mini. Her delusions of marriage grow stronger. She does not wish to see what is clearly before her eyes."

Padmini opened her mouth to refute Rumbha's rude prediction when a vicious look crossed Rumbha's face and her sister-in-law whispered under her breath, "Widow."

"Unclean," echoed Deepali.

Padmini fled inside the dark, dank room, her fears making her hands shake. As she took deep breaths to calm herself, the pungent scent of the fresh cow dung she had spread across the floor earlier stung her nostrils. Though they would never speak it to anyone outside the family, her sisters-in-law taunted her with her secret shame. How much longer could she hide the fact she was a widow? If Nursoo discovered her first bridegroom had died, would he refuse to marry her? Not all Khasiyas forbade widow marriage. And yet, wasn't it true that her widowhood could prove bad luck for her husband? Should she not tell Nursoo the truth and let him decide if he were willing to take the risk? Despite her guilt about her deception, Padmini knew she would say nothing. She feared too much losing Nursoo and remaining in Baijnarn, the bane of her family.

Determined not to let her sisters-in-law corner her like a frightened beast in the *ghar* house, Padmini tucked her basket closer and crossed the small quarters back to the courtyard. She did not even look to where Deepali and Rumbha sat, but settled before the grindstone just beyond the entryway. As she pounded the wheat kernels with the wooden paddle, she tried to forget Rumbha's allusions to her ruined marriage prospects. Instead, she concentrated on the night she met Nursoo.

He'd caused a great stir when he and the sahib had moved to her village. The sahib, Holt Atley, had purchased the village from the two Brahman families who still lived there, but whose impoverished status had left them little say in village matters. At first, Nursoo lived with the sahib, but later he built his own modest home in the village. But the two continued to work closely together for years, and many, including Padmini, admired Nursoo for his close relationship with the powerful and wealthy sahib. When she grew old enough to care, she would watch for glimpses of the handsome *shikaree*. At night, when she was allowed to leave the seclusion of the women's quarters to gather wood and bring water from the well, she would search him out and watch him with girlish infatuation. Until the day her childish game came to an end.

He was setting a "victim," a young goat, for the morning's hunt as she watched him from behind a wall of tall grass, admiring his youthful strength as he climbed the tree to check the *machan* that would be used as a shooting platform in the morning. The hour growing late, she tried to slip away soundlessly, but he heard her. At first he aimed his gun at her, thinking her a tiger. But her gasp warned him, and he held his fire only to say he must be dreaming the vision of female beauty before him. She immediately ran away, frightened that her scandalous conduct would be discovered.

The second time she saw him, she was at the well, and he asked her for a drink of water. He held his cupped hands below her brass pot and she poured water over them, as he sluiced his face and neck, then drank. She was so intent on providing a steady stream that she allowed her veil to slip. He looked up then and smiled, saying her name softly.

Oh, such a wonderful, tender smile he had given her. She had smiled in return, trying to show her heart's desire in her look of admiration. When she'd noticed her veil, she had been so frightened she'd dropped the urn and fled—then endured a beating by her mother for having forgotten one of their finest pots at the well.

A painful pinch to her arm vanished Padmini's memories. As if her thoughts had come to life, her mother stood before her. Alarmed by the hateful expression that marred her mother's already haggard features, Padmini dropped the wooden paddle that had lain idle in her hands for too long.

"I see Rumbha is telling the truth for once. My lazy daughter is again daydreaming and ignoring her work."

"*Maji*, I have just started to prepare for the evening meal."

"You lazy girl, your brothers will be in from the fields soon and expect their food to be ready. What have you prepared for them?"

"I thought Rumbha and Deepali—"

"You did *not* think, as usual. You sit and daydream about a husband that will not be."

Padmini felt ill at her mother's words. "Is that true, *Maji*? Did father tell you something new?"

Padmini felt her fear hang suspended between them, as her mother examined her from hooded eyes. "Bah! Your father dreams of riches. His greed will leave me with you as a yoke around my neck for years still."

"Has he called off the wedding?" she asked, alarmed.

A sharp slap across her face answered her questions.

"Do not be stupid. Who else but a worthless Khasiya would have you? Your father merely bargains for what he has no right to ask. He may ruin his peace of mind in the next life for his greed in this one." Her mother pursed her lips into a scowl. "You are as insolent as ever, my daughter. It is time you stop your daydreams and work like the rest of us."

A hand made clawlike from years of hardship grabbed the silver necklace and ripped it from Padmini's neck. Her mother weighed the jewelry in her hand. With a vicious smile, she tucked the necklace in her skirt. "I will keep this until you have earned the right to wear it. Get back to work, lazy Padmini."

Tears filled Padmini's eyes as her mother carried away the necklace. She knew better than to plead for what was hers. Any rights she had depended entirely on her mother's whims. As she watched the older woman disappear with her only treasure, Padmini felt as if she'd lost more than the precious silver.

Nicky battled with her conscience as she stomped down the road toward camp, digging her boot heels into the dirt. The enticing smell of curry and roasting chilies wafted around her, almost conquering the stench of cow dung cooking fires. Women dressed in flowing skirts and veils of bright colors, balancing enormous earthenware jugs on their heads, swerved out of her path with the grace and elegance any prima ballerina would envy. Before an open doorway, men clustered around a *hookah* pipe rapidly discussing village matters in their native tongue with the intensity of opposing factions in Parliament.

She'd done the right thing, she comforted herself. Hadn't her brother taught her the maneuver, skimming discreetly over the details of the male anatomy while making his point about a man's vulnerability? Hadn't he trained her to defend her virtue, practiced with her until the move became almost a reflex? And yet Keane had failed to prepare her for the total incapacitation she'd witnessed after she shoved her knee in that vulnerable spot between Holt's legs. Off balance, she hadn't even hit him hard. She'd assumed he'd get right up, but he'd just lain there, writhing in pain. . . .

Oh for heaven's sake, the man had forced himself on her! She would not regret what she'd done. She'd been protecting herself.

Or had she merely vented her anger because she'd responded to his kiss, betraying Drew?

Nicky pressed her lips together, remembering the soft, seductive touch of his mouth. Though she'd spent a great deal of time around men, thanks to her uncle, none had ever looked at her like Holt had—as if he were watching a truly desirable woman. For an instant, his kiss had made her forget everything, the tiger hunt, his lies to the natives, even Drew. But then the thing had turned ugly, and he'd forced himself on her in a way that had frightened her and yet tantalized her as well. Nicole shivered. It was best to stay away from Holt Atley—a very dangerous man.

Nicky rounded the bend toward camp, concentrating on her steps to divert her aching conscience. Here, on the outskirts of town, single-room stone huts with slate roofs lay in a cluster on the hillside. The rancid smell of animals and humans living at close quarters almost overpowered her. It was no wonder the Indians spent most of their time outdoors, often preferring to sleep under the stars rather than under their roofs. The first night their party had camped here, Nicky had been stunned by the sight of white-sheeted men dotting the hillside as they slept, looking much like gardens of linen that had sprouted before each doorstep during the night.

Approaching her tent, the sight of a rider barreling toward camp caught her attention. The horse was winded and sweating, as if its rider had traveled quite a distance at a fast clip. When she recognized Drew, her guilt threatened to overwhelm her. Nicky fought off her sense of shame over the kiss. She would forget the disastrous morning. Once they set out on the hunt, Holt Atley need never concern her. In all probability, she'd never see the man again.

She smiled and waved to Drew. He returned the gesture, then dismounted, instructing a native to take care of the lathered horse. Watching him dismount, she noticed for the first time he had on the same clothes he'd worn the day before. It was quite odd, really. Drew was always so meticulous about his appearance. Apparently their primitive surroundings had forced even Drew to compromise his unbending standards.

"I'm sorry I'm late, darling." Drew clasped her two hands within his larger ones. "I was having a quick look around camp this morning. Just give me a moment; I won't delay us much longer."

"You needn't rush." She watched his dark brows draw together over his pale eyes. Seeing no way to get around the truth, Nicky explained, "You're not the holdup. The natives, I'm afraid they've left us high and dry. Some superstition about the tigress." She shrugged her shoulders. "They refuse to go on the hunt."

"We must organize something immediately!" The distress she saw on his face surprised Nicole. Frowning slightly, she listened as Drew continued, "If your uncle gets wind of this, he's sure to call the whole thing off. I'll have to arrange for other servants."

"Actually, I've already discussed that with the guide." Drew's blue eyes widened as Nicole added, "He's recruiting them now."

A cool smile lifted the corners of his thin mouth. Drew leaned forward and caressed her cheek with the back of his hand. "That's my darling. You're just as anxious as I am for this hunt to succeed. I'll go look for the guide and see how he's managing, shall I?"

Without waiting for an answer, Drew turned and walked away. Odd again, she thought, watching him nearly run down a native blocking his way as Drew sped to the village gates. Somehow, she'd thought he would feel the same as her uncle about the loss of help, that he would retreat rather than experience discomfort. And here he was rushing to regroup. She walked to her tent and drew back the flap ready to scoot inside. Well, his help was certainly appreciated.

Holt hefted the strap of the Hall's carbine high up on his shoulder, giving a passing member of the *panchayat,* the village council, a quick nod in greeting. After he'd managed to recover his wind—as well as his pride—from the blow delivered by Miss Marshall's knee, he'd acted quickly. If the Marshall party planned to continue to hunt Enchantress, Holt couldn't afford to sit around and lick his wounds. He had plans.

With the familiarity of a native, he wound his way through the maze of alleys separating the piled-stone hovels at the edge of town, intent on retrieving his horse and launching into his strategy for defense. As he turned one corner, he caught sight of Nursoo, his tall figure huddled against the wall of a hut. The deep-seated sense of danger that Holt had developed as a soldier and a hunter clicked its warning inside his gut. With a step so quiet that it would not disturb a tiger at twenty paces upwind, he crept toward Nursoo. The Indian turned when Holt came up directly behind him. He held his finger to his lips in a gesture of silence. A familiar camaraderie pulsed between them as their eyes met. Holt gave a short nod. For this instant in time, they were once again partners.

Following Nursoo's example, Holt leaned flat against the stone wall and listened to the haunting buzz of furtive whispers coming from around the bend. Two things about the hushed murmurs drew his attention immediately. The men spoke in English, and Morgan's unmistakable Irish brogue dominated the discussion.

". . . the raja be wantin' his messenger . . . see the goods . . ."

"I'm afraid that's quite impossible," answered a man's voice with a clipped British accent. "He'll have to trust me. The raja need not worry. Delivery will be when and where I said. He'll get his treasure, and I'll get mine, just as we planned."

Holt heard Morgan speak in the Korku dialect, a talent that had thus far gained him the position of intermediary for any illicit deed from here to Oudh. A native replied heatedly in Korku, apparently not trusting the Brit. Holt felt a tingle down his spine as he exchanged a knowing glance with Nursoo. Damn that double-crossing snake of an Irishman! Holt had sensed a Korku tagging along was a bit fortuitous. That Irish misbegotten dog was up to something.

"Not good enough, lime-juicer—"

"I told you not to call me that!"

Morgan's voice dropped lower and Holt had to lean forward to catch the words.

". . . seen her meself. That's a real tigress yer after. She'll be one hell of a wedding present. Maybe if I tagged along until . . . ready to deliver, to look after the raja's interests."

"Would he trust you?"

"I've worked for the raja before. Remember? T'was me who introduced ye. And I have me friend . . ."

"All right, then. As it so happens, I have a perfect excuse for you to join the hunt. The guide, Nursoo, is looking for more men. You and the native join up with the hunting party. You keep an eye on the raja's . . . present. In fact, you might be of some help. I might be able to use you should there be any complications."

"Now yer thinkin', man. Cost ye a couple a quid, but I'll do a good job for ye."

"Of course, I didn't think you'd help out of the goodness of your heart. Don't worry, Morgan, you'll be adequately compensated . . . depending on how useful you turn out to be."

There was a soft scuffle of feet followed by silence. Holt pushed off the wall and glanced around the corner. The street was empty, except for Harrington's retreating figure.

Holt stood watching the Englishman walk away. "Well I'll be damned!"

Nursoo nodded his head. "It is a most difficult circumstance. Very ill-advised for the memsahib's betrothed to be involved with that jackal."

Holt turned to Nursoo. "*I* hired him. *I* paid the Irish bastard to work for *me*!"

Nursoo appeared startled. "An unwise selection, Holt sahib."

He gave Nursoo a look of contempt. "Yeah, well, my first choice had a prior commitment . . . in the enemy camp!" Holt swore under his breath. "Damn that cheating cur to the devil. Damn *you* and this stupid hunt!"

Nursoo nodded his head sadly. "It is also difficult for me that we are working at cross purposes."

"There's other ways to make money, Nursoo," Holt said, anxious for a solution. "The man-eater at Askot. We could hunt it down together, just like old times. The government's offering plenty to destroy that menace."

"My share would not be two hundred rupees."

Holt grabbed Nursoo by his shoulders, shaking him as if he could rattle some sense into him. "I'll give you the blasted money! I'll lend it to you! I'll make you slave for it for the rest of your life if that's what it takes. Swallow that Hindu pride of yours and let me help you."

Nursoo's dark eyes clouded. With a swing of his arms, he jerked free. "I do not need charity. Nor will I put myself in debt like Padmini's father, whose fear of the moneylenders eats at his heart until he stoops to blackmail. I can provide for my bride." He lowered his voice and added softly, "If I could not, I would not deserve her."

"It's not the same as borrowing from a moneylender, Nursoo. You're my friend . . ."

"Perhaps you will remember that when I lead the *hankwa* for the tigress."

"You ask too much." He examined Nursoo's expectant face, then shook his head. "I can't. I just can't, dammit."

"I thought of you as a brother, sahib . . ." The words trailed off like an accusation.

"I thought the same, Nursoo," Holt said with equal censure. "I thought the same."

When he turned to walk away, Nursoo stopped him with a hand at his shoulder. "There is something that I do not understand about this plan of the British sahib's."

"What's to understand?" Holt ground out between clenched teeth. "He's selling Enchantress to some Korku raja."

"No. I do not believe so." Holt was about to argue, until Nursoo held up his hand for silence. "When he spoke of the tigress, the jackal's tone was strange, as if he did not speak of an ordinary tigress—"

"Enchantress isn't ordinary—"

"As if he spoke not of an animal at all." Nursoo looked straight into Holt's eyes. "I do not believe the British lord trades for Enchantress. I believe he delivers a woman."

4

"A woman?" A prickle of recognition stung the back of his neck, but Holt dismissed it immediately. "Right," he said caustically. "A British lord comes to India to trade dancing girls and concubines to some highland raja. He brings his fiancée along to boot. Maybe she's even involved? She could pick 'em out for Herringbone. 'Here's a pretty one, Harry dear. Let's take her.'" He shook his head. "You've been smoking the dream stick, Nursoo."

"I do not take of the poppy, as well you know, sahib. It is the manner in which the jackal spoke that makes me believe they discuss a woman."

"You and I both heard him. It's a wedding present. A 'real tigress' he said."

"The white tigress is one of a kind."

"Exactly, a prize—"

"Then why must the Korku *see* her? What is to compare?" The Hindu's brows knit together. "But such an examination is often done with women—"

"And other valuables."

Nursoo remained silent for a moment, considering Holt's words.

"What do you care, Nursoo?" Holt asked. "Even if that bakeheaded Brit were knee-deep in the slave trade, what concern is it of yours?"

The Indian looked up, surprised. "If the British sahib trades women, we must stop him."

"We?"

Nursoo nodded. "There is no one else. That fat superintendent, Sewgolam, he concerns himself only with terrorizing those who cannot pay their rents. Holt sahib, there are few enough women in our villages." When Holt said nothing, Nursoo bristled. "Why protect them from suttee or from death at the hands of their parents at birth if you allow them to be sold to some untouchable raja in his jungle kingdom?"

Holt grimaced. It was true. Widow burning and infanticide were the two things Holt had actively worked to change in the Hindu culture. Widows from a high caste never remarried; they followed their husbands to their destinies in ritual burnings on the funeral pyre. Despite the abolition of the practice by the British government three decades ago, fresh suttee stones appeared every year to commemorate new suicidal burnings.

Female infanticide was another fact of life in the north. Hypergamy ran rampant among the Rajputs and Jats. The honor of a family often depended on the marriage of daughters to youths of a superior sept than their own. And these grooms didn't come cheap. The payment of a bridegroom price and the inordinate expenditures in marriage entertainments and dowry could seriously cripple a man's resources if his quiver were full of daughters.

The sumptuary laws advocated by bureaucrats living thousands of miles away in England wouldn't stop the killings. Of that Holt was sure. Putting a cap on the money spent on weddings would never change the ambitious soul of a Thakur. Holt had done what he could to stop the practice —often going to such lengths as witnessing births as a representative of the British government and keeping detailed notes on the increase or decrease in the female population. In Baijnarn and the surrounding villages, his actions had made a difference. But the number affected ranged in the thousands.

Holt returned Nursoo's challenging gaze. It was no wonder his friend felt protective of the women in the village.

Infanticide and widow burning had kept the number of females to about twenty percent that of the male population. Nursoo was just one of many bachelors who had searched in vain for years before finding a bride. And while many never made a marriage, Holt could not truly call Nursoo's engagement a success. Padmini's father had been willing to contract her to Nursoo—at a price. Unfortunately for Nursoo, the price had been high, too high for him to produce the money.

Until the Marshalls showed up hunting Enchantress.

Holt turned away. "Fat Sewgolam aside, your coconut's missing the milk if you think Herringbone's selling women." He shouldered past Nursoo. "Damn sakes! That ass-brained aristocrat is here with his fiancée and her uncle. He's some blithering British lord, not a slaver!"

"I will keep my eye on him, just the same," Nursoo called after him.

Holt stopped, addressing Nursoo from half the length of the stone hovel away. "You do that. I'll be watching Enchantress."

Following the twisting alleys to his original destination, the grove outside the village where his Arabian grazed, Holt navigated his way to the village bazaar. Lost in his own musings, he nearly collided with a Sannyasi mendicant seated in meditation, dreaming away life under the thralldom of intoxicants. As Holt turned past a corn sellers stall, where a holy cow nibbled unrestrained, he thought how those drugs provided easy answers for the ascetic. He could use a few answers himself—like what the hell was Herringbone doing trading Enchantress? What could a poor Korku bastard give an English lord to motivate such an act? Certainly not money, the highland natives had none. They were barbarians, their jungle world completely untouched by any civilized society, British or Indian.

Another riddle wormed its way into his consciousness as he pounded his way through the market and beyond—one that did not concern Herringbone or Enchantress, but a sphinx of a woman named Nicole. He could still picture her, aiming her rifle with ease at the leopard, her movements graceful, assured. With the same expertise, she'd uncocked her rifle and lowered the gun, courting death as surely as any Sannyasi who gave up material life to reach his gods. But her strong resolve after she'd recovered from the fright of the leopard attack—the same assuredness she'd demonstrated when she'd spoken of her desire to shoot Enchantress—had nothing to do with martyrdom. It was pride, pure and simple. She wanted to prove herself the best, to boast of her kill and display Enchantress's pelt across some pastel wall at her English estate, and the consequences be damned!

Yet, as he reached the outskirts of town, Holt saw a sizeable crack in his theory of Nicole's boastful intent. He stopped, as if the thought were a puzzle that required all his concentration, and he could no longer guide himself along the well-known path to his horse. If ever she'd hungered for a prize, it had been dished up before her that first day, waiting only for the gentle squeeze of her finger at the trigger. Even if she didn't have the skill to shoot the leopard, she hadn't even tried. She'd lowered her Purdy, choosing the cat's life over her own, however unintentionally. Why pass up such a trophy only to fight for the right to kill later?

Why, indeed.

Holt gazed up at the horizon above the haze of the hills to where the majestic peaks of the Himalayas reached like jagged, white-tipped fingers toward the heavens. What a bundle of contradictions she was. She'd turned her back on a leopard to rabidly pursue a tiger, as if her life's goal depended on the trophy. She'd lain vulnerable in his arms after a leopard charge, then stood to shake his hand and introduce herself with a smile—as if she'd not just escaped the jaws of death by fractions of a second. She wore trousers and lugged a man's rifle . . . but to Holt, she looked more feminine and alluring than any other woman he'd met.

He shook his head, losing the battle in his mind to make sense of her actions. How could you understand a woman who hiked through the jungle without an escort—as if she feared nothing—but shriveled under her uncle's heated up-braiding with a look of such vulnerability it had touched something deep inside Holt? Just thinking of her eyes, glazed with an expression of remembered pain, he experienced the soft tap at his heart again. She'd reminded him of someone . . . something.

An image flashed in his mind—Jani as he'd found the lemur, far from her Madagascar home in a bazaar in Delhi, boxed in a cage of bamboo almost the same size as the le-mur's small body, so she was forced to crouch down on her haunches. She'd been near death, starved and mistreated; her liquid brown eyes had pulled at Holt until he'd paid the exorbitant fee asked by the peddler, not bothering to haggle for a reduced price. He'd bought the lemur reflexively, with-out thinking. It had been the same when he'd lied to Marcus Marshall about the leopard kill. The haunted expression on Nicky's face had caused a sick tightening in his stomach. He'd been willing to do anything to wipe away that pained expression—that dull look that reminded him so strongly of the abused lemur's eyes.

Jani had been small, needy of care . . . of affection. Could the impervious Miss Marshall require the same?

Nicky stared up through the canopy of trees. Their intertwined branches leaked glimpses of the darkened sky beyond, creating the illusion of a heaven clothed in star-trimmed lace. The smoke from the cooking fires drifted with the evening's stingy breeze, stinging tears from her eyes, while the scent of jasmine and fragrant orchids weighed the sultry air so heavily she could almost taste its blossoming flavor. A growl rumbled deep in her stomach. Dinner was late.

After two days of travel, there were still no signs of the tigress. Nursoo said she was warier than others of her kind. They may need to journey farther up the foothills to the rockier terrain of the Kumaon hills before the *hankwa* could commence. When he found her lair, Nursoo would set the "victim" they'd brought with them, a young buffalo bull, and the few servants they'd been able to hire in Baijnarn would be augmented by natives from neighboring villages. Many beaters would be needed, as well as *rokhs* or stoppers, whose duty it would be to climb the trees near the waiting hunters and route the tigress, funnelling her down the path to the sportsmen as the beaters rushed her from behind.

Nicky gazed into the forest darkness beyond the lights of their camp. Despite the jungle chatter, the insects, frogs, and birds that harmonized to create music as seductive to Nicky as a lullaby, she could not curb her growing anxiety. The tigress lurked out there, somewhere. It would be up to Nicky to kill her and hand her up to her uncle like a bribe, hoping to earn his permission to carry out her own plans. Fear of failure haunted her conscious thoughts, as well as her dreams.

Stuffing her hand in the pocket of her favorite hunting trousers, she fingered the rubied locket she'd brought outside with her and thought of the miniature within its gold case. She would never meet that grand lady, but surely there would be others of her family. There had to be someone— someone Nicky could talk to, who would understand . . .

Still rubbing the locket, she walked to one of the cooking fires and stared into its low flames, remembering just how little people did understand. Even her own mother had answered Nicky's questions with fear, hesitation. *Don't talk about it, darling. It was so long ago. It needn't concern you.*

But it *did* concern her. She was different, and unlike the others of her family, she looked it.

She thought back to one of her first memories—an incident involving a portrait of her father that hung in the main salon. The posthumous child of Nicholas Marshall, she had never known her father, or the older brother who had drowned with him in a sailing accident before her birth. In a romantic gesture, her remaining brother, Keane, who had inherited her father's title as Viscount Eldridge, had named her Katherine Nicole, after both her parents, stating she was the last thing their love for each other had created.

She had always been very curious about her namesake, Nicholas Marshall. One day, when she was five, her nanny had brought her into the salon to bid her mother and her dinner guests good night. Entering the room, she had immediately looked up to the portrait hanging above the mantel. It was a beautiful oil that Nicky had always thought was of her brother, except the hair was too dark. For some reason, she realized then for the first time who the man in the painting was. She'd been so excited, she'd begun dancing around the room asking everyone if she looked like him—her father. She resembled no one else in her family, all of whom had hair in various shades of brown and blond, nothing like Nicky's raven curls.

A stunned silence had filled the room and she'd sensed that something was wrong. But like the child she was, she'd insisted, her cries growing louder and louder. He has dark hair. I look like him, don't I? She remembered her mother turning pale and her nanny dragging her off to bed.

Later, her brother Keane had come to tuck her in, something he always did whenever he wasn't away tending the family businesses. She remembered the tender gaze of his amber eyes as he'd stroked her hair, so much darker than his own light brown curls.

"Why was Mother so upset about the picture?" she'd asked, confused by her mother's behavior.

Keane had looked thoughtful before answering, "It wasn't the picture that upset her. You just reminded Mother of something that's a little . . . difficult for her to accept. You see, scamp," he said, using his nickname for her, "you didn't get this beautiful black mane from our father, and Mother's friends tonight knew that."

"I don't look like him?"

He shook his head, smiling his reassurance. "You look like someone else. Someone very special." He reached into the pocket of his suit and pulled out a beautiful gold locket covered with brilliant red stones that shone like fire. "I asked Mother to let me give you this. It's yours now, scamp. Let me tell you a little about the lady inside, the Raj Kumari, our grandmother . . ."

Nicky nudged one of the rocks that rimmed the cooking fire and watched a few sparks fly and fade away with her memories. Keane understood her need to know about India. If it had been up to him . . . but over the years his many obligations had left him little time to help Nicky resolve her feelings. And her uncle, who had taken over the job of fathering Nicole, had always been opposed to her attempts to find out about the lady in the locket. Until Drew had proposed this hunt.

She tightened her hand around her gold case and prayed she would succeed in her plans. If she bagged the white tigress, her uncle would surely give her what she desired most. In the afterglow of a successful hunt, he would agree to take her to Rajputana, despite his arguments against it in the past. *I've gotten this far. Please God, don't let me fail now.*

When she felt a man's grip on both her shoulders, Nicky started. The soft "darling" and the warm breath brushing her throat as if for a tender kiss on her neck immediately identified Drew. Nicole tensed. Ever since the night Drew had visited her tent, things had not been right between them.

"It's a beautiful evening, isn't it, darling?"

"Yes, lovely," she answered warily.

Gently, Drew turned her to face him and lifted her chin with one hand, so she looked up into his deep-set, blue eyes. "A night for lovers, I would say."

Nicole felt herself blush at the delicate intimacy of his voice and tried to look away. There was something supercilious about his suggestive words. In the past, she had always loved his playful flirting, but his remarks of the last two days were disturbing—no longer innocent. Gone was the proper gentleman who would never dare to kiss so much as her hand in public. Nor did his comments strike her as heartfelt. In some ways, it seemed almost as if he were an actor playing out a part.

"Not shy still, are we, little Nicole?" Drew's smile mirrored the mocking edge to his voice. "I thought after the display in your tent, we were well past any silly prudishness."

"I'm no prude," Nicky mumbled to his chest.

She felt more than heard his deep chuckle. Drew patted her shoulder. "No, I would not have thought so—considering that kiss." He leaned close to her ear and whispered, "It was almost indecent, how you wanted me. A sweet maid like you, who would have thought it?"

Nicky felt her face flame once more, but not from any sense of priggishness. She thought of that night, when she'd clung to Drew to try and force Holt's image from her thoughts. Perhaps it was not Drew who had changed, but she. Maybe she imagined his baiting tone because she felt guilty after kissing another man.

"I never knew you could be so passionate." The seductive whisper barely reached her ears, but she felt its wispy breath against her cheek. "Such lust I felt in your arms that night." Again, laughter, soft and fragile against her face. "Does the wedding seem too far away for you, darling?"

When his head lowered to kiss her, Nicole twisted away. She didn't want the touch of his lips to recall another kiss— one whose passion made her fumbling embrace in the tent seem shallow and silly.

She didn't want to compare those kisses.

From the corner of her eye, she saw one of the Indian servants they'd hired approaching. Happy for the interruption, she nodded her head toward the servant to alert Drew. Hands joined, the Indian bowed to both of them and announced something in his native tongue. Drew responded in kind.

"At last, dinner is ready," he translated for Nicky, his smile showing he was not the least bit perturbed by her rebuff. Looping her arm over his elbow, he shepherded her toward the dinner tent.

As they walked, Nicole began to relax, anticipating the dinner ahead. Considering her encounter with Holt Atley at his home, it was no wonder she felt odd around Drew. Soon enough she would forget Atley's attack and she would no longer be so tense around her betrothed. In due time, everything would be as before.

Feeling better about the whole situation, she said, "I haven't told you, Drew, but I am very impressed with your command of the language here."

He smiled down at her. "I've spent a fair bit of time in India, although not so much in the north."

"So you've said. I'm sorry you've stopped your archaeological studies. Your search for the golden city sounded so exciting."

"Maharuta-l-Hind," he said, a bit wistfully she thought.

"I can't even imagine half the things you told me. Gold idols encrusted with gems. And rubies the size of a fist." She smiled up at him. "You made it all sound so marvelous. How can you give it up?"

"I haven't given it up, exactly." He pulled aside the flap of the tent for her to enter. "I've merely . . . postponed it."

"There you are, Nick, Drew." Her uncle stood up from his seat at the far end of the dinner table and waved them to their chairs. It was the first smile she'd seen on his face today. The entire afternoon he'd spent complaining viciously about the lack of sport, not content with the tame hunting for their evening meals. Her uncle's intolerance for things less than perfect ran not only to Nicky and himself, but to everything he took part in. Each day the white tigress remained hidden, his mood grew more foul. Nicole guessed the fine Portuguese wine they'd brought along with their supplies had helped ease his temper.

Uncle Marc nodded his gray head for the hovering native to start serving as Nicole and Drew sat down. "It's hunter's stew tonight. A mighty fine one by the smell of it, although to be perfect, it wanted a few doves."

Nicky arranged her napkin and waited to be served. Hare curry also made up the repast, and her mouth watered with the spicy scent of the cardamom and cloves. With a good hunter's appetite, she dug into her meal.

"Have you heard anything from the guide yet, Marcus?" Drew asked, breaking off a piece of *roti,* the Indian bread offered to him by a servant.

"No." Her uncle dipped his *roti* into the wooden bowl with one hand as he dished up a spoonful of stew with the other. "I imagine we'll be hunting pigs tomorrow, not tiger. Nick and I came across a fine sounder of wild ones today, scampering off to their lairs. Imagine they'll be gorging themselves in some poor fool's field tonight, fat and ready for our spears in the morning."

"I wish you wouldn't go, Uncle Marc. Nursoo said the land here is full of holes from rats and foxes. You could ruin your horse, or worse yet, break your neck."

Drew reached over and covered her hand with his. "We shall both be there to watch over him."

Her uncle snorted loudly, obviously taking offense at the frailty attributed to him. "Nick's a scratch for tomorrow. She's backed out of the hunt."

Drew's hand immediately tightened over hers. She looked up at him, puzzled. His face remained in the same friendly calm lines as before, except for a faint flare to his nostrils.

"Nonsense," Drew said. "Of course, Nicole will come. Pig sticking is terribly exciting. Why, your own Captain Shakespear proclaimed it the first sport in the world. You wouldn't want to miss that now, would you?"

It seemed strange for Drew to insist. He'd never been interested in her attendance at sporting events before. "Actually, the whole thing sounds rather childish. Men riding about, screaming, throwing spears like some Greek folk heroes. Why risk the horses for that?"

"I insist you come, Nicole."

Uncle Marc's chuckle from across the table ended the quarrel even before the tinders could spark. The gleam in his sharp brown eyes was warning enough for Nicky. Pressing her lips together, she waited for his sharp tongue, loosened by the wine, to take his ire of the day out on her. She vowed she'd say nothing. Let him say his worst; he'd not get a rise out of her. Not this time.

"She isn't so eager to please now that the noose is on, is she? Maybe the engagement was a bit premature, eh, Drew old boy?" He leaned over the table and whispered conspiratorially, as if Nicky could not hear every word, "Perhaps you would have been better off courting her a little longer before you agreed to ankle up the aisle." He gave her an exaggerated wink. "Seems Nick here has a flaw or two you'd not noticed in your haste, eh? Not too late to back out, is it? Could always go ducking elsewhere."

Complete silence reigned, a quiet that seemed, by its very stillness, to confirm her uncle's words. Nicole felt her face heat up, despite her deep desire to remain unaffected.

"To a great huntress." Her uncle lifted his tin of wine, continuing to bait her with the toast. "Ah! But what kind of wife will she make? Remember, Drew, it's not too late to reconsider." He ended his speech with a gratified swig.

She wanted to fight, to scream that he was being unfair. Why should she have to pay for the lack of good game? But instead she recalled every time she'd tripped on the train of her gown running down the steps of the grand stairway like a hoyden, every sampler she'd botched for her lack of patience, every man who had smiled past her to ask some other eligible young lady to dance. She remembered the looks of disdain she received when she arrived in her hunting trousers rather than a riding habit at some gathering. As was his talent, her uncle had spoken her greatest fear. That fear made her powerless, draining every sensible reply from her mind.

Had it been a mistake, Drew's love? An illusion that would dissipate like the morning fog when he came to see how totally incapable she was of the things that came naturally to other women?

From across the table, Uncle Marc's shining eyes laughed at her as he took another sip of his wine.

"Really, Nicole. I do wish you'd come."

At his soft words, she turned back to Drew. His kind expression caused a large lump to settle in her throat. Despite the pain her uncle's words caused her, apparently Drew gave them little credence. She smiled, the relief she felt almost stinging in its intensity. Suddenly, her irritation with Drew's teasing seemed rather childish and silly. Drew loved her. He would be her husband within the year. If he wanted her on the noxious pig hunt, it was little enough to ask of her. But before she could open her mouth to reply, Nursoo burst into the tent.

"I have found her, sahib. The tigress. I found her lair."

It was dark, the kind of pitch black possible only after the moon sets. Everyone in the camp lay quietly in their tents, asleep. Only one fire glowed dimly at the center of the camp, where Nursoo stood guard with the Korku.

Time to strike.

Holt moved swiftly, keeping close to the ground until the cloth cover of a *pal* hid him from Nursoo's line of sight. He prowled from tent to tent, then found the one he sought. Edging aside the *pal's* thick cloth, he slid soundlessly within. The raucous snores of the Irishman, as well as his stench, filled the small space. Without hesitation, Holt slipped the edge of his hunting knife under the Irish dog's chin at the jugular.

Morgan did not stir. His breath reeked of whiskey.

Crouching down at the head of the camp cot, Holt whispered in the sleeping man's ear, "Wake up, fool."

Morgan jerked awake. Holt pressed his free hand over the man's mouth and pushed his weight against the Irishman's struggling body. "Relax, Morgan. If you're real good and quiet, I might just let you live."

Instantly Morgan settled back against the bamboo bed, but his eyes looked wild and white.

"What's the matter?" Holt asked, his voice a bare whisper. "Afraid I might slice your scrawny neck in two?" Holt smiled. "God it's tempting!" Morgan's eyes widened as Holt pressed the tip of the knife against his skin. "No one double-crosses me, Morgan. No one."

The Irishman began to shake his head but stopped when he felt the knife prick his skin.

"You want to say something to me, Morgan?"

He nodded. Slowly.

"Now let me think. What would a weasel like you tell a man holding a knife to your throat?" Holt pretended to ponder the question seriously. "Maybe you'd say, you don't know what I'm talking about. Double-cross ye, lime-juicer? Why'd a smart fellow like meself go and do a fool thing like that?" Holt mimicked. He bent closer to the trembling man's face. "I don't know, you Irish dog. Tell me."

Holt lifted his hand from Morgan's mouth as he pressed the knife against his neck, making the Irishman stretch to avoid being cut. To Holt, that extended neck, bobbing from one swallow after another, made Morgan look like a turkey ready for the pot.

"Mr. Atley, I dinna know what—"

"Harrington." Just the name startled Morgan into silence. "I overheard your little talk, Morgan. And let me tell you, it riled me something fierce."

"But then ye knows!" Morgan pleaded. " 'Tis nothin' to our bargain, that affair."

"Do you take me for a fool? You're here to bag the tigress for Harrington. I'm paying you to stop the hunt. Seems to me like a conflict of interest."

Morgan instantly quieted at his words. His eyes shifted slyly and Holt imagined he was doing some fast thinking. Beads of sweat dotted the forehead of his overlarge head. He licked his lips. "Aye. Well, ye see, 'tis another tiger I'm after. Not the white tigress a 'tall."

"Now isn't that interesting. The *hankwa* tomorrow is for a rare white tigress. A prize worthy of a raja. Harrington hires you on—but somehow it's not Enchantress you're going to bag?" Holt's eyes narrowed. "That's pretty dim-witted, even for an ass-head like you, Morgan."

" 'Tis her mate, see?" He licked his lips again. "A huge brute. I'm after him for Harrington."

Holt dropped his knife and grabbed the lapels of the Irishman's grubby shirt. "The white tigress's mate is nowhere near here. I heard you say it plain, Morgan. You're after a tigress—the female of the species." Lifting Morgan's back up off the bed, Holt shook him. "You play me low, and you're a dead man. Do you understand? No matter what rat hole you crawl to, I'll find you, just like tonight. But next time, I won't ask any questions. Understand?"

Morgan nodded.

"Here's what you're going to do." Holt picked up the knife and slipped it back into the sheath at his boot where he could retrieve it almost instantly. "Nursoo's found Enchantress. He's got the bull tied up in her tracks and she's sure to take the bait. Tomorrow, they'll all be after her. I'm going to be in the jungle, watching. You got that?" Again, a nod. "And you, Morgan, are going to do your damned best to ruin this hunt so Enchantress escapes. Because if you don't, if that tigress gets shot tomorrow, I'll come back for you, Morgan. I swear it. I'll find you. And whatever they do to that tigress"—Holt's eyes narrowed on the Irishman—"I'll do to you."

"They'll not touch the tigress, Mr. Atley."

"I'll be watching, Morgan. Remember that."

They started for the *machans* at daybreak, Nursoo having announced that the buffalo bull was dead. The rose wash of morning sun bled through the thick clumps of evergreens, lighting a path on the grassy forest floor. With her Purdy balanced in the crook of her arm and a bearer carrying her gear and second rifle, Nicole trudged through the stands of *chir* pine, stepping over lantana, skirting the waist-high raspberry bushes and clumps of stunted bamboo, her eyes alert for any signs of the tigress. At this lower elevation, the morning air retained its sultry promise of the afternoon's moist heat, its thickness echoed in the dense foliage and cottony silence that enveloped the small troop of hunters as they wound their way down the narrow path.

With them came eight of the bravest villagers. They would act as the *rokhs,* climbing the trees alongside the hunting platforms, or as Drew called them, *machans,* and cautiously attracting the attention of the tigress to lead her down the path to where the hunters waited. While their pay would be double that of the beaters, Nicole hardly thought it worth the risk. Drew had recounted one story in which a *rokh* had placed himself too low in a tree and had attracted the tiger's attention too markedly. The tiger clawed him down, killing and carrying him off before the gentlemen could descend from their hunting platforms and attempt a rescue.

The soft crunching of leaves to her left made Nicole jerk to attention. Her fingers tightened on the trigger of her rifle and she peered through the shrubs, catching sight of a peahen as the bird scurried through the underbrush.

Drew gave her braid a playful tug from behind. "A bit on the edge, are you?" he whispered over her shoulder.

From his position up ahead, her uncle turned and signaled for silence. She and Drew fell quietly into step. In the early morning hours, the wild beasts prowled, seeking out their prey. The jungle was not a safe haven for conversation.

They arrived at a small clearing dominated by an enormous banyan tree. At the base of the tree lay the dead buffalo, its carcass now humming with eager flies. Ignoring the fresh kill, Nursoo supervised the construction of screens made from freshly cut branches. Nicole swallowed back the bile the putrid stench from the dead animal caused to rise up her throat and watched several natives, dressed in *dhoti* loincloths and turbans, monkey up the banyan onto its sprawling branches.

The tree made a perfect cover. Aerial roots as thick as trunks hung down from its limbs, creating the appearance of a dense tangle of trees connected to one mother trunk. Three *charpoys,* Indian bed frames strung with rope, were hefted up the tree and fastened into place. The natives cut down branches with their small wood axes and covered the frames. Above the *charpoys,* the workers strung bamboo poles draped with leafy branches that hung downward to conceal the hunters and their rifles. These preparations complete, Nursoo signaled the men to help the hunters mount the *machans.*

Ten feet off the ground, Nicole propped her gun against the bamboo pole of the screen, careful not to let the rifle fall through the floor of overlapping limbs that covered the *charpoy.* Her bearer settled in behind her, ready to hand her a second rifle should she need it. Beside her, she placed her pistol.

Through the cover of the leafy screen, she watched her uncle giving Nursoo last minute instructions before he too climbed up the banyan with a boost from one of the *rokhs* and settled to her left. Drew rested on her other side on a separate platform four feet away. The *rokhs* scurried up the trees on either side of the banyan. Each carried a small hand axe.

Nicky knew well what to expect. Nursoo had recounted the details last night over the fire while the men calmly smoked their cheroots and Nicky tried to subdue her roiling stomach. The beaters were already in place. Fifty natives equipped with sticks, pans—and anything else that could make a sharp noise or be used to beat a bush—formed a semicircle to the rear of where the tigress supposedly lay, preparing to sleep after her heavy meal. Three Indians with tomtoms, small native drums, would be stationed among the villagers, one in the middle, the others at each side. Nursoo would lead the group forward from the center. As the half moon closed in on the tigress, the beaters would herd her toward the banyan and the hunters' rifles.

Before it seemed possible, a hand signal originating with Nursoo reached Nicole. She gave her uncle and Drew the return signal, which would then travel from man to man until it returned to the *shikaree* on both sides and the *hankwa* would begin.

The jungle erupted in a din of shouts and shindy of drums. Nicole froze into place, not daring to even swat the persistent flies, enduring the black tree ants that climbed up her boots. She scanned the space immediately in front, then searched ahead to the bushes beyond. At any moment, the white tigress would show herself. Nicky must be ready. She must be the first one to shoot.

Nicky pulled the hammer of her gun from half to full cock. Her finger rested on the right trigger. She kept both eyes open.

A boar burst through a bush to her right. Nicky held her fire just in time. A shot now could very well scare the tigress back onto the line of beaters, ending in death for some poor native.

Like the thunder at the base of a waterfall, a roar filled the air. Nicole felt it tear through her, tingling inside her like a jolt of lightning. Ahead, a glimpse of ghostly white passed through the bushes just out of firing range. The soft "hish" of the *rokhs* and the gentle taps of their wood axes against the trees seemed a ridiculously futile method of routing a creature who could make the jungle tremble with the sound of its voice, but the very constancy of the tapping and hishing made clear the tactic was effective.

The white tigress broke through a screen of lantana. Nicole's breath stopped at her throat.

Enormous. Like an alabaster statue—not a living thing at all. But she moved. With a stealthy tread. Her large, whiskered head swayed left and right, as if she searched for something. She prowled toward a tree bearing a *rokh,* each step a dancer's move. Slow. Precise. Then she stopped. Nicky barely heard the *rokhs'* quiet "hish" above the ruckus of the beaters before the tigress turned away.

Her gun back in the crook of her arms, Nicole settled onto her heels to watch the ghostly cat. The chocolate stripes slicing through the white pelt and undulating with each step were a living work of art. The cat's piercing blue eyes, extraordinary. A sharp hiss to her left made Nicole turn to her uncle. The expression of blazing anger on his face brought her quickly around. Nicole immediately fitted the stock of the rifle to her shoulder. This was it. *Don't hesitate.* She aimed straight for the animal's back where a well-placed shot could pierce the spinal cord and cause instant death. Beads of sweat formed on her brow. Her hand began to tremble. She bit down on her lip and pressed her finger to the trigger, trying to control her shaking. She followed the tigress with the sights of her rifle, waiting for her to come within range.

A blood-chilling scream pierced the air.

5

"Dear God." Nicole watched a *rokh* crash through the branches of the tree just ahead of the tigress. The man grabbed frantically for some anchor to stop his momentum downward. For a catch of a breath, he managed to snatch a thin branch between his hands and hung suspended off the forest floor. *Crack,* the limb gave way. The *rokh* tumbled to the ground.

Still out of shooting range, the tigress became a blur of silver darting to the Indian.

Another scream.

Grabbing one of the aerial roots, Nicky scrambled to the jungle floor. She ran, her breath pounding in her chest, her handgun gripped between her fingers. Ignoring the shouts behind her to stop, she pulled back both hammers of her pistol, still keeping stride.

When she reached the tree, the tigress had fled. Only the man lay there, moaning in pain, his bare chest striped with four bloody gashes. Nicole dropped to her knees beside him.

Her uncle and Drew reached her at the same time. The beat of the tomtoms still filled the jungle. Her uncle fired two shots in the air, while Drew knelt down beside her to examine the bleeding Indian. Just then, the Irishman Morgan shimmed down the tree from which the *rokh* had fallen and joined the group huddled around the bleeding man.

Drew stood immediately. "What happened?"

"I dinna know. The blighter lost his grip."

"My God." Her uncle breathed the words softly, watching the man's life leak through his wounds—the tigress's work. "What a beast."

"What a prize," Drew corrected. Ignoring the dying man at his feet, he said something in Hindustani to the Irishman, irritating Nicole. Morgan spoke English. Whatever Drew was saying, he obviously didn't want Nicole or her uncle to understand.

They appeared to argue for a minute, until Morgan nodded his head curtly. Drew turned back to Uncle Marc. "I think we should go after her."

"Are you mad? This man's bleeding to death!" Nicky shouted.

"You want the tigress, don't you?" Drew faced her uncle. He pointed to Nursoo, who ran across the clearing, joining the group. "Ask him. If you miss your opportunity now, chances are you'll never find her again. That tigress will be long gone from this area. Who knows where she'll hide in these hills."

Her uncle stared at Nursoo as the *shikaree* removed his sash from around his waist and tore what was left of the unconscious man's shirt from his chest. "Is it true?" he asked the guide.

"Uncle Marc!" Nicky cradled the Indian's turbaned head in her lap as Nursoo balled up the rags that had been the man's shirt and tied them over his wounds with the sash.

"Yes, sahib. The tigress will flee. I can but try to track her once more."

"This is insane!" Nicole exclaimed. "This man is dying and the two of you are talking about a blasted hunt!"

Her uncle pulled at her arm. "Come away, Nick. There's a good girl. We can't do a thing for the chap now."

Nicole wrested her arm away. "I damn well plan to try!"

"Nicole!" Drew shouted. "You'll do as your uncle tells you."

Nicky looked helplessly at Drew. His eyes burned. A hunger emanated from them that she'd seen only once before. In the leopard's eyes. When the animal attacked.

Nicole shook her head. "I'll stay here."

Drew grabbed her wrists from the side of the Indian's head and pulled her to her feet. Her arms burned at the sockets, but she struggled until Drew's grip relaxed and he cradled her face between his hands.

"Nicole. Darling." His breath was uneven, a series of short, sharp gasps. "I have seldom asked anything of you." He spoke in a low voice, the message meant for her ears alone. "I am willing to give you everything I have, including my name. I ask nothing in return." His eyes still blazing with the lust of the hunt, he stroked the loose tendrils that had escaped her braid off her face. "This one thing I want. The tigress. It's a fantastic opportunity. Nicole, darling, don't make me miss this chance."

Nicky stared at Drew's loving features, his aquiline nose and strong brow, the dark curls that dipped to his deep-set pale eyes, and her anger drained away. Everything he'd said was true. Only Drew had accepted her without question. He'd never made her feel inadequate—never tried to change her. He'd arranged the hunt for the white tigress thinking it would please her. It was the same with the pig sticking last night. He'd thought she'd miss some wonderful experience if he didn't convince her to come along. He'd always put her first, before his own wants and needs. And when her uncle had made her question her adequacy as a bride, Drew offered only gentleness to assuage that hurt. Now, caught up in the excitement of the hunt, he desired the beautiful tigress as a prize.

"Memsahib," said Nursoo. He gestured to the many hovering beaters and *rokhs* who'd gathered around. "As you see, I have plenty of succor."

Nicole looked to the Indian, saw that he was well-tended by the other natives, and turned back to Drew. She gave a short nod.

His smile was brilliant, as if she'd granted him his legendary Maharuta-l-Hind rather than a farfetched chance to bag a tigress. "You won't regret this, darling." He kissed her soundly on her mouth, which utterly stunned her, then turned immediately to her uncle as if he'd not just committed a serious breach of etiquette. "We'll have to move fast. Her pug marks are clear enough. I'm sure Morgan here can find her for us."

Drew launched into action, instructing one of the *rokhs.* The man jogged back to the *machans.*

"We'll need only one or two attendants—more will only slow us down." Drew signaled behind Nicole. Nicky recognized the Indian who stepped forward immediately as the native who accompanied the Irishman. His skin was a shade darker than the other natives, more like the Doms than the Kumaonis of the village, and rather than a baggy cotton shirt, he wore a quilted jacket of brilliant red with his loin cloth. He, too, headed for the *machans* after orders from Drew.

When the two natives returned from the hunting platforms, Drew barked directions in Hindustani, then explained his plan to Nicole and her uncle in English. They would follow the tiger tracks as far as possible, then sweep around and circle her. Watching him now, so controlled yet boiling with excitement, he seemed different to Nicky. The subdued, well-mannered gentleman had vanished. In his place was a man with purpose, whose pale blue eyes glowed like ice, so cold they could burn. The sharp cunning of a trained hunter had replaced the aristocratic bearing. She found the change curiously alluring, yet at the same time repulsive.

She turned back to the injured native. Nursoo was almost finished binding his wounds with a cloth. The Indian was propped against him, held up by two other natives. Only an intermittent moan and the howl of a langur disturbed the jungle silence. The *shikaree* looked up and met her concerned gaze.

"If you wait but a moment, memsahib, I will attend you on the hunt."

"No need for that." Drew took her elbow and turned her

in the direction the tigress had taken. "We'll have the cat soon enough. This way, darling. You don't want us to miss our chance now, do you?"

"It's all right, Nursoo." She tucked her pistol in its holster and grabbed her Purdy from Morgan. The Indian in the red jacket already carried her second rifle. "We'll manage well enough."

Nursoo looked uncertainly at Nicole. For a moment, she thought she saw fear in his dark eyes, but then he said, "As you wish, memsahib."

Holt leaned against the bark of a *sissoo,* well hidden behind the blackwood's five-foot girth. In his mind, he relived the scene he'd just witnessed, trying to make sense of it. Could Morgan have actually pushed that man to his death?

He tightened his grip on the Hall's carbine in frustration. Everything had happened so quickly; he wasn't sure what he'd seen. He'd been shifting his gaze between Morgan and Enchantress, waiting for the Irishman to act—ready to intervene if he didn't. Yet, he thought he'd seen that slight motion. Morgan's shoulder against the man's back . . .

He couldn't be sure. Morgan had been hidden behind a screen of branches. Then all hell had broken loose—the Indian screaming, Nicole bounding down the tree with the ease of a panther, her long black braid trailing behind her as she sprinted to the Indian, her gun in hand. Holt had acted quickly then, cocking his own rifle and moving to cover her lest Enchantress turn back to attack her. Luckily, the tigress had fled.

The episode had left him shaken. He couldn't help thinking he'd had a hand in the man's injuries by his brutal threats to Morgan. *Whatever you have to do,* he'd said. Had Morgan included murder as a method?

Holt shook his head in disgust. One thing was certain. His association with the Irish dog had just come to an end.

As he watched the party disappear into the bush, Holt shouldered the strap of his carbine and followed.

* * *

"I've lost her, sir."

The Irishman scratched at the dirt, looking for clues to the tigress's direction. Nicole stared at the scar that split the man's cheek and pulled his mouth into an eternal grimace. His expression reminded her of an engraving she'd seen once in a magazine showing African masks carved from wood. Mr. Morgan looked just as demonic as those macabre faces.

Nicole tried to set aside her distaste for the man and shifted her attention to her boot, dragging it across the loose dirt in a circular motion, kicking tufts of grass, as she waited for instructions. Morgan, Drew, and the native conferred quietly. When they seemed to reach an agreement, Drew stood to address Nicole and her uncle.

"We'll need to split up. Marcus, you come with me. I am a bit familiar with the terrain here. Morgan shall lead Nicole. He's able enough as a guide."

"But why split up?" Her uncle's face showed a moment of trepidation.

"We'll double our chances of finding her. We'll circle around, rout her. Neither you nor Nicole have any experience tracking tiger. It's up to Morgan and myself to show the way." When her uncle shook his head, Drew added more persuasively, "Morgan here has worked for me before. There's really no need to worry. We'll keep well within shouting distance."

"But that tigress . . ." His expression remained clouded.

Drew placed his arm around Uncle Marc's shoulders, his whole bearing a monument of encouragement. "Nicole is a crack shot. You *know* she can outshoot either one of us." He chuckled softly before adding, "If anyone is in danger, it is we without her." He placed both hands on Uncle Marc's shoulders. "You've trained her well," he said in a voice full of admiration.

Her uncle looked at her. "What do you think, Nick?"

Few times in her life had Uncle Marc asked for her opinion. She could read in his face what he wanted—to go after the tigress—and his need for reassurance. The gooseflesh rose up her arms as she thought of hunting alone with Morgan, but her uncle's expression decided her. He wanted the cat as badly as Drew. Nicole could not deny him.

"It's a fine plan," she answered.

Her uncle stepped forward and looped his arm through hers. While he was not considered a tall man by average standards, he beat Nicky by a head. He lowered his face close, so their voices would not be overheard. "You're sure you'll be all right?"

They appeared troubled, those warm brown eyes that still sparked amber despite the bushy gray brows that heralded his age. It touched a spot deep within Nicky to see her uncle's concern. No matter how ruthless his demands, these moments of warmth reminded her of what really mattered —Uncle Marc cared for her.

"I can outshoot you blindfolded, old man."

A quick grin lit his face. "There's a good girl." He gave her a sharp slap on the back, then stepped over to Drew.

"We'll keep within shouting range, as you say, Drew." Nicky smiled at the authority back in her uncle's voice, as he continued, "If we've no luck, we'll meet at the site of the drive when the sun's straight overhead."

"Good luck, darling." Drew gave her a warm smile before leaving.

Nicole watched until the thick green shrubs shielded her uncle and Drew from view, then turned to the Irishman and the native who waited. "All right, Mr. Morgan. Lead the way."

The flat, pockmarked face made her shiver, as did his gash of a smile. "As ye say, Missy."

Nicole followed the Irishman's lead, while the native trailed behind. Her eyes scanned the vegetation ahead, doubly alert when approaching a bush or clump of vines that could hide the tigress. After a while, the rifle weighed heavily in her arms, and her legs felt leaden from the hike. She ignored the dull pain in her forearms and thighs, focusing on keeping herself sharp.

They traveled without comment, until they reached a fallen *semul,* a silk-cotton tree, that blocked their path. Morgan stopped and examined the ground around them. He was a short man, dressed in soiled trousers and a shirt Nicole suspected he'd not changed in a fortnight. Around his thin neck he wore a red kerchief that emphasized the disproportionate size of his head. His shape and scars contributed to the image of a dastardly creature. Obviously, it was the man's troll-like appearance that frightened her, causing her to distrust him. But despite what her logic told her as she waited, watching him patrol the area ahead, she couldn't help wishing Drew had heeded Nursoo's protests and not hired the man on.

Morgan returned to her side. He untied the kerchief from his neck and removed his dirty cap. A tumble of drab hair the color of mud flopped down to his beady eyes. "The tigress be ahead of us, Missy." He swabbed his greasy neck and forehead of sweat. "Ye go ahead and climb over the tree, real careful like. Me friend here will give ye a leg up."

Morgan signaled to the native and said something rapidly in a guttural language that sounded different from the dialect she'd heard Drew speak. The native looked at Nicole and a sharp cunning smile spread across his ebony face, showing a row of sharp, yellowed teeth. Unconsciously, she took a step back.

"Go now, Missy. He'll help ye." Morgan motioned to the trunk, still holding the kerchief in his hand.

Nicole stepped to the wide trunk that blocked their path and leaned her rifle against it. The native was already on his knees, her second rifle beside him, holding his cupped hands out for her foot. The yellow-toothed smile remained in place. Her heart thudded in her chest. A dull buzz rang in her ears and a prickly sensation rose up the back of her neck.

She turned sharply back to Morgan.

He held the red kerchief taut between his hands, stretched like a rope. A wicked grin erupted across his face as he balled up the cloth and dabbed once more at his forehead.

Nicole let out her breath. For one beat of her heart, she'd actually thought he'd had some nefarious purpose. The image had disappeared when he'd wadded up the kerchief and used it to wipe his brow. She shook her head; she was letting her fears get the best of her. Certainly it was the scars that made her attribute some evil motive to the poor soul. It was wrong to hold such a handicap against the fellow, but despite her best intentions, he made her uneasy.

"You're sure the tigress is out there?" she asked, hesitant to give Morgan her back once more.

He answered with his gap-toothed smile and a putrid puff of breath. "Take a look and see, Missy."

There came the sound of something crashing through the jungle behind Morgan. The bamboo and bushes rippled as whatever was out there moved toward them. Nicky picked up her rifle off the ground and cocked one hammer, just as Nursoo cleared the bamboo. She lowered her gun.

"I came as fast as I could, memsahib," he panted. "I thought you might have need of me." Nursoo looked directly at the Irishman.

She watched Morgan tie the kerchief back around his neck, the expression on his face difficult to read. She held in a sigh of relief. Somehow she felt safer with the *shikaree* present. "Morgan says the tigress is up ahead."

"Shall I go look, memsahib?"

"Ye saying she's not there?" Morgan growled.

Nursoo ignored the remark and waited for Nicole's answer.

With a quick glance to Morgan, she replied, "It wouldn't hurt to check her position. I would hate to find her close enough to attack."

"Do as ye like," Morgan grumbled.

It didn't take Nursoo long to return. "If the tigress was there, she is no longer."

Morgan stepped forward waving his arms wildly. "She was there, I tell ye—"

"I have found her trail, memsahib. There is a ravine up ahead. It is an excellent place to trap her."

Nicole cradled her gun once more in her arms. Her eerie sense of unease lifted now that she was no longer alone with the Irishman and his native companion. "Show the way, Nursoo."

All the fat's in the fire now, Holt thought.

Enchantress had trapped herself, well and good.

From his post on the precipice above the ravine, he looked down at the tigress as she rested among a cluster of ilex. Holt tipped his slouch hat back and wiped his brow with the back of his sleeve. It wouldn't take long for the Brits to find her in the dried up riverbed below. Half the party, Harrington and Marshall, trailed minutes behind him. They would track her pug marks to where she'd crept down into the gully, a gorge that dead-ended fifty yards back in a sheer wall of rock. The rest would be easy. Trapped inside, the tigress had only one way out—straight ahead into a volley of gunfire. Holt doubted even the powerful tigress could leap the twenty-five foot vertical up the ravine wall.

She was a sitting target.

Unless . . .

Holt eyed the group of tall walnut trees at the mouth of the gorge. Grabbing up his carbine, he headed for the copse.

"Nick," her uncle called in a hushed but excited voice, waving her over.

She hiked the last of the incline, past Nursoo to where her uncle and Drew waited at the edge of a dry gulch. The area was clear, except for a cluster of walnut trees providing a patch of shade. Nicole set her gun on the sandy ground and dabbed at the perspiration on her neck with her handkerchief, then stuffed the linen back into her pocket.

"By Jove, you made it." Her uncle clapped her hard on the back. He looked over to Drew beside him. "We were afraid you'd miss all the fun. Weren't we, Drew boy?"

"Yes. What took you so long?" Drew turned to Morgan. "I thought you were such a grand hunter, Morgan."

The biting sarcasm in Drew's voice surprised Nicole. She didn't believe her uncle and Drew had been waiting long. Could he truly be irritated with Morgan for the delay? Yet the look on his face as he stared at Morgan definitely showed anger.

The Irishman shrugged his shoulders. "Try I did, yer lordship."

"She's jolly well here now," her uncle continued, his expression one of happy expectation. He motioned Nursoo over, practically rubbing his palms together. "We've spotted the tigress. Followed her pug marks and spied her from above. She's holed up in there about fifty yards back, behind some holly." He waved toward the end of the ravine. "I've been saying to Drew here, we could go in from both sides and up the middle. She's sure to bolt as soon as she gets wind of us, but there's only one way out." His bushy mustache curved upward in a triumphant smile. "Straight at us. One of us is sure to bag her."

"Sahib, what you suggest is perilous. The tigress is a vicious beast. And very cunning. If the gentlemen and memsahib should miss, or the shot not be fatal, the tigress could attack."

"Well, we don't plan to miss, now, do we, Nick?" Her uncle gave her a jaunty wink.

"I do not believe the sahib realizes the danger to the memsahib." Nursoo looked pointedly at Nicole.

Her uncle pursed his lips together, as if someone had just told him his favorite mount had turned up lame. "Well, Nick and Drew can certainly shoot from up here where it's safe. I plan to have a better position."

Uncle Marc handed his rifle to the attendant and set out

for the edge of the ravine. Nicky followed, ready to hike down the incline to the dried riverbed below.

The ominous click of a rifle being cocked echoed loudly behind them. Nicole turned, following the noise up to the top of a walnut tree. She couldn't help a startled gasp at the sight that met her eyes.

Above them, balanced on the limb, was the American. His buff trousers hugged the taut muscles of his thighs. His dark curls were plastered to his head where the brim of his slouch hat pressed against his hair. He'd rolled up the cuffs of his native shirt, so that Nicole glimpsed the thick sinews of his forearms. He looked magnificent, a sentinel silhouetted against the white noon sky.

Their eyes met over the sights of his gun.

The Hall's carbine he held was trained directly on her.

"That tigress is a protected animal." His voice was low, but with a hard edge to it. "The first person to touch a rifle" —a slow, menacing grin inched across his face—"I shoot."

6

Something inside Nicky snapped. The tension she'd held within herself since she'd turned and found Morgan creeping up behind her erupted into a blazing anger.

Really, this was too much. First Drew and Uncle Marc arguing to continue a hunt that in her estimation had long since ceased to be sport—beginning with the damned *hankwa*. Driving an animal down to be slaughtered was not *her* definition of a good hunt! Then the poor man almost gashed to death, followed by that troll Morgan and his sinister looks. Now Holt stood perched in a tree, aiming a rifle at her like some latter-day Robin Hood.

Pulling her pistol from its holster, she didn't stop to examine why she trusted the American to hold his fire. She simply followed the instinct that told her this was another of his ploys to ruin the hunt and send her home.

"Shoot away, Mr. Atley." She cocked both hammers back with the palm of her hand and aimed for the man in the trees. "I certainly plan to."

Standing beside her, Andrew Harrington raised his rifle. Without the hesitation he'd shown when aiming at Nicole, Holt fired a bullet two feet in front of Drew, making the British lord jump back. As Nicole watched, her betrothed dropped his gun and raised his hands in the air.

Holt was reaching for the revolver he kept tucked in his waistband at the middle of his back when Nicole fired.

The branch above his head cracked. Shot loose, it tumbled down, knocking his hat off his head.

"Blast!" He crouched down, flattening himself against the tree branch, his revolver now trained on the party below. He searched out Nicole. She stood as tall as her elfin height permitted, her chin up, her breasts straining against the cloth of her shirt as enticingly as two apples outstretched to Adam.

She looked magnificent.

Except for the pistol she held aimed right at him.

"I don't want to hurt you, Mr. Atley," she called from the ground, her legs spread apart in an even stance, the second barrel cocked and ready to shoot. "But if you fire on my party again, I'm afraid I'll be forced to."

"You're here illegally." Still lying low on the branch for cover, his revolver at the ready, Holt tried to coax her with words. "That animal is protected by the Crown. As a representative of the Conservator's Office, I'll use force if I must to turn your band of butchers back."

"That's a lie!" Nursoo called out from behind the armed woman. "I have a hunting permit for the tigress signed by the Deputy Commissioner himself!"

"Shoot him down, Nick girl," her uncle called out, shaking a fist at Holt. "Threaten us, will you!"

She remained staring down the sights of her gun, but the expression on her face showed doubt for the first time. Encouraged, Holt argued, "She's one of a kind—you can see that for yourself. A rare white tigress. You kill her and you'll be destroying the rarest species of tiger ever to exist."

Holt saw her gun lower a fraction, before she straightened it back on him. He gritted his teeth. It was a face-off—him in his tree, Nicky down below at the edge of the gorge.

A roar like the crash of thunder erupted from inside the gully.

Immediately, everyone turned their attention fifty yards down the ravine to where Enchantress stepped out from behind a clump of hollies. As they watched, the tigress crouched at the foot of the twenty-five foot vertical that blocked her retreat. Her long white body tensed, and she leapt forward, scaling halfway up the steep incline before falling back into the bushes.

"Nick. The tigress!" her uncle yelled. "My eyes aren't so good at this distance." He pointed to the animal at the base of the vertical. "You shoot her!"

Holt watched her uncle steer Nicky, the only one holding a gun cocked and ready to fire, toward the ravine. He thought furiously of how to stop her without actually harming anyone, particularly not Nicole. But as he stared down the sights of his revolver, thinking to distract her with a few choice shots, he did not see a woman primed to shoot. Nicole stood with her gun lowered to her waist, an expression of anguish on her face.

"For God's sake, Nick," her uncle shouted. "Are you going to just stand there like some lily-livered ninny. Damn it all, shoot!"

The girl watched Enchantress as her uncle goaded her to fire with language that could have put a foot soldier to shame. Then slowly, she turned and looked up into the trees, directly at Holt. As their eyes met, Holt saw confusion reflected in her gold eyes, not the cunning of a hunter bent on killing.

Marcus Marshall turned to Harrington. "Grab up your gun, man. The tigress is getting away."

As soon as Harrington moved to bend down, Holt fired, shooting the gun farther out of the Brit's reach. Harrington immediately raised his hands again.

"Weak worthless cowards, both of you!" Marshall's face turned a deep crimson. "You deserve each other, you do!"

As Marshall ran back to the attendant holding his rifle, Enchantress leapt again. Holt saw the ghostly shape, large for a male tiger, astounding for a female, sail upward, as if propelled by wings. Halfway up the incline, her back paws found purchase on an overhanging rock, and she again pressed up, this time making the lip of the ravine with ease. As all watched, the tigress sprinted up the hillside. Marshall aimed, saw the tigress was out of range, then lowered his gun with a curse. Enchantress disappeared into the brush.

"By the ever-living jumping Moses!" Her uncle grabbed the bill of his hunting cap and slapped it against his thigh. He turned on Nicole. To Holt, she appeared to be doing her best at keeping her gaze level to her uncle's raging anger. "What the hell's the matter with you, girl? Why didn't you shoot?"

Holt barely heard Nicole's whispered response as he climbed down the tree, followed as it was by her uncle's biting tirade. Yet, despite the softness of her words, they echoed in his ears as he picked up his hat from the foot of the walnut and blended into the trees, making his way as quickly as possible from the Marshall party.

She'd said simply: "I can't."

It was the last thing he'd expected her to say.

The girl who'd jumped from the hunting platform, landing at a running sprint before the "gents in the trees" had time to close their hanging mouths shut, the lady who'd practically shot his hat off his head with the precision of an expert marksman—that same woman had held her fire, granting Enchantress her life.

"What are you doing, Mini?"

Padmini jumped back, only to find her young brother fairly whooping from the satisfaction of frightening her. Holding her finger to her lips, she pulled him away from the doorway that led from the kitchen into the main room where she'd been listening to her father argue with Nursoo.

Once outside, she admonished in a harsh whisper, "If you did not have the high squeaky voice of a woman, I would not have believed myself discovered by *Ma!*" Seeing her nine-year-old brother's shoulders droop at her slight, she felt ashamed. "I am sorry for my angry words, Sagi." She gestured back to the kitchen with a shake of her head. "Please, come with me. I cannot understand all that is said.

You, my brother, have the hearing of a chital deer. Perhaps your keen ears may help me?"

Sagi nodded, happy to assist his sister. Together they crept back into the kitchen and knelt beside the doorway. Soon the heated words filtered through from the main salon.

"All the conditions have been met. The *sagai* commitment cannot be repudiated," she heard Nursoo argue.

"There will be no wedding day, if I decree it so!"

Stunned by her father's words, Padmini almost missed Nursoo's booming response.

"The marriage negotiations are complete. The Brahman and Nai have already come and have been paid for their services."

"But you, Nursoo, are unable to meet the price we agreed to between ourselves, before the Brahman and Nai were sent for."

Silence followed her father's odd words, and then she heard Nursoo reply, "The tigress escaped. I cannot be assured that I will find her again. The money I would have earned—"

"Your incompetence is not my problem!"

"I offer four hundred rupees," Nursoo said more calmly. "It is enough."

"It is two hundred less than you agreed to!"

"By asking for such a sum, you took advantage of the fact I care for Padmini. No one else would accept these conditions!" A blistering silence followed before Nursoo asked in a lowered voice, "Is there nothing noble left in you old man that you would attempt to repudiate the *sagai* for money?"

"You should be made to pay! You, a Khasiya, a worthless hunter of meat, aspire far above your station seeking my daughter in marriage."

The blood rushed to Padmini's ears, so she heard no more. Somewhere in her unconsciousness, she understood her father continued to argue with Nursoo, but the voices were only a rush of words, the meaning of which she could not comprehend. Humiliation overcame her.

The gentle tug of Sagi's hand woke her from her stupor. With a nod, she followed him outside. They rushed through the courtyard, past their mother, whose shouted protests were weak only because Sagi, her favorite son, led the way. Her mother could deny nothing to her rascal son, the boy of everyone's heart. They dashed outside the village, running until the breath hurt in Padmini's lungs and the tears streamed down her face. She let Sagi lead, knowing he'd take her to their special place outside the village, a rounded clump of bamboo nestled within which was the small area Sagi had named his private fort.

While it had always been the reverse in the past, this time it was the young boy who comforted the weeping Padmini with the touch of his hand on her arm.

"It is not so bad, Mini. Nursoo is a great hunter, he will find the tigress and then you will be married."

"You mean sold." She wiped at the useless tears with her veil. "Six hundred rupees our father asks to be rid of me. Six hundred! I was surprised that Nursoo would forgo a dowry, thankful that Father would not fall into greater debt for my marriage, but I could not conceive that Nursoo would be made to pay. It is beneath our family's dignity to accept money for the marriage of a daughter." She looked helplessly at her brother. "Surely the moneylenders have driven our father mad with their threats for him to do such a thing!" New tears slipped down her cheeks. "Is my happiness so worthless to our father that he thinks only of his purse? He sells me off, like wheat, and if he does not get his price, he would rather have me rot in the fields than allow me the happiness of being a bride."

Sagi's eyes seemed to soften in sympathy for his sister, but then the dark brown face brightened. "But does it not show the hunter's great admiration for you that he chooses to pay such a grand sum?" Padmini felt her heart lighten at Sagi's words. "Why," he continued, "Nursoo argued fiercely for you against our father! I think he must love you very much, Mini." He gave her hand a squeeze. "As do I."

Padmini bit her lip and brushed away the fresh tears, smiling at her beloved Sagi. Quickly, before she lost her courage she bent down to remove one of the silver chains of bells she wore around her ankle. What did she owe her father now, she argued, even as she hesitated from committing herself to such a forward act. She tugged the chain off with renewed resolve. Certainly she should not care if she embarrassed him into the next life!

Taking her brother's hand, she laid the chain in his palm and closed his fingers around it. "Take this to Nursoo." Not wanting her brother punished should her folly be discovered, she added her cryptic message. "Tell him when the moon rises to be on guard for yet another tigress. Tell him to look carefully before he shoots, as he did once before." In her heart, she willed Nursoo to understand.

Nicky stood in front of the large canopy bed that dominated the guest chamber of the Deputy Commissioner's house in Almora. She held onto the thick bamboo bedpost with both hands. "I can't . . . *breathe!*" The last word came out a long sibilant whisper, as if the very breath were being squeezed out of her—which, in fact, it was.

"Well, that's a pitiful shame, my dear, as we have a good quarter inch to go before that delectable gown will fit."

Mrs. Tod pushed aside a white corkscrew curl from her pleasantly plump face. The matron, dressed in a black bombazine gown that emphasized rather than hid her voluptuous curves, reminded Nicky of the fairies from her volume of the Brothers Grimm. She was even shorter than Nicky's petite five-foot, two-inch height, with a rounder, softer shape and merry blue eyes. In the mirror before her, Nicky saw her companion grab the cotton laces of her corset as if they were reins. The fairy image evaporated. Mrs. Tod's look of determination reflected the granite purpose of Eldridge Manor's head groom when bringing a skittish horse under control. She gave another merciless tug.

"*Please* . . . that's quite enough!"

The matron "tched" softly. Glancing over her shoulder, Nicole saw a touch of disappointment in the woman's soft aqua eyes. Obviously, she'd thought Nicole made of sterner stuff.

"Short, light breaths, dear." She demonstrated, her large bosom heaving up and down like a bellows. "As a dog pants."

Nicole followed her example, ready to do just about anything to get the air she craved.

"That's right, dear."

Another sharp pull. Nicole gasped.

"There now. *That* ought to do."

The bedpost started to fade. Nicky blinked her eyes rapidly, trying desperately to keep the Ratcliffe's guest room, where she'd spent the last three nights, in focus.

"Arms up, Nicky!"

With military precision, Mrs. Tod tossed three petticoats, one after another, over Nicole's head. They billowed and floated down around her waist as she concentrated on her breathing.

"The color is just stunning!" Mrs. Tod eased the yards of gold silk over Nicky's head, emitting a satisfied chirp when she found she'd not miscalculated the corset size. The gown fit perfectly. After fastening the dress, Mrs. Tod turned Nicole around, then frowned. "Your color, on the other hand, is not."

"I thought blue all the rage this year," Nicole said shortly.

"Now, now." Clucking in a motherly fashion, she pinched the pale cheeks. "You'll be thanking me soon enough!"

Her busy fingers moved to puff the gown's off-the-shoulder sleeves. With a sharp tug, she brought down the neckline of the dress. Nicky watched the support of the corset prop her breasts up, emphasizing a creamy expanse of skin that threatened to blossom over the plaited silk of the gown's décolletage with each breath.

"Oh dear." Mrs. Tod smiled demurely as she pulled the material back up. "Mustn't be too scandalous. We wouldn't want people to think you indecorous." Biting her bottom lip, she appraised the results. After a shrewd examination, she tugged the material back down, again revealing a healthy amount of cleavage. She smiled slyly. "On the other hand, a covered candle sheds no light!"

After being plumped, powdered, and primped, Nicole stood before the large beveled mirror, while Mrs. Tod tucked a last curl into place. Nicky's mouth opened slightly in surprise. The woman in the glass could have stepped right out of the pages of *Godey's Lady's Book*. The dress had a double skirt, the upper portion of which had been looped up with large bows of black velvet to reveal the shimmering gold silk beneath cascading down to Nicky's matching dance slippers. Black velvet epaulets separated the plaited silk from the short, full sleeves, displaying the white skin of her bare shoulders. The plunging neckline trimmed with plaited gold silk fit like a second skin to her waist, then flared with the full double skirt, making her waist seem impossibly small. Her hair had been styled as elaborately as the dress. Parted through the middle lengthwise, then divided again, the front hair twisted away from her face in a rouleau. Mrs. Tod had pinned the back portion into a low puff at Nicky's neck, creating a regal effect.

She felt as if she'd swallowed butterfly wings that fluttered in her chest. For the first time in her life, she actually looked beautiful! Nicky turned and hugged Mrs. Tod, twirling her about in a two step until the constraining corset made her too breathless to continue.

Turning back to the mirror, Nicky felt awed by the foreignness of her appearance. She almost reached out to touch the beautiful creature in the glass, unable to believe it was only a reflection of herself. Mrs. Tod hovered behind, a knowing look on her cheerful face.

"I was right about the gown?"

Nicky smiled and nodded into the looking glass. "Absolutely."

Mrs. Tod had practically browbeaten her into wearing the dress, one that Nicole suspected her sister-in-law, Esmeralda, had hidden in her trunks. At home, no one had been able to rig Nicky up in such an elaborate costume—not her mother, nor her two sisters, not even Esmeralda, Keane's wife, whom of the four women in her life Nicky admired the most. Not when she spent most of her waking hours in loose trousers would she truss herself up in such a tight gown. But she'd met her match with Mrs. Tod. Now Nicky could understand how the matron had survived three husbands in the Indian jungle. She had a steel will and an iron constitution. Nicky smiled thinking of her poor uncle, whom Mrs. Tod had apparently selected as husband number four.

"Won't that handsome Lord Harrington be proud of you tonight." Mrs. Tod clapped her hands before her voluminous bosom. "He'll just eat you up with his eyes, he will!"

Nicky watched her reflection in the mirror frown as Mrs. Tod's words dissolved the image in her head. It wasn't Drew she'd pictured watching her sway across the dance floor.

She shook her head. She was hopeless, utterly hopeless. Despite all her attempts to forget Holt Atley, his handsome face and haunting green eyes would endlessly creep into her consciousness. For the first time in her life, she'd imagined herself surrounded by young men, envied by ladies, and it had not been Drew, her betrothed, she'd pictured vying for her attention. What in the world was the matter with her?

With the image of Holt Atley came the biting reality of their last meeting a week ago. "Band of butchers," he'd called them. And at the time, when her uncle had ordered her to shoot the splendid white cat, the label had seemed to fit. Nicole couldn't help wondering if perhaps she'd not misjudged Mr. Atley. Could actions she'd labeled as sabotage of her hunt for notions of male pride actually be concern for the welfare of a rare animal? Certainly his heartfelt plea for the tiger's life had made it impossible for her to shoot.

Nicky closed her eyes, trying to stop the pain welling inside her with her memories of her uncle's tirade. The return trip from the hunt had been absolutely wretched. Her uncle's temper had been tuned to a fever pitch while Drew remained pensively silent. Aside from Mrs. Tod, who'd chosen to come from Naini Tal to meet them in Almora, Nicole had been utterly alone for the past week. Even Drew had acted distant, as if she had failed him as well as her uncle by her decision not to shoot. If she didn't think of some way to regain her uncle's favor soon, she would end up home in England without ever seeing Rajputana.

Opening her eyes, Nicky sought the woman in the mirror, trying to find comfort and confidence in the sight. She plucked at the gold skirt and cocked her head slightly. She didn't look like herself at all—she looked pretty, beautiful even. What would Drew and her uncle think of her spruced up appearance? Would they be so surprised they'd actually forget to be angry with her? It would be a welcome relief from the glaring disapproval and silent condemnation she'd received since the hunt.

"All right, dear. Enough of this shameless display of vanity." Mrs. Tod gathered up her own reticule and fan and handed Nicole hers. "We were expected downstairs half an hour ago. This should be just the right time for an entrance!"

Nicole gave her reflection one last confident smile, then took a bold step toward the door—and quickly tripped over the train of her gown, almost stumbling to the floor.

"Oh dear," Mrs. Tod whispered, her fan held across her lips.

The picture of sophisticated lady vanished. In its place, Nicole again saw the awkward girl who stood propped against the wall, watching the other young debutantes dance. Disheartened, she looked to Mrs. Tod for support. The matron shrugged her plump shoulders, as if the misstep mattered not a whit, and gestured encouragingly toward the door.

Nicky picked up the skirt of her gown and took a cautious step forward.

It had been a humbling experience, to say the least.

Holt slouched down into the leather wingback chair occupying the corner of the commissioner's office. The armchair's thin stuffing was hard-packed beneath him, making it about as comfortable as a bed of nails. The only good chair in the room had Ratcliffe's skinny backside plastered to it.

Thinking about the last time he'd been in Ratcliffe's office, and how different the circumstances, Holt barely heard the commissioner drone on to the others in the room about the dangers of the hunt at Askot, the need for the *shikaree*, Nursoo, to accompany Holt, the Indian being the only other hunter in the district able enough for this particular project. Ratcliffe apologized profusely for any inconvenience this might cause the Marshall party in their quest for the white tigress, but certainly they could understand the circumstances—the pressing need for their guide's services?

Holt found Ratcliffe's oozing placatory tone about as annoying as the metal springs threatening to burst through the leather beneath him. He would have gladly missed the whole affair if not for the direct command from the Conservator's Office to be at Ratcliffe's beck and call in the days ahead. The commissioner had said he needed Holt at the ball honoring the British nobles in order to explain why the government was commandeering Nursoo's services. But Holt knew the real purpose for his presence here. He was the scapegoat should the Brits get testy over their loss of a guide.

He had to admit it was a small price to pay to get Nursoo off Enchantress's trail. After the *hankwa,* Holt had tracked the white tigress and her cubs to the Gori Ganga, where many animals had fled for food and water during the hot season. How long would it take before Nursoo picked up her trail? The Indian was good, too good. Though the commissioner didn't know it, Holt was the one who had requested

Nursoo's services. In the time it would take to track and destroy the man-eater, Holt estimated the Brits would lose interest in Enchantress. The hundred rupees the government paid for killing the man-eater would at least be a start toward the money Nursoo needed.

Holt adjusted the sleeve of his black tailcoat and picked at the bit of lint on the knee of his matching trousers, thoroughly bored, ready to go downstairs and drink Ratcliffe's excellent brandy. But when Marcus Marshall's words finally registered, he jolted to attention.

"I hunt alone," Holt interrupted, intending to squelch any ideas of the Marshall party tagging along on this particular hunt. The man-eater was just too dangerous and Askot too damn close to Enchantress's new den.

"Nonsense," Marshall answered, taking a relaxed puff of his pipe. "The *shikaree,* Nursoo, will be with you."

"That's different," Holt argued.

"The more guns the better," Marshall added.

Holt vaulted to his feet, addressing Ratcliffe. "This is absolutely ridiculous. We're not discussing a jaunt through the park. We're after a man-eating tiger. I need experienced hunters!"

"Are you suggesting we're not?" Marshall asked, incensed by the slur.

"Look, Mr. Marshall. This is not a social gathering to see who can outshoot whom." Holt could see his words had the wrong effect, but he was too angry for diplomacy. "There won't be any beaters or *rokhs* driving this tiger. No native will come near its hunting grounds. Whole villages have been abandoned by the threat of this man-eater."

Marcus stepped around Holt to Ratcliffe, knowing who held the power in the group. "Everyone in my party is a crack shot. Isn't that right, Drew?"

Holt watched Harrington smoke his cheroot thoughtfully then nod.

Marcus stood next to Ratcliffe's desk, hovering over the commissioner, his stocky body tensed with the same excitement Holt heard in his voice. "We could be of great service. Why, you're damned lucky we're about, Commissioner. My niece can shoot—"

"You're not bringing Nicole into this?" Holt shoved his way past Marshall to the commissioner, forgetting Enchantress for the moment. "He's talking about a seventeen-year-old girl, for God's sake!"

"She's twenty-one and *my* responsibility, Mr. Atley," Marcus corrected. "And a better shot than you'll ever be, I'd wager."

Holt turned to Harrington, willing to seek even the aristocrat's help to keep Nicole safely out of this hunt. "That woman is your fiancée. Do you actually condone her tagging along the foothills with a bunch of men, tracking a tiger that is responsible for the death of nearly one hundred natives?"

A slow smile spread across Harrington's face. He took another pull of his cigar. "I think she can do it," he said as if he were discussing a wager at the Calcutta Club. "She's certainly a better shot than I am, and I plan to come along." Harrington faced the commissioner. "I agree with Marcus. Our party could be of great value on this hunt."

Something in Harrington's expression made the hair stand on Holt's neck. He was using his influence to encourage Marcus and the commissioner to bring Nicole along! He didn't seem to care that he was putting the woman he intended to marry in mortal danger.

Holt turned back to Ratcliffe. "This is insane. These men may not be concerned about the girl's welfare, but I refuse to be responsible should any harm come to her. Nicole Marshall stays here, where it's safe!"

Jeffrey Ratcliffe watched Holt carefully. The more forcefully Atley argued to keep the woman out of the hunt, the more inclined Jeffrey was to include her. Perhaps with the girl along, Atley would be distracted. It might provide Jeffrey with just the opportunity he needed.

"I believe I've sufficiently inconvenienced Mr. Marshall and Lord Harrington." Jeffrey rose leisurely from behind his desk. "This conversation is at an end." Straightening his jacket, he looked directly at Holt. "If they wish to join in the excitement of the hunt," he said silkily, "I see no reason to deny them . . . or the young lady."

He watched Atley's green eyes narrow. "You and I both know," Atley warned in a deadly soft voice, "how dangerous this hunt will be, Commissioner."

Jeffrey smiled. Mr. Atley couldn't possibly guess just how dangerous Jeffrey planned to make this hunt for the obnoxious forest officer. "I agree with Mr. Marshall," he said, cutting off any further discussion. "The more guns the better." He looked evenly at Holt. "Your responsibility is to kill the man-eater and rid the district of its menace. Those are your orders. The rest you may leave up to me, Mr. Atley." He extended his hand toward the door. "Shall we retire downstairs, gentlemen. I hate to keep the ladies waiting."

Her entrance had been all she'd dreamed. She'd glided down the stairwell without mishap, the gold silk of her dress shimmering around her, her head held high—with only an occasional glance down to her feet. While she'd been unable to find Drew at first, she'd certainly gained the attention of several young men. The few women present, mostly wives and daughters of the officers and officials stationed at Almora, stared at her as well, Mrs. Tod said with envy. Even the commissioner's wife, Serena Ratcliffe, watched her closely, as if startled by Nicole's appearance.

She felt like a queen.

Until she saw her uncle.

He marched through the crowd, with Drew in tow. Nicole felt a sense of trepidation skid across her stomach, much like the time her brother had caught her putting a garden snake in her sister's bureau, but she squared her shoulders against it. Like the other gentlemen in the room, both men were dressed in formal black, her uncle looking endearingly stout and short next to Drew's elegant height.

She wet her lips, anticipating the opinion of the two men who mattered most in her life.

Would they think her beautiful, as beautiful as she'd believed the woman in the mirror to be?

"There you are, Nick." Her uncle stopped abruptly before her. She could tell by the gleam in his eyes and the bounce to his step that he was excited about something—something that pleased him. A little of her anxiety lifted at the good omen.

"Been looking for you everywhere," he continued. "I have splendid news, splendid." He took her hands up in his and smiled widely at her. "A man-eater, Nick. Just think of it. It's quite dangerous, of course. Cleared out a good bit of the district, the beast has." His eyes fairly sparkled. "But they need us, Nick, and we must do our best for the Crown."

While her uncle recounted how the commissioner had begged for their attendance, apparently in dire need of their talents in ridding the countryside of this scourge, Nicky's heart lifted. Once again she was in her uncle's good graces. Neither he nor Drew seemed to notice her dress, but that mattered little when her uncle pressed her hands within his and beamed at her with such approval. He spoke at length about preparations for the hunt, and Nicole took heart. She'd been given another chance! If she shot the man-eater, if she proved herself, then she could speak to her uncle about Rajputana.

"We'll need to prepare as soon as possible. Drew here has mentioned a few things he'll see to tonight, and I myself must get preparations under way, so I'm afraid you're on your own for the evening." Then as if actually noticing her for the first time, he wrinkled his brow. "Egad, Nicole, what do you have on?" Examining the full skirt of her golden gown, he lifted his white bushy brows, a look of distaste curling one side of his lip under his mustache. "I must speak to that woman your brother hired. Dear God, she's dressed you to look like a yellow dumpling."

Both men began to laugh as if finding the comparison highly amusing. Nicole's smile faltered. She felt a hollow coldness near her heart as she endured their laughter.

"Oh, I don't know," Drew said smiling, his glance flitting over her. "I think Nicole looks rather fetching."

At that moment, Mrs. Tod whacked Nicole's uncle on the shoulder with her fan and dragged him off to dance a reel, taking little notice of his rather loud protests. At Drew's wink of encouragement, they watched the elderly couple dance, and Nicole felt the tightness in her chest ease.

"Shall we?" Drew gestured toward the dance floor as the couples lined up for the next dance.

Nicole gave a short nod and swallowed. She knew from past experience that it would take all her concentration to look "half bad" out there, but she was game.

As she began the tortuous steps of the quadrille, trying to remember whether to pass right or left on the next beat, an odd thing began to happen. At first she wasn't sure they were watching her, the men and women surrounding the dance floor. Perhaps it was the elegant blonde beside her, Mrs. Ratcliffe, or the sophisticated gentleman to her left. But then she would catch a flick of a fan, a nod of an officer's head in her direction, and she became more certain. As if to confirm her suspicions, Mrs. Tod nudged her as she passed Nicole for the *chain des dames,* a knowing smile on her face. But it wasn't until after Drew and her uncle took their leave that she was completely positive. That's when the offers began.

It seemed as if every man in the district wished to dance with her.

And dance she did, through marches and reels, quadrilles and lances, endlessly dancing as if in one night she were making up for a lifetime of waiting and watching. An hour later, Nicky thoroughly exhausted from two quadrilles and a march, they stood two deep around her, the red-coated officers in dress uniform. She did her best to accept the flirtatious remarks of the young men, acting as if she'd done so a hundred times before. As one officer handed her a glass of punch, she listened to another's tales of his exploits on a bear hunt. Nicole bit her lip to stop from giving any helpful advice.

She grinned behind her glass. No one here seemed to care if she was a good shot or not. Instead, she could see from their admiring looks and warm smiles that they thought her only an attractive young lady on whom they chose to shower their attention.

"Excuse me, soldiers. This dance is mine."

The deep American voice behind her set a painful pace to her heart. She felt the warm touch on her arm and tried to steady her pulse with a deep breath. She did not turn to acknowledge him immediately, but took a minute to settle her shaking hands on her punch glass as the gentlemen around her protested against the intrusion.

Quite miraculously, Holt Atley stood at her elbow in attendance with the rest.

Her heart pounded with excitement—the same excitement she felt before a hunt. She wouldn't deny it. She wanted to see admiration in Holt's cool green eyes when she turned, the admiration that had been so notably absent from her uncle's and Drew's. So far, she had earned nothing but the American's disdain, failing to shoot the leopard outside their camp while trying to kill a tigress Holt argued was precious. She wanted to prove to this man that she was someone *important,* someone who merited his regard, despite her fumblings and displays of ill temper before him.

With a touch of guilt she thought of the growing distance between her and her betrothed. If Drew had stayed for but one more dance, she argued, she would have tried her newfound wings of beauty on only him. Again she pictured the lovely woman she'd seen in the glass upstairs, saw her reflected in the admiring eyes of the soldiers around her.

Yellow dumpling, her uncle's voice called out.

No! she cried back. Once and for all she would silence that voice and prove her uncle wrong.

Nicky turned slowly, she thought gracefully, and gave Holt her most charming smile—one she'd practiced endlessly in the mirror for just such a moment—but her lips faltered as soon as she saw him.

In her many fantasies about this man, she'd always pictured him in his buckskin trousers and cotton native shirt, still covered with dust from the red clay of the hills, his dark curls sweaty from the heat. But of course he was dressed in evening wear—the picture of elegance. Her surprise at the double-breasted dress coat and embroidered waistcoat, the sense of amazement she felt at seeing the black trousers and pristine white shirt, its collar folded neatly over a tie, seemed silly now. It was even more cabbage-headed to be stunned by how good he looked. She'd always known he was handsome as the devil.

She almost spilled her punch as she took a nervous swallow. The liquid settled into a ball in her stomach. Irrationally, she felt outmaneuvered by his splendid appearance. She had planned to charm Holt Atley, and sadly enough it seemed the reverse was more probable. Nicole's gaze slipped to his firm lips and an almost painful shock skidded up her spine as she remembered their kiss.

Holt took the glass of punch from her and gave it to Lieutenant Carlson at her right. He never said a word, never took his eyes off hers, as his fingers closed around her hand and he pulled her to him.

"Have a heart, Holt," the young man complained. "Give the rest of us chaps a chance."

"Sorry boys."

He guided her gently onto the dance floor. The lilting beat of a waltz accompanied their steps, and Nicole had to shake her head to adjust to the reality of the situation and not let herself slip into some silly fantasy in her head. *Chin up old girl,* she commanded, *don't dissolve in a puddle at his feet.*

"To what do I owe the honor, Mr. Atley?" Nicole smiled, thinking she'd attained just the right touch of suave polish to her voice.

"Call me Holt."

She arched her brows upward, recalling their first meeting when he'd refused to give his Christian name. "I was under the distinct impression you preferred a more formal address. Certainly you did before."

"Before"—his gaze rested on the plunging neckline of her gown then returned to her face—"you didn't look this good."

She felt herself blush, hated the lack of sophistication it revealed, but never let her eyes waver from his direct stare. She simply chose to ignore the flaming heat at her face. "What a gallant compliment," she said sarcastically.

His smile spread across his mouth like honey on warm bread. "I've been told I have a silver tongue."

"Sterling," she answered dryly.

Holt laughed, a chuckle from deep within his chest. He looked so handsome at that moment, he actually took her breath away. She frowned. It was the silly corset, of course. She took a few discreet pants as Mrs. Tod had instructed.

When she started to feel lightheaded, she searched for something stable to focus on, hoping to end her dizziness. She settled on his mouth, but quickly looked away because it made her feel soft and vulnerable in some rather odd places. Despite herself, she recalled the warm touch of his hungry lips on hers—causing all sorts of delicious sensations in the pit of her stomach—until she stumbled over his feet. Holt's graceful turn salvaged the step. He brought her closer, guiding her lightly against him as they danced.

She could just kick herself. This wasn't the way the thing was supposed to go, she tripping all over herself like a left-footed duck every time he smiled. She concentrated on the sophisticated lady she'd seen in the mirror upstairs, but the image was dimming.

Licking her dry lips, she smiled her practiced smile again. "Where did you learn to dance so well?"

He executed another expert maneuver, tucking her closer

to him. Nicole felt her breath catch once more in her throat. Blast the corset!

"In Boston. From my mother. Now, there's a lady who could dance."

She couldn't help it. She looked down at her feet, instantly aware that she could *not* dance. The lady in the mirror faded, then vanished completely, replaced by a girl in a gown that made her look like the doughy dessert her uncle had dubbed her. She kept staring at her feet until she felt Holt's hand tilt her face back to his.

"That's not what I meant," he said softly. "My mother was *the best.*" The hard lines of his face relaxed, and he smiled warmly, as if recalling a cherished memory. She'd never seen him smile before. Not like this. He could have such a mean-spirited smile, more a twist of his lips, a smirk, than a thing of joy. But this smile was soft and gentle. It transformed his face, making him look young and carefree. Suddenly, Nicky wanted desperately to know what made Holt Atley so happy.

"You danced often?" she asked.

He nodded. "I remember the parties. How we'd waltz together and she'd tilt her head back and laugh." He twirled Nicky in a quick turn, exaggerated, flamboyant, making her laugh like the woman in his memories. He smiled again. "I was her only dance partner. She had to teach me in self-defense."

"Your father didn't like to dance?"

His smile faltered. "We lived in Boston most of my life. My father lived in India."

"Oh. I see."

"He was a captain in the British Cavalry stationed here." He sighed, apparently begrudging the explanation but willing to give it just the same. "After a native skirmish near our bungalow, he shipped us both to my mother's family in Boston—for our safety."

Nicole refrained from saying anything more. She could see the conversation pained him. It was a kind of pain with which she was familiar. She thought of her brother, Keane. Yes, she understood only too well—people not having time for you, sending you away for others to take care of you. She swallowed her sympathy, knowing how badly she'd hate to be pitied, and smiled winningly at him instead. She wanted him to laugh, to wipe away his serious expression.

"Well, you certainly have a talent for it. Dancing I mean."

"Why didn't you shoot?"

She started. He meant the tigress, of course. Nicole felt some of her good humor drain away, wishing he'd not brought up the hunt. She didn't want to fight.

"Perhaps I should have." She sighed. "My uncle certainly made me sorry for it afterwards."

"Then why didn't you? You knew what he'd say."

She nodded. Holt had been there that first time, when her uncle had badgered her about the leopard—had even lied to make him stop taunting her. He knew well the price she would have paid for failing to meet her uncle's expectations. An uncomfortable thickness settled in her throat as she recalled Uncle Marc's angry words. *Fool. Incompetent.* The words drummed against her consciousness, a grating counterpoint to her own reproach: *Never hesitate!* But at the time, looking back at Holt's condemning expression in the trees, then watching the great white cat try desperately to escape, she'd been unable to shoot.

With only silence for an answer, Holt looked down and searched her face for the truth. She had a faraway look in her eyes, as if she were absorbed by her memories, and from the look of her what she recalled was not the least pleasant. Her lips were lightly pressed together, one soft corner turned down in a sad expression that gripped Holt's heart. He immediately looked up over her head, a simple enough task since her head barely reached his shoulders.

She was doing it again, making him want to protect her, to take away that hurt look.

He wasn't supposed to feel this way. When he'd asked her

to dance, he'd seen only a stunningly beautiful woman surrounded by men—a challenge. He'd been curious at the sight of the trousered kid turned elegant debutante, had convinced himself he wanted the dance only to make sure the two women were one in the same. He hadn't intended to ask about Enchantress. The last thing he wanted from the kid was something as personal as motives. It was enough she'd not fired. *Leave it cut and dried, Holt boy. No need to get overly friendly.* Yet holding her in his arms, watching her bite her lip in concentration, trying desperately not to step on his toes, it was hard to stay cool and detached. And then he remembered their kiss.

He stopped those thoughts right there and pulled her tighter into his arms. He closed his eyes and stepped with the music, humming the melody to try and distract himself.

"Uncle Marc told me we're to hunt a man-eater together."

He held his breath for a count, trying to stop the anger boiling inside him. It didn't work.

"Yeah. Looks like I'll have the lot of you tagging along. Lucky me." He squeezed her hand tighter than he'd intended. "Just stay out of my way, or someone might get hurt."

She stopped dancing right in the middle of the floor. "Thank you for the waltz, Mr. Atley." She turned to leave.

"Wait." He tried to pull her back into his arms, but she stood her ground, watching him. "Look, I'm sorry I said anything," he apologized. "It's just that . . ." He searched for a nice way to say the Brits should get the hell out of his life and mind their own business, then shook his head. "Let's just finish the dance, shall we? You're great at this. Where am I going to find a better partner?"

She couldn't help it, she laughed at the ridiculous question. She'd been amazed Holt would still brave the dance floor with her, she'd trod so often on his feet. "That is absolute rubbish and you know it."

"Well, at least you're a new face. Would you condemn me

to dance with Lilian Murphy?" He jogged his head toward a pouty blonde whose large puppylike eyes were practically devouring him.

"Oh my. She actually looks dangerous."

"She is." He took her in his arms once more and began swaying back and forth to the beat. Leaning over, he whispered softly in her ear, "She's tried to get me in all sorts of compromising positions—trap me into matrimony." He lifted his brows in an exaggerated manner, trying to make her laugh again—and succeeded. His smile deepened. "I'm considered quite a catch here."

"I suppose," she said with an impish smile of her own, "one could do worse in the wilderness."

"Thanks. That's a real vote of confidence."

He picked up the pace of their steps, enjoying the challenge of avoiding her feet on his toes. It was amazing how someone who looked so elegant aiming a rifle could dance like an ostrich. He was just starting to really enjoy himself, turning right and then left, losing himself in the music and the lily scent of the woman in his arms, when he noticed her breathing.

She was panting. Like an animal.

"Are you all right?"

"Could we stop, please. I'm feeling quite breathless."

He'd seen that look before—a damned corset squeezing the breath from her. Blast these foolish women and their notions of fashion. He steered her off the dance floor, taking her outside. She looked like she could use the fresh air. Her face was about the color of rice.

Outside, in the moonlight, the cool mountain breeze that made Almora a summer favorite seemed to help her regain a bit of her color. It was a real shame it did nothing for Holt's problem. Against his better judgment, he stole a peek at the lovely breasts that had brushed against him so temptingly while they'd danced. It was a mistake. He felt that traitorous part of him stand to attention. And then he started to remember all sorts of stupid things, like how sweet she'd tasted when they'd kissed, how soft she felt in all the right places . . .

"Damn," he mumbled.

"What?"

He looked into her questioning gaze, wondering what she'd do if he told her straight what his problem was. Maybe it was just the kind of kick in the pants she'd need to get away from him, before he did something they'd both regret. He should try it. *You see, kid, I got this burning ache . . .* But instead he asked, "You didn't answer my question back there."

She stared out over the moonlit trees. "Why didn't I shoot?"

He nodded.

She looked up at him; her expression reminded him of a child with a desperate need for answers. "What you said before, that the tigress is protected by the government, is that true?"

Holt thought of lying, but shook his head no. "Not in the way I implied. She's exempt from the reward normally given for tiger kills, that's all."

"Then why did you . . . ?"

Holt took her in his arms. "She is worth protecting, Nicole. No matter what the British government may or may not do to help the tigress. When you watched her trying to jump up the ravine, I saw it in your eyes. You knew she was different, special." And out of nowhere, the damning thought: *Just like you.*

"The tigress showed great heart attempting that leap," she whispered.

As he stared down at her, his hands on her shoulders, his lips a breath away, her eyes got a dreamy look. It made them seem more slanted and catlike. Panther eyes for sure. She really did look like a Rajput princess, Holt thought. Although seeing her dressed in that gold getup, her hair twisted in curves more complicated than the switchback paths up the Himalayas, made the idea of her being Indian royalty seem inane. The kid was a real aristocrat, he reminded himself. A Brit through and through.

He almost pulled away then, but in the shimmering light of the moon and the torches set for guests, she gave him that tentative smile of hers, the one that made him want to cradle her against him and say things would turn out all right.

He gritted his teeth.

Her smile wavered.

"Oh hell." Despite all the warning bells in his head, he took her in his arms and bent down to kiss her.

It was a slow kiss, filled with longing he didn't know he'd bottled up. It started tender, as if they'd discovered a wonderful way to apologize, then grew in intensity. At first she responded, kissing him with the energy he felt vibrating between them. What she lacked in technique, she more than made up for with enthusiasm. Holt rather liked that. But then she started to struggle, pushing against him, trying to remove her lips from his. He knew he should stop—but he also knew that if he kept kissing her, she'd stop fighting soon enough. He bent forward, arching her against him, deepening the kiss. Finally, he felt her succumb.

And then he felt her go limp.

"What the . . . ?"

She'd fainted.

Lifting her up in his arms, he pressed his lips together in a worried frown and searched the gardens for the privacy he'd need to execute this particular rescue.

"I knew I was good," he mumbled to himself as he carried her deeper into the gardens. "But, honey, I didn't know I was that good."

7

Padmini clutched her veil to her face as she waited in the darkness of the forest outside the village. She leaned against an oak, periodically glancing around its thick trunk toward the village. She knew in her heart he would come. He was her destiny, her life-comrade in fulfilling her holy duties. He must understand the message the silver anklet held.

She had dressed in her best *ghaghra,* the cotton skirt she fingered while she waited. Anxiously, she wished the matching bodice of red was not patched. She'd made certain the veil draped over her left shoulder successfully hid the flaw, wanting to look worthy of Nursoo in this their first true meeting. She had even stolen from her sister-in-law the black eye salve that lined her eyes and the perfume that scented the air around her with jasmine. It granted her confidence, the kohl, the perfume. Her hair design had given her the most pause. Should she wear it in a braid of odd numbered plaits, tied at the end with bright ribbons she'd saved for her wedding, or in a knot at the base of her neck? In the end, she'd left the black strands to flow loose to her hips, liking the symbol of freedom the hairstyle represented. It was a fitting tribute to her plans. This evening she would escape her father's house.

He has sold me, my father. The idea still stung her like the bite of a cobra, the pain swaying in and out of her consciousness with the snake's rhythm. *I and my family's dignity have been sold, like a bag of millet or a length of hemp rope.*

She knew that they owed money, knew that the moneylenders could take away the small inheritance her brothers must share among themselves. *Sagi's inheritance.* She could understand her father's desire to salvage the jewels, the land and house he'd inherited. But the voice she'd heard arguing with Nursoo from her post outside the main room had not been suffering the strain of finances, the compulsion of loss. It had been a voice edging on insane rage, filled with angry pride, shouting to Nursoo that he, a hunter, a killer for meat, must pay for the privilege of marrying into her father's esteemed family. And if he could not meet her father's price, the marriage be damned.

Damned as his daughter's happiness.

Why was she so cursed? Her first betrothal at the age of ten had ended in the death of her young bridegroom from a disease of the blood, years before the actual wedding or the *guana,* the reunion ceremony when the marriage would be consummated. She'd prayed to the goddess that her father would find another bridegroom. Without a husband, children, and a household to take care of, a woman was nothing. Yet, no new bridegroom came. And when she was sixteen, she despaired that it was too late, that the others of her village would discover her widow status and she would never marry. Then she had seen Nursoo and he'd sent his sister's necklace.

She raised her fingers to her neck realizing too late that it was bare. *Ma* had the silver gift, her only tie to Nursoo. Padmini's resolve to carry through her daring plan rekindled. She *would* marry him, despite her mother and father.

She had never been so near a man who was not related to her. Purdah required that she hide her face from the men of the village. She would gather sticks and cow dung for her family's fires at night and draw water from the well under the stars with the other women of the hill Rajputs. If she worked in the fields with her brothers, she would make sure her veil was draped securely over her head. But when she'd seen Nursoo, when he'd looked upon her and smiled as she poured water from the well into his hands, she had known Rama's ecstasy at meeting his consort Sita.

At the sound of brush breaking to her right, she turned and watched Nursoo as he cleared past a *bosanta* bush. Her heart stopped its pounding in her chest and for a moment, looking at his tall handsome figure walking toward her, she felt herself mounted up to the heavens. Their eyes met and she quickly lowered her gaze, gathering her wits for her daring proposition.

"You came," she said when he stood before her.

He lifted his hand. In it, he held the anklet with its tiny silver bells. "I was not sure . . . until I remembered our first meeting, when I nearly shot you thinking you were a tiger." He looked down at her. "Padmini, why have you—"

She held her finger to her lips, lightly pressing against the silk of the veil she held tightly across her face. Risking all to her wild plans, she took up his hand to lead him deeper into the forest before he could begin his protests over their meeting.

She brought him to Sagi's fort. Once within the bamboo walls, she knelt down on the dirt floor and invited him to do the same. The moonlight filtered through the tall bamboo stalks that made up the enclosure, casting barred shadows across the ground. Kneeling before her lord, Padmini silently examined Nursoo from lowered lids. He looked so handsome. His eyes were bright with intelligence, his mustache long and pulled around his face like a Rajput's. The bright blue *kurta* he wore was flawless. He was a warrior—a true hill Rajput, despite her father's slurs about his clan.

"You should not be here—"

She covered his mouth with her fingers, then, realizing her daring, she pulled back her hand as if burned and stared at the smooth ground. "I know this," she answered in a whisper.

When she looked up again, his dark eyes had softened. Although she still clutched her veil to cover her face, his gentle gaze encouraged her and she dared to look him straight in the eye.

"Is there something you need, Padmini?" he asked, in a voice so tender, so soft, her heart melted like *ghee,* the clarified butter her mother made. She nodded.

"What may I give to you, my heart. Merely ask and if it is within my power, I will make it so."

She did not hesitate. "I wish for us to marry."

"We will marry. It has been arranged—"

"I heard you argue with my father," she interrupted.

A frown darkened Nursoo's friendly expression. After a pause that seemed to Padmini an eternity, he said, "I truly wish that you had not."

He made to stand, but Padmini rose up on her knees and grabbed both his hands before he could part from her. "Why do you leave me now?"

He seemed to battle some demon within himself. Finally, he held her to his chest so she could not see his face, but she'd caught sight of his anguished expression and she knew the words before he said them.

"I am ashamed, Padmini."

She shook her head and pulled away. Looking into his deep set eyes, she sought to reassure him. "It is I who am ashamed. Of my father, of what he has asked of you." She dropped her gaze.

"I agreed to pay the sum. He has a right to expect—"

"He has no right to sell my happiness."

She said the words with a ferocity that surprised her. Too late, she remembered that Indian men did not like such show of spirit, that women should be quiet and compliant, dedicating their lives to their lords' happiness. If she could show such scorn for her father, would not Nursoo reject her for fear that she would rebel against her husband's tutelage as well? She peeked up from beneath her lashes, fearful now that he would send her away. But instead of the fierce expression she expected, she saw him only smile.

It gave her the courage she needed. Slowly she let her veil

fall away from her face and watched his eyes widen. She looked at him, she hoped with a seductive expression he could not resist, and moistened her lips so they would shine temptingly. "I want you to take me away from my father's village."

He shook his head. She placed her hand softly on his forearm. "Please, it is our right to be together."

His breath came in short, hard bursts, as if he had difficulty breathing. Slowly, he lifted his hand and trailed it through her hair, his long strong fingers combing back the veil until it fell away and pooled around them on the ground. He leaned toward her.

His kiss was like a union of the gods. She reveled in his lips against hers, his hands stroking her back, smoothing her hair. She pressed against him.

Abruptly, he pulled away. The look on his face, the breath pounding in his chest, made her feel powerful and loved. She felt her heart swell.

"Padmini," he whispered, his voice harsh and raw to her ears. "You are a shining brightness, like a tongue of flame. A lotus-eyed daughter of the stars, whose beauty shines a thousandfold." He brushed his fingers through her hair then framed her face in his hands. "You will be my bride, my *Apsara* on earth." His dark brown eyes clouded. "But you will be a bride proper, not an outcast who must hide from the vengeance of her father's family."

Her eyes misted over at the truth of his words. She had not thought beyond running away from her father's tyranny. Foolishly, she had ignored the consequences of her actions. A blood feud between their families would haunt them all their lives, as well as destroy the lives of their children. Seeing his compassion for her, the deep love in his eyes, she ached to tell him the truth about her first bridegroom, but fear sealed her lips against the words.

"But what if my father never sets the date," she cried. "What if we never—"

This time it was Nursoo who silenced her with the touch

of his mouth against hers. "Be patient," he whispered against her lips between soft kisses. "The date will be set." He pulled away and smiled. "You need but have the faith to believe."

She blinked back the tears that his tender expression brought to her eyes. He wrapped his arms around her and held her to him.

"We will be married, Padmini. It will be so."

Leaning against his strength, she echoed, "It will be so."

Serena took a vicious bite from her cuticle, then sucked the blood that oozed from the wound when she discovered she'd bitten too deeply. The nervous habit ruined the appearance of her long shapely fingers, but she gave into it now as she waited anxiously for her lover to appear. They'd made their assignation earlier that evening, dangerously agreeing to meet here in her husband's home, right under Jeffrey's long pointed nose. The very thought of initiating her bed to her lover's hot passion after years of cold copulation with Jeffrey thrilled her to the toes of her fine slippers.

Serena pulled the bodice of her white tarlatan evening gown lower off her shoulders until her rose nipples threatened to show over the cordon of flowers that decorated the neckline. She didn't want to risk any chance that her lover would hesitate to take her in Jeffrey's fine canopied bed during the soiree. The possibility of discovery, after all, would only make their passion sweeter.

"Serena."

She turned and found her lover behind her. Alone in the hallway, she was free to run to him, hugging his broad chest, threading her fingers through the dark curls of his hair. She clasped her lips on his, thinking of the taste of his rough tiger scar against her mouth. His hands instantly traveled to the curve of her breast, and his thumb circled the stiff tarlatan of her gown teasing the nipples until the tips creased the material. Serena drew away long enough to guide him inside the room and shut them within the darkened upstairs bedchamber.

"What took so long?" she whispered through nips and bites of his lips.

"I had to get rid of the girl. It took a while to get away. Serena," he moaned. "Serena. I need you."

She looked up into her lover's hungry eyes. In the soft moonlight streaming through the window, she smiled slyly, then dug her nails into the cloth covering his strong arms. "Prove it."

He chuckled. Grabbing her hand, he pressed it roughly to his erection. "Proof enough, my dear?"

She angled her hips to meet his and rubbed against him as he devoured her mouth with his. A low growl emanated from deep in his throat as he reached for the fastenings of her dress. He laved the tops of her shoulders with his tongue, and asked in a rough voice, "Have you found the papers yet?"

Serena felt a burning anger flood through her even as she continued her frantic kisses. "The papers. Always those silly reports." She skimmed her tongue across his lips and inside his mouth before whispering, "Why must you always speak of the geographical surveys?"

Abruptly, he pushed her away, ending their kiss. A hard light shone in his eyes as he dug his fingers into the flesh of her upper arms. "I would very much appreciate your help, darling." With both hands, he reached down to her skirt and began gathering the material so that the hem traveled upward, exposing her ankles, then her knees. "Your husband does not see fit to give me those reports for some silly reasons of confidentiality." He slipped one hand under her skirt, his fingers traveling up her drawers, then reaching inside to the moist curls. His thumb found what he searched for and she threw her head back, almost panting. "It would help me a great deal to have the reports, Serena."

Completely at his mercy, she leaned into his hand. "I'll find them, Drew. I'll find them."

* * *

Somebody was slapping her.

It was really quite annoying, the stinging taps against Nicole's cheeks. All she wanted was to stay within her womb of comfort and live the breathless kiss she was sharing with Holt. It was such a lovely kiss, gentle—then hot and urgent, then gentle again. But ignoring the tiresome swats only seemed to increase their frequency. She wanted them to stop, before they dissolved her wonderful vision. Without opening her eyes, Nicky fisted her hand and took a swing.

"Hey!"

A strong grip caught her hand midair. Her lids fluttered open and she stared up into a pair of eyes shaded by dark arched brows. By the flickering light of a torch set near the arbor post, she saw the eyes looked familiar and friendly, clouded with concern. The moonlight shimmering through the vine-covered arbor was captured in their depths of vivid green. They seemed to promise to make up for the comfort they'd stolen by banishing her hazy world. She smiled in welcome. Wanting ever so much for the kiss to return, she coaxed softly, "Please, kiss me again."

The eyes smiled back. Their corners creased and they filled her vision as Holt's dark head blocked out the moon and his warm lips met hers.

At first his lips conveyed only comfort—a soft touch against her mouth, a tender kiss on her forehead, really only a celebration of her awakening. But soon his firm mouth invited hers to part with gentle pressure, and she leaned up into the kiss, hungry to taste him again. With the brace of his arm warm against her back, she sat up from the wooden bench where she lay, feeling the cooling breeze against her hot skin as Holt's hand brushed up her bared back and his tongue traced her lips. Slowly, her dress slipped farther down her shoulders, his hand cupped her breast under the silk—

Nicky gasped. She shoved Holt away and grabbed up the

material of her gown just before it fell to expose her breasts completely. She looked dumbly at the gold silk she held crushed against her, unable to comprehend how it could lay lax in her arms instead of pressing the very breath from her as it had been all night.

Slowly, the realization came. Her dress and corset had been unhooked.

And she knew by whom.

"Good heavens, Mr. Atley," she gasped. "Whatever do you think you're doing?"

His arms crossed before him, he stared right back at her. "I wonder about that myself," he said, shaking his head. "Kid, you do the damnedest things to me."

She grabbed hold of her anger when she realized how easily he could derail it with his soft expression. "Stop calling me 'kid.' I'm hardly a child."

His eyes dropped down to where she held the silk against her breasts. "You got that one right."

Before she could protest against his lustful stare, Holt said, "Look. *Kid.* You were trussed up in that corset tighter than a tick in a dog's ear." He sank his hands in the pockets of his trousers before taking a step back and leaning up against the arbor post. "You passed out." He shrugged. "I had to loosen the damn thing."

Nicky felt her anger leak away, replaced by waves of guilt. A little of what had occurred before she'd fainted filtered through to her consciousness. She had set out to charm Holt. Deliberately. Intentionally. The flood of memories came. How he'd made her laugh as he twirled her across the dance floor like an expert, leaving her breathless. Holt smiling as he talked about his mother. And when he'd spoken of his father—his expression, one of pain. She'd known then, while they'd danced, that somewhere deep within him, he hid a loss similar to her own. At that moment, she'd felt a sense of kinship that she'd not shared with anyone else.

Yes, she remembered it all now, every incriminating detail. When they'd slipped outside to the garden, she'd wanted him to kiss her—had encouraged him. She had even kissed him back before the damned corset had wrested her last breath from her.

And she'd enjoyed it. Very much.

Nicky felt a stab of regret slice through her as she thought of Drew and her scandalous behavior with Holt. She couldn't blame Holt for the kiss. Nor could she be angry with someone who had unlaced her suffocating corset after she'd fainted.

Looking back to Holt, she watched him light a native cigarette and tried to think of how to respond.

"I was trying to help," he said.

"Yes," she answered softly, feeling his words load more weighty guilt on her shoulders. "I understand."

He shook his match out and took a deep puff. "And you slugged me." He stepped forward, shaking the cigarette at her like an accusation. "I swear to God, lady, you hit me *one* more time and you can roll up and *die* before I lift a finger to help."

"You needn't shout, Mr. Atley. I believe I understand the situation now."

"If you didn't always look so blasted . . . like some damn—" He stopped, then flung the unsmoked cigarette to the dirt. "Oh, hell."

Nicky watched him walk past her toward the lights of the commissioner's house. She didn't know what to say to make him come back; she just knew she wanted him to. Something about their conversation felt uncomfortable, unfinished. When she looked down at the dress hanging well off her shoulders, threatening to slide past her pale breasts, she understood why.

"Mr. Atley, wait!" She ran after him, almost tripping on the hem of the loose gown. When he turned back to face her, she slowed her pace and tried to approach with as much dignity as she could muster under the circumstances. She stopped two feet in front of him.

"I think you've"—her face heated up—"you've forgotten something."

He furrowed his brow. Nicky looked down at the material she held cradled to her breasts and prompted, "The dress?"

Holt stepped back, then walked around her in a slow circle. "Well, isn't this cozy." After an embarrassingly thorough inspection, he stopped and crossed his arms over his chest.

With a sinking feeling at the pit of her stomach, Nicole saw his smirk of a smile was back. And it looked as mean-spirited as ever.

"Doesn't this just beat all," he drawled. "You need me to button you up?" He "tched" softly. "Wouldn't it be a hoot if you marched right back in that salon with your dress hanging down to your waist."

"Mr. Atley, please"—she ground her teeth together—"button me *up*."

He stared at her for a moment then took out another *bidi* cigarette, making a great ceremony of lighting up. Every second or so, he would chuckle, as if he had thought of some private joke he found quite humorous. He blew the match out with one puff, then looked up and met her gaze. "It's tempting not to."

Nicole felt her face burn anew. As the smoke curled around Holt, his smile turned so diabolical, it made him look as if he belonged right where she wished him at that very moment.

"You don't think this is all rather childish?" she asked after his marked silence.

"Yeah." His smile widened. "Isn't it."

He turned on his heels and headed toward the house.

"Don't you dare leave me here like this!" She grabbed for his arm, just grazing the superfine material of his jacket.

Holt swung back to face her. "Sounds *real* menacing, kid." Cigarette in hand, he walked toward her until they stood only a foot apart. "You gonna pull a gun on me again?" With the toe of his boot he lifted the hem of her gown as if to peek beneath it. "Got one hidden under that tent?"

She swung at him then, but he flung the cigarette from his hand and captured her fist easily within his. He pulled her flush against him. "You know what the problem is, kid?" His lips were so close she could almost savor his breath, a seductive combination of cognac, tobacco, and the sheer sweet taste of him. "You *really* want to know why you and me are so spitting angry." Slowly, his hands relaxed their grip and he ran his callused fingers up her bare shoulders to her neck, his thumbs massaging the pulse points there. "It has nothing to do with the damned dress." His lips grazed her cheek; he gently nuzzled her neck, sending chills down her spine to her toes. "It's frustration, pure and simple." He blew the words softly into her ear, making her tingle. "That's what it is, kid." His mouth brushed against her earlobe, his whispered words a caress. "It's because we both want this something fierce."

He stroked her neck with his lips, then kissed the curve of her cheek. His arms wrapped around her, and his fingers found the bare flesh of her back. Nicole arched toward him, feeling his warmth surround her.

"God, I want you." He kissed her then, a fierce coupling of their mouths. His tongue plunged deep within her, touching hidden recesses until she could feel her toes curl. "I want you, Nicky."

She tried to push him away, knowing she had played a terrible game, and lost—lost herself and the happiness she'd coveted with Drew, whose kisses and embrace would never make her feel the hunger Holt could inspire with a look. But when he finally released her, he did so with such gentleness, she almost wished she'd not initiated her retreat.

Regret bitter in her mouth, she looked up to his face and found something more than mocking anger in his eyes— something much more tempting. It was almost hidden by his arrogant expression, but she saw it nonetheless. A hint in the soft curve of his mouth, a suggestion in his lingering glance, that he might actually feel the same aching need that raged within her.

She looked at him then. Really looked, until his cocky grin faltered and his expression turned serious. Their eyes met. She caught her breath.

Nicky stepped back into his arms, stopping only when she could feel the cushion of warmth emanating from his body. He tried to look away, but she steadied his face with a hand at his cheek, seeking his eyes, for the first time completely unrestrained in her manner. He had beautiful green eyes, flecked with gold and brown, but the dark green centers dominated. Staring into those eyes, she realized with sudden insight what it was she sought.

She was looking for herself, mirrored there within his gaze. What did Holt Atley think of her?

She looked closer, believing she'd find the sophisticated lady in the looking glass, the one she'd seen reflected in the officers' admiring glances. She didn't. In Holt's eyes, she saw something else. Someone else. Someone deep inside her who was . . . was what? Pretty? Courageous? She looked closer still. Somehow she knew that if she could *see* that person, know she existed without the mirror before her, she could . . .

Nicky felt as if some great truth lay within her grasp, a word on the tip of her tongue that through some trick of the mind she could not utter. And then the moment was gone.

She felt Holt's hands on her shoulders and she watched his eyelids drop slowly. She leaned forward; her head tilted up to receive his kiss as he lowered his mouth to hers. His tongue sought hers gently, softly now, and she welcomed him.

The kiss was tender, so tender. It made her wonder if its very tenderness were the reason she felt like crying.

When he pulled away, Holt said nothing. Neither spoke a word. He simply turned her around and began slowly lacing her corset.

*   *   *

Celibacy was impeding his ability to think straight. Why else would he be acting so strangely?

Holt laughed dryly, leaning against the cypress just outside the French doors of the Ratcliffe's salon. He might even look up his condition in one of the many reference books that filled the almira at his bungalow, books shipped to him courtesy of Professor Dawson in London. If he couldn't find any mention of his particular disorder, he'd publish a paper on it himself.

Of course he would have to think of a name for the syndrome. Recalling the year he had spent guiding Albert Dawson through his studies of the animal life in the Northwestern Provinces, Holt thought himself up to the task. The good professor had shown his gratitude by sharing his infinite knowledge with Holt, praising him as one of his best pupils, and on one occasion, even granting Holt the honor of naming a new species of orchid he had discovered, orchids being a special hobby of Dawson's. With his prior experience at the professor's side, and the years of his youth spent at Harvard, Holt felt able enough if he were called upon to name his current illness.

He could just picture it. Holt Atley, forest officer and naturalist, a victim of the deadly, debilitating disease . . . *Brainitis Celibacitis:* A reduced capacity in decision-making caused by long periods of enforced celibacy, which may lead to a strong desire to make mad passionate love to petite, pistol-packing females.

Funny. So why didn't he feel like laughing?

Pivoting on the balls of his feet, he threw a hard punch to the cypress behind him. The pain radiated up his arm to his shoulder, giving him something to think about besides gold eyes and raven hair—but not for long. He rubbed his raw knuckles, feeling the rough edges where he'd scraped the skin against the tree bark while he listened to the music streaming from the salon. He'd just escorted the now properly corseted and gowned Nicole back inside, no one the wiser for their little interlude.

Katherine Nicole Marshall. Bloody hell, even her name sounded regal.

A damned British aristocrat. A damned *betrothed* aristocrat.

Holt fumbled with a cigarette and began to smoke it furiously, inhaling the smoke deep into his lungs. Why her? The lady had so far threatened Enchantress, nearly unmanned him, shot at him—plague take it, the list was endless! And what did he do? What great defensive strategy had he taken? He'd kissed her—as if she were the only blasted woman left on God's earth. With his heart and soul in his eyes, so clearly there for her to see that she'd stopped herself mid-tirade to kiss him back!

Brainitis Celibacitis. Had to be.

But what was the cure?

He knew the antidote he would have taken last summer. He would have gone to see Maralys, his mistress of three years. But Maralys was gone now, returned to her family in Sussex after he'd made it clear he would not wed the military widow. He'd tried to explain why he couldn't marry. He'd tried for Maralys's sake, the lady who had faithfully seen to his needs during the long years of their relationship, to put it into words.

Hearing the music's lilting beat, Holt thought of his stiff explanation, of her sad pale eyes of cornflower blue as she'd listened. The waltz playing inside the commissioner's house flowed and ebbed, teasing other memories from him, until the blonde's sweet face faded and it was his mother he saw in his mind's eye. Beautiful, happy, laughing as he twirled her in his arms to the beat of the waltz streaming through the French doors, her green eyes sparkling, her dark hair gleaming under the candlelight.

Her face pale in death.

Painfully, the memories returned. His uncle standing stoically before Holt. The wet drizzle that characterized Boston in the fall dampening his greatcoat. "It was her Bible, my boy," his uncle had said, his proper Boston accent making him sound cold and distant despite the soft look of sympathy in his eyes as he'd handed Holt the leather-bound book. "Her most precious possession. I'm sure she would have wanted you to keep it."

The mourners slipped away, one by one, their black cloaks reminding Holt of winged ravens circling a kill. Alone, he watched the newly tilled soil on his mother's grave darken with rain. He stared at the Bible in his hands, recalling how each night his mother would read to him from the book, until he'd been old enough to read it aloud himself.

Until he'd been old enough to leave her and his studies at Harvard, disappointing her, running off for the adventure of the Mexican-American War.

Standing there in the rain by her graveside, his pain a swelling deep in his throat that threatened to choke him, he defended his actions. Hadn't she spent hours telling him about his father, a man Holt had not seen since his third birthday, painting romantic pictures of his heroic feats as a British cavalry officer in India? Hadn't she made Steven Atley seem bigger than life, a man to emulate—right down to his father's abandonment of her?

He flipped open the Bible, hunching over the pages to protect it from the faint drizzle. On the inside back cover, he ran his fingers over the dates there, stopping at one. *June 16, 1827, Delhi, India: Marriage of Miranda Hawkins Edwards of Boston, Massachusetts, to Captain Steven Taylor Atley of Yorkshire, England.* And then another: *July 26, 1828, Cawnpore, India, born Holt Steven Atley.*

The pages curled back and the book opened naturally to his mother's favorite psalm. Holt found a slip of paper tucked inside. Carefully, he unfolded the thin vellum, saw it was a letter addressed to him in Mexico. A letter his mother had never sent. His eyes skimmed down the lines that said so eloquently how much she missed her only child. Each word was a testament to his abandonment of her in her hour of need, as she slowly died from a debilitating illness of the lungs she had successfully hidden from him. He read on, forcing himself to accept this punishment.

It is written that no test is given that is too great, but I fear that mine perhaps is, Holt. I sit alone with only my Bible to grant me comfort, wishing you were here, safe beside me. I tell myself to be strong, that I must let you fulfill your dreams as I have your father, but I confess I pray each day for your quick return.

Holt folded the letter back inside the Bible, knowing God had not answered her prayers. Holt had come too late. His mother had died a lonely old woman while the men she loved left her to fulfill their own lusts for adventure.

Raucous laughter from inside the Ratcliffe home dissipated the morbid image of his mother's grave site. Holt stared out into the darkened garden. There was a time when he'd hated his father for choosing his military career over his family. For making Holt believe through his actions that war was romantic, worth sacrificing your loved ones for. If it were not so grand, so special, why would his father choose it over his family . . . over his son?

So he'd followed in his sire's footsteps, and made his own discovery: War was a living hell. He'd seen boys with their chest blown wide open. Men with their life's blood flowing from severed arteries no one could sew shut. The precious illusions he'd fostered all those years had been shattered, but it had cost his mother greatly, nonetheless. Yet, after his mother's death, when he'd gone to India to confront his father, Holt had found more than he'd bargained for. A land full of mysteries, seductive and enchanting. The five years he'd spent with Steven Atley, before his father had been killed by a leopard while hunting, Holt had come to know Steven and his choices. One night, over a bottle of arrack, his father had spoken wistfully of India, his mistress. He'd told Holt he regretted his marriage, admitting that he'd failed his wife miserably.

Yes, after ten years living here, Holt could understand why his father had stayed, always promising that next year

he'd join his family in Boston. *Next year, always next year.*
India was an enchanted garden, and like his father, Holt had
fallen under her spell. But it was a land too dangerous to
permit a normal family life.

That's what he'd told Maralys. He couldn't marry her; he
couldn't marry anyone. He'd never choose the route of his
father: marry, sire a child, then send the lot away to live in
safety elsewhere while he stayed within India's seductive
arms.

Holt sighed, shaking his head. Sick to death of his maud-
lin mood, he stamped out his cigarette and headed inside. It
was time to go back home to the village. Preparations for
the hunt would start before dawn.

Just within the glass doors, he almost collided with Serena Ratcliffe. When he stepped aside to allow her to pass,
she stopped him with her hand on his arm. Her pearl pink
tongue skimmed her lips, a gesture that Holt suspected was
calculated to be sensual.

"Aren't you going to ask me to dance?" She leaned
against him, her breast grazing his arm. She acted as if
they'd been intimate for years, when in fact he'd turned
down her advances from the first. Though she was almost
ten years his senior, it wasn't her age that deterred him. He
just had no desire to get involved with a married woman, no
matter how willing she appeared.

With thinly veiled distaste, he was about to say he was
leaving when he saw her glance across the room, watching
someone. Her smile widened and her dark blue eyes returned to him. It was a vicious smile that made him wary.
Serena Ratcliffe was a woman desperately hanging on to her
aging beauty. She took any rejection as a grave insult. Holt
searched the crowd, trying to discover what could make
Serena Ratcliffe look so triumphant.

Just across the room to his left, his eyes met the commissioner's. The man was staring at him as if he wished Holt
would drop dead on the spot.

It all made sense then. The permit, trying to kill Enchantress, insisting Nicole go on the hunt despite his protests. Serena, the little bitch, had never forgiven Holt his refusal. She'd said he'd regret it. Apparently, she'd found a way to get her revenge.

"Well," she asked, "shall we dance?"

Holt pushed her hand away. "Lady, you're poison."

As he headed for the front doors, the sound of her laughter followed him.

Padmini reached the darkened *ghar* house. Warily, she dropped her bundle of sticks by the entrance, trying to make as little noise as possible. When she'd left earlier this evening, she'd had no intention of returning. Now, if discovered, she must try to explain her prolonged absence—something she truly dreaded.

Leaning against the cool stone wall, her thoughts turned again to Nursoo. He'd told her he would return in a month's time with the money her father had demanded. He'd asked her to be patient, that they would have a lifetime together to make up for these few years apart, and she knew he was right. She would wait. She touched her fingers lightly to her lips where Nursoo had kissed her. At least now she would have wonderful memories during his absence.

Taking a deep breath, she entered through the door quietly. She'd come in through the back, avoiding her father and brothers, who slept on the veranda. But the person she truly feared was *Ma*. Although she'd planned to use the gathering of fuel as an excuse, the moon was high in the sky. Her explanation would hardly stand under her mother's stern examination.

Padmini climbed one step at a time, wincing as the wooden stairs creaked under her weight. She moved steadily, her heart's beat pounding stronger with each step. But when she reached the top floor, she saw her worst fears had come true. Her mother waited at the top; beside her stood a beaming Rumbha.

"*Ma*, I was—"

Her mother grabbed her arm, dragging her inside the darkened chamber. By the light of a single clay lamp, Padmini saw Deepali's smirking features. Her mother's fingers clawed deeper into Padmini's arm until it felt as if she might draw blood.

"I know what you were doing!" Her mother's harsh whispers echoed across the near-empty room. "Rumbha had the presence of mind to follow you. You little fool. You've compromised yourself! All the years we hid the death of your bridegroom go for naught. No one will have you now."

Her mother's twisted expression frightened Padmini. Never had she seen *Ma* this angry. "There was no sin to our meeting, *Ma*. I swear it."

Her mother's slap burned into her cheek. The blow sent Padmini reeling against the wall behind her. Padmini glanced to Rumbha. For the first time since her sister-in-law had joined her family, the woman looked concerned for Padmini's welfare.

"You have ruined your father's salvation!" her mother shouted.

"We simply talked, I tell you."

"Not even the lowly Khasiya will have you now."

"He will, *Ma*. He told me we would marry," she said desperately, trying to stem her mother's advance. "He promised on his honor."

Her mother struck her, again and again. Padmini dropped to the floor, retreating to the corner to escape her mother's blows. Across the room, Deepali and Rumbha huddled silently, their faces drawn in expressions of fear.

"You stupid, stupid girl." Her mother's hand landed another blow. "He promised on his honor? Those are useless words. The Khasiya has no honor. You have ruined this family!"

Padmini held her arms crossed before her face, trying to deflect *Ma's* attack. When her mother's words against Nursoo reached past her wall of fear, she rose to her knees.

Grabbing her mother's swinging arms, she held *Ma's* hands still. Her mother stared at her, nonplussed by her actions.

"You say the Khasiya have no honor? And what of the Bhanaris, our family's people? Speak to my father about his salvation." Out of control Padmini screamed, "He sold me!" Dropping her mother's hands, she pressed her fist against her chest. "He asked Nursoo for six hundred rupees to marry me."

Rumbha gasped. The shock of Padmini's words sent everyone into silence. Tears running down her cheeks, Padmini added, "A true hill Rajput would never accept money for his daughter. Do not blame my father's loss of honor on me."

Ma rose slowly to her feet. She turned to Deepali and Rumbha. "No one is to speak of this."

Padmini laughed harshly. "Another secret—"

"Be quiet girl. Do not question your father! You must be mad to even suggest such things." Her eyes narrowed on Padmini. "Yes, certainly your actions are a result of sickness. To speak in such a way, you must truly be possessed. What has the Khasiya fed you to turn you against your family?"

"If I am possessed, it is with nothing but anger for the lost honor of my family!"

"Padmini!" Rumbha warned her from across the room.

Her mother's expression turned smug in the lamplight, as if she'd just determined how to deal with her rebellious daughter. "Possession is a terrible thing, Padmini," she said smoothly. "The Dholi shall be sent for. Whatever it takes, we shall drive this spirit from you."

The
Capture

*Men are the actors and women are the persons
acted upon . . .*

> *The Kamasutra of Vatsyayana,* as
> translated by Sir Richard Burton

8

After only one day of preparations, the party of hunters and their porters set out for Askot, the man-eater's most recent territory. Climbing ridge after ridge, crossing the thick forests of ilexes, rhododendrons, and bracken, a few miles could mean a difference of three or four thousand feet in altitude. At the higher elevations, the outstretched limbs of ancient white oaks and horse chestnuts appeared to grope for the thinning air along with the out-of-breath wayfarers. As they hiked down to the tropical monsoon forest at the base of the foothills, the moist heat and sudden rainfall made travel equally unbearable.

Sandwiched between the deputy commissioner and Nursoo, Nicole crossed deep ravines, hiked the narrow sheepherder paths, battled the loose rocks, thick undergrowth, and trees. She never for a moment forgot that behind the next bush or cluster of stunted bamboo could be hidden a quick death—the man-eater. Yet each time she felt she could not take one step more, could not carry her ten-pound rifle one inch farther, she looked up the trail to where Holt trekked at a steady rhythm.

And she would march on.

Holt led with a confidence born of experience, a man in his element. The brim of his slouch hat pulled low against the sun, the shirt buttons of his cotton *kurta* opened at the neck, he looked like a hybrid of the gaitered and helmeted British hunters wearing their dusty shooting jackets, and the wool-capped natives dressed in loose *anga* coats and *paijama* style trousers. To Nicole, Holt seemed part of the rugged countryside, right down to the strange catlike creature that clung to his neck; a lemur, he'd called it. Along with the animal he toted his kit in a leather pack while the others of the party—Nicky, Uncle Marc, Drew, and Jeffrey Ratcliffe—could hardly keep up with only their rifles to weigh them down. Certainly the porters, each of whom carried a load of up to forty pounds balanced on the crown of his head, kept the party's pace slow, but still the hunters huffed and puffed, harassed and harangued, protesting the party's speedy ascent to Askot.

Holt ignored them. He pressed effortlessly on. He was, quite obviously, in excellent physical condition—an Atlas of strength and endurance.

The arrogant cretin.

Nicole bit her lip, having almost voiced her opinion out loud, and concentrated on keeping within the narrow track. Holt signaled the group to pass him, and they snaked up the switchback paths, halting before a large clump of blood-red rhododendrons. As the natives stopped to pick the fist-sized blossoms, chewing on the sorrel-tasting plants as they'd done periodically throughout the journey, Nicky glanced over her shoulder. For a moment, she watched Holt confer with Nursoo, but returned her gaze to the natives before he could catch her staring at him.

Cretin was only one of the many epithets that had come to Nicole's mind as the party journeyed from Lakhtoli to their next resting point, the village of Beninag. Watching the bearers enjoy the flavor of the blossoms she had found too sour for her liking, Nicky tried to quell her pent-up antagonism toward Holt. He was, after all, the man who just three days ago had held her in his arms and kissed her with such tenderness she'd wanted to cry.

"Out of the way, kid."

Nicole started at the deep voice behind her. She stepped aside, allowing Holt to pass her on the narrow trail. The expression of utter detachment in his eyes as he brushed past her to take the lead once more hit Nicky like a slap in the face. That was it. That was all. *Out of the way, kid*—his first words to her in two days of travel together.

The taste in her mouth turned as sour as the rhododendrons. At the Ratcliffe's party, Holt had fed a part of her that had been starved, a part Drew had never satisfied. Now he simply chose to forget her. He'd looked right past her, as if she wasn't worth the notice. Well, she couldn't forget, not when each time she saw Drew she felt nothing but guilt and uncertainty for their marriage. What would she give for even a tenth of the attention Holt showered on the lemur he carried on his shoulder? Kissing her in the moonlight, he'd made her feel beautiful. And now he'd taken that away. It hurt. More than she cared to admit.

As she continued up the path, Nicky tried to set aside her feelings of loss, focusing instead on her problems with Drew. Could they still have a happy marriage, despite a lack of passion? Would that aspect of love come with time? These were questions that remained unanswered even as the party arrived at Beninag, their halting place for the night.

Dropping her canvas bag to the ground, Nicky forced herself to enjoy the spectacular view of the Himalayas and dismiss her troubled thoughts. Beyond the terraced slopes of the foothills, the sawtooth outline of the nearest ridge rose straight into the darkening sky. Nursoo had named the highest peak earlier in the day, before the clouds had gathered to veil it from view, Nanda Devi—the Guardian Goddess. Watching Nursoo instruct the porters to set up camp at the pagodalike shelter built beneath a large tree, Nicole gave the *shikaree* an appreciative smile.

Thus far, Nursoo had been the only one to take any notice of her on this difficult trip. After their many hours traveling together, she considered him a friend. Drew and her uncle, who hiked ahead with Holt, were too busy discussing the upcoming hunt to pay her the least attention. Yet Nursoo often marched at her side when the narrow path permitted, behind her when it did not. He answered all her questions, sharing interesting bits of knowledge, such as how the earthenware pots tied beneath incisions in the bark of the fir trees would collect resin for the kerosene tins bound for Almora. The *shikaree's* friendship was a soothing balm to Holt's distance. But as she watched the American speaking to her uncle a few feet away, she realized it was not a cure.

Just then, Nicole caught sight of the lemur sprinting across the campsite toward Nursoo. She smiled and turned to watch the animal's amusing antics. As she took a step toward the *shikaree* and the delightful lemur he now held, her legs tangled in the straps of the canvas bag she'd absently dropped at her feet. Tired from the day's hike, she couldn't seem to get her balance. She cried out as her feet slipped out from under her.

A jumble of images, the tops of the pines, the darkening sky, raced past. She clasped the Purdy rifle she still carried as she tumbled backwards. When her back hit the ground, the air left her lungs in a harsh whoosh. She couldn't catch her breath. A stunning pain flared from the back of her head as she hit a rock. Spots of light floated before her eyes. Like a faraway noise, she heard the roar of the Purdy firing.

Almost instantly, Nursoo was at her side, kneeling down beside her. "Memsahib, are you all right?"

"I'm fine. Just a bit winded." With the *shikaree's* help, Nicole sat up. She touched the back of her head lightly where a sizeable lump had begun to swell. "My gun," she asked. "Was anyone hurt?" Shaking her head, trying to get the fuzzy world into focus, she looked around for her rifle.

Her gaze met Holt's disapproving glare. His green eyes shone with the fire of anger, a charge set and ready to explode. Standing over her, he shouted, "That gun could have killed someone!"

"It is all right, memsahib," Nursoo said as Holt turned to retrieve her rifle on the ground next to him. "No one was hurt."

"I had it only half-cocked—"

"Well it's broken now." Holt tossed the Purdy to the dirt

beside her, then turned to her uncle. "She shouldn't be here, Marshall. I've said so from the beginning!"

"It was an accident . . ." Nicky tried to stand and defend herself, but Nursoo held her back, shaking his head.

Her uncle stabbed a finger at Holt's chest to the beat of his words. "And I say you're wrong! There's no finer sportsman than my Nick."

"Sportswoman, Marshall. She's not a man; she's a woman. You seem to forget your niece's gender."

"It's not hurt her yet"—the jabbing finger now pointed to her—"Nick here's no simpering maid, like the rest of those ninnies. She's got more courage than any man I know! That time with the white tigress was a fluke. She can pull her weight just as well as Drew and I." He looked to Drew as if for confirmation, but her betrothed, like the commissioner beside him, remained a silent spectator to the argument.

"A woman has no place hunting a man-eating tiger!" Holt's voice rose to match her uncle's. "She should have stayed in Almora with her companion, where she belongs. She slows us down; it's a nuisance to find her separate quarters at night. Dammit, you saw what just happened! She could have been hurt!"

"Nicole is a crack shot. An experienced huntress. She's an asset on this hunt. How dare you insinuate she cannot hold her own? You were there the day she bagged the leopard!"

Nicole held her breath, waiting for Holt to tell her uncle the truth: She had botched that kill as well. So far, the supposed leopard trophy was all she had to her credit on this trip. If Holt set the facts straight, what would her uncle do to retaliate for the lie? As Holt's eyes narrowed on her, Nicole's pulse pounded at her temples.

"I remember the leopard," he said in a cold voice. "Most clearly."

When Uncle Marc's finger posed to continue its assault, Holt pushed his hand aside. "Mark my words, Marshall." Nicky felt Holt's glare slice through her. "She's a danger to us all."

Holt turned and walked away, leaving her uncle to release his parting volley. "You're wrong, Atley!" Marcus shouted. "She'll show you, she will. We'll both show you." Then, mumbling under his breath, Uncle Marc followed Drew and the commissioner back to the shelter.

Nicole felt Nursoo's hand at her shoulder. When he gave her a sympathetic smile, she stood, grabbing her gun and her bag from the ground. Without a word to the Indian guide, she marched off, ignoring the thudding pain at the back of her head.

In the *pal* tent she would occupy that night, away from the men in the trees, she threw her bag carelessly to the corner. Examining the Purdy, she saw that the sear holding the right hammer back had indeed broken. Though she had another rifle with her, the Purdy was her favorite, the gun with which she felt most comfortable. She placed it on the ground gently, then dropped to her cot, stifling a cry for the loss of her most reliable weapon.

For the longest moment, she stared at the canvas walls of the *pal*. What hurt most was the shattering of her silly belief that Holt cared for her. That night, when they'd danced and laughed together, he'd made her feel so special. Now, rather than give her the strength she searched for deep inside herself for the challenge ahead, his words only made her doubts grow.

When the party arrived at Askot, the village appeared abandoned. Rows and rows of stone two-story huts stood like silent sentinels on the hilltop. Not a soul passed through the flagstone streets. Not a dog or goat disrupted the unearthly quiet. Even the jungle at the bottom of the ridge seemed oppressively still. Nicky looked immediately to Nursoo for an explanation, but the Hindu shook his head, glancing warily at the empty whitewashed houses.

"The man-eater."

Nicole turned at Holt's chilling words. His face reflected

the same grim quality as his voice. Then she heard a faint chanting on the afternoon breeze followed by an eerie wail.

"Jumping Jupiter. What on earth . . . ?" Her uncle's eyes widened and he tightened his grip on his rifle.

Holt looked knowingly at Nursoo. The Hindu gave the American a short nod.

"Let's go," Holt said. After a few instructions to the porters standing next to their baggage, he turned up the first street toward the heart of the village.

"Hold up there," her uncle called out. "I demand to know what's going on!"

Holt and Nursoo continued up the street, ignoring her uncle's cries. His face flushed with anger, Uncle Marc nodded to the rest of the party and followed the two *shikarees.*

As the party of six climbed higher toward the center of town, the wailing grew stronger, more haunting, until Nicky knew for certain what it was she was hearing: the voices of women crying. No one spoke a word, but she could see from their wary expressions that the keening disturbed them all. Only Holt seemed unaffected, his expression merely a deepening of the anger that had characterized his mood during their four-day journey from Almora.

They passed several huts plastered with whitewashed clay until they reached the source of the mournful cries. Like the houses that surrounded it, the stone hut had two stories. The wooden door stood open. Nicole could smell the sharp pungent odor of incense, hear the chanting of a Brahman within. Several men of the village waited silently outside the threshold. On the quartzite flags in front of the hut, a bullock cart stood surrounded by several more men. The keening grew louder. A shrill cry filled the air.

"A funeral," Nursoo said softly beside her.

Holt approached a few men on the outer fringes of the group surrounding the cart. Though Nicole could not understand the men's answers to his soft words, she knew by their passionate responses and the tears in the eyes of one older native that they were all deeply upset.

A commotion at the door caught her attention. The group of villagers parted to allow two men carrying a pallet between them to pass. Nicole gasped when she saw the litter held the badly mangled body of a young boy, no more than ten years of age. The men placed the straw pallet onto the bullock cart and stepped away. Another cry pierced the sound of wailing as a woman ran outside the hut and threw herself on the boy's garlanded body. She screamed over and over, until several women, black cloths tied to their heads and thick black veils covering their faces, pulled her off the boy. Slowly, the cart proceeded down the street, followed by the procession of men. The screaming woman fell to her knees on the street, crying as the others tried to console her.

"What happened?" Nicole watched the distraught woman, obsessed with the word the woman kept repeating with such passion. "What's she saying?"

"My son," Nursoo translated. "My son."

Two hands grabbed Nicole's shoulders. Before she could cry out, Holt turned her around to face him.

"Is this what you wanted, Miss Marshall?" he asked with acid sarcasm. "To be a part of an exciting hunt for a man-eating tiger? A great thrill, I'm sure. I hope you got a good look at his latest victim."

Holt pushed her away. Nicole stumbled back against Nursoo. Her uncle and Drew stepped forward, protesting Holt's rough handling, but the American paid little heed to their words. When the woman still kneeling on the flagstones gave another shrill cry, the group fell silent, all eyes trained on her pain.

"When we start out in the morning," Holt said, "I don't want any of you to forget. The tiger is a man-eater, a killer. It craves human flesh. It's out there, waiting for its next meal to come walking up to it in the grass. If you're not careful." He gave each hunter a quelling glance. "If you're not on guard one hundred percent of the time," Holt turned and looked directly at Nicole, "you could be next."

* * *

Nicole picked up her pistol and checked it carefully. The funeral and Holt's dire warning had left her shaken. She wanted to go down to the river and wash up, hoping the cool water would help dissipate the disturbing images of the funeral as well as the heat, but decided the village well was safer. Gathering up her brush, soap, and a cloth, she made for the door of the stone hut, her pistol firmly in hand. For a moment, she thought of asking her uncle or Nursoo to accompany her, but dismissed the thought. The men of the group were probably meeting with the villagers now, discussing the sites of the tiger's previous attacks. It was still light out. If she hurried, she'd be back long before dark.

Nicole left the stone hut and turned down the flagstone street toward the outskirts of town. After the funeral, a guide had led them up the lofty heights to the rajbar of Askot's home. The rajbar owned the *zamindari* of Askot, the feudal holding that paid revenues to the British government, and had made arrangements for the hunters to stay in town. It wasn't safe to camp outside the village as they'd done during most of their trip to Askot. Not with the man-eater prowling for its next victim.

Finding the well Nursoo had spoken of earlier, she thought longingly of the cool waters of the stream outside the village. She wished she could strip off her hunting jacket and trousers and jump into the river in only her chemise. After the day's sixteen-mile hike up and down the foothills of the Himalayas, she wanted a bath desperately. With a sigh, she settled for a quick wash with her cloth. Deciding she was too tired to carry the bucket back up the street to the hut, she dragged the pail to a cluster of bushes, hoping for some privacy. Kneeling down facing the shrubs, she undid the top buttons of her jacket and carefully placed her pistol on the ground beside her. Even here at the fringe of the village, well within shouting distance of help, she didn't feel quite safe. The man-eater was out there, somewhere. He would strike again.

The faint shadow registered just as she reached for her

cloth. At first, it was only a flash of darkness, a suggestion of a shape, but then it solidified into something black and sleek and tall. Out of the corner of her eye, Nicole made out the cobra's long thin body. The hood swayed only a foot from her hand.

Instinctively, she held her hand still. Watching the serpent, its slit eyes both menacing and mesmerizing, she followed its movement. Back and forth, it rocked. Closer. She quelled her desire to snatch her hand back. The aching muscles of her arm screamed from the effort of holding her hand suspended before the venomous snake. Perspiration beaded on her upper lip. She could almost smell her fear. Slowly, she inched her free hand toward her pistol.

It was just out of reach.

She wanted to cry, scream in frustration. Instead, she steadied her breathing and watched the snake weave in its deadly dance. Ready to strike, ready to kill. Carefully, she stretched, reaching for the gun—still out of reach! *The gun Nicky! Get the gun.* She stretched a little farther.

The snake swung forward. A gun fired.

The cobra's head vanished. Only the body remained shivering on the ground next to her. Nicole scrambled back, watching the headless snake undulate toward her, still seeking her. With a muffled cry, she grabbed her pistol, aimed. She discharged both barrels into the snake.

The cobra went still.

"Don't worry. It's quite dead."

Holt watched Nicole's hands drop to her lap with her gun. She seemed to catch her breath before turning her head to face him. Not wanting her to see how shaken he was, Holt concentrated on reloading his carbine. If his aim had been off even a fraction of an inch . . .

It took every bit of control he possessed not to run to her side and cradle her in his arms. Instead, he placed the cartridge in its chamber and finished loading. Slowly, ignoring Nicole kneeling on the ground, he walked to the cobra's body. He gave the dead snake a kick.

"A black cobra. The most venomous of all. Takes an average of ten minutes to die after its bite. If you have the courage, and the strength, the only cure is to immediately hack off whatever it bites. If you're lucky, you only lose a hand or a foot."

He'd meant his words to scare some sense into her. Damn her hide, if she put herself at risk one more time, he'd kill her himself and get it over with! Why had she come to the well alone, for God's sake? He was about to say as much when he saw her face. Her eyes were wide. Her lips quivered. Holt held his tongue. She was upset enough as it was.

Shaking his head, he shouldered his carbine and offered her a hand up. Nicole stared at his outstretched hand as if she were actually scared to take it. "Go ahead," he said. *"I* won't bite."

Slowly, she reached out and laid her palm on his. Her hand felt cold. It trembled.

The poor kid was scared to death.

Holt lowered his gun and dropped down to his knees beside her. "Hey, it's okay." He clasped her hand warmly between his two. "You're all right."

Immediately, she embraced him. He hugged her tightly, making soothing noises in her ear as he stroked the hair that had escaped her braid. He knew he should push her away, but the temptation to offer comfort was too great. It was what he wanted most—to feel her warm and alive in his arms.

"Salaam." Holt lifted his ceramic cup to the smiling natives, his hosts, and took a healthy swallow. He could feel the arrack liquor he'd brought with him in his pack burn its path to his stomach even before he downed the last of the drink. With a friendly nod to the Katyuri man and his two older sons in whose shed he planned to sleep, the fleas permitting, he left the whitewashed stone hut. Nursoo should be serving up dinner just about now and Holt could use a

little sustenance to counter the arrack he'd drunk. Unfortunately, he just might have to face Nicole to get it.

She would be the death of him, of that he was sure.

When he'd seen her heading for the outskirts of town, he'd followed her, ready to give her hell for going off by herself. But then he'd caught her frozen posture, the cobra a mere foot away, ready to strike. There were very few things in this world that still frightened Holt, but Lord help him, that girl sure found them.

His expression grim, Holt turned toward the edge of town to where Nursoo had set up their cooking fires. Four days he had ignored Nicole, through the whole damn trip here. It hadn't helped. Every time he saw her, he wanted to take her in his arms and kiss her and . . . Yeah, that was the problem, that damned *and.* So instead, he'd stooped to downright meanness. He wasn't too proud of some of the things he'd said. It was frustration. Sexual frustration. He'd thought the quicker he took care of it, the sooner he'd be back to normal. But the time he'd tried—the Nat Gypsy girl he'd brought home the night after the ball—had been a perfunctory act that had left him wanting Nicole all the more.

So he took it out on the kid. Each day his comments became more snide. He hated every damn word of it. Sure, she should be anywhere but near the vicinity of a man-eater, but that wasn't the kid's fault. It was her uncle's—and that ass-brained Herringbone's.

Thinking of the British lord brought Holt his only satisfaction since starting out for Askot. He'd sure enjoyed the old aristocrat's expression when Holt had refused to let Morgan on the hunt. It had almost given him as much pleasure as telling Morgan to get lost or face charges for what he'd done to the poor *rokh.* He'd seen neither hide nor hair of Morgan or the Korku since.

As he neared the cooking fires, Holt's small flame of contentment was immediately extinguished when he saw Nicky seated beside Nursoo, the commissioner hovering behind them in the shadows, smoking his pipe. Her exotic features lit by the flames, she timidly petted Jani as Nursoo held the lemur out to her. Holt felt a jolt of longing burn in his stomach along with the arrack. As quickly as he could manage, he grabbed a bowl of curry and turned back to the shed. He just couldn't face her tonight. Not if he wanted to get any sleep before the hunt.

Nicky saw Holt take a plate and leave. The hot peppers in the curry suddenly felt as if they were carving a hole in her stomach. Holt Atley had her tied up in more knots than a sailor could brag of. One minute the man held her tenderly, granting only comfort—forfeiting an opportunity to point out one of her many blunders—the next, he acted as if she was a pariah.

"Do not let Holt sahib upset you, Missy. Though he is stubborn, he will come around soon."

She stiffened, hating her transparency before Nursoo. "I don't know what you mean."

"We have a saying in my country. 'A man doesn't have to watch the water for his heart to thirst for it.' "

Nicky stared into the fire, concentrating on scratching the lemur's soft coat as if the task had taken on monumental importance. Rather than address Nursoo's provocative words, she asked, "Her name is Jani? Did I say that right? Like the little boy's name, Johnny?" At Nursoo's nod, she continued, "It's a pretty name. Does it mean anything?"

Nursoo gave the lemur an affectionate pat. "It is short for *Khajana,* which means treasure."

Nicole smiled at the whimsical name. "Does Mr. Atley call her that because she is so precious to him?"

Nursoo shook his head, a devilish grin appearing beneath his mustache. "Holt sahib said he named her so because, 'She cost me a bloody fortune.' "

Nursoo said the latter half in a perfect imitation of Holt at his most caustic, making Nicole smile. "You two must be very close."

Nursoo's expression sobered. "I have known Holt sahib for ten years. We were great friends once, like brothers."

The curiously hurt look on Nursoo's face touched Nicole deeply. "And now?" she asked softly.

"We had a disagreement." Nursoo seemed to think a moment, then toss away his pensive mood. He smiled back at Nicole. "But I hope it will not last. For many years, we hired out as *shikarees* together. Holt sahib was known for his ability to deliver some of the most exciting hunts in our province, just as his father had before him."

Nicole's hand stilled over the lemur until Jani leaned up into her fingers, apparently not ready to forgo the pleasant petting. She continued her soft, rhythmic strokes. "But I thought . . . ?"

"Ah, *now* he considers himself a great protector. Particularly of the white tigress."

She looked up at the Indian guide whom she had learned to respect a great deal since her arrival in Almora. Perhaps Nursoo could help her decide who was right about the tigress, her uncle or Holt. Suddenly anxious to know his opinion, she asked, "What about you? You don't seem concerned about the tigress. If what Holt says is true, if she's so special, why would you agree to kill her?"

"Oh, she is indeed an extraordinary animal." He shrugged his shoulders. "But I am a hunter; my livelihood depends on killing one such as she. While more beautiful than most, she is a tigress, a deadly creature."

"Holt doesn't agree."

Nursoo broke a twig between his fingers and searched the area in front of him for another. "Holt sahib studies these animals for, I believe you call it, the London Zoological Society. He sees them differently than I. I respect his choice, if he would but respect mine."

Nicky remained silent for a moment. Holt *studied* animals? A naturalist with formal education? That surprised her. Vaguely, she recalled a faint memory of his bungalow, a table covered with sketchings of animals. He seemed to care for the lemur a great deal, and the animal was certainly attached to him. She knew he could be kind, despite his gruff exterior, knew from experience the gentleness of his touch.

Nicky shivered, shaking off her sensual thoughts of Holt. "What would make a man go from hunter to naturalist?" she asked softly, not realizing she had spoken aloud.

"In the case of Holt sahib, it was the influence of a London field biologist, a Mr. Dawson, who came from London to observe the beasts in their land. He hired us both. Almost a year, the sahib stayed. During that time, Holt changed. He was fascinated by the things the professor told us. It was like the sahib had opened my friend's eyes to a new world. Holt sahib asked so many questions that, truly I believe in self-defense, the good professor began giving him his books to read." Nursoo shook his head, as if still disbelieving of his friend's turnaround. "He learned everything he could. After the doctor left, Holt sahib sent away for more books and continued his studies of the animals with help from Mr. Dawson in London. He never again hunted for profit. He works for the government now. Charting new territories, working with the villagers, and observing animals. A forest officer." Nursoo smiled, a sly look coming to his dark eyes in the firelight. "You see, Missy. I know Holt sahib. I know him well." He pointed a finger to his eyes. "And I can see that which you cannot. He holds you in great esteem."

Nicky turned to Nursoo. "You are mistaken."

Nursoo chuckled. "Oh, I hear his words. But I, unlike you, know what is truly behind them." Nursoo leaned forward, toward Nicole. "He watches you as he does his animals." His voice lowered. "With a hunger to know more."

Nicole stared at Nursoo's fire-lit features, haunted by his words. Shaking her head, she grabbed the lemur off her lap and dropped it into Nursoo's hands as she jumped to her feet. "I have eyes too. Holt may study my actions, but not with admiration."

Intending to go back to the stone hut for the night, she turned—walking straight into the commissioner's arms, almost knocking his pipe to the ground. "Excuse me." Nicky stepped back, surprised she had not seen the commissioner standing behind her and Nursoo.

Commissioner Ratcliffe stepped aside, gesturing her by. "My fault entirely, young lady."

Nicole smiled her thanks and continued past, once again thinking about Nursoo's words: "a hunger to know more." She wanted to forget those words. They reflected too well her own feelings for Holt.

As Jeffrey watched the Marshall girl wend her way around the cooking fires, he once more congratulated himself for insisting that she come on the hunt. Yes indeed, the girl was proving the perfect distraction.

He'd chosen his spot well, just beyond the light of the campfire, but still within hearing distance. He'd caught bits and pieces of the conversation, enough to know the girl was taken with Holt, despite the presence of her betrothed. Perhaps Holt shared her feelings? She was certainly a beauty, despite her mannish attire.

Taking another puff from his pipe, Jeffrey watched Nursoo stand to leave, carrying the disgusting rodent Holt had insisted on bringing along with him. Left alone with his musings, he again thought over the discussion he had overheard, a bit surprised to discover that, even though it played nicely into his plans, the Marshall girl's fascination with Atley bothered him. It seemed every blasted female in the district was hot after the forest officer. Why were women such fools? The man really was a menace—one that Jeffrey planned to do something about.

It was still dark, just nearing dawn, when the party left to search for the man-eater. Wandering over the rough terrain, the company of eight included two villagers from Askot. As they neared the site where a goat had been set the day before as bait to lure the tiger, Nicole's fears ignited. She'd been unable to sleep last night. Disturbing images of Holt, snakes, and lunging tigers had haunted her dreams. As she trudged forward, not daring to fall behind, she tried to clear the haze from her head and keep alert. She knew from yesterday's experience that behind any moss-covered tree or bright raspberry bush lurked tragedy.

Nursoo had explained a man-eater would attack any easy prey. This particular tiger, an old male by the deep, squared, and splayed pug marks it left, had been happy to kill the goat they'd tied to a tree. Holt and Nursoo had built the hunting platforms directly above the kill last evening when they had left the goat. But although the party would wait for the tiger high up in the *manchans,* this time there would be no beaters to drive the cat toward them. No one but the hunters and the two natives, who had lost loved ones to the vicious animal, would dare to brave the jungle forest with a man-eater on the loose.

The sun was just bleeding through the mountain ridges on the east, painting the clouds a rich crimson, when they reached the site for the hunt. Nicole cradled her Purdy rifle in her arms as she awaited instructions. She'd chosen the gun instead of her other rifle despite the fact that only one barrel of the Purdy could fire. She felt more secure with the Purdy. Thinking over her past blunders, the leopard, the hunt for the white tigress, the cobra, she needed the added sense of security the weapon gave her. As Nicole waited, the men discussed strategy. When it came time to mount the hunting platforms, she stepped forward, anxious to get started—until she discovered who her shooting partner would be.

Holt cursed himself for insisting that Nicole shoot next to him on the platform. But he hadn't been able to decide what was worse: the two of them, alone, doomed to wait for hours side by side—or worrying about Nicole the entire time. Now, thanks to his own insistence, he was kneeling on a cramped four-foot wide platform with Nicole's thigh almost touching his, desperately trying to keep alert to something other than the way her pants molded the curves of her buttocks, the smell of lilies in her hair, the seductive tilt of her golden eyes.

What did you say to a woman who, a strong conscience not withstanding, you wanted to reach over and take into your arms for a long, slow kiss?

"Shove over," Holt whispered harshly under his breath. "You're in my field of view."

Nicole gave him a most chilling look, then inched over to the edge of the *charpoy* bed until Holt could see her boot almost touched the edge of the bamboo frame. He smiled to himself. *Atta boy, Atley.* Make her hate you. If she hates you enough, maybe you'll squelch the promise you see in those beautiful eyes.

But despite his resolve, Holt continued to watch Nicole from the corner of his eyes. She was staring dead ahead, focused on the small clearing where the dead goat lay. Her small white teeth bit the edge of her full bottom lip in concentration. It did little to reduce her appeal. The perfect fit of her tailored shooting jacket displaying her lovely breasts didn't help much; neither did the sight of her precious behind peeking out from beneath the peplum of the jacket as she leaned back on her knees. He looked away quickly, but her image seemed burned on the back of his eyelids.

Though she normally wore a cap, like the other Brits, she'd spent enough time in the sun without one that her complexion had turned a golden brown. More than ever, she reminded him of Indian royalty. He could almost picture her, a silk veil across her face revealing only a tempting peek of her seductive eyes . . .

Holt shook his head. He was losing his concentration. He didn't expect the cat to show up for a few hours yet, but he'd better keep alert just the same. Focusing on the ground before him, he tried to ignore Nicole pressed to his side on the platform.

Nicky counted to ten in her head, taking a deep breath on each count. She would *not* lose her temper. Not here. Not with her uncle one tree away and a man-eater close by. She forced her attention on the clearing. *Forget Holt.* This tiger hunt was important. She had seen firsthand what the animal could do; the natives of the village lived in terror of another attack. This was her last chance to undo her past mistakes—the leopard, her hesitation with the tigress. This was her opportunity to make good with her uncle. If she shot the man-eater, surely her uncle would be impressed. She might still reach Rajputana if she succeeded today.

The hours passed slowly, first one, then another. Her muscles cramped and tired, she listened to the forest sounds as Nursoo had taught her, but only the parakeets and pigeons crooned against the chanting of the cicadas. Nothing seemed to herald the coming of the man-eater.

Not until the sun almost crested the tops of the trees did the signs begin. This time, the animals' frightened cries of alarm were in no way muted by the din of tomtoms and shouting natives. The loud shrieking calls of the chital deer came clearly and in rapid succession, answered by the coughing barks of the langur. The noise echoed off the mountainside, following the tiger's progress. Holt tensed beside her, and she too raised her gun to the bamboo pole set as a shooting stand, aiming for the clearing.

As the monkey barks came closer, Nicole slowed her breathing, knowing from experience that it would steady her aim. She thought she saw a flash of orange through the bush. Out of the corner of her eye, she watched Holt's rifle slowly move across the clearing, as if he'd sighted and was trailing the tiger. But before the animal showed itself through the brush, giving them a clear shot, a gun fired from the platform beside them.

The cat sprang from the bushes. Its massive size hovered incredibly in the air before landing in the clearing. A volley of fire met the man-eater. It roared, rotating in a midair leap past scrub bamboo and ilex and disappearing into the forest vegetation.

Holt jumped from the tree. Nicole scrambled after him, but he signaled her to stay where she was and forged ahead in the direction the tiger had taken. She wanted to follow but made herself wait with the other hunters who gathered around Nursoo for instructions. The Indian guide at the lead, the company followed Holt's trail into the forest, until they came across the American kneeling above a set of tracks.

"Who the hell fired?" he demanded.

Drew stepped forward. "I thought I had a clear shot."

"Through the trees?"

After giving the British lord a look that conveyed exactly what he thought of the man's judgment, Holt signaled for Nursoo to examine the blood and pug marks. This was one of the reasons he'd wanted to hunt the man-eater without the "helpful" Brits. Amateur mistakes like Herringbone's could sabotage his efforts to destroy this deadly tiger.

Nursoo pointed with his finger to the ground where a distinct sliding appeared on the dirt. "The tiger drags the back paw."

"I knew I'd hit it," Lord Harrington announced triumphantly.

"You fool!" Holt came to his feet. "We have a wounded animal on our hands—twice as dangerous as before." Holt shouldered the strap of the carbine and addressed the group gathered around the pug marks. "We'll have to track it on foot." Turning to face Nicole, he added, "This is the end of the line for you, Miss Marshall. Nursoo will escort you back to the village."

"No!" Nicole cried. She turned to her uncle, seeking his support. "I can't leave now! We just found the tiger."

Marcus Marshall thought a moment, then stepped to her side. "I'll watch after Nicole."

"We're hunting a wounded man-eater. Think man!" Holt shouted. "You're risking her life."

When she saw her uncle hesitate, Nicole panicked. If he sent her back now, she would never prove herself to her uncle. She would go back to England a complete failure.

"I can shoot, Uncle Marc," she told him anxiously. "You know I can!"

Holt stared in disbelief when he saw her uncle soften. "She could be killed, damn it!"

"Don't send me back, Uncle Marc. You taught me how to shoot. You said I was the best!" She geared her words to her uncle, instinctively knowing who held her fate in his hands. Holt stood powerlessly aside as she continued in a voice filled with a yearning he couldn't understand. "Please, give me this chance."

"We're wasting valuable time," said Ratcliffe. "We need every available gun. The girl comes with us. Let's go."

"Right." Marshall gave a short nod. "We need Nick."

Holt felt an icy fear in the pit of his stomach. He couldn't believe it. The man was actually bringing his niece to hunt a man-eating tiger *on foot*. Did he have any conception of what lay ahead? Holt looked to Nursoo for assistance, but the Indian only stared back with a helpless expression on his dark face.

With a grim sense of foreboding, Holt led the group through the jungle brush, following the man-eater's trail. He'd do what he must to mitigate the danger to Nicole, but the task he'd set for himself might be beyond even his powers as a hunter. Silently, he tracked the tiger's prints to a thick area of jungle. Instructing the party to stay put and keep sharp, Holt went ahead to discover the tiger's exact position.

When Holt reappeared, Nicole felt her heart begin to beat again. She admitted that more than the concern over her abilities as a hunter churned her stomach right now. With Holt out of view, she'd experienced an overwhelming sense of fear for him. She'd been afraid something might happen, that he might get hurt and she wouldn't be there to help him.

"He's holed up in some thick raspberry bushes toward the far side of a ravine up ahead," Holt told the group. "I can't get a clear shot. We'll have to bring him out. We'll need to surround the tiger, then Nursoo and the villagers will throw stones." With a sharp look to each, particularly Nicole, he added, "Every one be ready. He could bolt in any direction."

Quietly, Holt and Nursoo guided each of their party to their designated spots, leaving Nicky and her uncle for last. Her heart pounding, she waited with Uncle Marc where Holt had set them, just above a steep lip of the ravine. It was hardly a place where the cat would escape to, and not a very good location to shoot from, but she vowed to do her best to protect Holt. She wasn't the least surprised that he and Nursoo waited at the most likely spot for the tiger's escape, directly opposite her and her uncle at the mouth of the dried up riverbed. He had set the commissioner and Drew to his left, the natives to his right.

When Holt gave the signal, she watched Nursoo beside him start to pelt the cat with stones. At first the animal didn't respond. But then the two natives added their stones and the tiger moved forward. Toward Holt.

Fear nearly choking her, she watched through her rifle sights, waiting for the tiger to clear the brush, her second rifle loaded and ready to fire beside her. As the man-eater neared Holt, its orange glow giving tempting glimpses of its position through the thick brush, her pulse accelerated. The cat kept moving slowly, prodded forward by stones from the natives.

To her right came the jolting sound of a gun firing.

The tiger dashed through the brush, directly at Holt. Just as it reached the point where Nursoo and Holt waited, Nicole fired. The cat veered left as it cleared the bush, dodging her shot. Scrambling up the side of the ravine, the man-eater escaped despite the rapid fire of guns that pursued him.

When the cat was clearly out of shooting range, another gun fired.

Her heart lodged in her throat as Nicole watched Holt fall to the ground.

9

Holt hit the dirt. "Bloody hell."

Someone had shot at him. Not at the tiger. At him!

He stared at the spot where a bullet had clipped off a branch—just about where his head had been seconds before—then turned back to Nursoo stretched out on the ground beside him. The Indian's eyes echoed Holt's suspicions.

"It appears you have made an enemy, sahib."

"Two guesses who. And they're both sitting pretty across the way."

Nursoo edged closer to Holt and peered through the bushes. "The British Lord or the deputy commissioner. Why would they choose to do such a thing?"

Holt could hardly credit the British official with murder out of jealousy, but he'd seen Ratcliffe's expression at the ball when Serena, his wife, had brushed against Holt acting like a lover. The commissioner had certainly looked ready to kill then. And Harrington. Holt knew the man was no friend and capable of double dealing, as he'd done with Morgan.

"It is not good placement for your enemies," Nursoo added as he looked across the scrub at the two Brits on their left.

Holt pressed his lips together in a grim line. "Sure looks that way." By placing the tiger between himself and their guns, he'd given either man the perfect excuse to shoot. Hunting accidents were common enough. But when he'd established their positions, he'd thought only of putting Nicole as far away from danger as possible. He hadn't thought himself a target. Now he knew better. What else could explain Ratcliffe or Harrington shooting at him as the tiger sprinted away in the opposite direction?

Slowly, Holt raised his head above the bushes he'd used as cover. When no gunfire followed, he stood. Nicky and her uncle broke through the brush behind him.

"Are you all right?" Nicole asked.

Her voice had a high-pitched edge he'd not heard before, not even after her narrow escape from the cobra. Dusting off his pants, Holt glanced at her. "You really look worried, kid." *Good. She owes me a couple of scares.*

"I thought you'd been shot, Holt!"

It was the first time she'd used his Christian name. Holt smiled. It sounded nice the way she said it, like she cared a hell of a lot what happened to him. His grin faltered. It sounded *too* good.

As the rest of the party joined them, Holt watched the two British gentlemen warily. Lord Harrington's amused expression disappeared when he caught sight of Nicole inspecting Holt for damage. But when Holt saw Ratcliffe, the satisfied grin on the commissioner's thin face told the tale. It was the same ruthless smile Holt had seen when Serena Ratcliffe had asked him to dance.

"Sorry about that, old man," Ratcliffe said. "I seem to have mistaken you for the tiger."

Holt nudged Nicole aside and stepped directly in front of the commissioner. Before anyone could stop him, he grabbed the lapels of Ratcliffe's shooting jacket and shook him. "What the hell were you trying to do, mister?"

Immediately Harrington locked his fingers around Holt's forearms, trying to pull him off the commissioner. Marshall sputtered around the two, attempting to help.

"That tiger was nowhere near me when you shot!"

"Now see here, Atley," Marshall said as they separated the two. Both he and Harrington held Holt. "The chap's explained it was an accident."

"As you say, Mr. Marshall." Ratcliffe straightened his jacket, a slight smile still on his face. "A most unfortunate . . . accident."

"You have to be ass-brained if you think I'm swallowing that—"

"Sahib."

The urgency in Nursoo's voice as he emerged from behind the raspberry cane stemmed Holt's attack. "Did you find the tiger?" Holt asked, anxious to finish the job they'd started.

Nursoo nodded. "The leg drags even more. It would be wise to follow now and attempt the kill, before the tiger recovers."

Shaking off Harrington's and Marshall's restraint, Holt narrowed his eyes on Ratcliffe. Now wasn't the time to confront the commissioner and the man's jealous delusions. The man-eater would certainly kill again if they didn't destroy the tiger today. He'd just have to watch his back.

Holt turned to the others. "We'll need to move fast. I'll lead. Nursoo, you make sure no one falls behind."

The party plunged into the forest, their pace fast. They followed the tiger tracks for miles. It seemed that, despite its wounds, the cat's energy was endless. Even after the sun had crested its zenith, the group of hunters pursued the man-eater.

Throughout the chase, Nicole relived the agony that had seared through her when she'd seen Holt hit the ground. Fear. Undiluted, heart-stopping fear. Nothing like the pity she'd had for the poor Indian gashed by the white tigress. When Holt went down, it was as if *she* had been hit, a piece of *her* torn apart. Whether it was through his soft yet fierce kisses or the tender smile he'd shared so rarely, Holt had made her care for him in a way she had for no other man, including her betrothed. She couldn't limit or define the emotions she had for Holt, but she knew they were frighteningly deeper than the physical passion she'd hoped to mimic in her marriage to Drew.

Dear Lord, what if something happened to him as she

watched, helpless to save him? She couldn't believe the commissioner had purposely shot at Holt. Yet, through a moment's bad judgment, the commissioner *had* almost killed him. The man who was made of muscle and bone, whose hard contours she'd felt pressed against her, suddenly seemed as fragile to Nicole as fine glass. She picked up her pace, determined to protect him.

Near dusk, the pug marks ended at a stand of evergreen *sal* trees with a thick cover of raspberry canes and thorny scrub grouse. Suspecting that the injured cat had taken refuge in the dense foliage, Holt and Nursoo circled around. No tracks led out of the heavily wooded copse. Following Holt's instructions, the group of hunters formed a chain surrounding the area, ready to flush the man-eater out of the grove together.

When Holt gave the signal, Nicole and the others stepped cautiously forward. Her uncle on her left, Nursoo on her right, Nicky scanned the tall grass and bushes, searching for a flash of orange. She listened carefully for any clues of the tiger's position. With each step, her fear of the tiger receded and a hunter's energy pumped through her veins.

Twenty paces into the grove, the commissioner bolted to the right. Drew dashed off behind him. Holt glanced at Nicole then back in the direction the commissioner had taken, as if trying to decide whether to go or stand guard over her. Nicole turned to follow but Holt stopped her. A shot blazed through the shrubbery. A great roar followed, then another shot.

"I got the brute," the commissioner shouted. Nicole could see Drew right behind Jeffrey Ratcliffe as he burst through the shrubs and rejoined the group. "Back there." The commissioner nodded his head over his shoulder. "Behind the bamboo. Shot him clean dead."

"You're sure he's dead?" Holt asked.

"Of course. Go get our tiger, Mr. Atley. The district is free of the man-eater."

Holt hesitated, examining the commissioner closely. In

that moment, anyone could see he didn't trust Jeffrey Ratcliffe. Holt turned back to the group.

"Everyone stay put. Except you, Nursoo. You come with me."

The two hunters left, following the commissioner's directions to the tiger's location. When Nicky's uncle started after them, the commissioner held him back with a hand.

"I advise you to stay here."

Uncle Marc didn't even break stride. "I'd like a look at the beast myself," he called over his shoulder, ignoring the warning.

"I'm going with you," said Nicole.

Drew grabbed her arm and swung her around to face him. "You stay here, Nicole. It could be dangerous."

Nicky twisted her arm free and ran after her uncle. She ignored Drew's calls to come back. She would not let Holt out of her sight. Not again.

When her uncle and Nicole reached the two *shikarees,* a reluctant Drew following close behind, Nicole saw the tiger's enormous length stretched out behind a clump of scrub bamboo beneath a *sal.* Though partially obscured from view, he appeared to be dead, certainly unmoving. Several yards away, Holt pelted the animal with pebbles. Nursoo stood on the side opposite, ready to shoot if necessary.

On the third stone, the tiger lunged out from the bamboo with a roar. Both Nursoo and Holt fired. Incredibly, neither shot stopped the beast. The Purdy already at her shoulder, Nicole watched the tiger leap again, high into the air, directly at Holt. She followed the tiger's arc with her sights. Holt dropped to one knee. She fired.

The tiger fell in a lifeless heap two feet from Holt. He lowered his head to his knee and released the knife he'd pulled from a sheath strapped to his boot. Nicky stared down at the tiger in front of him. The top of its head had been blown wide open.

"Good shot, Nick!" Her uncle raced to the kill. With a

begrudging nod of admiration, Drew went to investigate the tiger as well.

Nicky's chin fell to her chest. She took a deep breath and sent a silent prayer of thanks to heaven. When she thought she could move again, she hefted her rifle to her side and walked to where Holt still knelt, sheathing his knife while staring at the carcass. She held out her hand to him.

"You've saved my life more than once," she whispered, her voice shaking. "That's one I owed you."

With a wry smile, Holt pressed his hand in hers and came to his feet. "Miss Marshall, I think you just cleaned the slate."

By the time the natives had hoisted the four-hundred-pound tiger between poles and taken him to the village, word of the triumphant hunt had already reached Askot. When Holt and the others arrived, natives milled about the streets, chanting and dancing. A huge bonfire blazed in the public square. The relatives of the tiger's past victims gifted the victorious hunters with rice and wheat. The Rajbar of Askot presented each of the party with a Gurkha jungle knife. Dancing natives circled the square to the beat of the drums, while others passed around clay and wooden vessels filled with rice beer.

Holt accepted a drink, watching the dancers with a smile on his face, but his thoughts were on Nicole. She'd saved his life. Her skill, her reflexes, better than any he'd ever witnessed—perhaps even equal to his own—were responsible for stopping the man-eater that Ratcliffe had left wounded as a deadly trap. The commissioner he'd dealt with. During a private conversation after the hunt, Holt had let Ratcliffe know that he would be on guard against him. But he hadn't spoken to Nicole since they'd returned to Askot. Despite his desire to keep away from the temptation of her, he owed the girl an apology. The things he'd said, the insinuations he'd made about her during their trip here. God, if he could take back the words. Yes, at the very least, he should apologize.

Taking a last drink of the rice beer, he set the cup aside and went in search of Nicole. He'd seen neither her nor her uncle since they'd returned to the village just after dusk. He assumed she would be at her hut, getting ready to join in the night's celebration, and headed in that direction.

When he turned the corner at the edge of town, Holt found her face to face with her uncle. They stood on the flagstones before the stone house where she was staying. He stepped out to greet them, but stopped when he heard the two arguing. Still in the shadows, Holt leaned against the whitewashed wall of the hut neighboring Nicole's, not attempting to hide, but not making his presence known.

"You're daft if you think I'd ever take you to Rajputana!" Marcus Marshall shouted. From where he stood, Holt could not make out the older man's expression. Although the moonlight hit Nicole square on the face, Marshall's features were hidden by darkness. Yet, while Holt had to strain to hear his words above the music and revelry of the natives, the anger in Marshall's voice rang true and clear.

"How many times," he continued, his voice lowered so that Holt barely made out his words, "have your mother and I told you to forget about the past? Why would you want to go and seek out problems, Nicole? I simply don't understand."

"But it should be *my* decision. It doesn't affect you at all!" she shouted back.

"That's blasted ignorant, Nicole. Of course it affects me. Do you think for one instant my family was not *affected* by my brother's marriage? Jumping Jupiter, my father nearly died of apoplexy. But my all-knowing brother would hear none of it. Your father never would listen to reason—that's what killed him in the end."

"But—"

"He had responsibilities! *He* was the viscount! I *was* affected, my girl, more than you know! Your father got himself killed and then left me to fix his messes. And that's what

I've done, by thunder. After the Sepoy Mutiny, I had to work damn hard to stop wagging tongues."

Nicole remained quiet, as if she'd lost her taste for the fight. Though Holt could see her struggle to hide her pain, it was there in the lines bracketing her mouth and marring her lovely gold eyes.

"Well, you didn't do a good enough job, Uncle Marc," she whispered. "Not near good enough. I still heard the gossip, the vicious remarks—"

"Nicole—"

"Do you honestly think I was unaware of their prejudices?"

"Then why would you want to go to Rajputana?" her uncle pleaded. "You must see the thing is best forgotten."

"No. No, I do not see that at all."

Holt smiled, hearing the fight back in her voice.

Marshall threw his hands in the air. "What do you think Harrington will say about your wishes?"

"Drew knows how I feel. He has from the first. Unlike you, he's very understanding. And even if he weren't, frankly I'm not sure I care. I've been meaning to speak to you about Drew—"

"Understanding is he? You're so blasted stupid sometimes, Nicole. Too stupid to even be afraid. Think, girl. How do you see your fiancé treating these Indians? Hmm? With respect? Camaraderie perhaps? Asking them to join him for tea? Of course not you little fool! He treats them with utter *disdain.* A lower class—some no more than barbarians. They live like animals. He treats them as such. A backward people."

"You hate them as well," she said in a voice so soft, Holt barely heard her. "It is you who fear and hate them." She shook her head. "I've been so blind. I thought with the tiger kill, you would grant me anything . . ."

"Oh *please,* what have you really done, Nicole?" Her uncle spoke with such venom that Holt took a step forward, tempted to intervene. "You shot one tiger ten paces away—

any dunderhead with a finger to pull a trigger could have accomplished it. What about the white tigress? *She* was the greater prize! You think one lucky shot could make up for that blunder?"

Nicole looked about to respond. Her mouth opened to speak, but she said nothing. She simply stared at her uncle with a look of intense pain. Holt swallowed back the knot that formed in his throat just watching her. She pressed her lips together, as if fighting back a desire to cry. The lines of her face showed eloquently the kind of hurt that only someone you love dearly can deliver. In the moonlight, tears sparkled in her eyes as she turned and ran inside the stone hut.

Tears. Her uncle had made her cry.

Holt had never seen her cry. Not when she'd almost been killed by the leopard. Not with the cobra . . . never.

As Holt watched, the old man stripped off his hat and threw it to the ground. "By the ever-living jumping Moses! Damn all!" He gave the hat a kick.

Before he could think better of what he was doing, Holt stepped out of the shadows toward Marcus Marshall.

Nicole flung herself on the canvas and bamboo cot. She swiped back the tears from her eyes. She'd been a fool to think her uncle would understand her need to go to Rajputana. But what she had not anticipated, could never have foreseen, was his hate. He despised the natives here—he even sounded as if he hated her father, his own brother, for marrying Nicole's mother, a woman with Indian blood. On some level, did he hate Nicole as well?

She had lost a father before she was born. Her brother's attentions had dissipated with the birth of his own children. Had she lost her uncle's love as well?

There had been so much hate in her life, so many prejudices. Her uncle had mentioned the Sepoy Mutiny, the unsuccessful rebellion by the Indian troops resulting in the Government of India Act. But the legislation bringing India under the rule of the Crown almost two years ago was not the only result of the mutiny. Cries for revenge had been loud and frequent. Did her uncle actually believe he'd sheltered Nicole from the ugliness directed at anyone of Indian descent?

Sitting on her cot, surrounded by the smell of grass and wood fires, Nicole remembered her coming-out—postponed by a year after the mutiny's inception in 1857. When Nicole was eventually introduced into society the following year, Katherine Marshall decided against an elaborate debut for her dark-haired child and held a discreet fête at Eldridge Manor instead.

Nicole remembered well that party, the curious stares, the frilly pink gown her mother had chosen for her. The dress had made Nicky's complexion look dark, even more foreign. Lying back against her hard cot, Nicole gave a shallow laugh as she recalled how she'd stared back at her gawking guests until they'd turned away, embarrassed. The night had promised to be a total disaster until George MacCaffrey had asked her to dance.

He'd been blond and handsome with the kind of good looks that anyone would find appealing. He'd danced with her twice that evening, and Nicole began to see the whole affair as a success under the influence of his admiring gaze. When he asked her for a stroll through the gardens, she'd gone without hesitation.

He'd wanted a kiss. She remembered how eager she'd been to please him. She'd felt clumsy, of course, and a little foolish. But when he'd tried to touch her breasts, she'd pushed him away, shocked. At first he'd tried to coax her with his lovely smile, but she'd remained adamant that they return to the hall. Then the hateful comments had begun.

What they say is true, you really do think you're a man. And the airs you put on, pretending to be an Indian princess. You and your kind should all be put away somewhere.

Nicole shut her eyes against the painful memories. She wiped at her tears impatiently. Is that how her uncle thought about her? Inferior? Pretentious? She'd thought to prove herself with the tiger kill, but according to Uncle Marc, anyone could have killed that man-eater; it was no accomplishment at all.

Nicole flipped onto her stomach and dug her fist into the canvas. Would anything ever be enough for him? No matter what she did, it was never enough!

Someone knocked at the door, but Nicole ignored it, not wanting a witness to her pain. She would never see Rajputana now. Her dreams, everything she'd worked for, gone. Even her love for Drew was a fairy tale exposed as a myth by the feelings Holt ignited in her.

The knocking grew louder.

"I know you're in there, Nicole," Holt's voice called out.

Nicole caught her breath. She tried to quiet her crying. *Oh please, Lord, not Holt. Not now.* "Go away," she answered.

"Look, you don't need to open the door. I just want you to know we're heading out in the morning for a special trip. So be ready. We leave at sunrise."

Nicole peered at the door, rubbing the tears from her eyes. "Why?"

Silence, and then, "A surprise."

Padmini huddled on the floor on her reed mat as her body heaved with another sob. She took a shuddering breath and marveled that she still had tears inside her to shed. She had barely been able to climb the steps to the bedroom after the exorcism and had required the help of her two sisters-in-law.

The house still smelled of the black chilies the Dholi had burned like incense in the front room to ward off the evil spirits. Her cheeks burned where the Dholi had slapped her. Her head ached where he had pulled her hair, demanding that the spirit that possessed her identify itself. But the thing that pained her most was her finger where her father had squeezed it with iron pincers. She didn't think she could move her hand, it hurt so terribly, and she wondered if her finger was broken.

How she'd screamed for the Dholi to cease. She'd pleaded with her father to stop torturing her as well. That's when the Dholi determined the spirit was speaking, for surely an obedient daughter would not carry on so. Padmini had finally made up a story, telling all in the room that she was the spirit of a young girl who had died at the river earlier that spring—that she would leave Padmini alone if the Dholi would but stop the beating. The Dholi had then clapped his hands loudly to scare the spirit from her. He'd turned to her parents and announced the deed done, demanding his payment.

Now, as the others gathered downstairs in the kitchen for dinner, Padmini tried to rest. She would need her strength. She sensed that her mother was not finished with her yet.

A scuffling sound at the door drew her attention and Padmini looked up to see her sister-in-law, Rumbha, approach. She did so hesitantly, as if she truly believed Padmini might be possessed. Padmini smiled. Never had she thought to frighten the hardened Rumbha.

"You need not worry, *Bhabhi.* I made up the tale of the girl. I was never possessed."

As Padmini watched, Rumbha's expression changed from one of trepidation to one of knowing. "I am not a silly woman to believe in spirits."

Padmini's smile widened for she knew Rumbha was indeed superstitious. "Come closer, *Bhabhi.*"

"I cannot stay. Here." Rumbha stretched out her hand. In it, she held an orange.

Padmini looked at the precious fruit longingly, knowing she could never peel it. She looked down at her aching hand in despair.

With an impatient sniff, Rumbha knelt down beside her and began peeling the orange. "If you are smart, Mini, you will do as you are told." She broke off a section and pushed it into Padmini's good hand. "If you are wise, you will make no more trouble until the Khasiya returns for you, if he ever does. There." She dropped the peeled orange on the mat beside Padmini and stood to leave. "I know that in the past, I have been unkind, but I never . . ." Rumbha straightened, as if thinking better of her apology. "Deepali and I are deeply disturbed by what is happening in this family. We will try to help you when we can, but do not expect much. *Maji* watches all very carefully."

Padmini felt her throat tighten with thanks to this sister-in-law whom she had never truly known before now. "I thank you, *Bhabhi*."

"Do not thank me. Just make certain *Maji* never knows about the orange." Rumbha gave her a thoughtful look. "I can do little to help you, Mini. But I will pray for the Khasiya's quick return."

After Rumbha left Padmini ate the sweet fruit, finishing it quickly then hiding the peels. She stared up at the rafters of the room and thought of Rumbha's kindness. Despite the agonies of the day, something good had come of it: Rumbha's friendship. It gave her strength to remember happier times, the fort and Nursoo's loving touch. Thinking of Nursoo and his words of love, she drifted into a deep sleep, her only place of safety.

Holt avoided the town square, expecting it would still be crowded with celebrating natives, as he made his way through the streets toward his hut. There was a lot he hadn't understood about Nicole's conversation with her uncle. Why was Marshall so adamant that she not visit Rajputana? Was he suggesting Nicole had Indian blood? It didn't make sense. She was an English heiress, betrothed to a lord. In the short time he'd gotten to know the prig Harrington, Holt knew the nobleman would never marry a woman with "tarnished" bloodlines. He'd stake his life on it. No, more likely there was some family scandal involving an Indian, evidently a Rajput. A mistress, perhaps? He couldn't even be sure he'd heard Marshall correctly. Holt had been a good

distance away. But her uncle's criticisms of her hunting had
been plain as a pikestaff. It seemed the old Brit had a particular talent for tormenting Nicky. Marshall had totally de-
based her quick shooting. He'd made it seem as if anyone
could have killed the man-eater, when it was Nicole's damn
fine talent that had saved Holt's life.

With a stab of regret, Holt recalled all the arguments he'd
made against her coming on the hunt. Though in truth he'd
just wanted to keep her safe, in many instances his words
had been as cruel as her uncle's. Well, now that he had
Marshall's permission for tomorrow's excursion, he'd make
it up to her.

Turning up the flagstone street, Holt caught sight of Nursoo on the veranda of a stone hut, sitting half in the moonlight, half in the shadows. Balanced in his palm, a strand of
silver sparkled with the soft light. Holt heard the quiet tin-
kling of bells like those worn by Indian women around their
ankles as Nursoo turned the silvered object, examining it.

Holt's exuberant mood for the morning's trip faded. It
had been like old times with Nursoo at his side during the
hunt for the man-eater. Yet the barrier of Enchantress still
stood between them. Though he'd steered the party clear of
Enchantress's trail on the trip to Askot, Holt suspected
they'd not forgotten the white tigress. He knew for certain
Nursoo would again attempt a *hankwa* to bag her once the
party returned to Almora if the Brits were willing to pay.
How could the one lasting friend he'd made during his ten
years in India turn on him for money?

At that moment, Nursoo looked up and the shadows fell
from his face. He didn't seem to see Holt. His expression
looked sad, almost despondent, as if the worries that held
his attention were too great to bear. Glancing down at the
silver jewelry in his hands, he said, "Padmini."

Holt tried to harden his resolve against Nursoo, concen-
trating on his friend's disloyalty. But the sight of the
Hindu's pain was too great a stumbling block for his anger.
Something had deeply disturbed Nursoo. Holt walked to-

ward the veranda. No matter how much he willed himself to do so, Holt couldn't forget ten years of friendship.

Nursoo looked startled when Holt crouched down beside him, as if he'd not heard Holt's approach. Holt frowned. He thought never to see the day he could successfully sneak up on the *shikaree.*

"Sahib." Nursoo began to stand, but Holt gestured him to stay seated. "Is everything all right? Do you have need of something?"

"Funny. I was just about to ask you the same thing."

Nursoo said nothing, but Holt thought the sadness in his dark eyes and the lines around his mouth deepened as the Hindu watched him. Holt copied his friend and sat back against his heels, Indian style. He turned the Khasiya's hand over. The soft chimes of the bells echoed in the night.

"Padmini's?" Holt asked, looking down at the anklet nestled in the Hindu's palm. Nursoo nodded. "You look worried. Is something wrong with her?"

Nursoo peered past Holt at the moonlit night. He seemed to think as he narrowed his dark eyes. "Since we left Baijnarn, I have had these . . . dreams. They haunt me like visions." His troubled gaze met Holt's. "I think she is in trouble. I feel . . . pain." He closed his fist over the anklet. "Padmini's pain." Nursoo shook his head. "Holt, my friend. I must confess to you. If the British sahibs wish to continue their hunt for Enchantress, I will seek her out. Though after today's work, it is not in my heart to do so." He gave Holt a grin. "It was like old times, no? You and I, hunting side by side . . ."

"Yeah, like old times."

"I would truly wish to stop my part in hunting the tigress, but I cannot. I must have the money to free Padmini."

"Free her?"

"I cannot explain, sahib. It is something I do not truly understand, these dreams, but I fear for her safety."

Holt examined Nursoo. Was he suggesting something supernatural? Though many Indians believed in black magic and spirits, especially in these secluded foothills, Holt had always found Nursoo to be a man of logic, not prone to superstition. Yet, looking at him now, he certainly seemed disturbed by his nightmares. Then again, hadn't his own instincts warned Holt numerous times of trouble?

Holt sighed. It was time he stop chastising Nursoo for his choices and help his friend. For the first time, he was able to see Nursoo's side of their disagreement. Nursoo could never think of Enchantress as a precious animal, as Holt did. Nor was he betraying Holt for money. Somehow Nursoo had linked the hunt for Enchantress with rescuing his bride from some evil. It was up to Holt to change that.

Standing, Holt dusted his hands off on his trousers. "If Padmini's in trouble, we'll just have to help her."

Nursoo looked up, rising as well. "We?"

Holt nodded. "Why can't we work together on this? Like old times."

"You would help me find the white tigress?"

"No. But I know how you can earn the two hundred rupees you'll need."

"Another man-eater?" Nursoo asked. "I did not even kill today's. There will be no reward fattening my purse."

Holt shook his head. "No, not as a hunter. The two villages I own, your family's village and Baijnarn, when my father was alive we could manage things between the two of us. But now, I'm gone so much of the time, I've had to put off many of the improvements I've planned. I would like to hire someone to manage things. Why not you? In fact," he said as the idea gained appeal, "I would rather hire you, who have a vested interest in the welfare of both villages, than some Banya who cares only about revenues. You could start right away. I've wanted to build a well at your family's village for a long time now, so the women don't have to travel to the river to gather water. You could manage that."

Nursoo shook his head. "I don't know anything about building wells or managing villages. I know how to hunt."

"Hire someone who does. You just make sure it gets done

and they don't steal me blind." When he saw Nursoo's look of doubt, he challenged, "You don't think you can do it? I'm willing to bet the money you need for your bride that you can."

Nursoo looked at Holt stunned. "For this you would pay me two hundred rupees?"

Holt clapped his hand on Nursoo's shoulder. "When I found out you were hunting Enchantress, I was so angry, I couldn't even think straight. I wanted nothing to do with you. But the last week, tracking side by side, covering each other, talking strategy—I realized that's the way I want things to stay between us. I'd give you the money because I'm your friend, but if you won't accept such an offer of help, you'd certainly earn it working for me."

A full smile flared beneath the Hindu's mustache. "Holt sahib, my friend, I too desire that we never be opponents." Nursoo pocketed the anklet and took Holt's hands in his in a warm handshake. "You need my help. I would not trust a Banya to look out for your interests. We say in my village that when two Banyas come together, they rob the world. You can trust a snake before you should trust a Banya. For you, Holt sahib, I will do my best at this . . . managing."

Nicole waited for him outside her hut just before dawn, her gear piled next to her. She caught sight of Holt making his way toward her with two mountain ponies trailing by their tethers. Nicole looked down at the dirt, trying to hide her eyes, knowing they were red and swollen from crying.

When Holt reached her, he asked, "I assume you can ride?"

"Of course."

He looked down at her trousers. "Astride?"

"Any objections?"

Expecting a caustic remark on her mannish ways, she was surprised by Holt's pleasant smile. "Not a one." Poking her bags with the toe of his boot, he said, "You won't need any of this. Just some water and your gun." He patted the sack strapped to one of the ponies. "I brought all the provisions we'll need."

"Where are the others?" Nicole looked past him, expecting to see the rest of their party joining them. No one but a few natives appeared to be up as yet. She looked back to Holt for an explanation. He smiled that wicked, lovely smile that had made her toes curl as they'd danced at the Ratcliffe's ball.

"It's just you and me, kid."

"My uncle knows about this?"

Holt nodded.

"I cannot believe he'd agree to this."

Holt's smile turned enigmatic. "Oh, I found him in a very agreeable mood last night."

Nicky raised her eyebrows in surprise. Before she could challenge his statement, Holt stepped closer, making her look up at him guardedly. "I told him I had something special to show you." He placed a hand on her shoulder. It felt surprisingly comforting. "Something I thought would please you, very much. But I told him I'd show it to no one but you." There was a soft, tender look in his green-gold eyes that gave a special quality of warmth to his words. "Your uncle wanted *very much* to make you happy, Nicole. I told him this might do it."

She couldn't help the choking feeling deep in her throat even as she held back the flood of emotion she felt at Holt's words. "My uncle wanted to please me?"

He smiled. "Oh, yes."

"Last night? You asked him last night?"

Holt nodded. "After the festivities."

Nicole was astounded. He'd spoken to her uncle after their fight. And Uncle Marc had wanted to *please* her. Nicky felt her heart lighten just a bit; the heavy feelings of rejection she'd toted since last night's argument lifted. Perhaps he was sorry for what they'd said to each other. Maybe he'd spoken out of anger and shock over her request to visit Rajputana rather than out of actual hate for her heritage.

Nicole smiled for the first time since last night's horrid meeting. With her uncle's approval, Holt was going to show her something special, something to please her. Nicole scooted her gear back inside the hut, then walked to her pony. She climbed onto her horse with a step up from Holt. "Lead the way, Mr. Atley," she said.

"That I'll do, kid." Holt answered her smile with a warm grin as he mounted his pony. "You just make sure you can keep up."

Nicole rode beside Holt, enjoying the sight of the hills, green with the budding crops of grain and fruit trees. The cart road's accessibility to the sturdy mountain ponies made the going faster and more comfortable. As Holt led her down the open ridge on which Askot was built, into the tropical vegetation where the Gori poured into the Kali River, he described the changing landscape. Acacia and *sissoo* bloomed dramatically like spots of flame on the hillside. Iris and wood anemone added their reddish purple hue to the valley's palette. Holt knew each plant, each jungle sound, and unlike the trip from Almora, this time he shared his knowledge freely. He pointed out the temple to Vyaghreswar, the tiger-lord, where natives worshipped in hopes that the deity would rid their village of the man-eater. Too often, they came across piled stones surrounded by offering jars and flowers that marked the site of the tiger's attack. At each whitewashed temple they would dismount and Holt would give Nicole petals to toss into the small niche, then ring the bells hanging from the arched opening. She reveled in the mystery and mysticism of the small ritual.

When the sun was almost straight overhead, they reached the river valley. Holt dismounted at the base of a steep incline. He unloaded his gear and took out of pair of field glasses. After searching the overhang, Holt stopped, focusing the glasses on something. He smiled, then handed the field glasses to Nicole and pointed up the ridge.

"There, on your right."

Nicole focused the glasses on the spot. At first, she only

saw a bit of greenery, but then she caught sight of something white, and a bit of orange. She focused again, following the movement.

Her breath caught in her throat.

There, up on the ridge, was the white tigress. Before her, frolicking like kittens, were two yellow tiger cubs.

"Her name is Enchantress," she heard Holt say as she watched one cub playfully track and pounce on the other. "Well, that's what I call her anyway. I've been studying her, sending reports about her to a friend in London."

Nicole kept staring through the glasses. The tigress and her cubs looked close enough to touch. "She's beautiful," she whispered, as if the animals might hear her and be frightened away by her words.

She could feel Holt lean closer to her, saw him out of the corner of her eye staring up the ridge. "Look at her eyes, Nicky. A clear crystal blue. I've never seen anything like it in the wild."

While Nicole watched, he continued to describe the tigress and her cubs. How the female of the species would let her young feed first from a kill, before she would eat. "They're the only ones of the big cats who do that in the wild. Real motherly love." He described how the cubs used their play as a precursor to hunting. That they would stay with their mother for two years while she taught them how to survive in the wild. He explained how he'd trailed the tigress here, to the Gori valley beyond Askot, after the hunting party had driven her out of the foothills. Nicole regretted her part in running the tigress and her family from their home.

"When I found out you'd hired Nursoo to hunt her," he said, "I telegraphed the London Zoological Society. If I couldn't stop the *hankwa,* I was going to capture the tigress for their zoological gardens. I thought she'd be better off. I didn't want to see her killed." Nicole felt a sharp pain pierce through her at his damning words. "But I couldn't do it," he continued. "I know it would be bad for mankind to lose her. But to Enchantress—a cage or dead, what's really the difference to her?"

"I wouldn't want to be locked away," Nicole whispered.

She felt Holt lean closer, until his mouth was almost against her ear. "You see, Nicole, when you didn't shoot Enchantress, when you let her escape"—the words were soft flutters against her skin—"your instincts were right. The tigress deserves to live. It was your uncle who was wrong."

She lowered the glasses then turned to stare up at Holt, awed by his words.

"You did the right thing," he repeated.

She pressed her lips together, putting down the glasses. The emotions she felt were almost overpowering, threatening tears. Her throat was thick with gratitude for Holt's gift. *You did the right thing.* She looked back up to the niche where she'd watched the tigress clean her cubs with long strokes of her tongue. *Yes. I did the right thing.* Turning to Holt, she whispered, "Thank you."

Holt looked into those hungry eyes. They needed so much reassurance. After witnessing her uncle's bombastic harangue the night before, he could understand why. But at this moment, it wasn't her gratitude that touched him. In her eyes, he saw something that answered the need he'd been denying for days—a hunger over which he no longer had control.

"Nicole." He lowered his mouth to hers.

Nicky pressed herself to him, feeling a freedom she'd never experienced. She opened her mouth under his and in the same moment opened herself. All her secret fears he'd seen, witnessed, and soothed. She had nothing to fear from Holt.

When he lowered her to the bed of fragrant pink thyme, it seemed natural to wrap her arms around him. She barely realized what they were doing. She was conscious only of his tender kiss, his lips molding her. How gently those lips touched and caressed the corner of her mouth then slipped seductively to the curve of her neck. She inhaled sharply as a liquid warmth radiated up through her stomach, infusing her with a glow that made her feel lighter than the hot moist air of the valley. His hands searched and found every inch of exposed skin—her wrists, her neck, the lobe of her ear. But when those persuasive fingers began to unbutton her jacket, Nicole felt herself fall harshly back to earth.

Holt stopped, as if sensing her hesitation. He propped himself on his elbows and looked down at her, stroking the short curls that had escaped her braid. There was a thoughtful smile on his lips and his eyes had turned a deep green, darker than the *sal* trees around them.

"I've shown you what I brought you here to see," he said. "Shall we go back?" He followed the line of her lower lip with his finger. "Before I show you too much?"

Nicole studied his handsome face. The chiseled planes reminded her of the beautiful alabaster Greek statues in the gardens of her brother's estate. She watched his eyes. Even as his expression remained calm, waiting for her answer, his eyes seemed to hold a fire deep inside them, a promise of a passion that made their past kisses tame. Though she feared allowing Holt to finish what they'd started, she feared stopping him even more. Rajputana, she may never see—but what Holt offered now was hers for the taking.

She took up the hand he'd used to unbutton her jacket. It looked strong, tanned, with long blunt-tipped fingers and calloused palm. As she held it, she recalled that this was the same hand that had comforted her after he'd killed the leopard. The same hand that had helped her up after he'd shot the cobra. The hand that had expertly led her as they'd danced, twirling about the Ratcliffe's ballroom, laughing as she'd never laughed in a man's arms. Slowly, she brought Holt's fingers to her mouth and kissed each one, then placed his palm on her breast as she reached for the buttons of her jacket.

Holt watched her, excited by the decision she'd just made. He felt the breast beneath his hand, warm, soft, and he stroked the tip covered by the linen jacket with his thumb.

He heard as well as saw her sharp intake of breath caused by his touch. Reaching for the jacket, he helped her slide it off her shoulders, and kissed her warm skin as the material slipped down, stopping at the valley between her breasts. There was no corset now to impede his progress, just the soft barrier of her cotton chemise, which he removed easily. When nothing barred his view of her glorious breasts, Holt stopped, staring at their round and upright shape. Nicole gasped, and Holt looked up. Her eyes were huge, wide with fear. He smiled, trying to reassure her, then pulled her into his arms. "It's all right, Nicky." Though it pained him to even think it, he heard himself say, "We can still stop if you like."

He felt her head shake against his shoulder and a sense of relief flooded him. To stop and return to Askot was the last thing he wanted to do. Her consent silenced for good the warnings that knocked at his conscience. They were meant for this. Since that first day when he'd kissed her in his bungalow, he'd known that eventually they'd make love, had said as much to Nicky in the garden when he'd held her partially clad body in his arms. No, there would be no stopping now. Together, they removed her trousers and drawers. His own clothes soon followed, though he kept on his pants, afraid his arousal might frighten her.

When they were kneeling in the grass, Nicole naked, Holt wearing only his buckskins, he lowered her to the ground, kissing her lips then smoothing a path with his mouth to her neck and shoulders. Heat melted through Nicky's muscles, followed by a chilling shock as Holt's mouth closed over the tip of one breast, then the burning began anew. She wanted to feel his chest against her stomach; the crisp black hair that followed the line of his muscles excited her as it gently rubbed her skin. Nicky arched up against Holt. Her breath came in sharp, shallow pants. She needed something. What, she didn't know. But she sensed Holt did.

He tasted her salty skin, smelling the lilies in her hair. What he felt seemed basic, beyond control. Logic or conscience could not stop what the feel of Nicole against him did to his soul. He leaned over her, kissing the side of her breast as he cradled the other in his hand. Slowly, he licked and kissed until he found the rose center with his mouth. He swirled his tongue around it, then sucked softly. He felt her press against him. Her hands floated over his back to his shoulders, like butterflies searching for a resting place. With his free hand, Holt trailed a path up the inside of her leg. Nicole seemed fired by his touch. She reached for his face and brought his lips back to her mouth kissing him like she wanted to devour him. Tentatively, he reached up and cupped his hand between her legs. Finding her moist opening with his fingers, he stroked her. The kiss became feverish.

She pressed against him and he made a soft shushing sound against her lips as he reached inside her soft recesses. In a gentle rhythm he caressed her and teased her. His fingers entered and retreated, circled and caressed, as she spread her legs for him, reveling in the passionate strokes. He captured her soft whimpers with his mouth.

When he could stand no more, when he felt he might lose control, he pulled away to remove his trousers.

Nicole looked up, her eyes glowing gold with the fire he'd awakened within her. "Why are you stopping?"

He couldn't help himself. He smiled then looked down to where he strained against the material of his trousers. "Nothing's going to happen if I don't take off my pants."

She looked puzzled, then her face turned as bright a red as the acacia blossoms. For the first time, Holt realized Nicole blushed with considerable frequency. It reminded him she was young, untried—a virgin still.

He closed his eyes. He took two long breaths. What the hell was he doing? Then he felt Nicole's warm hand against his chest. She was kneeling beside him now, naked except for the tiny pink blossoms of thyme caught in her hair. Soon her mouth followed the trail of her hand. Her tongue grazed his nipple, kissing and sucking as he'd done to her. The blazing hunger reignited. But still, he had his doubts.

"Maybe this isn't such a good idea." Even as he said it, he caressed the back of her head, relishing in the moist kisses on his chest as he felt Nicole's small hands at the waistband of his trousers. "Maybe we should stop?"

With the same determination she'd shown before, he heard Nicole say, "No, I don't want to stop. I want to . . . finish."

When she unbuttoned his trousers and his erection burst free, Nicole's hands stilled. In broad daylight, he could do little to stop her from seeing just how much he wanted her.

"Are you frightened?" he asked.

She looked up, meeting his eyes. "A bit."

Taking her hand, he gently placed it at the opening of his trousers. "Don't be," he answered softly, then leaned over her, guiding her slowly to the ground. As he lowered his lips to hers he said, "I'll try not to hurt you."

She seemed to think about his words, staring up at him with her heart in her eyes. "I trust you."

Holt marveled at how she could touch something deep inside him with just a look. Now more than ever, he wanted Nicole with a burning need he had to satisfy.

Pressing himself against her, his skin gliding over the warm moist flesh beneath him, Holt began a different dance from the intimate waltz they'd shared at the Ratcliffe's. He smoothed his hands down her shoulders and rested his palms on her breasts. He rubbed the tips with his thumbs and kissed each. He could feel her squirming beneath him.

"Does it feel this way to you, like you're going to burst," she panted. "Do I make you feel the same?"

"Yes," he breathed against her breasts.

"Good."

He smiled. He reached up and stroked the soft tendrils of hair from her face as he lined his hips up to hers, thinking that even in this Nicole did not want to be outdone.

"Open your legs, Nicole."

She met his gaze. Her look was serious, so serious it made him pause. Watching him, she inched her legs open and wrapped her legs around him, the gesture one of complete trust. Slowly, so as not to frighten her, he fitted himself to the opening of her womb.

"This may hurt."

She nodded. Then closed her eyes and said, "Kiss me, Holt." She locked her legs around him and did the same with her arms at his shoulders. "Make me forget the pain."

He had never before been with a virgin, but he knew what to do. Stroking the recesses of her mouth with his tongue, he slowly built the fires of her desire, increasing her passion until she would relax and forget what lay ahead. Caressing her breast with one hand, he slipped his other hand between their bodies. With the same rhythm of his tongue in her mouth, he soothed the path he intended to follow. When Nicole gasped against his lips, her sweet breath coming in sharp bursts, when the moisture at his fingers let him know she was beyond pain, Holt fitted himself to her and plunged within, bringing them together in one powerful stroke. The obstruction was there, as he'd known it would be. He burst through, making them one. Then began his rhythm.

She was so moist, tight. It seemed he had pent up within him a desire so strong it would break through his control. But he held his breath and gritted his teeth, and teased himself within her, praying he'd not leave her dissatisfied. He could feel her breath against his neck when she arched up, bringing him deep inside her. He reached between them and placed the pad of his finger against her most sensitive spot. She sucked in her breath and her eyes burst open. Holt watched the desire blossom into fulfillment in her gold eyes as he caressed her gently.

Immediately, he felt her muscles contract around him and he caught his breath, almost losing control. But he held on, determined that she should feel the depth of the climax he knew he'd find for himself. Determined that they should reach that point together. Soon she started to whimper, pressing up to meet his thrusts, until he felt her plunge into her release. He quickly followed.

Nicole lay back on the bed of thyme, her eyes closed, a soft smile on her lips. Propped up on his side, Holt watched her. In the same tone of admiration she'd held when she'd spoken of the tigress, she whispered, "Beautiful," then leaned against him with a sigh of satisfaction.

Holt played with the end of the long braid, as fat and thick as his largest paint brush. Nicole nuzzled him, and a hard knot formed in his chest. Another of this nymphlike creature's tendrils had wrapped itself around his heart. With a certain amount of surprise, he realized how devastated he would be when she left him—back to her fiancé and future, Lord Andrew Harrington. A secure lot awaited this British heiress, filled with endless luxuries Holt could never offer. But despite the logic in it, Holt knew their parting promised pain. He hugged her to him. Now, he would feel that much lonelier in his jungle kingdom.

After a while, he realized Nicole had fallen asleep in his arms. He smiled and for a fraction of a second, allowed himself to think what it would be like to always have her at his side. He shook his head at his fanciful thoughts and looked at the gathering cloud cover. They should head back now, before they were drenched by one of the many storms that plagued the foothills. Leaning over, he kissed her awake. Nicole opened her eyes slowly, her rosy cheeks and mouth looking as soft and pink as an orchid.

"Nicole, we have to go back now." He smiled down at her.

Nicky looked at Holt and felt her heart contract. In his eyes, she saw a special warmth; his touch made her feel cherished. What they'd shared had been wondrous, a bonding she would never experience with another man. *So this is love,* she thought. And even as the idea formed in her mind, she felt another wave of emotion squeeze her heart. She reached up and touched his mouth lightly with her fingertips in amazement. Holt loved her. *He loves me.* Just as she loved him.

Never had she hoped to find this kind of love in her life—the kind she suspected her brother shared with his wife. The same love that had displaced her in his life. Now she could understand her brother's devotion to his family and forgive him for turning from her. She had found something just as wonderful. She marveled at how her life would change with Holt beside her. She would never again feel frightened or alone. Holt would be there, loving her. He was so handsome. Truly, extraordinary. Her heart swelled with pride.

Nicole reached up and cradled his face in her hands, meeting his gaze. "I love—"

Holt kissed her; he didn't want her saying words she would regret later. He put everything he felt into that kiss, knowing that it must and *would* be their last. But before Nicole's enthusiastic response made them even later for their rendezvous with the group, Holt pushed her away gently.

"Come on, let's go. The others will be waiting."

"Oh dear." Nicole tensed beside him.

"What's wrong?"

She looked at Holt with a horrified expression as if she, like Holt, had just realized how wrong their lovemaking had been. "How will I ever tell Drew?"

That stopped him cold. "Honey, I suggest you don't tell Harrington anything about this."

"Oh no! Not about . . . that." She colored sweetly then, following Holt's example, she began dressing quickly. "That was something very special I don't plan to share with anyone." She smiled, her heart in her eyes. "I mean about us."

Holt held his breath as he buttoned his trousers and pulled the *kurta* shirt over his head.

"How will I ever break our engagement? Drew has been wonderful to me."

Holt listened, a sinking feeling in his stomach as he watched Nicole finish dressing.

"I'm sure he'll find someone, of course," she continued. "It's just that he has been so giving."

"Nicole . . ."

She faced Holt then, a wondering smile on her lips, her gold eyes glittering with happiness. "Oh, I know it's only right. He should find someone who makes him feel this happy. It was wrong, our relationship—"

"Nicole."

"—I see that now." Nicky stepped closer to Holt, placing her small hand on his chest. "We only shared a certain camaraderie. I suppose that would have been enough for a marriage before"—her eyes grew darker—"but certainly not now." She reached up and stroked his cheek with her cool fingers. "I'll just have to explain to him how I feel."

"Nicole." Holt grabbed her hand and pulled it away from his face. The trust he saw in her eyes hurt—the love and happiness cut even deeper. "Nicole, what are you talking about?"

"About us, of course. I can't possibly marry Drew." She laughed nervously, then added in a soft voice, "Surely you knew I wouldn't marry Drew now? Don't be upset, Holt. It was all wrong from the beginning. You see, I thought I loved him, but I was truly only thankful. I would never make him a good wife—"

"You'll make him an excellent wife."

The smile on her lips slipped just a bit. "W-What?"

Holt watched doubt leak through her shining expression of love. "Nicole, don't break your engagement to Lord Harrington over this."

"This?"

He could see the pain dawning across her face. Holt dreaded it, but knew there was no way she could give up her secure future with Harrington just because she and Holt had made love. "Nicole, Lord Harrington will be a grand husband for you."

"I don't . . . don't understand." She was shaking her head, as if denying what he was saying.

"I can't marry you, Nicole."

His words drove through Nicky with the same numbing pain she'd felt when she'd fallen and hit her head. She searched his face, trying desperately to find some contradiction between his words and what he actually felt for her. But his cool green gaze revealed nothing. Suddenly, Nicole saw herself in a way she had never wanted to. The ugly duckling. People laughing at her. Oh it hurt. Nothing in her life had hurt so much. Nothing her uncle had ever said to her could touch the place Holt's words were ripping apart now.

"I'm sorry, Nicole. Truly sorry."

She backed away, still shaking her head as if she could make his words go away. He was sorry? She was dying inside and he was sorry? With a strangled cry, she turned and ran, as fast and as far as her legs would take her.

"For God's sake, Nicole," she heard him shout after her. "Where are you going?"

She didn't answer, just kept running toward the stand of trees ahead. She wanted to hide. Something very special inside her was dying, and she didn't want anyone, especially Holt, to see.

10

Holt watched Nicole run. The look of betrayal he'd seen on her face was carved on his conscience. He'd made love to her knowing he couldn't offer her anything except pleasant memories. Now even those would turn bitter with her pain.

How could he have let this happen? At thirty-one, he wasn't some untried schoolboy who couldn't control his desires. He knew better than to seduce young virgins. But since the day he'd met Katherine Nicole Marshall, his sense of good judgment had abandoned him. God, her devastated expression when she'd realized what he was saying to her, that the special moment they'd shared was just that, a mere instant in time. He'd almost told her then he'd marry her if that's what would make her happy.

Holt stared bitterly at the floor of pink thyme—the blossoms crushed where he and Nicky had lain together. Of course the girl would think herself in love and be ready to break it off with Harrington. She was young and without a lick of sense. She didn't realize what the commitment she suggested entailed. Would she really want to leave England, her genteel life as a country heiress, and live in a small stone house in a village that smelled perpetually of cow dung? How would she feel over the years with the same Indians her uncle had labeled barbarians as neighbors? No, the kid hadn't thought that far ahead.

Holt clenched his fists to his sides warring with the voice inside his head that shouted she wouldn't care. *It's her uncle who's prejudiced, not Nicole. She would be happy to stay with you here, a part of your life in these forests.* He shook his head, concentrating on the buttons at the neck of his *kurta* as he fastened them slowly. He must be mad to forget the hard lessons of his life, to even consider for a moment the possibility of marrying Nicole.

Looking up, he was dismayed to find she had already disappeared into the trees ahead. He started a slow jog toward her, intending to give her some time to herself, but not wanting her out of his sight too long. All he needed now was for her to get lost.

As he reached the perimeters of the wooded grove, Holt felt a teasing prickle at the base of his neck, as if he were being watched. He spun around, but only the dark clouds hovering on the horizon boded ill. It wasn't the first time he'd felt that odd tingling. Since they'd left Askot at dawn, he'd been nervous that someone was following them, looking for Enchantress's lair. He'd thought perhaps her uncle had broken his promise and come after them. At one point in the journey, he'd actually searched the immediate area, but found nothing. Then he'd lost himself in the joy of answering Nicole's questions about village life in these hills, something about which he considered himself an expert. Now again, he dismissed his sense of unease, more concerned with following Nicole's footsteps into the jungle before the storm hit.

Nicky swatted away the swarm of butterflies she'd disturbed, dispersing the yellow cloud that surrounded her. She could not for a moment enjoy the beauty on display as the delicate wings fluttered out of her reach. She was having trouble enough stomping and clawing a path deeper into the forest of cedar and blackwood, away from Holt, without this blur of umber to hinder her progress.

How foolish she must have sounded to him, speaking of love like a naive schoolgirl. How blithely she had planned to remove Drew from her life, when Holt had never intended to let her into his. She had thought what they shared magical, had equated it with love and a lifetime together. Marriage.

To Holt, it had meant nothing. Nothing.

Nicky scrubbed the tears from her eyes, cursing her blurred vision. She wanted to find some place deep within these woods where she could hide. No, not hide—disappear. Holt, damn his hide, would not be a witness to her pain.

A choking sob escaped her and tears threatened anew. A part of her railed that what had happened wasn't possible. It wasn't possible that the love she'd reveled in for those glorious moments in his arms had, in fact, never existed. It was a loss that went so deep, it threatened to engulf her like the tall looming trees surrounding her. Best to think only of moving forward. Hop over that log, kick aside this bush, and damn the thorns! Sweep the vines and grass from the path. These things could not hurt her. And yet the tears slipped past her guard and down her cheeks just the same.

Nicole tripped on the root of a tree and fell headlong into the dirt. To her absolute horror, tears flooded her eyes. For a moment, she huddled on her scratchy bed of leaves and loamy soil, giving in to her pangs of anguish. What a sight she must be, she thought miserably. The skin of her hands and face was riddled with bloody scratches where the thorns and bushes had slapped against her. Her jacket was torn, showing her chemise underneath; her face was covered with dirt and streaked with tears. The image of herself prostrate on the ground shamed her. Stumbling to her feet, she cleared the tears from her eyes with the back of her hand, and searched the thicket around her. Holt Atley would not find her on her knees in the dirt.

Nicky began climbing a sturdy-looking tree whose spreading branches linked with its neighbor. She dug her boot heels into the rough red bark, and shinnied up the barrel trunk. Reaching the lowest branch, she hoisted herself up onto it and smiled with satisfaction when she stood on the thick branch. Holt Atley would not find her at all.

Hitching herself up onto the next limb, she found a stout

branch and slid on her stomach to its outer reaches until she could just touch the branches of the next tree over. Taking a deep breath, she rose cautiously to her knees, then inched her feet beneath her, almost losing control and tumbling to the ground. When she regained her balance, she eyed the sprawl of branches of the neighboring tree. The purchase she sought looked ominously far, but she was determined to get out of this forest and back to Askot without Holt's escort.

On the count of three she catapulted herself forward, grabbing at the prickly branches of the next tree until she had one clenched between her hands like a rope. The wood snapped. Nicole careened into the branches just above the trunk. Limbs slapping her, the tree's rugged bark cutting into her arms and face, she smacked into branch after branch. She managed to keep her grip around the broken limb that swung her to the center of the tree, until she landed on a large bough like a sack, her legs and arms hanging on either side of the limb. After she steadied herself and caught her breath, she brushed her hair from her eyes and looked to the next tree over. She reached for the branch above her, ready to climb higher.

No, Holt Atley would never find her.

"Nicole!" Holt shouted, hiking through the trail she'd left with his rifle in his arms. "Nicole!"

Overhead, another cloud covered the sun and a corresponding sense of alarm settled over Holt. A storm in the valley now could prove a disaster for them both.

"Damn it, Nicole. Answer me. Now!"

Only the howling wind returned his cries.

Battling his rising fears, Holt reminded himself that, with the exception of an elephant, nothing could have left a more conspicuous trail than Nicole. He expected he'd catch up to her soon. Still, the cloud cover made him uneasy, as did the ominous silence of the forest ahead. Where the hell was she!

"What the . . . ?"

He scouted around the base of a *toon,* a cedarlike tree common to this area, where Nicole's footsteps suddenly disappeared. It wasn't possible, yet the half-moon marks of her tracks vanished at the trunk. He took a closer look and found where Nicole's boots had dug into the rough red bark as she'd climbed the tree. Stepping back, he searched the branches above him. A drop of moisture landed on his cheek. Then another. "Damn."

Quickly, he shouldered the rifle and climbed the *toon.* Yet, even at the top, he couldn't see any signs of Nicole. Holt scrambled down and circled the area, his worries doubling with each step. He shouted her name over and over, but it only echoed unpromisingly up and down the Gori Ganga. Standing in the middle of the silent grove of *toon* and *sissoo,* interspersed among the tall ironwood trees, he listened for any sounds, any clues, of Nicole's direction, but heard only silence. Finally, he took off his slouch hat and wiped the perspiration from his forehead, leaning against the tree where all traces of Nicole had vanished.

So, Katherine Nicole Marshall had outsmarted him. Had outsmarted herself.

A storm was coming, and she was out there, somewhere in the middle of the Indian jungle. Alone.

As clouds obscured the sky, Nicole's forest turned into a gloomy cavern. The jungle of bamboo and other shrubs gave way to stands of bent and twisted boxwood trees. The moss-covered branches spread above her like arthritic arms, blocking out the sky and casting an eerie greenish glow on everything around her. The dark and silent trees seemed threatening. The ghastly iridescence of their moss altered even the beauty of the orchids that hung from their trunks. Nicole tread softly, as if fearful of disturbing whatever evil hid within this jungle.

The spatter of rain leaked through the cover of the trees and Nicole began to regret her decision to seek refuge in the forest. She could hear the rush of the Gori River and anxiously turned to retrace her steps. By now, she would expect Holt to be somewhere well away from the glade where they'd left their horses. She would find her way up the gorge, back to Askot and her uncle, without Holt's help.

Nicole had no idea how many hours passed as she trekked through the silent stands of gnarled boxwood, climbing over boulders, winding her way through the menacing trees. Completely drenched, she admitted she was nowhere closer to finding her glade than when she'd turned back. She could no longer hear the river, and the trees were looking frighteningly similar. The heavy rain had plunged the forest into splenetic darkness and somewhere along the trail she had lost her way.

She kept moving, but couldn't escape the sensation that she was traveling in circles. The feeling became so intense, she finally tore off a piece of her chemise and tied the bit of cotton to a thorn bush before continuing ahead. With the rain pelting down through the trees, it seemed as if some current were dragging her deeper within the center of the jungle like a whirlpool. Even her footsteps disappeared into the muddy soil, as if the forest had determined to absorb any trace of her passage. The very sounds of the jungle disturbed her, attaining an irritating cadence that became haunting. *Lost, lost . . . lost.* The word echoed in her head, matching the beat of the cicadas and frogs.

The rain poured down in a deafening torrent. She sought refuge in a niche between two large boulders. Though the temperature was sultry, she felt a chill deep within her bones and looped her arms around her knees as she huddled among the ferns. Terror, dark and biting, nudged at her, but Nicole thrust off her sense of panic, confident that when the rain stopped she would once again find the river and her sense of direction.

When the downpour finally ceased, it did so as abruptly as it had begun, but the hours spent in darkness had taken their toll on Nicole. Wanting only to find some landmark, some familiar trail, she climbed out of her niche and did the worst thing possible: She ran, frantically and without care for her direction.

She ran until her breath wheezed in her chest, until the pounding of her heart became painful. And when she felt she would collapse from her fear and exhaustion, she ran on. Panic boiled in her veins like a poison, making her pulse race with her heart. In her head, a voice called with the rhythm of her steps: *Find your way out, you must find your way out—before it's too late.*

Nicole tripped, careening into the mud. When she looked up, what she saw radiated chills down her body. There in front of her was the strip of cloth she had tied to the too-familiar thorn bush.

Holt galloped into the center of Askot, drenched in sweat and rain. After an hour of searching in the downpour, he'd finally admitted he would not find Nicole without help. What he'd thought a shallow grove had turned into a dense jungle of boxwood. She could be anywhere, lost deep within those thick woods.

Coming up the gorge had taken valuable time and Holt's insides were strung tighter than catgut. Each passing hour, the sun fell lower past its zenith. Though he'd raced up the bridle paths to Askot, coming dangerously close to sending himself and the sturdy mountain ponies to perdition, he knew a search party would not make it back down before dark. Refusing to admit even the possibility of failure, Holt focused his mind on what supplies they would need, how many people to recruit, a strategy for finding Nicole.

As he expected, her uncle waited at their rendezvous point, pacing on the slate flagstones of the village square. Beside him, the others of their party, the commissioner, Harrington, Nursoo, and their porters, milled about, until Nursoo shouted and pointed toward Holt. The group gathered around the uncle, with the exception of Harrington, who stood back slapping a leather quirt against his thigh as he watched Holt approach.

"Where have you been? I expected you back hours ago." Marshall sputtered the questions as Nursoo held the pony's reins and Holt dismounted. "Did the storm catch you unawares, man? Where did you leave Nicole? Is she safe?" When Holt didn't answer immediately, a desperate look dawned on Marshall's face. "Where is Nicole!"

"Lost." He didn't have time nor the inclination for diplomacy, but Nursoo's startled look made him realize his shortness was ill timed. "I came back for help," he explained. Peering toward the sun on the horizon, Holt felt every muscle in his body tense. His concern for Marshall's sensibilities and his own culpability in the man's eyes vanished and he shouldered past him. "We'll need to search for her—in the dark by the look of it."

Holt began instructing the natives on what they'd need for their rescue mission. But as he finished making arrangements for fresh horses, a hand jerked him around from behind.

"What are you saying?" Harrington stared at Holt, his blue eyes wide in disbelief. His grip bit deeper into Holt's arm. "Are you telling us you were out *alone* with Nicole and you've *lost* her?"

Holt pushed Harrington off, startled to find his hand in a fist ready to take a swing at the Brit. He was even more surprised to discover himself fighting the urge to do just that. For a moment, they faced each other—Holt with his hands clenched at his sides, Harrington with his knuckles white around the quirt—until Holt felt Nursoo's warning hand on his arm. He shook his head, disturbed by the depth of his animosity. He knew he'd always harbored this antagonism toward the Brit, even before he'd overheard Harrington's nefarious plans for Enchantress. Since the day he'd met the man in the woods and discovered he was engaged to Nicole he'd been set against the British lord. Now he understood the reason. This man, because of his title, his influence, his station in life, deserved Nicole and would have her as his wife.

Taking a deep breath, Holt faced Nicole's future husband, giving him his due. "We were in a glade," he explained. "We argued and Nicole disappeared into a grove of trees. I went after her, but the rain made it impossible to find her."

Harrington's eyes narrowed and one slim eyebrow arched upwards. "You were in a glade together?"

"Lord in heaven," Marshall said under his breath, "help us find her."

Harrington whipped around to face Marshall. "You'll have to do better than pray, Marcus," he said viciously. "This man has *lost* your niece!" He extended his hand toward Holt with the righteousness of a barrister pointing out the accused. "In the damn Indian jungle, no less!"

Once again intent on Nicole, Holt ignored the British lord's displays of temper and instructed Nursoo on his plan. But the gentleman would not be put off. He swung Holt back to face him.

"What did you do to make Nicole run away?" Harrington's eyes blazed. He grabbed Holt's shirt with both hands. Holt had never seen the sophisticated Brit out of control as he was now.

"If anything happens to Nicole, I'll kill you, Atley. God help me, I'll kill you." He shook Holt by the collar. "You will not ruin my plans for Nicole. I will *not* have everything I've worked for destroyed by the likes of you! Where's the girl, damn it!"

With one swing of his arm, he dislodged Harrington's grip and stepped back. A sixth sense clicked its warning inside him. "Your concern is a bit late, don't you think? *You* insisted Nicole come on this hunt in the first place!"

Instantly Harrington retreated, the eyes once again cool, on guard. He turned back to Marshall, as if wary of rebutting Holt's silent accusation.

"This is your fault, Marcus," he said. "If you had for once thought of Nicole as a woman, rather than a chip off the old block, none of this would have happened. I demand to know what the girl was doing with this man unchaperoned?"

Marshall seemed lost for a moment, as if he'd just come to understand what a tremendous error in judgment he'd made. He looked to Holt, searching for an answer there. "He said he'd make her happy," Marshall shook his head and Holt felt doubly damned by the old man's desolate expression. "I just wanted to make her happy," he finished softly.

"How could you let her go off like that?" Harrington sputtered. "Think of her reputation!"

As Harrington continued his tirade at Nicole's uncle, Holt watched in disbelief. He was acting as if Nicole were an object whose value had just been reduced beyond repair. *My God,* he thought suddenly. *He doesn't care about her.* And then, the damning truth: *Not like I do.*

A blazing anger erupted within him, directed at himself as well as Nicole's betrothed. She should have better than this arrogant popinjay, who despite his good name and influence, would never love her. She deserved better than anything Holt had to offer as well. But most of all, she merited a timely rescue rather than this useless examination of her moral fiber.

Mounting one of the fresh ponies Nursoo brought forward, Holt signaled to the others to do the same. He stared down at Harrington from atop his mount. "Listen to me, Lord Harrington. Nicole's life is in danger. Now, you can sit here spouting righteous anger about her lack of chaperone or you can mount up on a horse and help us find her. We're wasting time; its almost dark, and I guarantee it's easier to find a button in a sand dune than someone lost in the Indian jungle by night."

Harrington stared at Holt for a moment, then grabbed his gun from an attendant and mounted up on the horse next to Holt.

"I'll find Nicole." He brought his horse alongside Holt's until the hindquarters of the horses banged up against each other. Andrew Harrington smiled viciously when Holt veered away to control his spooked pony. "But I'll do it alone."

The Brit snapped his quirt against the pony's flanks and rammed past Holt. Despite the fact that Holt had never mentioned Nicole's location, Harrington disappeared down the empty streets of Askot as if he knew exactly where he was going.

The touch was cold, cold as death. Nicole felt waxy smooth scales on her neck then a moist prodding as the snake nosed past her braid. Its weight slithered across her shoulder. An involuntary shudder skidded across her skin. She held her breath and watched out of the corner of her eye, sensing when the snake's head emerged off her shoulder and down her arm. It stopped, raised up, and swung back to face her. The snake's forked tongue flicked out from scaly lips. Nicky shut her eyes in terror and felt something slick and wet brush against her cheek with a featherlike touch.

Holding back her scream, Nicole waited as the snake continued down her arm, inch by slow inch, then traveled down the tree where Nicole had been resting. In the dim moonlight that slipped stintingly through the web of leaves above, she could see the snake was twice as long as Nicky was tall and as thick around as her calf—truly a creature of the devil. When the serpent had moved completely away, Nicole stood and ran blindly in the opposite direction.

Something moist and rubbery snagged her around her neck and Nicole fell screaming to her knees. She ripped the creature from her, but found in her hands only a few wet jungle vines. Sinking to the ground, she held the vines clutched in her fingers, her arms hugging her belly. Night had fallen on the Indian jungle. She was wet and absolutely miserable—and her nightmares were coming to life.

She thought of all the creatures that haunted these woods. Nursoo's words came back to paint vivid pictures of great horned beasts covered in armor, enormous bears that could kill with one swipe of their clawed paws, and panthers so black you could not see them until they'd locked their jaws around your neck. The deafening sounds of the jungle proved their existence, and when a roar echoed down the gorge, Nicole rolled to her stomach and grabbed unconsciously for the pistol she'd forgotten.

The shrieks and howls, the barks and caws that filled the night spoke of the terrible consequences that awaited a single misstep. Suddenly, Nicole caught sight of luminous eyes blinking at her from her right. She rose slowly and backed away, then once again ran unseeing into the night.

"Nicole. NICOLE!"

Holt peered through the smoke of his torch at the stand of ironwood trees. The meager light showed no more than a few paces ahead. His throat ached from the hours spent shouting into the darkness. To his right and left, he could see the flickering lights held high by Nursoo, the commissioner, and Nicole's uncle. Their cries blended and echoed with his own down the length of the Gori Ganga. Their only answer—the tread of animals scurrying into the night as the party approached.

"NICOLE!"

Hearing no response, Holt experienced an aching guilt over his seduction of Nicole. Once again, an Atley had conquered a woman's heart—and destroyed her. Incredibly, history had repeated itself, and at that moment, his crime seemed much more heinous than his father's.

"Damn it, Nicole," Holt muttered under his breath as he searched ahead. "Come on girl; show your skinny little hide!" Then to himself, "Dearest God, don't let me fail her now. Not again."

Holt continued into the bowels of the jungle, his concentration focused on the circle of the torchlight as he cleared his mind of useless recriminations. Regrets would not save Nicole. And deep within him, Holt knew she was out there, alive, waiting for him. If the Indian vision of destiny was correct, Holt would find her. Their story wasn't finished.

Out of the corner of his eye, Holt caught sight of a sliver of white. He whipped around, and with the torch above his head, peered through the inky darkness, searching for the source of color. Concentrating so as not to miss it, he scanned the area ahead until he found it, a bit of cloth hanging on a thorn bush. Edging closer, Holt crouched down at the shrub—the strip of cotton had been carefully tied there. Taking the cloth in his hand, he rubbed it gently between his fingers, remembering its texture from that afternoon when he'd helped her to undress. Nicole's chemise.

Holt ripped the cotton from the bush and vaulted to his feet. Raising his face to the sky, he cried, "NI-COOOOOOOOOOOOOLE . . ."

Lost. Nicky felt the bark's sting against her cut palms and forehead, uncaring of any threat that might be slithering down to greet her. *Lost.*

And dismally tired of being afraid.

Turning around, she leaned back against the tree and challenged the darkness, "Eat me, if you like. I don't care anymore! Do you hear? I . . ." she slid down the trunk to the forest floor, "don't . . . care."

A tear fell down her bruised cheek. Nicole swiped it away with a finger, amazed that she had any tears left. She was worn out, hungry, and achingly weary of the fears that gnawed at her. At this moment nothing seemed worse than the nightmares she'd been fleeing since she'd lost her way in the jungle.

Let them come, she thought. Let the animals devour her, if they liked. She hoped she gave them indigestion.

Crouched at the base of the tree, Nicole giggled softly. *Indigestion?* She imagined the grimace of distaste on the face of any forest creature who might find her *not* to its liking.

She hoped to give them indigestion?

Nicole fell back against the floor, smiling. Her hunger,

her thirst—even her deep weariness, seemed to ebb. She scooped handfuls of leaves and flung them in the air. Weak giggles bubbled into cleansing laughter as she rolled in the soft layers of bark and leaves. When her chuckles subsided into soft hiccups, she settled back into her loamy nest and stared through the branches overhead. She gazed at the sliver of moon hanging in the indigo sky, and a calming peace fell over her.

She had a curious thought as she lay there in her den of leaves, watching the crescent moon: She was lost—but hadn't she lived with that same fuzzy sense of disorientation all her life? Wasn't that why she'd wanted to come to India in the first place? To find her bearings? To find herself?

Nicole crossed her arms under her head, inhaling the earthy scent of wet soil. Yes, she had come on this hunt in search of a lost legacy, tired of spending a lifetime with a part of her undefined. Wouldn't it be ironic if here, in the Indian jungle, she finally resolved the conflict inside her caused by that missing history?

She thought about the early days of her childhood, when she'd first come to understand her family's secret heritage, a lineage that she, a dark-haired child in a family of blond, amber-eyed Marshalls, alone betrayed. Even her mother, the daughter of a Rajput princess, had inherited the light hair and eyes of Nicky's grandfather. Nicole had spent a great deal of time learning what she could of India and the Rajputs, without letting her mother or uncle know of her studies.

If her father had lived, surely he would have helped her. He'd married her mother without a thought to her Indian blood, if what her uncle said was true. But Nicholas Marshall had died before she'd even seen the light of her first morning in this world. Her mother was too weak, too frightened of her past to help Nicole; her uncle, completely disapproving. When she'd made love to Holt, she'd thought he would help her . . .

Nicole suppressed the exquisite pain thoughts of Holt

brought her. As always, she was alone. Her search for her past would be a solitary journey. Perhaps that was the only way it could be accomplished.

With her fingers, Nicole traced the outline of her eyes, knowing they were large and almond-shaped, then spread her hands across her high cheekbones. How could her uncle and mother expect her to forget a past that she faced each day in the mirror? Sitting up, she crossed her legs and took her braid in hand. Untying the ribbon at its base, she released the thick ebony curls, stringing her fingers through hair she knew was strikingly similar to that of every Indian woman in the villages she'd visited.

The bark of a chital deer skidded up the hills. Nicole reached inside her pocket. Throughout the night, each time she'd heard a jungle noise that frightened her, she'd grabbed for her missing pistol. Her uncle had taught her to define herself by the gun. But now, she reached for something much closer to her heart.

Nicole traced the elaborate ruby design of her grandmother's locket with her thumb. Flicking the gold latch, she pictured the image of the gold-veiled woman inside as she gently pressed her fingers to the miniature.

She was Indian. No matter what her mother and uncle said. A Rajput.

Leaning back against the tree, Nicky listened to the caw of a peacock as it echoed down the glen. The langur monkeys' howls followed from deep inside the jungle, and then a distant roar . . . Enchantress perhaps? Searching to make a kill for her cubs?

A kill. In her head, she heard Holt's deep somber voice: *Sometimes I sleep in the trees to prevent tiger attacks.* Her heart beat faster.

The trees.

Nicole scrambled to her feet, pocketing her grandmother's locket. During their trip down the ridge from Askot, Holt had told her that often while on charting expeditions he would sleep in the trees if there was no forest bungalow about, to keep safe from animals prowling the night. With a swiftness that belied the hours she'd spent scouring the jungle forest, she climbed up the trunk, reaching for the lowest branches. Although there was no *manchan* to rest on, Nicky found a wide bough that forked into a comfortable niche, and fit herself into the curve of the branches.

Folding her arms across her, she thought of the coming day for the first time with optimism. She would make it—without her uncle, without her gun—she would live through this night. And when she did, when she found her way back to Askot, she would finish out her quest.

This time, no one would stop her.

Nicole woke to the sultry heat of the tropical morning. The sun was just a suggestion through the cover of the leaves, but in the pale light of dawn, she felt as if she could see for miles. The gloomy forest had been transformed into a magical kingdom. Ferns flowed from every crevice, every tree. Their green fronds glistened where crystalline droplets of water captured the morning light. Moss blanketed the rocks and tree trunks. From these green beds flowered pearly grasses of Job's Tears. Begonias of brilliant reds and yellows dotted the carpet of green as well.

Nicky scrambled down the tree, a sense of triumph bursting within her. She had faced her fears last night, had lived with them for endless hours until she knew their taste, their smell, their clawing touch. Today, she could conquer anything, her uncle, Drew—even Holt. And *certainly* this jungle maze.

After slaking her thirst from a water-logged crevice, and cleaning what dirt she could from her face and hands, Nicole searched for a lookout point. Once she'd jumped to the ground and seen the endless trunks and shrubs from the level of the forest floor, she'd known immediately she was too confused to chance moving ahead without some directional references. She could hear what she thought was the distant Gori River, but couldn't be sure it wasn't merely the river's echo bounced off a ridge. What she needed was a better view.

An evergreen-type tree, whose massive trunk had enough ruts and holes for footing, became her ladder. Slowly, she climbed up the bark, her hands shaking from the effort of pulling herself up by the time she reached the first branches, a good twenty feet off the ground. Determined to see above this haze of green, she scaled the limbs, inching closer to its conical top. Finally, above the tree line, she had the answer she sought. She knew where to go.

It took her nearly two hours to reach the valley she'd seen from atop the tree, but when she stepped beyond the forest into the meadow where three ponies grazed peacefully near the remains of a campfire, an almost painful joy suffused her. She'd made it; she'd found her way out of this vortex jungle. And now she'd discovered help.

A familiar snap-click of a gun cocking beat its cadence from directly behind her.

Turning slowly, Nicole found herself facing the hideously scarred Morgan, his gash of a mouth twisted in its perpetual grimace. The red-coated Korku stood directly at his side.

"I knew ye'd be out sooner or later. I said it before; yer a real tigress." He motioned with his gun toward the horses in the glade ahead. "Just step ahead there, Missy. Yer future husband be waitin' fer ye."

11

"Drew!" Nicole wrested her arm from the Korku's grip and stumbled to her fiancé.

"Nicole. Thank God you're safe."

Drew's arms tightened around her; his voice sounded hoarse, charged with concern. In his embrace, her fears of the Irishman and his gun seeped away. She leaned against him, her legs drained of their power by lack of food and rest. As he lent her his familiar strength, Nicole considered the possibility that she had been wrong about love. Perhaps that tender emotion was not the burning desire she felt in the American's arms. Couldn't love just as well be this man's supporting arms and comforting embrace? Why couldn't true love be a lifetime of kind words and companionship?

"I tol' ye we'd find the girl, yer lordship. T'ain't a thing in this jungle that Korku can't track."

"You fool, Morgan. Nicole found you!"

"Now that t'ain't quite right. We kept our eye on 'er, we did. Just like ye tol' us. We been following her—"

"Shut up!" Drew kept his pale eyes on Nicole, as if she alone mattered on this earth. "What ever possessed you to go off with Atley, darling?" he asked. "Without me or your uncle?"

Nicole didn't answer, thinking over Morgan's odd remark. She frowned. Why would Drew ask that horrible man and the native to follow her?

Drew grabbed her by her shoulders, almost lifting her off the ground. She could see her silence had upset him greatly.

"What did he do to you, Nicole? Tell me what happened when he had you alone?"

The image of Holt bare-chested above her, his lips spread in a sensual smile as he leaned down to kiss her, pierced through her. Nicole shook her head, as if by denying her intimacy with another man she could somehow make it not true. She buried her face against Drew's shoulder, deeply ashamed. A small voice within her challenged: *What are you going to tell Drew now?*

She considered confessing. Morgan may have seen her with Holt in the glade. But she discarded the thought quickly. Drew was too intent on his questions to know anything about her indiscretions. She need not wound him with the awful truth. And then the thought arose: *Can I still salvage my relationship with Drew?* She could tell him that Holt had taken her to see the white tigress. The American trusted only Nicole with the location of the cat's den because she had let the tigress escape. That reason alone might assuage Drew's suspicions. The tigress was unique. Certainly Drew could understand how tempted she would be to see the animal again, even if it required riding down the gorge with Holt. But then she remembered how keen Drew was on bagging the tigress. If she told him the cat's den was nearby, she'd be condemning Enchantress and her cubs to certain death.

"Nothing happened, Drew," she said. "Mr. Atley merely wanted to show me the game around the gorge," she finished in a flat voice. The excuse sounded weak, even to her, but she didn't want Enchantress or her cubs hurt. Of all the choices she'd made since she'd tangled with the American, sparing the tigress was one she could never regret. When she looked up to meet Drew's pale blue eyes, she knew by his expression that he didn't believe her.

"Nicole." He stroked back the hair from her face. Running his thumb along a scratch on her cheek, Drew shook his head sadly when she winced, as if her pain hurt him as well. "You were with that man, alone, for quite some time."

The look in his eyes softened, and he coaxed, "Did Atley do anything to hurt you? To make you run away?"

Seeing the expression on his face, Nicole felt truly cursed. Such gentle emotions radiated from Drew, he tempted her to throw herself in his arms and tell everything. Instead, she tried to pry herself away, denying herself this comfort, but Drew wrapped his fingers tight around her wrists and held her steady.

"I was perfectly safe with Mr. Atley," she answered. She would not hurt Drew with the truth. Nor would she marry him with the lie. She would pay, as she must, for her mistakes.

Nicole leaned against Drew once more. She was infinitely tired, weary to the depths of her soul, but ready to move on with her life, to put Drew and Holt Atley behind her. Meeting his penetrating gaze straight on, she said, "Drew, I lost my temper over a disparaging remark Mr. Atley made concerning my hunting skills. I ran away and became lost in the woods." She forced conviction into her voice. "Mr. Atley did nothing more than"—she smiled at the ironic truth— "make me feel the fool."

Drew stared down at her. Nicole didn't allow doubt to show on her face until Drew sighed and looked away.

"I *was* worried." Drew's eyes narrowed, and his voice attained a sharp edge. "I've caught him staring one too many times as if you were some morsel he planned to feast on. I certainly wouldn't trust that man to keep from compromising you if given any encouragement." Wrapping his arms around her, still holding her wrists, he hugged her. His actions forced Nicole's arms back, behind her. The position was awkward, and Nicky had to lean against Drew to regain her balance. "But I felt sure you'd not betray my trust, Nicole. Dear God, I spent a miserable night searching for you. I thought you'd been killed. Or worse."

Nicole flinched, hearing the anger in his voice—anger directed at her. Behind her back, Drew crossed one of Nicole's wrists over the other and pressed them together. "I can't risk losing you, my dear." He locked his fingers around her hands like a set of manacles, then looked up over his shoulder to the Irishman. "Bring that strap of leather from my saddlebag, Morgan."

Nicole started. "What are you doing?" She struggled against Drew's grasp, but he held on tightly while Morgan came back and restrained her hands with the leather. "You're tying me up?" she asked, disbelieving.

"I won't have you running away again, Nicole."

"I wouldn't run from you, Drew."

"Not before, perhaps. I, however, have my doubts now."

"Drew, you're scaring me. Is this some kind of punishment because of what happened yesterday?" She again considered the possibility that Morgan had seen Holt make love to her in the glen.

He laughed. "Hardly. Call it a bit of security, my dear."

Drew pressed Nicky to him, crushing her breasts against his chest. He leaned forward and whispered in her ear, so only she could hear, "I've wanted to plow your sweet little body for such a long time." He glanced over to the Korku, and added softly, regret coloring his words, "But I'm afraid our friend here might object."

Nicole stood perfectly still, shocked and horrified by Drew's crass words.

He chuckled in her ear. "Have I shocked my sweet Nicole? You still don't understand, do you?" He dug his fingers in her hair and pulled sharply, forcing her head back. Drew ran one finger across her mouth. "Dear God, girl. Here you stand, tied before me, and you still look at me with that childlike innocence that pleads—Drew make everything right." He shook his head. "You're so deliciously naive. It's tempting . . ." He looked back at the Korku. "But I'm afraid this is one treat I must forgo."

Nicole silently watched Drew's pale eyes as they lost their dreamy appearance and narrowed on her. Her heart pounded in her chest as she realized she had more to fear from Drew than from the animals that had stalked her in the night. This was her fiancé, the man she was betrothed to —and yet, he was not Drew at all. The way he stared at her, as if she were a costly gun he assessed for its worth, made her skin prickle and the hairs at the base of her neck rise.

"How many times," he whispered, "did I try and get you where I have you right now? The pig sticking for one—well that was certainly a patch job. But the hunt for the white tigress, now there was a marvelous opportunity. And yet, you managed easily enough to evade our Mr. Morgan here."

For a moment, her concentration wavered, as if the morning's fog in the glade had seeped inside her head and clouded her thinking. Each instance Drew recounted slipped into a notch within her mind like the ramrod of her Purdy driving the powder down the barrel. Drew, avoiding her kisses, then taunting her for them. Drew, insisting that she go pig sticking. His rabid desperation to follow the white tigress on foot when he'd never really shown any enthusiasm for the hunt before. His insistence that she travel alone with Morgan into the isolated woods . . .

"How positively ironic," Drew continued, a hint of glee in his voice, "that when I thought I'd lost you to this wretched jungle, my plans should finally *succeed*. Such irony, my dear, such delicious irony. I plotted and planned, but in the end, I had little to do with your disappearance." He stroked the curve of her cheek with a finger, and she flinched, pulling her head away from his touch. He merely laughed at her efforts. "I must take some credit for insisting that you be included on this hunt, but truly, you did my work for me."

"The trip to India, the hunt." Nicole thought of how she'd worried for the tigress should Drew know the location of Enchantress and her cubs. With growing alarm, she saw it was not the tigress he hunted. "You didn't want to kill the white tigress."

"I don't give a damn about the animal. Actually, I don't care for the sport at all. It seems a dreadfully dangerous way to achieve a thrill, and in the end, one has but a scraggly carpet of fur to measure and boast of."

She frowned. "But the tiger scar on your arm . . ."

Drew laughed. "Ah yes, the ladies do love the tale of my manly exploits. I must disappoint you, my dear. I've never been within scoring distance of such a beast. This"—he pointed to his forearm, now hidden under the sleeve of his coat—"was a childhood accident." Drew turned and shoved her toward the horses as the Korku and Morgan looked on. Nicole stumbled, almost falling to the ground until Drew pulled her to her feet with a jolt that left her arms burning in their sockets and her wrists raw from the leather straps that held them. "No, it is you and your uncle who care for the great sport of hunting tiger," he said from behind her. "In order to get Marshall here, it had to be a fabulous catch. Something that would make him forget his fears of this country and the blemish it represents to his exalted family name. The white tigress did just that."

Nicole dug her heels into the ground. Drew whipped her around, still holding her close to his body. She faced the man she'd agreed to marry, who had romanced her for the past year with unstinting kindness, searching for a motive for his outrageous actions. Despite his ugly words about plowing her, she sensed the look of hunger she saw in his eyes had nothing to do with sexual desire. "What do you want Drew? Money? Are you planning to ransom me to my family?"

"Nicole"—he held her shoulders roughly—"I came to England looking for *you* . . . *you* are my key to Maharutal-Hind."

The awe in his voice frightened her. It didn't seem quite sane. "The golden city?"

"Will be mine at last, bought and paid for with the delivery of the great-granddaughter of the Maharana Amar Singh. A Rajput of the Sun Line. God, you were *elusive*, girl."

"The s-sun line?" Drew's words mesmerized. He spoke with such authority. Could he truly know the answers she had searched for all her life?

"You sound surprised. Didn't you know, my dear? You are part of a proud and noble race. Many would pay treasures to be part of such a powerful clan—some would even kill. Your cousin, the Princess Usha, took her life rather than be forced into marriage with the lowly Korku raja who stole her from her family." He picked up a strand of ebony hair and twirled it thoughtfully between his fingers. "Lucky for him, I found a reasonably good replacement."

"Replace . . ."

"I deliver you, and the Korku tells me the long guarded secret of his tribe—the location of Maharuta-l-Hind."

Her response died on her lips when she saw his calculating smile. Taking a step back, she tried to ram her knee between his legs, as she'd done to Holt, but Drew pulled her flush against him. Nicole twisted desperately until he yanked her arms back. She gasped, unable to breathe for the pain that flared through her.

"Don't make this any more difficult than it has to be, Nicole." He hiked her bound wrists farther up her back, forcing her on her tiptoes to avoid the pain of her arms ripping out of their sockets. "I expected you'd be less than enthusiastic about my plans, but your cooperation will make things easier for you. I have my regrets as well. It is truly a shame we never married, as I planned. I could certainly have used the money. But your family would not let the thing be rushed. Oh, no. For you, their dark little angel, there must be a grand ceremony. And the raja grew impatient." In one move, Drew whirled her around and pushed her to the ground. Nicole rolled to her back, despite the pain she felt, anticipating another attack. But Drew merely loomed above her. "When your brother and uncle began suspiciously sniffing out my finances, I was forced to act. I'm afraid they would rather object to our courtship if they discovered the true circumstances of my living. After an appropriate period of mourning for you, my dear, I shall have to seek out another heiress, if I want the funds to begin excavating." He kneeled down beside her. "Though, I dare say, I'll never find one so charming as you."

Laughing, Drew stood and walked to the horses, searching the saddlebags. From within the bag, he withdrew the Gurkha jungle knife given to them by the rajbar of Askot. "Let's get started," he said to Morgan. "Before her uncle and the rest come sniffing around."

Drew extracted the knife slowly from the leather sheath, then tested the edge with his thumb before advancing on Nicole. Terrified, Nicky tried to get to her feet. Almost immediately, she was captured from behind and pulled up to face Drew's attack. She could smell Morgan's putrid breath behind her as he held her still. With the knife, Drew sliced off both sleeves of her shooting jacket. He grabbed her ragged collar and cleaved the jacket completely open before ripping it off her. Morgan guffawed behind her, and Nicole shut her eyes, unable to watch Drew staring at her with only her chemise to cover her. She didn't open her eyes until she felt the weight of Drew's coat on her shoulders. Stunned, she watched as he began hacking at the remnants of the jacket he held, stabbing and shredding it, then examining it as if he were an artist looking for any blemish in his work.

"That ought to be convincing," he said. Turning to Morgan, he asked, "Did you find the kill?"

The gnome nodded. "Over yonder. Lots of pug marks and blood. Apparently that tiger had himself a real hard time catching the sambar."

"What did you do with the deer?"

"Tossed it in the river down a ways. No chance of anybody finding it."

Drew nodded. "Excellent."

Taking the knife, he stared at Nicole, riveting her with his pale eyes. "For you my dear." With the knife, he sliced a thin cut along his forearm. Nicole almost gagged as she watched his act of self-mutilation. Drew smiled tightly, pain etched in the lines of his mouth as he held her shredded jacket to his arm and let the blood soak into the thick linen.

"I would have used your lovely limb, but I'm afraid to mar the merchandise."

He tossed the bloodied jacket to Morgan. "You know what to do."

Morgan nodded and left.

After he'd wrapped a cloth tightly around his arm to stop the bleeding, Drew tried to pick up Nicole. She fought him, kicking him with her feet. Drew's slap across her mouth knocked her to the ground of the meadow. Her hands tied behind her, she couldn't break her fall. For a moment, the world went dark, her breath wheezed in her throat. When her vision returned, Drew was staring at the Korku, who watched them with an expression that looked surprisingly like anger on his face.

Drew crouched down beside her. "It's useless to fight me, Nicole," he whispered harshly. "You're only making things worse for yourself."

Still stunned by her fall, Nicole lay lax as he picked her up and carried her toward the ponies. "That's much better, my dear," he said. "Now." He lifted her onto a pony and mounted up behind her. "Shall we go meet your bridegroom?"

Holt crushed the bloodied piece of cloth in his hand. The group of hunters, Nursoo, the commissioner, and Nicole's uncle, clustered around him, all staring at the crimson stained sleeve in deathly silence. At his feet, where he'd found the strip of linen, lay a trail of pug marks—tiger tracks he recognized as belonging to Enchantress.

Marshall began shaking his head, slowly at first, then faster, as if warding off the nightmare Holt held in his palm. "No," the man whispered. "It can't be. My Nicole can't be dead."

Holt stared at the cloth, then at the tracks. To believe that Nicole had died such a heinous death tore at his soul. For a moment, his guilt overwhelmed him and Holt swore under his breath, cursing himself to eternal damnation. Nicole dead, a victim of Enchantress's lethal jaws? But even as he formed the thought, something inside Holt denied the possibility. It conflicted too strongly with what he knew of the tigress and man-eaters in general. Holt took a deep breath, concentrating on piecing together the evidence before him.

Holt threw the cloth down. "Something's not right here."

Nursoo turned Holt aside and whispered, "Sahib, perhaps you and I should search to find the girl." He looked over his shoulder at Marshall. "Before the uncle sees . . ."

What's left of her, Holt finished the gruesome phrase. "Those are Enchantress's pug marks," he said, as if the identity of the tiger itself should refute the evidence of such a grisly death. "She's no man-eater."

Nursoo nodded; only he and Holt were familiar enough with the tigress to recognize her tracks. "It would be difficult to believe this is the doing of the white tigress. She is young, healthy—she would have no need to seek human flesh." Nursoo met Holt's gaze. "But, Holt sahib, there are other reasons a tiger kills."

Holt tensed, knowing Nursoo spoke the truth. If Enchantress had come upon Nicole unexpectedly, she might have killed in self-defense. Many tigers had developed a taste for man's flesh in such a manner. Or if game were scarce and Enchantress had trouble feeding her cubs, she might hunt anything. Nicole had left without her gun. An unarmed woman was easy prey.

"No!" Holt shoved past Nursoo. "Your niece is alive, Mr. Marshall. She needs our help and I intend to find her."

"But the jacket . . . ?" Marshall asked.

"It could mean anything," Holt said. "She could have been cut and the sleeve torn off by a bush—"

"Dear God, Atley, this is low, even for you," the commissioner called out from behind him. "You'll have this man believing there's hope, just to save yourself the trouble of his recriminations." Holt swung around to face Ratcliffe. "You'll not escape blame," the commissioner continued. "Not this time. This is your doing. You led the girl here—

only you and God know for what purpose—and *you* left her here to die by this vile creature's jaws!"

"That's enough, Commissioner."

"Not nearly! She's dead. Tell him how you let her die! Explain to that poor man what torture you let his niece suffer! How long did that poor girl live? How much of herself did she watch the tiger devour, before she found the blessed relief of death?"

"Shut up. Shut the hell up! You don't know what you're talking about."

The commissioner picked up the sleeve Holt had thrown to the ground. He shoved the blood-soaked linen at Holt. "I speak of this, Mr. Atley. Proof of your heinous crimes against women!" The commissioner's eyes narrowed and he added under his breath, "And I've no doubt blood was shed before you left the girl," he hissed. "The blood of her innocence!"

Ratcliffe's accuracy stunned Holt. Though the man had been dead wrong about Holt's relationship with his wife, in this Holt could not argue with him. His hands shook; the blood pulsed in his veins as if it would rise up and choke him. Ratcliffe had deduced Holt's dishonor toward the innocent Nicole, but Holt refused to believe the man's prediction of her death.

"You're wrong, Commissioner." Wrapping his fingers around his rifle until his knuckles turned white, Holt stared at Ratcliffe. He thought of the commissioner's deranged jealousy and what it had led the British official to do. "I told you before. You're wrong about a lot of things."

"Wrong, am I?" Again, he waved the bloodied sleeve like a trophy. "At last, I have the means to destroy you, Atley. When I'm finished with you, your days as a respected forest officer will be nothing more than memories. I'm just sorry that a young girl had to die to accomplish your demise." Spinning about on his heel, the commissioner picked his way through the jungle. He, at least, had ended his search for Nicole.

Holt turned back to Marshall. Though he could not refute he'd harmed Nicole deeply, Holt would not accept her death. Not, as Ratcliffe suggested, because he would save himself recriminations. Those he deserved well and good. He would always carry the weight of her suffering on his conscience. But he couldn't quite live with the thought that Nicole was gone. Until he had irrefutable evidence to prove it, he would not give up his search.

"Mr. Marshall." Holt hefted the rifle strap to his shoulder. "Nicole is out there, somewhere, alive. You can return to Askot with the commissioner and seek his style of vengeance, or you can help me find her. Which will it be?"

Marcus Marshall stared blankly ahead. The night had been long and tiring for all. Nicole's uncle showed the strain of their sleepless twenty-four hours more vividly than the others. As if just coming out of his stupor, he raised his eyes to Holt.

"That night," he said in a voice made hoarse by hours of shouting and lack of rest. "After my fight with my niece. You had some strong words for me, Atley." At Holt's nod, Marshall continued, "At the time, I thought you were right. Tell me now, sir, and it had best be the *bloody* truth. What did you show my niece? When you took her down the gorge, what did you find there that you could show no other, but that would make my Nick happy?"

Holt examined the older man, saw the weary lines of his face, the lifeless look of suffering in his eyes. He had to believe the man's search for Enchantress was over, that his words would not harm the tigress and her cubs.

"I showed her the white tigress," Holt answered. The man's eyes widened just a fraction—in surprise or calculation, Holt could not guess. "At her den with her cubs," he continued. "I thought if Nicole could see the cubs with their mother, she would understand her hesitation to shoot. I wanted her to know that her decision not to kill such a magnificent animal was right. That, instead of scorn, her actions deserved admiration."

Marshall stared at Holt for a moment, then lowered his head and nodded. Silently, he raised his hand to his eyes and brushed away a tear. He then squared his shoulders and looked up at Holt. With a sobering sniff, he said, "Let's find her, shall we? I don't want Nick spending another night out here alone."

Holt closed his eyes with relief, then turned to Nursoo beside him. The two exchanged a meaningful glance. If there was ever anyone Holt would want tracking beside him under the circumstances, it was Nursoo. The Hindu smiled, and Holt knew he shared his thoughts.

"Let's go," Holt said.

Together the three men followed the pug marks. Each scanned the area ahead, alert for clues of Nicole's fate. They hadn't traveled far when they found what they were looking for.

Holt knelt down beside Nursoo. He heard Marcus Marshall's intake of breath when the old man caught sight of the shredded jacket on the ground in front of them. But while the Indian and Marshall examined the remnants of Nicole's coat, torn as if by the claws of a tiger, Holt stared elsewhere.

"Over there." He motioned Nursoo to where the dirt was blood-soaked. Both *shikarees* studied the ground, and Holt pointed to the drag marks in the soil. "I'd say Nicole has put on a little weight. What do you think?"

Nursoo nodded. Stepping over to a thorn bush, he retrieved a few short strands of brown. He rubbed the coarse-looking hairs between his fingers then held them out for Holt to see. "Sambar."

Holt picked up similar strands in the dirt beside the reddish circle in the earth. They felt sticky with blood. As if reading each other's minds, both hunters began to scour the area.

"What is it?" Marshall called, following first Holt and then Nursoo. "What are you looking for?"

"For something that is notably absent." Holt turned to

Nursoo. Under the Hindu's impressive mustache stretched a toothy grin.

"The young memsahib's prints," Nursoo finished for Holt.

"Not a trace of Nicole's footprints anywhere, yet there's plenty of blood and pug marks. And here," Holt pointed to where the dirt had been gently brushed as if passed over with a branch of leaves. "I'd say whoever *was* here, went to a good deal of trouble to hide their tracks and the deer's."

"Sahib!" Nursoo called from twenty paces away where he'd gone to search while Holt spoke to Marshall. Immediately both men raced to the Indian guide.

On the ground, imbedded deep and clear in a soft patch of clay, were two hoof prints.

"Very sloppy." Holt's elation at Nicole's escape from Enchantress's jaws vanished, replaced by a gnawing fear. He met the Indian guide's worried gaze.

"The memsahib, she is in great danger."

"Wait one minute," Marshall said in stunned disbelief. "Are you saying someone has abducted Nicole?"

"Mr. Marshall, I'm almost certain she was taken. Whoever rode that horse left those pieces of Nicole's coat next to a set of pug marks, near a fresh kill. They went to a great deal of trouble to remove the kill, probably a sambar weighing two hundred pounds, and brushed away the deer tracks and their own. Except for these two prints." Holt pointed to the hoof marks in the clay. "I don't think Nicole was ever here. There are no tracks, no signs of her—not even a strand of hair—only a bloodied and torn jacket. In this province, revenge or the disappearance of an incompliant wife is often attributed to a mysterious tiger. Normally, no questions are asked." Holt turned to Marshall. "I think someone was counting on that."

"But why would anyone want to take Nick?"

Why indeed, Holt thought. Though he knew his judgment could be clouded by his distaste for the man, he couldn't help but think of Harrington's odd flight from Askot. While they'd spent the night searching for Nicole, they'd not once come across the British lord. Why hadn't Harrington come with them and where the hell was the man?

An odd reference knocked at the back of his mind. Relying on his instincts, Holt closed his eyes, bringing the message forward until he recalled Harrington's odd bargain with Morgan for the tigress. He again heard snatches of the conversation between the Brit and the Irishman.

That's a real tigress yer after, Morgan had said. *A real tigress.* Holt had assumed they spoke of Enchantress. But Nursoo had thought . . .

"Bloody hell." Holt whipped around to face Nursoo. "The Korku, the highland raja—Nursoo, do you remember saying Harrington wasn't after Enchantress?"

Nursoo's eyes darkened. "The British lord was to deliver a present of great worth to the Korku's raja, a wedding present . . . you thought the white tigress. But I"—he pressed his lips together—"I believed it was a woman."

"Dear God, this is crazy," Holt whispered, shaking his head in disbelief. Harrington couldn't have such nefarious plans for Nicole. Yet, instinctively, Holt knew the phrase ringing in his head had significance.

"And it is normal for the British lord to deal with such as Morgan and the Korku?" Nursoo argued. "The ancient hill tribes of the south never have contact with the British sahibs."

"Just a moment, gentlemen." The pitch of Marshall's voice seemed to increase with each word. "Are you implying Lord Harrington had something to do with this?"

"The man Harrington hired for your hunt, Donald Morgan, he's a pretty seedy character. How well do you know Lord Harrington?"

"He is an aristocrat, a lord of the realm," Marshall sputtered. "He wanted to marry Nick."

"Wanting to marry Nicole hardly qualifies him as a decent marriage prospect," Holt said, thinking of himself. "Come on, man. His family, his finances, his reputation—all

those things you Brits spout about incessantly—what of those?"

Marshall shook his head. "I don't know; let me think. I met him at the Chadwick's, then at White's." His voice rising in defense, he added, "For God's sake, he wanted to marry her from the first." Marshall looked up at Holt. "She was *twenty-one.* The girl had no other prospects."

"Nicole?" A seething anger began to build deep within Holt. "No one but Harrington courted her?"

"No." Marshall shook his head, then his face turned bright with color. "Don't you understand! You heard us argue about it. Didn't you realize? Nicole has Indian blood," he said, as if he'd just informed Holt that Nicky had leprosy. "Her grandmother was an *Indian.*" Again, he said the word as if it were some horrible flaw. "And she wouldn't let the thing die. She would talk to anyone about it . . . the men, they seemed disinterested. Then, after the Mutiny . . ."

Suddenly, Holt understood the curious look of pain he'd seen so often in Nicole's eyes and her need for reassurance. Dear Lord, the prejudices she'd had to live under, with only this hardened man to guide her. His anger raged again. "And to help things along," Holt added in a deadly soft voice, "to make her life really easy, you taught her how to be a man, and made her forget she was a woman."

The color drained from Marshall's face. "How dare you!" he said in a whisper. "Who are you to judge me like that? I was like a father to that girl. My Nick was the best!" Marshall struck his fist to his chest. "I *made* her the best she could be!"

Shaking his head, Holt said, "Not nearly, Mr. Marshall. Not nearly."

"Holt sahib." Nursoo placed a warning hand on Holt's shoulder. "He said the memsahib has Indian blood. Perhaps this is why she was taken?"

Nursoo's words seemed to suspend time for Holt. *She looks like a Rajput princess.* How many times had Holt

thought Nicole resembled Indian royalty? Yet, he'd always
discarded the possibility, even after overhearing her curious
argument with her uncle, because he'd believed the aristocratic Harrington would never wed someone of mixed
blood. But if Harrington had never intended to marry her?

That's a real tigress yer after, Morgan had said.

Holt turned to Marshall. "She wanted you to take her to
Rajputana. Who the hell is her Indian family?"

"I don't know!" Marshall shouted. "And I don't give a
damn."

"Well you better start thinking, old man, if you want us to
find Nicole. Who is her family?"

"I don't know, I tell you!" he shouted, exasperated. "I
suppose they must be in Rajputana somewhere. Her grandmother lived in some palace there."

"A Rajput of the plains," Nursoo whispered. "Then it *is*
the memsahib the Korku wanted."

"Listen, Marshall. Unlike in jolly old England, the blood
of a Rajput is prized here. Such women are protected and
coveted for their marriage value. If Nicole is related to an
important family, she could be of great value to a Korku
raja, claiming to have Rajput status."

"I don't know what you're talking about. Is this some
kind of white slavery?"

Holt nodded. "My guess is Nicole's halfway to the central
hills, on her way to becoming a bride or concubine to a
Korku raja."

"This is incredible." Marshall shook his head. "I'm not
sure I believe you. Are you suggesting Lord Harrington is
behind all this?"

"Why isn't he here looking for her? He's not familiar with
this area and yet he went off on his own to find her. 'You'll
ruin my plans for Nicole,' " Holt said, repeating Harrington's exact words before he'd left Askot. "A rather
strange way to look at one's betrothed." When he saw Marshall's jaw go slack in thought, Holt continued, "Harrington
doesn't strike me as the type who would marry someone

with Indian blood and you don't seem to know a hell of a lot about him. Add that to the fact the noble gentleman has completely disappeared, along with Nicole, and I think you get trouble."

"Dear God, what have I done?"

Holt placed both hands on the older man's shoulders, knowing what he was about to suggest would be difficult for Marshall to accept. "I'm going after Nicole."

"Of course. We must—"

Holt shook his head. "Not *we*, Mr. Marshall. I want you to go back to Almora. Nursoo will lead you there."

"But—"

Holt tightened his grip on the man's shoulders. "Mr. Marshall, if I'm right about what's happened to Nicole, if she's been abducted for a highland raja, I'll need to move fast. Alone."

The light in the brown eyes died as the fight left Marshall. He nodded. "Though it pains me to admit it, I'll only slow you down. Go then. And bring her back safely." Marshall grasped Holt's hand on his shoulder. "Don't let anything happen to her."

12

The silk veil fluttered against Nicky's cheek, covering her like a shroud. The *orhna's* gauzy material, weighted down by its thick trim of gold, trapped her breath hot against her mouth. Through its crimson pattern, Nicole saw Drew's look of satisfaction. The filmy cloth made his face appear red, as if tinted by a thin coat of blood.

"Beautiful, simply beautiful, my dear. The Thakur will be pleased."

Drew reached out to touch her cheek. Nicole struck his hand away with her bound ones. His lips curled and he grabbed her wrists, digging his fingers into the swollen flesh under the leather bindings. For the past three weeks, she'd been forced to wear the punishing straps night and day. She'd had her hands free for only a few hours a day as the group had crossed the jungle forests of the Kumaon and the desert plains to their destination, the central highlands of India. After her second attempt and near escape in the *sal* forests at Jalapur, Drew had also bound her ankles. Trussed up like a brace of doves, Nicole had ridden the trail up the Mahadeo hills on horseback, dreading each day that brought her closer to the Korku viper's nest—the Puchmurree plateau.

Nicole winced as Drew pinched deeper into her skin. The cool gold jewelry she wore clamped like shackles around her wrists and ankles stung the cut and bruised flesh. With one hand, Drew lifted the veil off her face.

"I wanted one last look before you entered the seclusion

of the *zenana,* where only your husband will appreciate your beauty." His pale blue eyes, almost colorless in the noon sun, examined her like a prized cow. "Red truly does become you, Nicole. An appropriate color for a bride in India —the color of joy."

"The color of blood."

Drew's smile tightened at the corners of his mouth, but he ignored her remark. In the past three weeks, her baiting him had cost Nicole dearly. When he'd captured her after her first escape, Drew had beaten her nearly unconscious before he'd gained control of himself—but she would not cower before him in silence, despite her very real fears. She had found courage the night she had spent in the forest alone, enough, she hoped, to get her through this crisis as well.

"It really is too bad I couldn't deliver you unscathed." Still holding her wrists with one hand, he stroked her bruised cheek, making her skin crawl. The herbal-scented black paste the village women had applied to her lashes and eyes only emphasized the yellowing bruise he caressed, as did the *tika* mark of red powder on her forehead. "Let us hope the ceremony of consummation occurs under the cover of darkness," Drew said. "That way the Thakur will not be offended by these flaws."

"You bastard." Nicole shook the veil from her head. The silk fluttered to her feet and pooled on the ground between them like a puddle of red. "You think I'll docilely march to slaughter? That I'll give myself in marriage to this . . . this Thakur?" From behind her, Morgan grabbed her shoulders and pulled her away from Drew. "Your hill chief will soon find out he got no bargain in me," she threatened. "The first chance I get, Drew, I'll escape. And when I do, you'd best watch your back. For I'll not let you reap the benefits of your perfidy. I'll see you justly punished!"

"Nicole, my dear, you seem to forget the charming traditions of this country." Despite his polite words, there was a clear threat in Drew's voice. "Should you prove a recalcitrant wife, more likely than not you'll find pincers on your fingers and an exorcist pulling that lovely thick hair from your head to remove the evil spirits that possess you." He cupped her cheek and Nicky jerked her head away. Morgan yanked her back, clawing his fingers painfully into her arms.

"Nicole, darling," Drew continued in a honeyed voice, "we are in the heart of India, in hill country untouched by British hands. You'll never escape the life of the *zenana.* And for my delivery of you, a Rajput bride, the Thakur will repay me with what I desire most in this world—information that will help me find the secret location of Maharuta-l-Hind. Ten years I've waited." Drew's eyes attained a desperate gleam. "I have hocked everything I own, everything Nicole, and spent it looking for my dream city. Think of it, the legendary walled Maharuta-l-Hind, a city so magnificent as to be the fabled work of *jinns.*" His voice dropped, becoming soft and lilting. "A thousand temples lined its streets. Buried deep inside them will be gold deities with ruby eyes, silver idols embedded with sapphires purer than a mountain stream and more sparkling than diamonds. Not only will I be rich as Croesus, I will receive the recognition I *deserve.* I will go down in the annals of archeology as the man who made one of the greatest discoveries of our time!" He lifted her chin with the crook of his finger. "You see, Nicole, it truly is worth the risk."

Nicky twisted away from his touch. "May you rot in hell with your riches and fame!" She spit in his face.

Instantly, Morgan doubled the painful pressure on her shoulders, while Drew, like the aristocratic gentleman he'd always posed as, took out a white handkerchief from the pocket inside his hunting jacket and wiped the spittle off his cheek. Without a word, he lifted the red veil off the dirt and draped it once more over her face. "Take her away, Morgan. Before I ruin everything and kill the bitch."

Morgan pushed her to the saffron-colored palanquin and its bearers. A dozen beggarly looking Korkus dressed in patched, multicolored, quilted coats surrounded the enclosed litter. Belted at their hips with heavily embroidered yellow leather were various swords and daggers. Some retainers even carried matchlocks that appeared no less deadly for their antiquity. At the head of the motley group, beside one of two elephants adorned with a faded red and gold cloth, stood the Korku Indian in his familiar carmine coat. As Nicole watched, he grabbed the lead elephant's trunk and climbed atop the animal's neck like an experienced *mahout* ready to lead the parade up the hills to his Thakur's village. With a menacing look to Nicole, Drew followed the Korku and climbed inside the *howdah,* the basket strapped to the kneeling elephant's back.

Nicole almost tripped and fell to the ground when Morgan pushed her forward, making it clear he'd not stand for her dawdling. Once settled behind the bright orange curtains of the palanquin, she felt the litter rise off the ground and, like a boat in stormy seas, sway forward.

Though her hands were still bound before her, she managed to pull off the suffocating veil. She fell back against the pillows of the litter. A heavy lethargy weighted her limbs on the worn silk as if she'd expended her last burst of energy fighting Drew and Morgan. Despite all her efforts, the nights spent plotting her escapes, the days she'd argued and cajoled her abductors to free her, Drew's plans progressed toward success. That morning, the village women had bathed over three weeks of sweat and dirt from Nicky's hair and body, then, following Drew's instructions, had dressed her in a silk sari of the deepest ruby red. The gold choli they had made her wear beneath supported her breasts as effectively as any corset. They had colored her hands and feet with henna and covered her with hammered gold bangles and glass beads until Nicole felt like a sow ready for slaughter. Lying now against the pillows of the Thakur's palanquin, the strong scent of attar of roses nearly gagging her in the sultry heat, Nicole saw clear parallels between the destiny Drew had set for her and the fate of that pig.

As the company of servants marched up the red sandstone hills of the Mahadeo range, she thought of the cousin

Drew had told her of, Usha, who had killed herself rather than submit to the Korku raja. For Nicole, there could not be such an escape—her will to survive was too strong. Yet her mind was running out of alternatives. Again she calculated the chances of her plan succeeding. If she could convince the Thakur she came as his willing bride, she gambled that the guard set against her would be more lax and she could escape. She worried now she'd ruined her chances by her threats of escaping. Would Drew warn the raja of her intentions? And could she convince the jungle ruler otherwise without compromising herself when she could not speak a word of his language?

The tenuousness of her scheme did little to settle Nicole's fears in the hours that passed. The heat became almost unbearable behind the silk curtains of the palanquin, and Nicky thought she'd expire before she ever reached the Korku raja's village. But when the litter at last came to a halt, the pounding of her heart as the blood raced through her veins proved she was very much alive.

She heard voices shouting in Hindustani as well as the strange guttural dialect of the Korku. Nicole parted the saffron curtain an inch. Outside, the natives gathered around like circus spectators. The village women, dressed in white cotton mantles and blue skirts, the backs of which they had pulled up between their legs and tucked into the waistband at the front, stood in a group, staring and pointing at the palanquin as they spoke excitedly among themselves. Nicole thought sadly that if this were in fact a carnival, she, apparently, was the main spectacle.

A hand reached through the curtain and clamped around one of her arms. Nicole struggled until Drew emerged from beyond the silk barrier. Her heart skidded to her throat when she saw the Gurkha jungle knife in his hand.

"Put the veil back on, Nicole."

When she hesitated, Drew cursed her. Grabbing her wrists, he used the knife to cut through the leather thongs. Nicole pulled away and rubbed her chafed wrists as she stared at him warily. He jerked his head to the floor of the palanquin where the swathe of red silk lay. "The veil, Nicole."

Picking up the *orhna,* Nicole again covered her face with the gauzy cloth. Drew pulled her roughly from the litter and Nicole stumbled to where the Korku and Morgan stood waiting. Held securely between Drew and the Irishman, Nicky stared up the path where a beautiful white horse with silver trappings and its rider walked regally among the natives. The tall fair-skinned man atop the horse stood out among the shorter, ebony-skinned Korkus. He appeared young, no older than twenty-five. Unlike the natives around him, he was dressed regally in a brilliant turquoise jacket with a jeweled turban. Beside the horse strolled a Brahman, his ceremonial *dhoti* loincloth bagging to below his knees. The Brahman's head was shaved clean, except for a topknot at the crown. Bare chested, the high caste Indian wore a cord of twisted cotton from his left shoulder hanging down to his right hip. When Nicole looked back to the Thakur, she noticed he wore a similar cord.

"Look at him," Drew said snidely under his breath. "Your future husband, my dear. The offspring of some Rajput wanderer and his Korku whore. He surrounds himself with his ragamuffin servants and a bloodsucking Brahman, wearing the sacred thread of the twice born, the high caste Hindus, as if he were a true Rajput. But you can see the blood of his people in him, Nicole"—Drew stared down at her—"just as you can see the Rajput blood in you."

Nicky felt the rising fire at her cheeks, wishing she could speak to this Thakur and scream out the injustice being done to her. Drew's grip on her shoulder tightened as he turned back to the young lordling. "Don't be fooled by the tall, fair appearance. Look at the prominent jaw, his thickened lips." Drew chuckled softly. "He probably purchased the sacred thread he wears from the Brahman beside him." He smiled coldly. "Blue blood is a marketable commodity here in the hills. Like the Herald's College back home, the

Brahmans are the final arbiters of the purity of caste. The cost is high to ennoble the race, but our friend here is willing to meet the price." He leaned closely to her ear and whispered in a cloying voice, "That's why he, like many of his kind, seeks a bride with higher claims to Rajput descent. I plan to pass you off as just such a woman."

"Drew, if there is anything decent left in you—"

Drew's thumb dug painfully into the soft skin above her collarbone. "Be quiet," he said softly.

The Thakur dismounted before them and Nicky felt her hands begin to shake until she clasped them together. Behind the screen of the veil, everything looked distant and dreamlike, as if she could just pinch her arm and wake up in her bed back at Eldridge Manor. The Korku beside Morgan stepped forward and, pressing three fingers to his forehead in a *salaam,* bowed to the Thakur. From the glances the chieftain gave her, Nicole assumed the Korku spoke of her to his raja.

Suddenly, the Brahman responded harshly in Hindustani to something the Korku said. A look of stunned surprise crossed Drew's face as he stepped forward to intervene. But the Korku motioned him back, then grabbed the knife he carried at his belt and pointed its tip at Drew. In short barking words, he held the group's attention. The Korku accented his message in Hindustani with frequent jabs of his dagger at Drew, who stepped back out of range and raised his hands in a gesture of conciliation. The Korku's speech became heated. While Nicole could not understand his words, from his face and gestures she could see he spoke against both the Brahman and Drew. Drew and Morgan interrupted frequently, as if refuting the Korku's words, but then the native said something that seemed to rob the very words from their mouths.

Nicole glanced from Morgan to Drew, anxious for an explanation. A clear threat hung in the air. Drew stared at the Korku as if transfixed. When the Korku's gaze fell on her, his eyes narrowed in cunning. He said something slowly and distinctly, speaking as if he were pronouncing her the vilest creature on God's earth.

Morgan cocked his rifle and raised it. Before he could fire, he arched his back, and a strange choking sound came from deep within his throat. His rifle slipped from his hands and, stiff as bamboo, he fell forward, landing on his stomach in the dirt. The teak handle of a native dagger jutted out from the middle of his back.

Drew grabbed the jungle knife from his boot, but immediately half a dozen natives were upon him, restraining him.

"You bitch!" Drew's pale eyes glowed with the fury in his voice. "You rutting whore! You've ruined everything!"

After a sharp command from the raja, the natives silenced the struggling Drew with blows to his head and stomach. Nicole looked for a means to escape, but saw that she too was surrounded. She watched the raja as he stepped forward. He stood before her, his dark eyes narrowed with disdain, his very look a criticism. Taking the veil in one hand he ripped it from her face. When he saw her, his eyes grew wide, then calculating. For a moment he stared at her, then he reached up and cupped her chin in his hand. He said something to the Korku. The native responded with a smile that displayed his yellowed, feral teeth. Again, the Brahman objected, but a comment from the raja silenced him. With one final command, the Thakur mounted his horse and left the smiling Korku with Nicole.

From beside her, Drew began to chuckle and then laugh, a venomous cackle that made the skin of her arms tingle. Nicole turned and watched as Drew received another blow to his face. Still chuckling, he wiped the blood from the corner of his mouth with his shoulder and looked up to Nicole.

"Congratulations, my dear," he said. "You've just been demoted from wife to whore."

Nicole stared at the silk-covered wattle and daub walls. Compared to the thirty odd huts that made up the Korku village, the raja's fenced and multi-roomed home appeared palatial. She waited in what she assumed was the main chamber. Brightly colored pillows and rugs covered the floor. A large silver water pipe, a *hookah,* stood next to the velvet ottoman-style chaise where Nicole sat. The room was a collage of reds and yellows, giving it an exotic and festive ambiance that clashed with Nicole's feelings of anxiety.

A young servant girl entered and left a silver tray of sweetmeats and wine on a small carved teak table. The room smelled of attar of roses, the same suffocating scent the native women had rubbed into Nicole's hair that morning. With an odd feeling of nostalgia, she recalled the soft scent of orchids and rhododendrons carried by the evening breezes in the Kumaon forests. An almost chilling sense of loss filled her as she reexperienced the pungent odor of the crushed thyme when she and Holt had made love. What she had thought would become painful reminders of Holt's betrayal were now cherished memories of happier times. No matter what became of her here in the Korku village, she had at least experienced love once.

Through the doorway entered the Thakur, the village chieftain who called himself a raja. His extraordinary height as well as enigmatic dark eyes held Nicole. He was indeed a handsome man. His white turban framed a strong face with an aquiline nose and heavy jet brows. He wore his beard parted and combed against his cheeks. Picking up the two silver goblets of wine that the servant girl had already poured, he gave one to Nicole. With a smile he raised the cup to his lips and gestured for Nicole to do the same.

Nicky nearly choked when she gulped down what was not wine, but rather a strong liquor. The Thakur merely smiled and seated himself at her side on the divan. He downed the liquid as if it were water before replacing the cup on the tray beside them. In a low voice, he whispered in Hindustani in Nicky's ear. Prickles of fear traveled up her spine as he wrapped one arm around her shoulders.

"I don't suppose you understand English?" she asked. "If

you did, I could explain that I don't think I can do what you think we're going to do."

He took up her hand and placed a kiss on the inside of her palm.

"That's answer enough," she said to herself.

The Thakur took her cup from her and placed it next to his on the silver tray. He leaned forward until Nicole fell against the red velvet of the divan. He hovered over her, his chest only inches from her own. Again, he said something in a soothing voice, as if trying to calm a frightened doe. Even though Nicole did not understand him, his words had a smooth rhythmic lilt that spoke of pleasure. With the back of her hand, he caressed first her hair and then her cheek, before he placed his lips against the side of her neck.

Nicole's breath became trapped in her lungs. If she ever wanted to see her family and home again, she would lie quietly and submit to the Thakur's lovemaking. Judging from the look he'd given her before he'd ripped away her veil, he was not a compassionate man who would set her free if aware of her plight. She recalled Usha, her cousin, and her untimely death. Submitting now could be Nicole's only means of escape—of surviving.

Yet, despite her words of logic, when the Thakur's breath rasped harshly in his throat, she wanted desperately to push him off. When he reached for her breasts, she batted his hands off her, trying to move out from beneath him. He stopped his gentle kisses and sat up, looking at Nicole as she rose as well. His dark eyes watched her as she shook her head. She hoped he understood her reluctance.

The Thakur's lips curled into a snarl. He pushed Nicole back onto the divan and dove on top of her. Through the material of her choli, he pinched her breasts as he bit the skin at her neck. Instinctively, Nicole fought back, trying to shove him off her. The powerful odor of attar of roses choked her and she gasped for breath as she fought. He seemed to find her efforts amusing and continued to claw at her clothing. When he reached up under the sari, moving the silk material of her skirt aside to grab at her thigh, Nicole cried out for him to stop. The intimate act she'd reveled in with Holt was something she couldn't repeat with this stranger, no matter what the consequences.

She bucked against the tall Thakur. He ripped her choli in half, parting the material. Taking one breast in his hand he pinched her, hard, making Nicole cry out in pain. He laughed then bit her other breast viciously, enough so that Nicole knew he'd drawn blood. She screamed, over and over. The air seemed too thick with the smell of roses to breathe. The Thakur reached between her legs, careful to avoid her kicks, and rubbed the most intimate part of her body. Tears streamed down her face as she choked back her sobs. He pinched her intimately, then laughed at her cries. Nicole fought, but his strength was phenomenal. When he plunged his fingers inside her, she felt as if she were being split apart the pain was so intense. Screaming out of control, she raked both hands down the Thakur's cheeks leaving twin trails of blood.

The Thakur rolled off the divan to his feet, shouting as he held his hands against his cheeks. Immediately, four guards streamed into the room, followed by the Korku in his red coat. The Thakur continued to yell, pointing to Nicole, who held the torn choli closed over her breast. A guard instantly pulled her off the divan and pushed her to the Korku. His harsh dark eyes glowing with hate, the Korku back-handed her with enough force that, had she not been forcibly held by two guards, she would have been thrown to the ground. After another strangled command from the Thakur, Nicole was dragged from the room.

By the light of the dying sun, Nicole picked her way barefoot up the rock-strewn path. With one hand, she held closed the torn choli bodice, clutching the sari to her with the other. The white and naked branches of the trees stretched like ghostly claws as she stepped over the fetid and rotting plants creeping across the path. Korkus armed with daggers and matchlocks walked on either side of her, herding her forward.

Before the sun disappeared on the horizon, the troupe reached a tree-enclosed glade. At its center raged a gigantic bonfire. Nicole stared, transfixed by the ghoulish sight in the glade. Like grasping fingers, the flames of the bonfire licked skyward, reaching high above the Korkus' heads. Beside the fire, natives with their axes worked on the carcasses of two sambar deer, cutting strips of meat and handing them to waiting Korkus. Everywhere Nicole looked, the trees in the glade were covered with long strips of flesh. Meat hung from their limbs like decorative garlands. The smell of raw and half-cooked deer filled the air and Nicole gagged as she saw several Korkus swallowing bits of meat as if they were great delicacies.

The encouraging jabs of her escorts urged her past the bloody glade to where a crack in the cliffs created a natural aisle. With sterile interest, she noted the majestic entryway to the gorge. The green velvet of the mango grove stretched like a canopy leading three hundred feet back to an enormous, red sandstone cave. There, at the entrance, waited the Thakur with his horse; the Korku and Brahman stood like two sentinels at his sides. Nicole felt her fear rekindle with the ferocity of the bonfire in the glade. At the Thakur's signal, the natives grabbed hold of her arms and dragged her forward.

The cave opened through a natural arch in the cliff, running straight into the bowels of the hill. At the entrance was a conical black rock, ominously covered with vermillion. Straight above the stone, on the lofty cliff, a flag flapped curiously in the evening breeze, its white surface made luminous by the rising moon. Forced into the cave by the Korkus, Nicole stepped into a stream at the threshold. The water oozed red where a thin dross from minerals percolated up from the ground. The red, sticky water covered her feet as she waded across.

Inside the cave, Nicole stared in astonishment at the

torch-lit walls of an enormous hall. Every inch of stone appeared carved with images. Hundreds of faces, each representing some figure of Hindu worship, peered down at her from their lofty heights. At the end of the immense cave was a giant pillar, rounded at the top, with the image of a man carved on the front. At the base of the pillar were offerings of rice, flowers, and grass.

"Well, well. It looks like you're not even worth a decent tumble, Nicole."

Nicky turned to where Drew sat, his hands tied and resting on his knees as he leaned against the wall of the cave. In the eerie light of the torches, she could see that he had been badly beaten. His normally immaculate clothing was torn and filthy.

Drew looked pointedly at her bodice. "Don't tell me you refused his royal highness here?" He nodded his head to the Korku raja behind her. With a guttural command from their lord, the natives pushed her toward Drew. Losing her balance, Nicole landed on his lap.

"You always were overly affectionate, my dear." Drew laughed as Nicole scrambled off him, feeling as polluted by Drew's touch as the Thakur's. "I should have guessed at certain propensities."

"You're disgusting." Nicole clutched the sari to her. When she tried to get farther away, a menacing wave of the guard's dagger made it clear she should stay put. She sat beside Drew against the wall.

"Come, Nicole. Why so prickly? I only speak the truth. Did you not open your thighs willingly for Atley?" When she looked sharply at Drew, he chuckled. "Surprised? Oh yes, I know all about the little interlude in the glade. You see, dear Nicole—you had an audience. Our Korku friend followed you and witnessed your tender coupling. Just think of it"—his voice fell low and taunting—"as you lay beneath that rutting bastard, moaning your lust, the Korku's dark eyes watched you—"

"Shut up, Drew."

"Disturbing, isn't it?" His voice regained its hard edge. "Well, it wasn't nearly as disconcerting as finding out I hadn't delivered the virgin bride I had promised." Drew looked back to where the Korku waited at the mouth of the cave. "He staged it well, our little friend did, waiting until the last possible moment to tell his tales. But whatever he tried to accomplish against the Brahman, he did not succeed. As you can see, despite the Brahman's poor advice to marry you"—Drew nodded to where the Thakur lay prostrate before the pillar, the Brahman chanting beside him— "it's the Brahman who controls our lordling. He has the power to give the Thakur the thing he wants most in this world—support of his Rajput status."

"That's why they killed Morgan?" Nicole asked. "That's why I was no longer . . . acceptable. Good coin for your vile exchange? Because that . . . that . . . Korku animal recounted some sordid tale about me?" When Drew nodded, Nicole began to laugh, an ugly sound that made Drew stare at her as if she had gone mad.

"You mean it's not true?"

"Oh no, Drew," she said, almost relishing the look of distaste on his face. "It most certainly is true. But don't you see?" she asked. "You who love irony so well. Don't *you* understand?" Abruptly, Nicole's laughter ceased. With all the venom she had dammed inside her, she told him, "You wanted to . . . oh, let's see. What was that charming phrase you used? *'Plow* me?' But you managed to restrain yourself, so that you could purchase your dream city with the blood of my virginity. And all the while you were delivering tarnished goods." Echoing the words he'd spoken when he'd abducted her, she said, "I find that *ironic* indeed."

Nicole leaned her head against her knees, away from the frigid stone. She stared at the faces of the carved images and wrapped her bare arms around herself. The walls felt cold enough to suck away the last of her warmth. Everything about the cave chilled her—everything seemed foreign and distant. Sadly, she thought of her dreams of finding her family in Rajputana. India had turned fearsome and horrible in her eyes, and she wished herself home.

Gripping her arms with her hands, digging her nails into her cold flesh, she thought of how both Drew and her quest had betrayed her. "To think I actually felt disloyal to you." She whispered the words, almost to herself, then stared hard at the man beside her. The light of the torches reflected off the deep mountain stream that cut through the cave, making his face shine almost iridescently. "You never cared a farthing for the living hell your schemes would bring me." She heard her voice rise in anger, then shook her head, wondering if anger were even worth the effort. "I thought you loved me. Quite pathetic isn't it?" She glanced up to watch his reaction, but saw none. His cold colorless eyes just stared back at her. "Here's more of your 'delicious irony,' Drew. It was *you* who gave me the opportunity to fall in love with Holt Atley. I would have remained faithful to you —my *noble* fiancé—if you would have paid but one whit of attention to me during this trip. You're a fool, Drew." Falling back against the stone, she added, "We both are."

"*Touché,* my dear," he responded softly. "*Touché.*"

"They're going to kill us, aren't they? Like they killed Morgan."

"Oh much better than that. We are to be sacrifices to their goddess, Kali." Drew pointed his bound hands to a particularly large carving on the cave wall depicting a four-armed woman. Her teeth bared in a ghastly snarl and her tongue protruding, she carried in her hands what looked like a sword, a shield, a strangling noose, and a gigantic hand severed at the wrist. Around her neck was a strand of skulls; girding her loins, a string of more severed hands.

"Is she not charming?" Drew asked. "The great goddess Kali, consort to Siva the Destroyer, the god carved on that giant phallus our Thakur worships so diligently."

Nicole started when Drew named what the beautifully carved pillar represented. With a wicked grin, he continued,

"Oh, the *lingas* are quite tastefully done. One would hardly guess they represent such a scandalous subject by their form. But no matter how stylized, it is a phallus"—his eyes traveled up the carved *linga* —"a cosmic pillar, the symbol of the male power to create." Drew turned back to Nicole. "But our interest is with the great god's consort, the fearsome Kali." Drew gestured to the four-armed figure carved into the wall. "The story goes that the demon Raktavija's blood produced a thousand more of himself with each drop that touched the earth. Kali vanquished him by piercing him with a spear and drinking his blood before it ever reached the ground. But she developed a great thirst through her feat, and now her followers must appease that appetite with blood—the blood of human sacrifice." He leaned back against the stone wall and sighed. "No simple knife in the back for us, I'm afraid. We are to make the 'Manful Leap,' Nicole. If we boldly cast ourselves off that sheer cliff outside, above the sacred brook, all our sins shall be forgiven and we shall be married to angels."

As Nicole watched, mesmerized by his tale, Drew's eyes narrowed, as if he were concentrating on his words, actually calculating their chances of attaining heaven. "Ah, but if we hesitate, if we should prove fainthearted, then our lot shall be in hell. And if we should turn back in terror"—his head lolled to the side and he smiled sadly at Nicole—"I'm sure we'll get a helpful . . . push."

13

Nicole stared at the line of torches that lit the side of the craggy ridge. In the black of night, the points of light appeared like a stairwell to the heavens. At the very top of the footpath, a white flag flickered like a moonlit beacon, drawing Nicole's eyes to the cliff's sacrificial rock. Icy fingers feathered across her skin as she thought about the "Manful Leap" that would catapult her two hundred feet to the blood-stained rock below.

The revelers from the glade now circled a roaring fire set in front of the cave entrance. They danced to the beat of drums, their bodies jumping in a series of frenzied steps to the siren call of the bamboo pipes. Silhouettes crossed the backdrop of fire like dark ghosts, the shadows at their feet flitting in and out of the flames. The orange glow of the fire reflected off ebony faces, illuminating them into demonic masks.

"Not much of a religious ceremony, wouldn't you say?" Drew asked over the din of chanting natives. "I believe this little affair has something to do with a pestilence that threatens the community. Ergo, a celebration to pacify their gods —and an excuse to get bloody foxed."

Just outside the ring of the fire, a few feet away from the grove of mangoes, Nicole and Drew sat tied up on the ground together. The Korkus had set them back to back, their hands strapped between them.

"There is a certain beauty to their wildness," she said.

Drew snorted. "Barbaric aborigines. Look at them,

gorged on meat and pulling at the pot of *mhowa* spirit. The lot of them will be out cold by morning. Only the Thakur, under the watchful eyes of the Brahman, I might add, seems concerned with ceremonial purity."

Nicole lifted her face to the evening's breeze. She could feel the same whisper of breath at the curve of her breasts where the choli gaped open. It was nice; she was beyond feelings of modesty. "It never ceases to amaze me how free you are with your judgments, Drew. As if you believe yourself a cut above these people."

"Nicole, dear. *I* find it hard to believe that you could have any sympathy for a group of heathens who are about to make us living sacrifices."

"I thought you an adamant supporter of human sacrifice, Drew. Or was I an exception to your normally strict code against moral turpitude?"

He laughed. "Why Nicole, your scorn sounds almost adult. What happened to the child who just a few weeks ago looked at me with such little-girl eyes, beseeching my acceptance like an adoring daughter? Has the cub grown into a tigress so quickly?"

"My sudden maturity," Nicole said bitterly, "was forced upon me."

After a marked silence, Drew answered, "We all pay the price for our mistakes, Nicole."

"And what was my mistake? Other than believing a single word that passed your lips?"

"Living in a fantasy. Believing that dreams could come true. You should have been suspicious of a gentleman of my background choosing to marry a woman of Indian blood. Your sisters married merchants—rich ones, but of the working class just the same. Did you believe yourself so special as to attract the interest of the gentry—you, who with your dark looks practically herald your Rajput blood?" When Nicole tried to interrupt him, Drew's voice overrode hers. "Your sin, Nicole, was your naiveté—just as mine was greed."

"I am the daughter of a viscount! My father didn't count my mother's Indian blood against her."

"Then he was quite a stupid man, my dear, for look what it has gotten you. Ah," Drew said, his tone light as if with anticipation, "at last. It appears our hosts have not completely forgotten us."

His red coat discarded, the Korku walked toward them dressed in only a *dhoti* loincloth. The sweat gleamed on his near-black chest and in his hands, he carried a wooden bowl.

"Drink deep, Nicole," Drew instructed. "The *mhowa* spirits will make the night pass all the quicker."

The Korku kneeled before her, his jagged teeth catching the firelight. He held the wooden bowl to her lips. Nicole hesitated. Though she was thirsty and tempted to numb the hours ahead, she was equally unwilling to drink anything offered by the Korku.

"Go ahead," Drew encouraged. "It's really not so bad. Almost like whiskey if you get a good batch."

Nicole met the shining dark eyes of the Korku with misgiving. This man could do her only harm.

"Are you sure it's safe to drink?" she asked Drew.

"I certainly plan to indulge. It may be the last thing I enjoy in this lifetime."

The Korku shoved the bowl to her lips again, but still Nicole refused to drink. Drew said something to the Indian in the native's tongue and the bowl was quickly offered to him.

Nicole strained to watch Drew over her shoulder. From the little she could see, he appeared to take a rather long pull before leaning back against her. "There, Nicole. Perfectly safe. Quite delicious actually. Wouldn't mind a bit more myself"—Nicole could almost hear the smile in his voice—"but I thought it ungentlemanly to drain the bowl."

Nicky took a tentative sip. The liquor tasted a little harsher than the one she'd drunk at the Thakur's house, with a slightly bitter aftertaste. Before she was ready, the

Korku tipped the bowl to her lips again, so that some of the liquid spilled down her chin. With an angry jerk, he grabbed the back of her neck and forced her to drink another swallow.

The *mhowa* burned its trail down her throat to her stomach. Closing her eyes, Nicole leaned back, achingly tired. Drew was right about her sins. At twenty-one, she had expected life to grant her a fairy tale ending, like those in the stories her brother had read to her when she was a child. She'd acted naively in her desires to marry, first Drew, and then Holt. Well, she'd learned. Somewhere on the trail after her abduction, she had exorcized such simpleminded innocence from her heart.

A tingling warmth spread across her fingers and up her arms. Nicole's heart began to flutter like a bird's wings. "I feel strange, Drew." She narrowed her eyes on the fire, trying to clear her blurring vision. "Am I drunk already?"

"At a guess, Nicole, I would say there was enough poison in that cup to drug a troop."

"Poison?"

"*Datura.* A favorite with these people in their rituals. You'll have marvelous hallucinations I understand. Of course, if you take too much, as I'm afraid you probably have, it's quite toxic."

"Poison? Doesn't seem—" Nicole licked her lips. Her throat burned and the inside of her mouth felt dry as ashes. She was having trouble concentrating on making her mouth form the right sounds ". . . doesn't seem to . . . affect you."

"Of course not. I only pretended to drink. Not a drop of the vile liquid passed my lips. I plan to keep my wits about me until the bitter end, in case there should be a chance to escape."

"You . . . you *told* me to drink."

"I would like to say I acted for purely humanitarian motives. A merciful way to die and all that. However, under the circumstances, I'll admit I have absolutely no interest in your escape. Quite the opposite, considering what you know about me."

Nicole tried to swallow. The blood pounded at her temples with the force of a mallet against the native's goatskin drums. "Drew." The figures dancing before the fire blurred into inky spots weaving before the orange background of fire. "Drew—don't think . . . *ever hated* you . . . as—as much as *now.*"

His chuckles ricocheted off the sandstone walls of the gorge. Each wave of sound intensified, increasing in volume until his laughter became the only sound she heard. She fought viciously against her restraints, until a native cut them. She held her hands to her ears, trying to protect herself from the deafening noise. Drew's cackles boomed louder, but then a distracting sensitivity made her drop her hands to her lap. As if she'd never felt her own skin, she concentrated on her fingers, rubbing her thumb against each tip, tracing the edges of her nails. Staring at the sky, she saw the stars glow as if they would explode into a thousand brilliant fireworks to color the night.

Deep inside her, the jungle drums absorbed the cadence of Drew's laughter. They continued to beat, catching the rhythm of her heart, threatening to snuff it out as well. The pounding increased—thump, thump . . . thump, thump—faster and faster, until she thought her heart would explode with the stars.

Her skin was on fire. Wanting desperately to rip her clothes from her body, she clawed at the sari. But then she saw the gargoylelike faces leering at her, watching her as they relished her pain. She screamed.

The black void of the night devoured the sound until there remained only dark, abyssal silence. Nicole searched around her for Drew and the Korkus. Gone. It was as if her surroundings had been a colorful backdrop on stage at the Drury Lane Theater. Her cries had ripped an opening in the canvas and she'd stepped through to the blackened stage behind. She could see nothing. The only sound she heard was a faint rhythmic beat—the sound of a heart.

The heartbeat grew louder, closer. She searched out its source, saw him. An enormous yellow tiger. Stalking her.

Even as she thought of escape, the cat's tremendous power drew her. His graceful stride showed his strength, a force that called to her. His eyes were even more mesmerizing. They shone a deep green, the color of the leaves above and the grass beneath her.

Nicole shook her head, trying to clear her blurring vision. It was no longer a tiger prowling toward her but Holt. He held a hand out to her and she backed away, afraid of his touch and her response to it—yet, she ached to reach out and grasp the proffered hand just the same. He smiled, that seductive twist of his lips that made her forget reason. Tentatively, she reached out for his hand.

Holt vanished. In his place, the green-eyed tiger examined her with a hungry look. Nicole sucked in her breath as an unexpected wave of desire swept over her. She stared down at her hands; they glowed with a blazing light in the moonlight, pearly, iridescent. Shocked, she held her hands out, closing and opening her fingers. White. Whiter still. *Has the cub grown into a tigress . . . tigress . . . tigress.*

The night grew day-bright and achingly familiar. She examined her challenger through new eyes. Rebelling against the yellow tiger's magnetic scent, she growled deep in her throat. She assumed a defensive stance. He approached, confident of his welcome.

With a vicious snarl, she attacked. Both reared up on their hind legs. She growled and clawed until the yellow tiger gently boxed her neck and head in a mock battle. She sensed he didn't want to hurt her, and her fears receded, but the burning hunger remained.

He stood still, watching her, offering no welcome—but no resistance either. He seemed to challenge her to retreat, almost taunting her with the opportunity. She paced around him warily. When she moved in closer, he stretched out lazily, waiting for her. His scent, the incredible perfume of his body, made her dizzy. She circled closer.

Hesitantly, she nuzzled him. It was just a touch, a soft one, but with it came the raging call. Boldly, she rubbed her body against his, brushing against his flanks until almost every inch of him had touched her. He caressed her with his cheek, then licked her face until an agony of desire welled up inside her. With the moves of her body, she tried to convey her message. Stay, stay with me, love. Her neck entwined with his as she brushed his cheek, watching the stark contrast of her white against his yellow—

Noise, everywhere noise. She looked around her, startled out of her passion. The yellow tiger was gone and dark menacing creatures, standing upright on their hind legs, surrounded her. They crept forward, inching toward her. From their hands came the grating noises, the sharp clanging of metal, the harsh beating of drums. She raised her claws and pulled back her ears, snarling. They skulked forward, unafraid, shouting at her. She lunged. A few stepped back, but soon they converged on her with their deafening noise. She backed away in terror.

They drove her, forcing her up the mountainside, up a path lined with fire. She leaped and charged, finding no escape until she made the exhausting climb to the top of the cliff. Panting, she looked behind her. The dark animals pursued her. She stared at the cliff across the chasm, anxious to reach a place of safety. Crouching down on all fours, she prepared to jump.

14

"For God's sake, Nicole"—Holt grabbed frantically at her ankle and wrist—"don't jump!"

Standing on a shallow ridge directly beneath the cliff's edge, Holt used all his power to control the direction of Nicole's fall. As she leaped with incredible strength, he guided her into his arms, hoping to catch her. Outnumbered by the Korkus, he'd been waiting until the natives drank themselves into oblivion before making his move. But when he'd seen the Korkus drive her up the path, he'd quickly changed his plans. He'd climbed up the opposite side to a small saddle of rock below the precipice, ready to steer Nicole to safety. But he'd never anticipated her jump. As her body slammed into his, Holt lost his footing. The two cascaded down the face of the cliff together.

Ten feet below, Holt landed with an agonizing thud on one of the many small ledges where clumps of brush grew on the cliff's face. He absorbed the shock of Nicole's body hitting the ground with his. One arm wrapped around Nicole, he clawed at the ground with his free hand, grabbing roots and grasses. He managed to stop them from rolling forward—inches from the edge.

Straddling him, Nicole began scratching his face with her nails, snarling like an animal until he grabbed both her wrists. "Stop it, Nicole! It's me. Holt."

She stared at him as if just recognizing him. For the first time, Holt got a good look at her face. The moonlight showed a yellow bruise under her right eye, while the left was covered by a red mark of a fresh blow. The bodice under the torn sari was ripped open, revealing angry crescent marks on her breasts. Her lips were cut and bleeding, the pupils of her eyes dilated to the point where only a thin band of gold remained of their color.

He groaned and hugged her to him. "What have they done to you?"

A shot clipped a rock two feet away, sending a spray of gravel into the air. Holt pulled Nicole up flat against the cliff wall. Taking her hand, he edged across the narrow shelf of rock. "Keep low. We're getting out of here."

Amidst a bombardment of gunfire and spears, Holt and Nicole ducked and charged across the face of the mountain to its darkened half. To Holt, Nicole's balance appeared extraordinary as she made her way down the rocky terrain without a stumble. The two descended into the gorge, the Korkus fast on their heels. In the tangled nest of mango trees at the base, Holt tried to lose their pursuers, dodging around trees, seeking the denser foliage at the heart of the grove.

When the sound of enraged Korkus robbed of their sacrificial victim became only a dim threat, Holt stopped. Panting for breath, he leaned against the trunk of a mango with Nicole.

Suddenly, Nicole stilled.

"What is it?" he whispered. "What do you see?"

Like an animal sensing danger, she backed away, glancing left then right. Holt watched her lift her face to the air as if seeking the direction of their threat. She froze, then jerked her head around to their right. Almost too late, Holt saw the black figure out of the corner of his eye. He ducked. The Korku's dagger flew past his shoulder. Thunk. It sank deep into the tree behind him.

Before Holt regained his feet, the Korku had Nicole by the throat. The Indian held her against his naked chest, his forearm in a choking grip across her neck, the point of his short sword tucked under her chin.

Still crouched on the ground, Holt met Nicole's wild eyes. The rim of white surrounding her enlarged pupils reminded him of a cornered animal. He forced himself to concentrate on the Korku behind her, pushing back his fears for Nicole in order to save her. His hunter's instincts sharpened into focus as he watched the native's rabid grin. His pulse slowed. Holt's hand inched down to his boot. His eyes turned back to Nicole's. In the scanty moonlight that percolated through the leaves, he watched her carefully. Nicole glanced down to his hand at his boot.

With a shout that sounded like a strangled roar, Nicole bit into the Korku's wrist. The native dropped his sword. Releasing Nicole, he grabbed his arm with a high-pitched scream that echoed down the gorge. Nicole ducked to the ground and Holt sent his knife straight into the native's chest. The Korku clutched the hilt. His face froze in a mask of agony and he fell to the dirt, driving the blade deeper into his heart.

Holt grabbed Nicole's hand and zigzagged through the trees ahead. When he thought it safe, he doubled back and headed west. Once they cleared the grove, he found his way easily to the small cave, one of many that riddled the hillside, where he'd left his horse and gear.

On seeing Holt, the horse gave a soft whinny. Nicole stopped and when he pulled her forward, she jerked her hand out of Holt's.

"Come on, Nicky, we're going inside." He urged her toward the mouth of the cave. Incredibly, she backed away, hissing.

"I know what's wrong, kid," he said to her in what he hoped was a soothing voice despite his own panic. "I know something they gave you is making you feel strange. But you have to trust me." She didn't answer, too frightened by the pony. Thank goodness he'd left Jani with Nursoo at Askot. If the pony upset Nicole, the lemur would certainly have been trouble as well. Holt could see she wasn't budging until he got the horse out of her way.

When he had Nicole safely hidden behind a clump of bamboo, Holt led the pony into the cavern. He'd searched out this particular cave as a secure resting place, suspecting that Nicole might not be in any condition to travel after he rescued her. Its narrow opening hidden by tall bamboo, the cave expanded into myriad passages, some of which flowed into a spacious underground chamber. Once he had the horse secured and a candle lit, Holt went back for Nicole. She huddled in the bamboo, hunched against the hillside. The glazed look in her eyes gripped his heart and Holt picked her up, cradling her against him as he maneuvered down the cave passage. She lay still in his arms, too still. Her breath against his neck was her only sign of life.

Inside the chamber, he spread a blanket for Nicole in a niche opposite the horse. After making her comfortable, Holt picked up the lighted candle off a protruding rock to bring it closer. The candle slipped from his hand. It sputtered out against the cool earth. Holt swore under his breath, trying to calm his shaking hands as he relit it. The image of Nicole's hissing flashed in and out of his mind. It took several tries before the candle set to flame.

Grabbing his leather sack and water bag off the saddle horn, Holt knelt down in front of her. Opening the bag, he took out a small tin of ointment he kept in his kit and a chamois cloth, then poured water onto the cloth. As he wiped the dirt from her face, her skin burned through the chamois—but it was the seductively large pupils, narrowing minimally in the candlelight, that worried him most.

"Listen to me, Nicky." He swabbed her brow and cheek with frantic swipes, trying to steady his voice as he spoke. "You drank or ate something that's making you feel sick. We have to find a way to help you."

Her glazed eyes stared ahead unseeing.

"Talk to me, Nicky. Tell me what happened. Nicole, can you hear me?" Holt grabbed her hands and pulled her to her knees in front of him, cupping her face in his palms. "Answer me, dammit!"

A thin line of red was smeared across her lips—the Korku's blood. As he watched, she touched the tip of her tongue to the blood.

"Don't, Nick," Holt whispered. He took her chin in his hands and wiped the blood off with the chamois. "Don't," he repeated. Then, to himself, "Don't panic, Atley—not now."

The last of the blood gone, Holt coaxed, "Tell me what hurts most? If I know what hurts, maybe I can help you."

Nicole watched him, wide eyed, but in silence. Holt brushed her hair back off her face, trying to soothe her. He could only guess at what visions haunted her in her obviously drugged state. From the enlarged pupils and feverish look, he feared the worst—*datura,* an alkaloid like belladonna used by the natives. As an officer of the British government, he'd often investigated poisonings by roving hill gangs of their robbery victims—and, he'd seen people die from too much of the drug.

A thundering fear beat in his chest. This was nothing like the leopard and the cobra. He couldn't grab his gun and shoot the *datura* from her veins. Poisoned. Spunky, childlike Nicky, warm, sensuous Nicole—she was too special. She couldn't die. He wouldn't let her.

"To hell and back, Nicky," he vowed to himself as she watched him through unfocused eyes. "I'm prepared to follow you that far. God help me, I feel as if I already have. So don't even think of leaving me."

Holt opened the tin and dipped the chamois into the cleansing ointment. With soft pats of the cloth, he dabbed at the cuts and scratches, feeling every blemish like a laceration on his soul, knowing that these were only the minor scars Nicole wore from her abduction.

Your mistakes, Atley. The poor kid's paying for your mistakes.

Holt cursed under his breath. As he had for the three weeks he'd been following Nicole's trail, he wished he had the power to turn back time, to undo the harm he'd caused her by his callous treatment of her. He'd failed Nicky miserably—stripped her of her virginity, then of her pride when he'd told her he'd not marry her. If he'd bothered to reason with her, explain his situation in India so she could understand, she would never have run away, leaving herself easy pickings for Harrington. And how often had he failed her since? He'd lost valuable time trying to find her exact route to the central highlands where the Korkus made their home. In the weeks he'd tried to intercept Harrington, he'd slept little, mostly in the saddle as he rode. He'd crammed food in his mouth only when he thought he'd drop from hunger if he didn't stop to eat. And still, he'd been too late—too late, at least, to spare her the abuse she'd suffered. Now he must wait and see if he was too late to save her life.

Nicole looked past him frantically, imprisoned by the demons in her head. Both her hands came up to his face as if in supplication. Holt leaned forward, making it easier for her to reach him, then started when she raked the tips of her nails softly down his cheek.

"Are you still with me, Nicky?" he asked softly.

She stared ahead, intent on the feel of his skin under her fingertips.

"What is it?" He rubbed his thumb across her bruised lips. "Do you want to tell me something?"

She bit his thumb lightly, then licked the pad with her warm tongue. There was a feverish glow, almost a hot look of desire in her eyes. As she rubbed her cheek against his hand, like a tigress against the flank of its mate, a surge of heat filled his loins.

Holt shook his head. "Feels too good, Nicky." He pushed her away. "And honestly, I don't deserve it."

With as much detachment as he could muster, he continued to clean her cuts and scratches. When he passed the chamois down a long gash across her bared throat, her breath came in soft puffs of delight. The gesture seemed incredibly feline.

"Lady, you're scaring me," he whispered.

The lids of Nicole's eyes drooped, creating a picture of sensual pleasure. Another whisper of breath escaped her lips in a soft chuffing sound. Holt held his breath. He knew that sound; had watched tigers chuff in the jungle, a noise he'd determined was some sort of greeting for the big cats. What the hell was going on?

More than a little disturbed, Holt concentrated on the gash along the slim curve of her throat. He'd never seen anyone act like this, half awake and half dreaming. She was there, in front of him, touching him, and yet . . . she was not.

Her skin felt hot to the touch as he swabbed her throat. He feared that, whatever the *datura's* cycle, Nicole would get worse before she got better. He pulled the material of the sari aside an inch to finish cleaning her cut, careful not to expose too much of her lovely shoulder. With a shrug, Nicole continued the movement of the material, slipping it off her. Holt's mouth went dry as she pulled the choli apart, baring her breast to him. A dreamy look in her darkened eyes, she took his hand and placed the chamois he held on one of the many half-moon marks that marred the white skin.

An incredible mixture of rage and desire welled up within him. Rage for the obvious abuse she had suffered, desire for the soft line of her breast and the rose nipple. As he watched, she let the choli fall with her sari to the ground. Holt sat back on his heels, remaining perfectly still. Nicole reached out to caress his chest. Her nails grazed his skin through his shirt. Holt closed his eyes, for one moment letting himself enjoy the feel of her hand stroking his chest. She nuzzled his neck, seeming to enjoy his scent. His arms came around her and he touched the supple skin under his fingers as he ran his hand up her back. He sucked in his breath when Nicole's tongue lapped at his neck, gliding a trail up to his lips. She flicked her tongue along the edge of his mouth then traced his lips.

Holt opened his mouth to her kiss. With an anguished cry

he folded her into his embrace and kissed her with all the feeling he had pent up inside himself.

"Come back to me, love," he whispered between frantic kisses, hoping through passion to make her react. "I'm here, Nicole. Feel me here with you."

Holt pushed her gently to the ground. He nibbled on her ear, breathed in the sweet scent of roses at her neck as she rubbed her body against his until every inch seemed to have touched and stroked him. He kissed the bruise under her eye, then cherished with his tongue and lips the cuts on her breasts as if he could wipe away the pain with his caress. His hand reached up and cupped one breast as she arched beneath him.

His palm filled with the warm weight of her breast, Holt stopped. "What the hell am I doing, Nicky?" He looked down at her. Her eyes were closed and her breathing ragged. He shook his head. "I can't help you this way."

Leaning up on his elbows above her, he brushed back the fine hairs that curled around her cheeks until she opened her eyes for him. "God knows I don't deserve it," he said softly, "but if you could say one word, just a word, to show me you know where you are—who you are." He traced his fingers up the curve of her cheek, then leaned forward and whispered in her ear, "Come back to me, Nicky. Please, come back to me. Listen to me, love. You're not safe where you are. I'm holding you here in my arms, and you're not safe. And it's killing me. It's killing me. Because I don't know how to help you"—he hugged her tightly—"and I'm scared."

Suddenly she froze. Arching against him, she threw her head back. Holt's breath lodged in his throat as he watched her eyes dart right, center, then right again.

"Nicky? Dammit, Nicky, don't do this!"

She gagged. Then stiffened. Her eyes rolled up into her head as she fell limply into his arms.

15

The light of morning did not reach the dark recesses of the cave. The glowing stub of a candle remained Holt's only light as he tended Nicole, but he had seen the red streaks of dawn staining the sandstone cliffs of the gorge when he'd gone out for more water the hour before. Holding the edge of the chamois to her mouth, he let a few drops seep past Nicole's cracked lips. As he watched, she swallowed in her sleep. He rocked back on his heels and yawned, rubbing his hand over his bare chest. He'd given up his shirt and the spare he'd brought for Nicole's use. Stretching, he eased muscles that burned with every move.

Nicole moaned. Immediately, Holt dropped down beside her.

"Daddy," she said in a soft, childish voice, her head rocking back and forth in troubled sleep. "Daddy . . . I look like Daddy."

"That's right, Nicky," he whispered close to her ear as he had done all night, reassuring her. "Just like him. The spitting image."

She seemed to find comfort in his words and nestled down against the shirt he'd wadded into a pillow. Her hand at her cheek uncurled so that the backs of her fingers gently brushed her pinkened skin, making her look childishly young. Poor kid, Holt thought. She seemed tormented even in her dreams. He pressed his larger palm over hers, lacing their fingers together as she continued to sleep.

Staring at their linked hands, he wondered at how easily

her small one fit in his—as if she were a part of him. Overnight, he felt as if she had become just that. It didn't seem to count that they'd joined before. Oh, he could still remember her sweet kisses and the feel of her hips pressing against his, but he also remembered the misunderstandings that followed. Seeing her sick and delirious, raging at her to fight whatever demons tortured her, feeling her pain like a bullet in his gut, those experiences had brought them closer than any joining for sexual pleasure.

Holt raked his free hand through his mussed hair. The bargains he'd struck last night—with any god who would listen. He'd never touch her again. He'd get her home and keep her safe from him and this wretched land. *Take me, not the kid. She's faultless* . . . anything to bring her back to consciousness. But when her breathing had stilled and the tone had returned to her muscles, he still could not rest. Even in his state of exhaustion, he'd waited and watched, hoping to see the flash of gold hidden beneath her slightly bruised eyelids.

"I bet your dad was real handsome, Nicky," Holt said, taking a wisp of hair and rubbing it between his fingers. "He sired one hell of a beauty." He picked up the long strand and stared at its length. "You know, I don't think I ever told you how much I like your hair." He laid the ebony tendril along the edge of the shirt he'd put on her after discarding the torn sari, and watched it coil down to her hips. He'd taken great pleasure in combing her hair when she'd finally drifted off into a safe sleep. Thick, black as a moonless night, it was truly extraordinary. Trailing a finger down the wavy skein of black, he shook his head. "Who'd of thought something so small as you could grow this much hair?"

He'd been talking to himself all night, keeping himself company against his fears for Nicole. He'd told her just about everything he knew concerning India, his interest in zoology and native customs. Then, late into the night, as he'd almost drifted off to sleep beside her, he'd talked about himself. He'd even told her about his mother, explaining to

Nicole how important it was for her to go home, as his mother had eventually done. Now more than ever, he could see she wasn't safe in India.

With his thumb, he caressed the silky skin at the corner of her eye and thought of ways to make her understand how much her safety meant to him. How responsible he felt for having failed to protect her. The best thing he could do for her now was to get her back to her home in England—not to propose marriage as she'd asked. But would she think him bigoted like her uncle? Would she believe he'd rejected her ancestry when her Indian blood only made her more seductive to Holt—a man half-British, half-American, who'd given up everything to stay in this country?

Holt wound a strand of hair around his finger thoughtfully. It smelled pleasantly of attar of roses, a popular scent with the native women, but he preferred the lily scent she usually wore.

How to make her understand why he had to leave her? He watched the ebony wave uncoil and slip from his finger. How could he explain something he found so hard to accept?

Holt sat back against the cave wall, still holding her hand as if letting go would allow her to slip again into unconsciousness. Nicole moaned, clutching his fingers tighter, and he whispered reassurances. The cycle, repeated as it had been through the night, triggered in him a memory, and the words he had searched for came.

"You know, kid. Sometimes, when I'm out charting, I come across a deer or a monkey that's been hurt, and I try my damnedest to save them. Sometimes I do . . . but not always." One at a time, he pressed her fingers over his palm. "I've seen lots of things die. I've seen my share of men die in war, a few from hunting accidents. I've even seen people I care about die. My father—he was killed by a leopard. I wasn't there when it happened, but I arrived soon afterwards. He was still alive, and in a lot of pain. That cat had ripped him up pretty badly." He smoothed his thumb over

her torn nails. "It was hard, *really* hard, watching him die."
He struggled to keep his voice steady. "I buried him in
Lucknow. Did I tell you that already?" He squeezed her
hand. "Yeah, I think I did."

All the pain Holt had experienced at the death of each of
his parents rose up inside him. He saw Nicole again as she'd
appeared last night, stiff as bamboo, her eyes darting around
the room. He leaned closer. "It's a part of this country,
dying. But you see, Nicky, it's like this. I've never been
terrified by it before . . . not like I was last night. Even
with my father." He kissed her parted lips, then her forehead, rubbing his mouth lightly across her warm skin.
"Hey, lady," he whispered. "Don't scare me like that
again."

He barely felt the flutter of lashes against his chin. When
the soft tickle registered, Holt looked down and watched
Nicky strain to open her eyes. For one beat, his heart
stopped and he gripped her hand. "Nicky?"

Nicole stared at the portrait on the wall as it grew smaller
and smaller. She raced to the mantel, jumping to reach the
frame before it disappeared completely. Everyone laughed
and pointed as she tried to keep the painting of her father
from fading away. It was about the size of her doll when
Nicky managed to knock it off the wall and into her hands.
Even as she held it, the frame shrunk until it turned into her
grandmother's locket. Nicky closed both hands around the
miniature, trying desperately to keep it from disappearing as
well. But when she opened her hands, they were empty. Her
uncle and Keane stood with her sisters and mother huddled
beside them, watching her sadly, shaking their heads as if to
say she should never have tried to stop the portrait from
disappearing. She started to explain how important the picture was to her, but when she saw the tiger all words left
her.

It didn't seem possible that a tiger could prowl across the
salon, padding over the red and green scenery of one of her
mother's prized Aubussons, but the animal appeared quite

at ease with its elegant surroundings. It came closer and she stretched her hand out to pet it. The beautiful cat rubbed against her palm, and she smiled threading her fingers through its fur. The beginnings of something pleasant unfurled inside her. But then the tiger snarled and bit her hand. A piercing pain slashed through her. "No, don't. Please, Holt . . ."

"I'm here, Nicole."

Roses. Everywhere, the smell of roses. Attar of roses in suffocating strength. The raja kissing her—biting her breasts, hurting her. She tried to kick him away, but he grabbed her hands and held her down, laughing at her . . . Drew laughing at her . . . attar of roses.

"Nicole! Dammit, Nicole. Wake up!"

She sat bolt upright, and immediately regretted it. Every muscle screamed with pain. She closed her eyes and fell back against Holt's arms. Like a rifle with a double load of powder, her head felt ready to explode. When she opened her eyes, Holt sat beside her, propping her up. He looked as tired as she felt and breathed in heavy pants. When she saw his eyes, she immediately thought of the tiger.

"You kissed me."

Holt heard the deadened voice. Acid pain boiled inside him. She had no idea what they'd been through together. To her, everything would be just as it was before. She would remember only their fights. She might even despise him for his betrayal in the glade at Askot. Unlike Holt, she hadn't experienced the hellish night that would always make him feel as if she were a part of him. She'd slept right through their struggle for life together.

"Yes. I kissed you." And as he said it, he knew it was the last time he'd have that privilege.

Nicole had thought it was the raja kissing her. Had it been a dream? The shrinking portrait and the disappearing locket? The locket. Nicole stared down at the man's shirt she wore. She'd been stripped of everything she owned by Drew when he'd had the village women prepare her for the raja. Her grandmother's gold locket was gone. She was alone now. Truly alone.

A powerful scent wafted to her. Roses. Attar of roses. Gagging, she held her hand up to her mouth.

"Nicole? Are you all right?"

"Water." She tried to stand, but her legs buckled.

"Wait a minute." He helped her back to the blanket. "Take it easy."

She gulped a couple of breaths, trying to still her roiling stomach. Her surroundings finally registered. A cool dark cave that gave their voices a slight echo, a candle melted almost to the rock it sat on, giving off a stingy glow, a horse pawing the ground across the cave. Focusing on Holt, she realized he was bare chested. Somehow, the impropriety of it didn't spark a response. She simply stared down at the shirt that covered her to her knees and tucked her legs beneath her.

"Drew—the Korkus?" She crossed her arms around herself. "What happened?"

"That bastard, Harrington, escaped when the Korkus chased you up the hillside. The natives are long gone as well." He gave her a curious stare. "You don't remember anything?"

She shook her head, trying to push back the wall of fog around her memories. Slowly, images paraded through her mind. Meat hanging from trees. Dark bodies undulating to the drums—Drew laughing—attar of roses.

"Please." Nicole rose up on her knees. The room grew blurry and she lowered her head, feeling the blood rush back. "Please, get me some water. I need water."

He'd expected strange behavior, some disorientation. All these were symptoms of the drug she'd been given—nausea was common. He'd just have to help her through it as best he could. At least she knew who she was. "Nicky, look"— he rocked back on his heels and reached for the water bag— "if you just—"

"No, no—not to drink!" She slapped the skin away. "I need . . . to bathe."

Holt grabbed the bag before all its water spilled. A bath was the last thing she needed. "Look, lady. You try to take a bath right now and you'll find yourself on your backside with your head spinning—"

Every bit of color drained from her face and she lunged forward, retching. Holt grabbed her, and held her tightly, supporting her as her body heaved. The scene reminded him powerfully of the first time they'd met.

"Please." Her voice was almost a sob, and it hurt him to hear it catch like that. "It makes me sick to smell myself."

"Okay," he said softly, holding her from behind. "All right. You want water? I'll get it for you. But do me a favor and rest here for a bit."

Settling Nicole on the blanket, Holt used the indentation in a rock like a basin, filling it with the water from the skin. When he returned with more, Nicole was kneeling over the rock, wetting her hair. He dropped the water bag beside her and leaned up against the wall next to his pack. Looking down, he saw she'd opened it. Silently, he watched as she lathered her hair with soap. She didn't ask any more questions: How they'd gotten here; how he'd found her. Nothing. It was as if none of that mattered anymore. She just scrubbed and scrubbed.

"You're going to rip it out by the roots if you keep doing that."

For a moment, she looked like she was actually contemplating the prospect. But instead she finished rinsing, then held a lock of hair to her nose. Shaking his head, Holt turned back to his pack, searching for his spare pants.

"I want to go home," she said abruptly.

"I thought we'd wait here a day or so." He tossed her the pants, then hunted for something to anchor them around Nicky's slim waist. "Until you get your traveling legs."

"I'm fine. We can leave right now."

Holt stopped his rifling. "We're safe here, Nicky," he said gently. "The Korkus won't be back."

Staring straight ahead as she braided her wet hair, she didn't seem to hear the words he'd meant to be comforting. "I want to leave. No more waiting."

Holt frowned. At that moment, she seemed as distant as the Kumaon, as cool as the rock surrounding them. "Okay, kid. Whatever you say."

Holt watched her pick at her food. You'd think he'd served her bugs the way she examined every bite, as if searching for feelers and legs. Two days of travel, and the kid had hardly touched food. She looked so tiny, frail even. The pair of pants and shirt he'd given her practically swallowed her up.

Holt took a bite of stew and chewed. He could have stuffed a piece of wood in his mouth for all he cared. What had happened to Nicole during the three weeks he'd searched for her? She acted so strangely now, as if she had no needs, no wants. Even food was superfluous. She talked only when spoken to, stared straight ahead as she rode in front of him on the pony, never showing any interest in the dramatic scenery of the sandstone hills. Her behavior was so unlike the girl who'd shot question after question at him as they'd ridden down the gorge at Askot that it gave him the chills. It seemed as if she was tucked up inside herself—like the black curls she'd wadded up inside the brim of the slouch hat he'd given her for protection against the sun. The only thing she showed any interest in was bathing. Over the past two days, he couldn't remember seeing her hair dry. It was either hidden under the hat, or freshly washed and still wet.

Across the fire, she lifted her fork, grimaced, then lowered it without taking a bite. With lazy strokes, she pushed the stew across the tin plate.

"You might try putting some of that in your mouth instead of decorating your plate with it."

Silence.

Holt dropped his fork against the plate with a tinny clank. "Look, is there something wrong with the food? You don't like stew?"

She edged a few lumps together with her fork. "It's fine."

"For God's sake, Nicole. The stuff's not—" *Poisoned.* Suddenly, he understood. She couldn't forget the poisoning she'd suffered at the hands of the Korkus. She was *afraid* to eat.

Holt stood and emptied his plate into the fire. He felt utterly powerless to help her. "I'll see to the horse."

His lips pressed together to bite back any further comment, he led the pony through the abandoned village toward a mud and grass shed at the rear. He was acting like an absolute fool. He had no right to be angry at Nicole because she wouldn't eat. His anger couldn't help her.

Holt tied the pony's reins and watched it devour a handful of sweet grass. He stroked the horse's mane and gave its withers a pat. If Nicole were an animal, he'd know what she needed—to be held and nurtured. He'd whisper to her softly and smooth her hair as he'd done the night she'd been given the *datura.* He'd hold her against his chest, keep her warm, make her feel safe . . .

Holt turned, punching the daub and wattle walls in frustration. The horse startled and a chunk of the mud mixture crumbled to the floor. Dammit, why couldn't he get through to her? He was a man who'd gained the trust of wild animals. Why couldn't he reach the one woman he cared for so blasted much!

You had her trust once—and you betrayed it.

Holt shook his head. Could she ever trust him again? What could he do to help the silent woman back there if she didn't? She wasn't Nicky, dammit—just her shell.

Seeing that the horse had enough fodder for the night, Holt backed out of the shed. Outside, he lit a *bidi* cigarette, and stared up at the moon as if the answers to his questions could be found in the dark, star-studded heavens. He remembered how difficult it had been to gain Jani's trust. At first, the lemur had refused to eat anything he offered, bananas, leaves, even insects he'd painstakingly captured alive. He'd stayed awake nights, drifting off to sleep with his hand extended and holding tempting food. After two days of being confined with him in his house, Jani had finally scurried out from beneath his bed and taken a piece of fruit from his hand. Each day, the animal had stayed longer within his reach, until one day she had crawled up onto his lap and fallen asleep. Once he'd gained Jani's trust, the lemur had flourished. Couldn't he do the same for Nicole?

He ground out the cigarette beneath his boot heel. He damn well planned to try.

Back at the campfire, he found only embers burning low and bright. Nicky was nowhere in sight.

"Nicole?" Holt swallowed his panic. Looking down, he saw her plate filled with food she'd not eaten. She'd dodged him before and Holt knew from past experience the girl could be tricky if she didn't want to be found. In the moonlight, he scanned the village square, searching among the ten odd huts that still remained standing, but saw nothing of Nicole. He raced to the hut where she'd put her blanket, thinking perhaps she'd been tired and had gone to bed. The hut was as empty as when they'd arrived. Hating the anxiety, the instant dread that rose up each time she was out of his sight, Holt ran toward the stream, hoping she'd gone there to wash up after supper.

He found her kneeling by the edge of the brook. In her hand, his hunting knife gleamed with light reflecting off the water. As she slashed tufts of her hair, she grunted with the effort of sawing through the thick tresses.

He ran to her and dropped down beside her. "What the hell are you doing!" He snatched the knife out of her hand. She lunged for it, but he held it out of her reach.

"Give it back. Give me back the knife!"

Holt flung the blade from him and grabbed Nicole's shoulders. He gripped her chin between his fingers, making her hold still. Tears bordered her gold eyes. For the first time since she'd woken that day in the cave, he saw emotion on her face: anger, defiance—and something edging on despair.

He touched the hair she'd sliced off. The jagged edges of the one swag hung unevenly above her shoulder while the rest flowed past her hips. Holt dug his fingers into her skin, knowing he was hurting her but unable to check his anger. He'd washed and combed that hair. Stroked it when he'd thought she was dying—twined it through his fingers when they'd made love.

"How could you do it?" He looked at the mats of curls around them. He could see clumps circling like dark lilies in the river's currents. "How could you mutilate yourself like this?" He threaded his fingers through the shortened strands, feeling their loss deeply. "What's the matter with you?" He grabbed her shoulders and shook her. "What the hell's happening to you? Are you crazy?"

"Yes!" she screamed, cuffing his hands off her. "Yes, damn you! Yes!"

She threw herself on him, pummeling him with her fists. Holt pushed her down and they rolled one over the other to the river's edge. Nicole crawled out from under him, groping for the knife on the grass inches out of reach. Holt grabbed her legs and pulled her away, but she flipped onto her back and kicked him in the chest with both feet. Losing his grip, he fell backwards into the water.

When he waded back to the shore, Nicole stood on the grass, panting for breath, her knuckles white around the blade handle.

"I can't stand it anymore," she screamed at him. "It's making me ill, I tell you." Holt stared at her as she shook her head wildly. "It's making me sick! Can't you see that? I can't eat; I can't sleep. The smell. I can't stop the smell." She covered her eyes with the back of one hand, and a deep, shuddering sob escaped her lips. She fell to her knees, the hand clutching the knife slack at her side. "I try to wash it away. But I . . . I can't! No matter how hard I try, I *still* smell it."

He walked carefully toward her, stopping a few feet away. "Smell what, Nicky?" He knelt down and smoothed his hand over hers, then pulled it from her face so he could see her eyes. "What do you smell?"

"Roses. Attar of roses." Her words came in jarring sobs. "They put it in my hair—for the raja. I have . . . to get rid . . . of the smell. Oh God, Holt. Help me." She reached out to him, the knife still in her hand. "Please . . . help me."

Holt wrapped her in his arms. Her body shook against him and tears stung his eyes. It was on the tip of his tongue to explain that her hair didn't smell like roses, not anymore, not since the first time she'd washed it back at the cave. But what good would it do to confirm her fears about her sanity —even if he shared them?

"Shhh." He hugged her tighter, pressing his hands to her back. "Hand me the knife, *bacchi.* I'll help you."

He took the blade and faced her midnight hair. A swatch at the side had been hacked up to her shoulder. He reached to stroke it like a wound that needed soothing, but stopped. Instead, with the knife he sliced through the first handful. He continued to cut, up past her shoulders, trying to even up the ends she'd mercilessly slashed. Kneeling in front of him, she cried the entire time, but he sensed they were tears of release. Whatever had happened to her, the smell of roses in her hair was a painful reminder. He thought of the half-moon bruises on her breasts. Of course, there would be memories. Bad ones.

As he trimmed off the last piece, he tossed it in the stream. It was only hair, after all. He watched it float away until it disappeared, then turned his attention back to Nicole.

Holding her shoulders, he brought her around and cupped her face in his hands. She looked slightly boyish with her shorn curls, but her wide gold eyes appeared larger than ever. As he studied her, she smiled, a small, rather fragile smile. To Holt she'd never looked more beautiful.

"I'm not through," he said. She nodded, then sniffed. "I'll be right back. You stay put, *bacchi*."

He found the sliver of soap buried at the bottom of his saddlebag. It had been a gift from Maralys. She'd teased him about smelling like his horse when he returned from charting expeditions, and he'd always bathed with the sandalwood bar for her. Since she'd gone back to England, he used it rarely; the Nat Gypsy women cared only about the scent of your money. But he still enjoyed the fragrant soap on occasion—a reminder of happier times. It would come in handy now. With it, he would wipe out more than the smell of roses; he planned to dispel a few nightmares as well.

He knelt down before her at the edge of the stream. Taking her hand, he placed the soap in her palm then wrapped her fingers around it like a treasure. He guided her hand up to her nose, so she could smell its powerful scent. "We're going to take a bath, *bacchi*. And I promise, you'll not smell the roses again."

Slowly, so she could stop him, he reached for the buttons of the *kurta* shirt she wore. When he saw her stiffen, he rested his palms on her shoulders, then caressed her skin with one finger, drawing a trail along the sweep of her neck to the graceful curve of her ear. He leaned close, and whispered, "Did he kiss you, *bacchi*?" Gently, he placed his lips on the sensitive skin behind her earlobe. She shuddered.

"No . . . I mean, yes. Yes, he did."

"You mean, he didn't kiss you like this." Holt pressed his lips lightly on the tip of her chin, then traced his opened mouth across her skin. She tasted clean, fresh as river water. His mouth hovered over hers so that their lips barely touched and they shared a breath. "He didn't kiss you like you were precious, so valuable, he'd rather die than cause you harm."

She shook her head and Holt felt the soft curls brush against his cheek. He brought his hands up to her face and tilted her head back so her gold eyes shone with tears and moonlight. Looking down on her, sketching small circles on her cheeks with his thumbs, he asked, "Did he touch you, *bacchi?*" He placed one hand lightly over her breast, then more firmly. He watched her close her eyes and a tear slip down her cheek as she bit her bottom lip. Tracing the nipple of her breast with his thumb, he felt her rise to his touch beneath the cotton. "Did he touch you like this?"

"No." She started weeping, her eyes still closed. "He hurt me. He *wanted* to hurt me."

"Nicky," he whispered, hugging her tightly. "Nicky, I won't hurt you. *Shhh,* don't cry, my heart. I won't let anyone hurt you again."

With a low groan, she reached up and twisted her fingers through his hair. Holt bent down and matched his lips to hers, kissing her with the tenderness he'd bottled up for her. She met his kisses with the frenzied energy she'd used when cutting her hair, clutching at him, her desperation communicated by every touch.

"No, Nicky." He pushed her away gently, holding her so he could see her face. "Not like this."

She reached for him, but he placed a hand firmly on her shoulder. Nicky stilled, watching him with wide, pleading eyes. "I want to forget."

He undid the buttons of the *kurta,* then lifted it over her head. "You will, love. You will."

He stroked the warm skin of her exposed breasts. She'd lost weight, but her breasts were still as full and tempting as the first time he'd seen them. He took one in his hand, molding its softness in his palm and bending down to caress the nipple with his tongue. He heard her suck in her breath and he smiled. He felt the same.

He had a little trouble removing his wet clothes, but soon enough he faced her without them. She sat across from him, watching, until he reached for her pants. The too-large trousers slipped off her quickly. They knelt together, naked, bathed in the moonlight. He passed a hand over her shimmering skin, enjoying the feel and sight of her. "You're beautiful, *bacchi.*"

She looked pleased for a moment, then turned away. Holt frowned.

"Come on." He grabbed her hand and pulled her to her feet, toward the water. Once they both stood knee-deep in the stream, he placed both hands on her shoulders and pushed. "Sit."

She fell back with a splash and gasped. "It's cold!"

Holt heard the first hints of a strangled laugh. But she cut it off, looking embarrassed by the sound—as if she had no right to it.

Holt clipped the water with his hand, splashing her. "I know it's cold. I tested the waters first, thanks to you."

He soaked her mercilessly until she splashed back in defense and her laughter flowed as naturally as the stream. When they were both wet and gasping for breath, he took her hand and pulled her back into his embrace. Feeling the touch of her breasts against his chest, he lowered her into the water, holding her suspended over the current, kissing her face and neck as the water soaked her hair.

When he felt himself losing control, he sat her up, a little away from his touch. She sat cross-legged in the stream, looking up at him. Grabbing the soap, he held it up for her to see. "A bath, remember?"

He massaged the suds of sandalwood into a rich lather. She leaned back against him, her eyes closed, a soft smile on her face.

"Can you smell the sandalwood? I want you to concentrate on that scent. It's what your hair will smell like from now on."

When he thought the scent of sandalwood was fixed strongly in her mind, he leaned her back against the current, propping her up with his arm. One palmful at a time, he poured water over her hair, rinsing the soap. "I bet back home, you have a lady's maid who does this." She nodded and Holt dribbled a few drops on her lips then licked them.

Nicole laughed. "She doesn't do that."

"Exactly," he said, deepening the kiss. "I'd hate for you to confuse the two of us."

"There's not a chance of that." She giggled again, a light, encouraging sound that made Holt's heart warm. "She is old and gray and fat as a Christmas goose."

Holt smiled. "Well, I'm surely not fat."

The gold of her eyes deepened. She turned in his arms to face him. With one slim finger, she traced the lines of his muscles across his stomach, then looked up. "No, you're not." Her brows knitted together in a serious expression. "You're quite beautiful."

Holt caught his breath at the look of raw longing in her eyes. He leaned down and kissed her gently. "Let me show you a few other differences, love."

He kissed her, leaning back into the current, letting it flow over them. She wrapped her arms around his neck and he pulled her up into his arms without releasing her lips. Picking her up, he stood and ran back to the hut with her cradled against him, both laughing like children.

Inside the hut, he laid her down on the blanket. "You smell so good, Nicole."

"Yes." He could hear the smile in her voice, the release of fear as she molded his shoulders with her hands. "I smell like you."

She opened her mouth against his lips; his tongue smoothed over hers, leading her into deeper pleasures. With his hand, he brushed her breast in a gentle caress. Her nipples were hard, tempting. He reached down and took one between his teeth, rubbing the nub with his tongue. She arched against him, stroking her hands across his back until he felt himself grow even harder with desire. He reached between her legs for the dark curls, and threaded his fingers through them before reaching to stroke her with his thumb. Nicole moaned softly and Holt felt his own passion ignite at the sound.

He spread her legs apart with his knees, needing to feel

himself inside her, wanting to make them one again. But as he fitted his hips to hers, she stilled.

"Will it hurt?"

He stopped. Propped up on his hands above her, he looked at her, hoping the dim light from the entrance was enough to let her see as well as hear his reassurance. "I told you, *bacchi,* I'd never hurt you, not again. Trust me." An uncharacteristic need welled up inside him. "Please . . . trust me."

She reached up and traced his face with her hands, as if reading his expression with her touch. "I do," she whispered. "I can't seem to help myself."

Holt groaned. With his lips, he told her he loved her. With his hands, he tried to make her feel how precious she was to him. When he reached between them, she was wet, ready for him. Slowly, he entered her. She sighed softly and then, when he'd brought them together without pain, a quiet, "Yes," slipped past her lips.

He made love to her with gentle passion. Each touch, every move, Holt used to overcome her painful memories. When he whispered to her to tell him what felt right, she did. He taught her to touch him until he'd thought he'd die from the caress of her small hands. The explosion of sensations he felt when Nicole quivered beneath him and he followed her to fulfillment was just as awesome as falling over a cliff again, but this time they fell wrapped in each other's arms. The experience was a celebration of life. Afterwards, Nicky turned and huddled against him.

"What does *bacchi* mean?" she asked softly.

He rolled over until he hovered above her. His thumbs charted paths down her cheeks. "It means"—he grinned—"kid."

She pressed her lips together into a straight line. "How terribly romantic."

He laughed, dropping down beside her and spooning her to his side. "I thought so."

Sometime around midnight, when he felt her deep rhythmic breathing, Holt combed his fingers through Nicky's shortened curls. He estimated that when her hair dried it would bounce up just below her ears. But the length of her hair didn't matter. He'd been given another chance—Nicole trusted him. Now he could help her.

He cradled her closer, and heard her sigh in her sleep as she buried her cheek against his chest. He smiled.

It was a hell of a lot nicer than a lemur on his lap.

16

"The Khasiya has not returned! Certainly the girl is cursed with ill luck," Padmini's mother argued.

"Do not worry so, wife. I know the Khasiya. He is obsessed with our daughter. He is but trying to get the money."

"It has been too long. Almost a full moon has passed since he sent his messenger—"

"With the news that he works diligently to earn the money at another village! I am not concerned. He will return."

Padmini continued to sweep the courtyard with her stick broom, listening to her parents debate her future. Though they stood at the threshold to the rear entrance, glancing at her as they argued, they spoke as if she were not present, as if she mattered not at all—which certainly she did not. She'd learned as much after the Dholi had come to their home to exorcise the evil spirit that had caused her to challenge her mother.

As she cleared the courtyard, Padmini thought sadly that in a way the exorcism had cast a spirit from her, but it had not been the tormented spirit of a young child, but that of a woman—her own. She felt so empty inside, afraid that something had happened to Nursoo and that he would not return to take her from this torment.

"Husband, I am worried. You know the girl has been compromised," *Ma* said in a harsh whisper.

"We will use this to our advantage. I will ask the Khasiya for one hundred rupees more—"

"How could you even suggest such a thing? Are you mad? We will lose everything!"

Her father slapped her mother. Padmini looked on, fearful for *Ma,* but too frightened of her father to intervene. He had been drinking that evening. He was always in an evil mood when the arrack was in him.

"It is the moneylenders who will take everything, wife! I have not enough to pay the interest even. Unless I give the vultures something soon, you will give up your jewels as well as this house! The Khasiya is our opportunity to pay them off once and for all." He looked at Padmini in the corner. "The girl is comely. He will return for her."

Padmini watched her mother shake her head, but that was all the opposition she showed her husband. Like Padmini, her mother had learned never to question.

"Do as you think best, my husband. I shall take the girl to the priest and pray to the goddess that her luck changes and the boy returns."

Padmini's mother turned to follow her husband into the *ghar* house. Staring down at her stick broom as the evening's shadows lengthened across the courtyard, Padmini thought her mother's words rang true in her soul. Indeed, she was cursed. Perhaps the ill luck that had killed her first betrothed would take the second. She tried to shake off her fears. Truly, if Nursoo did not return soon, her parents would lose all patience with her. She shuddered. She did not think she could survive another beating.

"Mini!"

Sagi's whispered call brought her out of her gloomy thoughts. She turned, but her smile of welcome died on her lips as her brother gestured anxiously from around the corner of their house. Looking back at the doorway, Padmini saw her parents were no longer within sight. She leaned the broom against the whitewashed wall and followed Sagi.

Once around the corner, her brother smiled proudly at

her, then dropped to his knees urging her to do the same. He held something behind his back. "I brought you something, Mini."

She returned his impish grin, kneeling beside him. His youthful excitement helped lessen her grim mood. "A present, Sagi?" He nodded. "For me, dear brother?"

"Yes! Close your eyes, Mini!"

Padmini leaned back against her heels and waited with her eyes closed, thanking the goddess for Sagi. Her brother's giggles as he scrambled behind her brought a smile to her lips. A familiar weight rested at her neck. She gasped. Before she even touched the silver necklace with her fingers she knew Sagi had returned Nursoo's gift to her.

"Oh Sagi!"

"You like it?" he asked anxiously, dancing around her to witness her reaction.

"Yes, but how did you ever—"

"I took it from *Ma's* things." Before Padmini could protest, Sagi added, "She will never know it is missing. She buried it deep within some old clothes like trash! You need but hide it from her or wear it under your blouse where she cannot see it."

"Sagi, you are the dearest brother . . ." She took his hand in hers and squeezed it tightly, unable to express with words how much his gift meant to her.

"I just wanted you to remember," he whispered. "I know *Ma* has no faith in Nursoo. But you and I know he'll come back to you, Padmini. You need not be sad, just patient."

"You are right, dear brother." She fingered the silver necklace. Strangely enough, Sagi had echoed Nursoo's very words to her the last time she'd seen him. "I need but have faith."

Nicole stared down at the wilted cluster of flowers she held. Their heads lolled over the grip of her fingers like swooning ladies. The soft petals looked faded in the sunlight, no longer bright and vibrant as they'd been when she had gathered the blossoms. Nicole picked a brown-edged petal off one poppy and dropped it to the ground next to the rock where she posed for Holt. The experiences of the past month had shown her that life was short, and like the petal, easily plucked from you.

Nicole played with another flower and looked to where Holt sat bent over a pad of paper. "May I see now?"

"No."

His dark head focused on the pad, Holt continued to make effortless strokes across the page with a charcoal pencil. Watching him, she felt a gentle squeeze around her heart. She remembered the touch of those strong hands, the way the green of his eyes deepened each time she caught his glance, as if he wanted to make love to her here in the sweet-smelling grass. They'd done that often enough in the past two days. Nicole blushed, then raised her chin, refusing to feel anything but joy when she thought about making love with Holt.

"Much better, *bacchi*. I like that."

Nicole smiled, wondering what he would say if he knew what thoughts shaped her expression. He had probably guessed. Things had changed so between them since that first morning when she'd woken in his arms two days ago and he'd made such sweet love to her that she'd actually wept from the joy of it. He seemed to understand what she needed even before she did. He'd sheltered her at night, held her tenderly in his arms as they rode together, made her laugh. Every time they made love, she felt more alive. In two days, the nightmare of her abduction seemed just a little less present, a bit more manageable. The smell of roses was gone and only the memories of sandalwood, made fragrant from the heat of their bodies, remained.

Watching Holt as he leaned against the trunk of a *sal*, sketching, Nicole experienced something she hadn't felt since she was a child—the feeling of being cherished. For that reason alone it seemed irrelevant that he never spoke of marriage. The tenderness and concern he showed her through his loving attentions was commitment enough. She'd put such stock in marriage before and look what it had gotten her: Drew and his malicious schemes.

Nicole sat back against her rock and closed her eyes. She let the sounds of the forest lull her in the warm sun. *To the devil with marriage and other fairy tale endings,* she decided. *I've grown up.* Life was short—unpredictable. Let whoever wanted make their moral judgments on her actions. She planned to enjoy life.

As the sun rose high above her, Nicole swept the perspiration off her forehead with the back of her hand. She looked at Holt. "You had best hurry. I'm fading as fast as these flowers."

Holt didn't bother to look up. "You'll last."

Nicole sent a puff of air upward; a few shortened curls scattered. "It's hot."

"Complain, complain."

"I cannot believe your other subjects sit so long and still as I have."

"Nope. They don't." He looked up, added a line down on the pad, then squinted his eyes at her again.

"I can't imagine they sit around waiting for you to get every line correct."

"With animals, I usually take rough sketches, observe a lot, and do the rest from memory later." Holt stood. "All right, Lady Impatience. Off the rock and have a look."

Nicole skipped over and pulled the pad from him. As soon as she saw the dark, exotic woman sketched on the page, her heart plummeted and her warm thoughts of a moment ago vanished. With a few bold strokes and feather-like touches, Holt had created the image of a beautiful woman that looked like her . . . but not like her. The woman in the picture was exceedingly Indian.

Nicole dropped the pad back into Holt's hands. "You're not very good."

He stared at her in surprise then pointed to the portrait. "It's a damn fine picture."

"It doesn't look a thing like me."

"It looks a hell of a lot like you."

"The eyes are all wrong, the mouth"—Nicole grabbed the paper—"even my hair. It's too straight and long." She slapped her hand against it, smearing some of the charcoal. "You drew it like it used to be. I don't look like that!"

Almost as if she were watching a stranger, Nicole saw herself throw the pad to the ground. As she stared at the jumble of paper on the grass, she felt like crying. Instead she turned without a word of apology and headed back to the pony.

"What the . . . ?" Holt watched Nicole march off. Shaking his head in disbelief, he picked up his pad and fixed the bent pages, trying not to smear the delicate lines further. The woman on the paper was almost an exact replica of Nicky. So he got a little carried away and drew her hair long and flowing rather than the bobbing curls she had now, but somehow it had seemed more in character with the enchantingly exotic woman who had come to life under his pencil. Holt tore out the page and placed it carefully between two clean sheets in the pad. He was damn proud of the picture. He didn't usually draw people and thought it rather good. Why would it upset her?

He found her back by the horse, packing up, cool and silent. After tucking the pad in his saddlebags, he came up behind her. Putting his hands on her shoulders, he slid them down her arms, conveying his concern through his touch. He turned her around. Her pale complexion startled him and he tilted her face up to meet his. "You're white as cane, *bacchi*. My picture has you this upset?"

She shook her head. "It's just that . . . it reminded me of something, something precious I lost."

"Anything I can do to help?"

"No, it's gone now. Drew took it from me—a locket that belonged to my grandmother. I don't expect I'll ever see it again."

"I'm sorry, *bacchi*." He thought of his mother's Bible on

his nightstand back at his bungalow. "I know how special something like that can be."

She leaned into his arms, then reached up and kissed him. He tried to savor the feel of her lips but she pressed against him with mounting energy. When she grabbed at his shirt and began pulling it up his chest, he stilled her hands.

"Hey?" He reached up to smooth a tear from her face with his finger. "What's this, *bacchi*? You're crying?"

"No . . . I . . ." She buried her face back against his chest.

Holt hugged her, stroking his fingers through her hair. If he'd ever thought it could have this effect, he would never have asked Nicole to sit for him. But he'd enjoyed sketching her. He'd looked forward to other attempts even as he'd captured her whimsical expression as she held the flowers. With an artist's eyes, he'd focused on her more interesting features, the exotic tilt of her eyes, the full curve of her mouth, her high cheekbones—all the things that made her Indian.

Holt's hand hovered over her head for a moment as he realized the significance of that last thought. Slowly, he lowered his fingers to her thick, shortened curls and continued his rhythmic strokes. *Her most Indian features.* She had never told him about her Indian blood. They had never spoken about it. She didn't even know that her uncle had revealed her ancestry to Holt. Could that be what had her so upset? The fact that the picture made her look more Indian?

"You know, *bacchi*." He tried to make his voice sound casual. "Whenever I saw you, that first time with the leopard, out on the hunt for the man-eater, you always made me think of a Rajput princess." Nicole stiffened against him. "Then I'd look at your trousers and shirt—not to mention the 'I am a British lady' voice that could freeze the blood in your veins—and I'd think I was crazy."

Holt rubbed small circles on her back with his palm. He waited for her to admit her heritage to him, but after a few minutes of silence he guessed she would not. He would have to be more direct with his questions. Trying to get her to relax, he continued to hold her as he asked the one question he sensed she wouldn't want to face. "Nicole," he whispered, "why did you cut your hair?"

She looked up. "You know why. I told you . . . about the raja. What he did. You know what happened."

"I just thought . . . all that long black hair. Your hair was the thing that reminded me most of the Rajput women." He gave one curl a tug. "It was your most Indian feature. You think maybe that's why you cut it, *bacchi*?"

"Indian feature?" Her eyes grew wide; she pulled away. "What are you talking about—"

He placed a finger across her lips and shook his head, realizing she was going to deny her Indian ancestry. "Don't lie to me, Nicky. Don't *ever* lie to me." But despite his warning, he watched a calculating slant appear in her gold eyes, like someone hedging a bet. With a burst of anger, he realized then that she still didn't trust him, not completely.

"Dammit, Nicole." He grabbed her by her shoulders. "Your uncle told me all about your Indian ancestry! I already know!"

"Well, then." She tugged herself free. "There's nothing left for me to say, is there? My grandmother was Indian. A distant relation, but a blemish nonetheless. I hope it's not a bar to our current relationship—"

"Shut up, Nicole."

"—or do you have something against bedding Indian women?"

"Shut the hell up!"

Even as he shook her, his every word emphasized by an angry jerk, Holt realized how much he loved her. Her cold words sliced through his insides as cleanly as a jungle knife. Bedding her? For Christ's sake, every time he held her, kissed her, made love to her, he told her how much she meant to him. He wanted them never to reach Almora. The thought of losing her, just when he finally had her back, made him grab her and hug her fiercely, as if he could stop the inevitable by the tightness of his grip.

"God, how I wish . . ." Holt closed his eyes. *How I wish you were completely Indian, free to stay here with me, and not some English lady anxious to go home.*

When he released her, he wanted to shout that he loved her, that it was his greatest desire that she stay by his side. But he couldn't. Nicole was more English than Indian—she must return home. What good would it do to confuse her decision to leave with words of love. There were, however, ways in which he could help her and he set himself to the task—even as he subdued the small voice inside him that said he had other, more selfish reasons, for making Nicole face and accept her Indian heritage.

"Nicole. What's the real reason you came here to India?" He gave her hand a squeeze. "I think you had an important one, and it wasn't anything to do with hunting."

Nicole looked away, but not before Holt saw a sheen to her eyes that spoke more of pain than anger. "My family," she said in a very small voice. "I came to find my *grandmother's* family," she corrected herself, as if wanting to distance herself from the familial connection. "To find and meet my grandmother's people here in India." She clenched her fists to her sides and cried in an anguished voice, "But I don't care about that anymore. Why should I?" She blinked back the tears in her eyes that told Holt she cared very much. "They were right. My uncle, my mother, they were right. It has brought me nothing but pain. I told everyone I was the granddaughter of an Indian princess, and they laughed at me. I told Drew, and he sold me to some hill raja, passing me off as some upper caste bride. My Indian blood has brought me nothing but misery." Her voice dropped down to a whisper. "I want to forget. I want to go home and forget."

"It wasn't your ancestry—"

"I was abducted and sold because I looked like a Rajput Indian."

"Nicky—"

"I don't want to talk about it. Please!"

Nicole's arms circled him as she buried her head in his chest. Holt held her, biting back any further comment. He'd let it go. For now.

"You can't seriously suggest I eat this?"

Nicole stared at the round ball of dough that used to be a porcupine. After cutting it open, cleaning it, and stuffing it with herbs he'd gathered, Holt had covered the thing in a thick paste of *atta* flour they'd purchased with other supplies at one of the villages. He was now bent over a shallow hole he'd lined with mud, filling it with rocks warmed in the fire. He lowered the porcupine inside, then topped it with burning wood.

"That looks utterly disgusting."

"Actually, it's quite tasty, *bacchi.* I think you'll be surprised."

"I'll be surprised if I eat it," Nicole mumbled.

Holt slapped his hands together, then wiped them on his trousers. He grinned at Nicole. "Spoken like the prig Brit you are, lady."

"Since when is it priggish not to relish biting into a pin cushion?"

"My apologies I couldn't drum up some good old English food for you, like deviled calf livers and pickled ox tongue. Perhaps a jellied eel or two?"

Nicole tried to suppress an answering smile. "Actually, I prefer my livers fried. The devil sauce goes better with kidneys." She managed to keep her voice level. "Deviled grill and kidneys makes an excellent hunting breakfast. And I've tried jellied eel and it's quite nice, thank you."

"And you're afraid of one delectable pin cushion?"

Nicole pursed her lips. "You get used to those other things."

"Yeah?" Holt walked over to his pack and hunted through it before pulling out a *bidi* cigarette he'd bought from the natives and lighting up. He sat down next to a sapling and leaned against it, stretching one leg before him and resting his arm on the bent knee of his other. "Well, you'll get used to this too."

Nicole just stared suspiciously at the smoke rising from the pit.

"I've been told," Holt said, "by some very discerning clients, that porcupine tastes 'like well-fed suckling pork.'" He said the latter in the perfect imitation of an English gentleman and Nicole laughed.

"Which clients might those be?"

Holt took another puff and let the smoke curl out from his lips. "I used to hire out as a *shikaree*. With Nursoo."

"And now you work for the government protecting animals?" Wanting to confirm Nursoo's story, she asked, "That's quite a turnabout. Why did you stop hunting?"

"I don't believe in that sort of thing." He looked up and met Nicole's eyes. "Not anymore."

Nicole sifted sand through her fingers, trying to keep her voice casual as she asked the questions she'd thought about for so long. "Nursoo says it was a field biologist from London that changed your mind."

Holt smiled. "Is that what you and Nursoo talked about all that time? Me?"

She threw a fistful of sand, none of which landed past Holt's boot. "Conceited cretin." In her most haughty voice she said, "We spoke of you on one occasion as I recall. Otherwise we discussed more interesting matters."

"Now that really hurts, *bacchi*. Personally, I can't think of a single thing more interesting than you."

Nicole looked up at Holt, surprised. "For a man who spends most of his time outside civilized society, you can certainly be charming at times."

Holt laughed. "That's because I was brought up in 'civilized society,' and I got my fill of it around eighteen." Holt took a puff of the *bidi,* and watched Nicole thoughtfully for a moment. "The old Indian got it wrong, *bacchi.* I was for quitting way before Professor Dawson came."

Nicole drew small circles in the sand next to the fire and watched Holt from the corner of her eye. "Because of your father's death?"

Holt started in surprise, then took another pull of the *bidi,* squinting against the smoke. "So you heard that, did you? I thought you were unconscious."

Nicole stood and walked over to Holt. She knelt down in front of him. "It was like I was dreaming the story as you told it. About your father—your mother. How you grew up with your mother's family in Boston. And when you left, to fight in the war against Mexico." Wanting to wipe the wary look from his eyes, she reached out and took his hand in hers. "You must have missed your father very much. I'm sorry Holt—about everything. I know what it's like to grow up without a father."

Holt stubbed out the cigarette and pulled her onto his lap. "Is that why you're here with your uncle, *bacchi*? Your father gone?"

"He died before I was born." She nuzzled against his neck. "But I suppose it's worse for a boy—to be without his father, I mean."

Holt gave her a gentle squeeze. "Don't you worry about me. My mother was the best. And me and the old man had some five years together before he died. I didn't quit because of my father's death, Nicky. Hell, I face those same dangers every time I go off tracking."

Leaning against him, enjoying the feel of the warm night and Holt's arms around her, she listened to the beat of his heart as well as his words. "Then why did you stop hunting?"

Holt seemed to think a moment as he played with the fingers of her hand. "It started to remind me of the war too much—useless killing. Half the time the men who hired me would leave the dead animals where they fell, slapping each other on their backs, congratulating one another on a great shoot." Holt looked thoughtfully at the fire. "All I could see were those dead animals lying there left to rot." His eyes turned a dark angry green. "I wasn't so keen on that sort of thing after a while."

Nicole stayed silent for a moment. She'd never really thought about hunting in those terms. For her and the rest of the British aristocracy, hunting was a way of life. And though everything she'd shot had eventually ended up on their table at Eldridge Manor or the table of a tenant, Holt had showed her an entirely different side to hunting. When she'd seen Enchantress with her cubs, Nicole had realized the importance of preserving such a majestic animal. But for Holt the desire to protect went much further.

"Hey, come back to me, *bacchi,*" he whispered in her ear as he began kissing her neck. Nicky looked up with a smile and Holt followed the curve of her mouth with his thumb. "You looked sad," he said. "I don't like to see you un-happy."

"Then you'd best kiss me again, good sir."

"You're going to make me burn my porcupine," he said between kisses as he lowered her to the ground.

She wove her fingers through his hair. Leaning up, she whispered against his lips, "It shall be a devastating loss to us both."

Holt laughed and kissed her on the mouth. Covering her with his body, he pulled her shirt from the waistband of her trousers and reached underneath. Nicole moaned as the tips of her breasts crested with his touch.

"Nicky. Sweet Nicky."

The way he called her name spoke of pleasure and love. As she kissed his neck, tasting the saltiness of his skin, Nicole breathed in the scent of leather and horses—and a hint of sandalwood. The hard muscles under his shirt brought back memories of passion. But when he laced his fingers through hers, and hugged her, she felt more than desire. It was as if she were the most loved woman on earth.

Holt traced his lips around the curve of her eyes, then

kissed each softly. In a low rough voice, he whispered, "Beautiful are thine eyes—black-pupiled and unmarked." Slowly, he unbuttoned her shirt and pulled it up over her head. Kissing the skin between her breasts, he took both in his hands, adoring her with his eyes. "Firm and full and fair, are thy two breasts, like silver goblets from whence I long to slack my thirst." His palms glided down her torso, reaching her pants. With one hand, he rubbed the material between her legs. "Thy secret parts," he whispered in her ear, his breath making her shiver with heat as much as the thumb that caressed her, "swell with my touch." His hand returned to her naked breast and Nicole moaned. "The nipple lifts gracefully, smooth as the fruit of the palm. To whom will these breasts of thine, fit for a strand of pearls, grant their touch? Shall it be I who mounts thy broad secret parts and reaches heaven?"

She stared up at him. "That sounds suspiciously like poetry, Holt Atley."

"A very loose translation." He kissed the tip of her nose and smiled wickedly.

"It's beautiful."

"There's more." His hands trailed down her hips to her legs. "Thy thighs are like elephant trunks, straight and firm."

She wrinkled her brow. "Elephant trunks?"

Holt leaned up on both elbows. "Hey, to an Indian I have just described the epitome of female beauty."

Nicole laughed until Holt's kisses robbed the very laughter from her. When he hovered over her, a tender smile on his lips, she stared up in wonder.

"You make me laugh," she said. And as she realized the beauty of it, she closed her eyes against her tears. She threw her arms around him and held him fiercely. "Oh, Holt. I thought I'd never laugh again."

Holt set her gently on the ground. He cradled her face in his hands, waiting for her to open her eyes and look at him. "I made you a woman, Nicky." He leaned down and kissed her on the mouth. "It's only fair that I help you find the child in you again."

Nicky blinked back her tears and smiled. "Show me the woman, Holt."

Holding her gaze he unbuttoned his shirt, then tugged it over his head. Nicole reached up and placed her hands flat against the muscles of his chest. She thought of how much she loved this man, how at this very moment she could be carrying his child. The idea made him even more precious to her and she swirled her fingers through the hair of his chest, reaching to touch the skin beneath. Holt took off his trousers, then reached down and pulled off Nicole's. He studied her in the moonlight, and she saw all the words he'd spoken of her beauty reflected in his eyes.

As he stroked the curve of her breast, Nicky sucked in her breath, feeling the familiar glow of passion spark deep inside her. The pad of his thumb traced ever tightening circles around one breast as he watched her. Smaller and smaller, the circles brought his thumb closer to the tip, teasing her. Nicole bit her lip. She closed her eyes with a moan when Holt's thumb reached her nipple, stoking the spark inside her into a blazing fire.

In one smooth motion, he reversed their positions, pulling her on top of him, so she straddled him. Nicole looked down on him, confused, until she felt his hard length press between her legs. Instinctively, she leaned forward and Holt plunged deep inside her, making them one. Nicole gasped. She'd never felt so full, so good.

"You're a perfect fit." Holt placed his hands on her waist, centering her on him.

"Perfect?" Nicole giggled softly, then caught her breath when Holt moved gently beneath her. "I'm still trying to figure out how you got *that* in *me.*"

"I'll admit to a few doubts"—Holt reached for her breasts, stroking the tips as he moved beneath her—"but according to the *Kamasutra,* a tight fit is better than a loose one."

"Kama . . . ?" Again she gasped, but determined she should carry on a conversation despite these wonderful sensations if Holt could, she asked, "What are you talking about?"

Holt sat up, grabbing her legs and wrapping them around his hips as he did so, until Nicole sat on his lap facing him and he remained deep inside her. With a soft sigh, she grabbed hold of his shoulders and rubbed her breasts against his chest. Feeling him thick, swelling within her, she forgot all her questions. "That feels wonderful."

"The *Kamasutra,"* he whispered into her ear as he rocked her slowly on his lap, making Nicole shudder with pleasure, "is to lovemaking what *Godey's Lady's Book* is to fashion." He bit gently on the lobe of her ear. "It tells you all the dos and don'ts."

Nicole started laughing at the ridiculous comparison of the stuffy manual explaining when gloves were needed and the erotic contortion she was currently in.

Hearing her laughter, Holt said, "You see, Nicole. Even being a woman can be fun."

Nicole sobered instantly. Pulling a dark brown curl off his forehead, she stared into his loving gaze. She'd never felt so close to anyone, never been more intimate.

"I love you, Holt," she whispered softly.

An ominous silence followed.

She saw the hesitation in his eyes. It was almost as if he wanted to answer her, but could not. As if he were afraid to say the words. Nicole hid her face at the curve of his neck, not wanting him to see her disappointment. His every touch told her that he loved her, even if he couldn't say it out loud. She kissed him then, moving against him once more. Though sad for his silence, she urged him to show his love in other ways. Holt returned her kisses with a tenderness that left her breathless.

When they lay sated in the moonlight, gently stroking each other's bodies, Holt said, "The porcupine is probably charred beyond hope."

"A shame. I was really looking forward to it."

"I could catch another."

She shook her head. "Not necessary." Propping herself up on her elbow, she looked at him. "Tell me more about this *Kama . . . Kama . . .*"

"Kamasutra."

"Yes, *Kamasutra.*" Nicky drew soft lines across his flat stomach. "Is that where you learned all . . . all this?"

Holt laughed. "Hardly. Following the rigid caste system here, the *Kamasutra* has some very strange rules." Holt inched down her body, kissing a path down her shoulder to her breasts. "There are eight kinds of embraces, four gentle and four reserved for more passionate moments. Eight kinds of love bites." He nipped at the taut skin at her stomach, then his lips continued down past her belly button. "Just as many ways to make love with your mouth." He proceeded to demonstrate.

Nicole gasped. "Oh, my."

Holt looked up wickedly from between her legs, then kissed the inside of her thigh. "There's even positions like 'the splitting of bamboo' where—well, it's a little complicated to explain."

"No, don't stop. I want to hear," she said a bit breathless.

"It doesn't matter." He moved back to hover over her. He kissed her on the mouth then brushed the hair from her face. "Those rules don't apply to us."

The way he said it, with his heart in his eyes and a catch in his voice, gave Nicole's pulse a jolt. "Why, Holt?" she asked, sensing how close he was to expressing his love for her. "Why don't the rules apply to us?"

But the moment had passed and he merely shook his head. He rolled on top of her and started kissing her again.

"They just don't," was all the answer she got.

Nicole woke to the sound of a baby crying. At first, she thought she imagined the sound, but then the haunting wail grew louder. When her eyes fluttered open, she found Holt wide awake beside her. He held his finger to his lips.

Holt grabbed his pants, not bothering with his shirt or boots. Nicole dressed quickly. The sun had just crested the trees and a rose glow colored their makeshift camp. The pony, hobbled nearby, snorted as he pawed the ground for grass. After fastening his pants, Holt loaded and cocked his gun. Before he could tell her to stay put, Nicole signed her intention to come along. His jaw stiff and his lips pressed together in a grim line, Holt nodded once and headed for the river. Nicky followed.

The shrill cries of the infant grew stronger as they approached a copse near the riverbank. Nicole had to squint her eyes against the rising sun ahead before she caught the flash of white. Someone had tied a sheet in the trees, creating a makeshift hammock.

"Blast," Holt muttered under his breath. Tucking his revolver into the waistband of his trousers, he ran ahead.

When Nicole caught up to him, Holt was already reaching inside the low-slung hammock. Nestled within, a newborn baby wailed. Holt retrieved the tiny infant, cradling the child in his arms, his hand supporting the head like an expert.

"For heaven's sake." Nicole stared at the squalling baby boy. "What's a baby doing in the tree?"

"I'll explain back at camp."

Nicole watched the screaming infant. In an unconscious gesture, her hand went to her stomach, covering the place where she hoped her own child had already taken root.

"Oh, please." She held her hands out to Holt. "May I carry him?"

Holt watched her a moment, then gently placed the baby in her arms. "You have to hold his head up."

Tucking the babe against her chest, she laughed. "I'll have you know I am the proud auntie to nine nephews and nieces, most of whom I see on a regular basis." Her smile widened as she cooed down at the baby. "Knowing my siblings, there will probably be another on the way by the time I reach home."

Holt watched as the baby's cries quieted to soft hiccups in Nicky's arms. He felt a warm ache in his chest seeing how naturally she held the newborn. She liked kids; you could see it by her smile and the gentle noises she made. He'd always dreamed of having lots of children—but then the realities of his situation had made it clear he would never have a family.

"Come on," he said more roughly than he'd intended. "Let's get back."

At camp, Holt grabbed his shirt and moistened a corner with water. He held the cloth to the baby's lips, encouraging him to suck while Nicky rocked him in her arms. But the baby just turned away, screaming. He tried again.

"The poor dear," Nicky cooed. "This baby can't be more than days old."

"More like hours. He wasn't there yesterday when we made camp. I'd say its his first day out."

"Why was he all alone? Did someone abandon him?"

"You don't usually see this sort of thing so far west. In Bengal it's quite common. If a newborn doesn't take to its mother's breast, then it's exposed to the elements each day for three days."

"How barbaric!"

"The parents will be back at nightfall. Then in the morning, if the child still refuses its mother's milk, they'll leave it again." The baby's face bloomed crimson as he wailed his protests against the wet cloth, shaking his head and fists with violent jerks. "At the end of three days, they believe that a child who doesn't nurse is a demon and the parents cast it into the river."

"Dear Lord! Thank goodness we found him in time!"

"Nicole," he said, watching her try to calm the baby. "We wouldn't help the boy by taking him from his parents. If we can coax him to suck, we have to take him back."

"But such cruelty shouldn't be rewarded with a child!"

"It's their son, Nicole. What right do we have to take him?"

"We're not taking him; we're saving him."

"Would you have the boy grow up in some orphanage?"

"No—"

"Or raise him yourself in England where he'd be exposed to twenty times the prejudices you encountered? Look at him, Nicole. He's black as coal. He's Indian. He belongs here with his parents."

She still appeared unconvinced. Holt stopped trying to force the cloth to the baby's lips and concentrated on Nicole. "I promise you, *bacchi*. If we can get him to nurse, this child will be as cherished as any other baby by his parents. Don't make him an outcast, living for the rest of his days in a society and culture that despises him." When she looked away, Holt took her chin in his hand and turned her to him. "You once told me you thought it better that I let Enchantress die than cage her. I think we're talking about the same thing here."

Nicky stared down at the child. Holt heard her sniff, then wipe the corner of her eye with the back of her hand.

"Here, give me that." Nicole took the cloth and rubbed it against the baby's cheek. The baby continued to turn his head away from the cloth. Finally, Nicky gave Holt back the shirt. She rubbed the back of her finger against the boy's downy cheek, and the baby turned his head and started groping the air until he found her finger and latched on, sucking with satisfying smacks and gurgles.

"Well, I'll be damned. Hey, that's pretty good. Where did you learn that?"

She smiled gently. "I told you." She offered the wet cloth, which the baby now accepted with choking grunts. "Nine nephews and nieces."

A fountain of urine erupted from the boy's tiny penis, soaking Nicky and almost popping Holt in the eye. Both he and Nicky burst into laughter.

"And that's happened to me often enough as well," she

said, laughing as Holt used a dry edge of his shirt to clean them.

Spreading their blanket on the ground, Holt helped Nicky place the baby in the middle gently. Leaning over the child, she continued to coo softly, snapping her fingers and smiling to get the baby's attention.

When she looked up at Holt, her eyes were soft and sad. "How can a mother leave a child like that?" she asked. "It's barbaric."

Holt watched her play with the baby for a moment, before saying, "These people really think the child may be possessed. It's part of their religious beliefs."

"But it's unnatural to deny a child!"

"It's amazing what we do out of fear, Nicky. If we're scared enough, we even deny our own flesh and blood." He stilled her hand over the infant. "Or our heritage."

Nicole lowered her hand slowly. "Why do I feel as if we're no longer speaking of this child's parents?"

Holt knelt down beside her. "Nicole, I wasn't the only one doing the talking the night you were drugged. You had these nightmares, about your father, about your dark looks and your search for your ancestors. It seemed to haunt you even in your dreams." He took up her hands. "You came here to find your Indian family. If I thought you could go back to England a whole and happy person without doing that, I'd be the first to put you on a boat back. But out of fear and ignorance, you're denying something that meant enough to you once that you fought convention and your uncle to get here." He touched her shoulder gently. When she didn't say anything, he added, "Come on, *bacchi,* open up that cage."

Nicole picked up the baby and held him tightly. Smoothing a hand over his cheek, she said, "There was a time in my life when finding my grandmother's family would have been a dream come true. Now . . ." She shook her head, then looked up to Holt. "I'm frightened."

"Hey, don't forget." He smiled gently. "I'll be with you."

Nicole looked up into his eyes. His expression reminded her of that time in the commissioner's garden, when she'd felt a strong connection between them. In his eyes she'd seen something very special about herself. Now, in broad daylight, it was there again, a strength—or was it a belief in her strength?

"Drew said," she hesitated, almost afraid to tell him. "He said I was a Rajput of the Sun Line."

Holt's smile widened. "That would be the city of Udaipur in Rajputana. I can take you there, Nicky." He took her hand in his. "Let me show you the way."

The
Prize

*Pardon witless maiden's feelings! but beneath the
    eye of Heaven,*
*Only once a maiden chooseth, twice her troth may
    not be given!*

Book V, Woman's love,
The Mahabharata, the Epic of Ancient India,
condensed into English verse by Romesh Dutt

17

All the others meant nothing, Drew. It is you who gives me warmth, life. To have you gone all this time, with no warning. Don't you care for . . . no. I cannot even think it. You love me. You must! Please, come back to me, soon.

Serena penned her name and leaned back against the ebony armchair. She picked anxiously at the lace of her silk wrapper and stared down at the letter, the second she'd written that day. Her thoughts on Drew, she folded the delicate, scented paper, and added it to the stack neatly laid in her letter box. Letters she would never send. Even as the comfort of writing them dwindled with Drew's prolonged absence, Serena wrote longer, more often, like an opium eater who required greater doses to achieve the drug's soothing effects.

After locking the drawer of her escritoire and placing the key behind the clock on the mantel, she made her way by the light of an oil lamp to the upstairs bedroom—the guest bedroom. The day Drew made love to her in Jeffrey's bed, she had quietly moved her things down the hall. Jeffrey, glowering but accepting, had said nothing. On occasion, she would find him at the door of the guest chamber where she slept, waiting, watching, reminding her of the beggars who lined the streets of the city . . . and she would pay her tithe. He was her husband, after all.

Rounding the newel post at the top of the stairs, Serena heard a scraping sound. She stopped. The servants had long retired, yet a light shone momentarily from beneath the library door, then again, as if someone paced before a dim candle. She frowned and stared down the hall to where she thought her husband slept soundly, but who else but Jeffrey would be in the library at this hour?

She walked to the door. Tonight, she felt so empty even Jeffrey's cloying advances would be welcome. She needed to be loved, and at least Jeffrey made his feelings for her obvious. In his own pathetic way, Serena knew her husband worshiped her, was insanely jealous. That was why she'd made sure he knew about her lover, even if she had misled him about the man's identity.

Serena wrapped her fingers around the cold knob, but didn't turn it. An eerie sense of foreboding flooded her. For a moment, she stood there, the lamp in one hand, her fingers resting on the door handle.

The door swung open. A hand grabbed her arm, pulling her inside. Her scream never sounded beyond the warm palm pressed against her lips. She tried to rip the hand from her mouth and call for help.

"Hello, Serena," a familiar voice whispered in her ear.

Holding back her cry of joy, she turned in Drew's arms, almost dropping the lamp she held. Immediately, she saw the change in him. Dirt covered his sweaty face. His clothes, torn and filthy, reeked most foully. Only his smile, as charming as the devil's own in the lamplight, remained the same. When she looked beyond Drew's cherished features, she saw her husband's normally tidy domain was in no better condition than her lover. Books lay on the floor, pulled from their shelves in haphazard fashion; piles of papers littered Jeffrey's desk and the surrounding carpet.

A tap on the door, started them both. A feral, almost hungry look replaced Drew's charming expression as he stared at the door.

"Memsahib," called her husband's steward from the other side. "Is there anything you have need of?"

Serena laid her hand gently on Drew's arm, before stepping to the library entrance. He moved behind the heavy wooden door and Serena opened it just a crack to excuse the steward for the evening, making certain he would not trouble his master from his needed rest. After closing the door, she turned back to Drew.

"Nicely done, my dear. If only you'd been as able at the other task I set for you."

Without another word, he grabbed the lamp from her and moved to her husband's desk, setting it next to the candle burning there. Serena stood at the door, puzzled by his brusqueness. Whatever was the matter with him? Didn't he know how much she missed him? Why hadn't he taken her in his arms and kissed her? Bewildered by his hostility as much as his appearance, Serena walked slowly toward the bureau. She gasped when she saw Drew jamming Jeffrey's onyx and bronze letter opener into the lip of the drawer.

Serena dropped down beside him, trying to grab the letter opener from his hand. She could see from the scratches in the dark walnut that he'd been about the deed before her arrival. "Are you mad? What are you doing?"

He pushed her aside and Serena tumbled to the Turkish carpet. "Something I should have done ages ago," Drew replied. "Instead of relying on your worthless services." After a grunt of effort, he popped the lock and slid the drawer open. He removed the strongbox inside and laid it on top of the walnut desk. Slapping the letter opener against his palm, he stared at the heavy lock.

Serena watched Drew warily. Something was terribly wrong. Picking up the hem of her wrapper, she rose to her feet. Drew had never looked at her this way, as if . . . as if he loathed her very touch. She had to make him understand that he had hurt her. Then he would hold her and stop this silly search.

"Drew darling, you must not speak to me this way. I've missed you for so long. Please, leave this silliness for later, after we've—"

Drew grabbed her shoulders and jerked her roughly. "The key. Where does Jeffrey keep the key?"

Serena shook her head, frightened by the wildness in his eyes. "I—I don't know."

"You'd better start thinking, darling. My patience has just about run out."

"But I don't know where Jeffrey keeps his keys," she said. "Stop this, Drew. You're hurting me."

Serena tried to hug him, but Drew kept his arms locked at her shoulders. Tears of frustration welled in her eyes. Now surely he would be sorry for his ill treatment of her. She looked up into Drew's face, hoping that once he saw her tears he would regret his abuse of her. But when their eyes met, his lips curled in obvious distaste.

"You always were a stupid bitch, Serena," he snarled under his breath.

He swung her aside and Serena fell against the edge of the desk hurting her hip. A choked sob escaped her as she watched him pick up the letter opener, then begin jabbing it into the lock of the strongbox. After a moment, he turned his efforts to the top drawer of the desk, managing to pry it open. Serena stood aside, crying softly and biting her knuckle. When he found a key hidden under some papers in the front, he chuckled as he fitted it to the lock of the strongbox. It clicked open.

"A stupid bitch married to a fool," he whispered.

Drew rifled through the papers in the box, glancing through page after page in the lamplight. Serena felt something sick and painful unfurl in her stomach. The words "stupid bitch" ripped through her over and over.

"At last!" He lifted a stack of papers triumphantly. "The geographical reports I asked you for." His eyes were feverish. To Serena, he looked as if he hadn't slept in days. "They were here all along." He waved the rolled-up papers at her and she stepped back, crying louder. "But you couldn't bother yourself to find them for me, could you?"

She looked at the broken drawer and box and clutched

the lapels of her wrapper together. "I didn't know you wanted me to break into my husband's things!"

He grabbed her wrist, twisting it painfully. "I told you how important these papers were to me. Dear God, how long have I had to plow your thighs for *nothing*."

"Don't say such things!" she screamed. "You'll be sorry for speaking to me in such a manner. I'll make you regret it, Drew." She looked up at his face and said almost desperately, "Please, Drew." She tried to pull him to her for a kiss. "Please, don't make me do anything I'll regret." She shook her head, crying harder. "Not to you, Drew."

He released her. He folded the papers, then tucked them into his coat. "Oh, *do* shut up, Serena. Dear God, you make me ill. All the time I invested in you—a complete waste. Oh, I admit to needing your body at times. I thought I was engaged to a delectable young virgin, you see. It seems I was mistaken on quite a few counts, not the least of which was your usefulness." She felt his cruel look stab through her. "Your insatiable appetites were quite wearing, Serena dear. From now on I suggest you stay with darling Jeffrey between your ever-parted legs."

"Why are you saying this to me? You love me." She ran to him, began pounding her fists against his chest. "You love me!"

He clamped his hand over her mouth, making it difficult to breathe and impossible to talk. "Shut up, you old witch. Do you want your husband coming here to find us?" Serena's hands clawed at his fingers, but his grip only tightened.

Leaning forward, he whispered in her ear, "You're asking the wrong questions, Serena. You should ask rather, why did I say all those worthless words of love to you in the first place." He patted his coat where the papers lay. "For this! Geographical reports that map out the unexplored areas between here and Bhopal—including possible archaeological sites. By God, if only you'd helped me from the first. If I hadn't believed you when you said these reports were no-

where to be found, I might have avoided my stay in hell."
His nails dug cruelly into her cheek, making her cry out.
"Do you know what I've been through? Months of agonizing travel on the run. I was nearly a human sacrifice for a pack of Hindu idolaters. Hell, Serena. A living hell I would cheerfully send you to for your lying and incompetence."
He pushed her away and turned toward the door.

Tears almost blinding her, she watched Drew stop to pour himself a brandy and slam it back.

"God, I needed that." He shook his head, looking her over. "I still can't believe I managed it. How did I make love to your skinny body again and again? Pity such a grand effort was for naught."

Deep sobs racked her body. She wrapped her arms around herself, seeking the comfort of any touch, even her own. "You d-don't love me?"

He laughed. "No Serena. Any time I showed even an ounce of enthusiasm for your body, it was Nicole I dreamed of. A luscious, *young* woman." He poured himself another.

Slowly, she reached into the opened top drawer of the writing desk, searching with her hand toward the back.

"I've always found you tiresome. You see, my dear, you have this nauseating habit of whining—and you're quite insatiable. A bit of a drain, if you know what I mean."

"You look at me now l-like I'm a thing to disdain. You m-make me feel ugly." Serena wrapped her fingers around the cold metal.

"Not ugly, my dear. Just a bit worse for wear." He finished his drink and stared at her pensively. "Old. You're just old."

He replaced the glass and turned to the door.

"Drew?"

When he ignored her, a clicking sound echoed across the room. Drew swung back around. His dirty but beautiful face registered surprise at the cocked revolver aimed straight for his heart.

"I love you, Drew."

"Dear God, Serena, don't—"

"I always have." She pulled the trigger.

The force of the shot propelled him against the wall near the door. He looked at her in utter shock and staggered toward her. She fired again. Then again.

When he fell to the ground, she dropped the gun and ran to him. Splotches of red spread through the cloth of his coat and shirt. Placing his head on her lap, she smoothed away the beautiful chestnut curls she'd loved, remembering the feel of his lying lips on her skin. She leaned over him, weeping.

The door burst open. Jeffrey stood there, speechless, the servants crowding behind him.

"Ramu, call the constable," her husband's quiet but firm voice instructed. Serena sensed Jeffrey as he knelt down beside her, then touched her shoulder. "Come away, Serena."

She shook her head, threading her fingers through Drew's curls. Jeffrey didn't understand. No one understood.

"I loved him, Jeffrey." Her hand caressed Drew's dead face as she hugged him closer. "I loved him so very much."

Looking back at the blue-tiled terraces and golden minarets glittering in the sun, Nicole could see how the walled city of Udaipur had earned the name "City of Sunrise." When she and Holt had toured the palace grounds that morning, the rising sun had ignited in a blaze of color the whitewashed maze of arcades, balconies, and marble casements. At the lake below, what Holt called the loveliest in all of India, palaces and pleasure houses floated on the placid water with the grace of lily pads. That afternoon, while Holt met with the British Resident, Nicole had boarded the Maharaja of Udaipur's barge under the walls of the main palace. She watched women in gowns the colors of the rainbow dip their brass jars at the water's edge as the barge headed for the sparkling Jagmandir, the island palace that had sheltered forty-two English women and children from saber-wielding mutineers during the Sepoy Mutiny.

Now it housed one old woman and her attendants: Her Highness, the Maharani of Jaisalmer—Nicole's great aunt.

When the barge reached the island palace where she'd been told she would meet her grandmother's sister, Nicole stared up in astonishment at the life-size elephants of yellow sandstone that lined the entrance. Posts and pinnacles sparkled with glass, amber, and jade. In a bas-relief above the entrance was a gigantic image of the sun, father of the Rajputs, the symbol of her family's line.

Ushered silently down the halls, Nicole stared at the arabesques of colored stones depicting cranes, antelopes, and horsemen hunting tigers. The carved window screens shielded the interior from the summer's heat, which even at this hour threatened to suffocate the unprepared. Nicole, dressed in a corset with its stifling accessories and a muslin gown borrowed from the British Resident's daughter, blessed the breeze off the cooling waters of the lake. With her hair held off her face by a simple satin ribbon, Nicole felt totally English and completely out of place in her exotic surroundings. But she would not turn back now. She suspected Holt was right—she could not be whole or happy without accomplishing the one thing that had brought her to India in the first place. With his help, she'd put aside her fears and come.

Three weeks ago, en route to Udaipur, Holt had sent a message to her uncle, informing him of their plans to meet here rather than at Almora. Nicole expected her uncle to arrive any day now, giving her but a few days in the city of her ancestors on her own. She intended to make good use of her time. With the aid of the British Resident, Holt had obtained for her this audience with the maharani. At the time she'd been elated. Now, marching down the colorful halls to the receiving chamber, she felt equal parts dread and longing for the meeting.

When she entered the lavish quarters covered in Oriental rugs and Chinese tapestries, Nicole's eyes focused on the elderly woman lounging on a couch at the room's center.

Dressed in a beautiful sari of turquoise, the woman was surrounded by a bevy of servants seated on hassocks beneath the dais.

"Come closer, my dear."

Nicole started. "You speak English?"

She smiled. "Yes. I was taught by a *munshi,* a . . . tutor. It was the request of an eccentric old woman and my brother saw fit to grant me this wish before he died. But please, do step nearer. My eyes are no longer so sharp."

At the edge of the carpet, Nicole removed her slippers, as Holt had instructed her to do. She stopped directly before the dais and executed a low *salaam.* The maharani, apparently impatient with these elegant gestures, urged her up onto the dais. Nicole hesitated a moment, unsure of the dictates of etiquette, before she complied.

The maharani's pale blue eyes focused on Nicole. "So it is true." She took up Nicole's fingers into hands that shook slightly with age. "Aisha's granddaughter." The older woman's smile mellowed to one of heartfelt joy.

Entranced by her relative's friendly expression, Nicole returned the lady's smile. The maharani looked little like the young woman painted in the locket. Gray streaked the white hair beneath her veil. Her pale eyes were a soft, opaque shade, rather than the crystal blue Nicole suspected they'd been in her youth. But her expression—the smile, the shape of the eyes—reminded Nicole of her grandmother. Or perhaps it was only the comfort of her grasp that made this regal lady seem so familiar.

"I have come a long way to hear my grandmother's story," Nicole said. "I thought if I came here, to the land where she was born . . . no one in my family speaks of her."

The woman nodded. "So it is with us." For a moment, the maharani looked sad, but then the smile returned. "Of course you shall hear of Aisha. And who better than I to retell the tale. But first . . ." She said something to the young girl beside her. Instantly, the girl rose and spoke a command to the women around her.

The maharani gestured to the pillow on the floor beside her. Nicole made herself comfortable as servant after servant came forward. Each carried a tray piled with fruits and exotic delicacies to tempt the palate. One girl held a silver basin beneath Nicole's hands while another poured rose water from an elegant, long-necked vessel. Nicole smiled as she smelled the scent of roses and felt no responding sickness. *Holt made that possible for me, just as he made this meeting possible.*

After washing and drying her hands, Nicole followed the maharani's example and took a bonbon off one tray. She proceeded to unwrap the thin silver foil before the maharani reached over and stilled her hands.

"No. You eat it all. The *paan*—what you call betel leaves —is covered with pure silver. Good for the heart."

Nicole bit into the silver ball. The acrid tartness that flooded her mouth almost made her gag. As quickly as possible, she swallowed the wine she'd been offered, then grabbed an orange from another tray, hoping to cleanse her mouth of the *paan*'s powerful flavor.

"You have come a long way, Aisha's granddaughter. Did you really travel so far only to hear of my favorite sister?"

Nicole glanced down at the orange she peeled in her lap, away from the maharani's intense eyes. She didn't know quite how to explain the feelings and needs that had driven her so far from her home.

"I was told I look like her," she said, choosing the most simple explanation.

"Yes. Very much so. You look as I remember her when she left us."

Nicole cupped the orange in her palms. "I don't really look like anyone else in my family. In England, they would talk about me, about my dark looks." She smoothed her fingers over the waxy skin of the fruit, uncomfortable speaking about the prejudices against Indians to the maharani.

"When I asked my mother about her, she seemed fearful for me. She wanted me to forget my ancestry." She looked up warily. "As she had."

A chill of pride came to the lady's eyes, but she said nothing. Nicole continued, "My brother showed me a picture of my grandmother and told me she was a Rajput princess, a Raj Kumari." Nicole met the maharani's stare. "I felt I needed to know more . . . more about my heritage."

The cold look of hurt pride melted as her aunt met Nicole's gaze. A gentle sadness replaced it and Nicole thought that perhaps this great lady understood what had driven her niece half a world away from her family's country estate. The maharani reached out and clasped one of Nicole's hands. "You look a little lost, Aisha's granddaughter."

Nicole focused on the concern and understanding she saw reflected in the pale eyes. "I think I am."

The older woman gave her hand a squeeze of reassurance, much in the way Nicole's mother often did. And then she smiled her warm, heartfelt smile that made her seem so much younger than her papery skin and blue-veined hands indicated.

"She was full of life, our Aisha. She was my older sister by eight years and everyone's favorite—especially my father's, who took her everywhere with him, delaying her marriage until it was the talk of Udaipur and beyond. But he loved her so, he did not care what others said. He always complained that from some trick of the fates, she had been born a girl, for she had more daring and spirit than any of his sons." The maharani shook her head, a bemused expression on her face. "Her Rajput blood showed well. In the end, it was her spirit that took her from us."

"What happened?"

The maharani's smile deepened, but by some twist of her lips the expression made her look more melancholy than happy. "She fell in love."

The lady sipped the cool wine they'd been served, as if

needing a moment to collect herself before she continued. "When I was eight and Aisha but sixteen, there was much trouble in our region from the Maratha clans. Your grandfather was here to deliver a message from the British raja in Bengal. I believe it was the Marathas he came to speak about. He was very young, not much older than you I suspect, and very handsome. He had the sun in his hair."

Nicole nodded. "Blond, like my mother."

"We, my sisters and I, watched him from the balconies above the palace where we often looked undetected at visitors. Aisha saw your grandfather and claimed to have fallen instantly in love. How we laughed. For she was at the time betrothed to another."

Nicole stopped chewing her slice of orange. Her grandmother's engagement and love for another lent an eerie resemblance to their lives. She too had been engaged to Drew when she'd fallen in love with Holt. She wondered if Holt's and her story would end as happily.

"But Aisha would dare anything," said the maharani. "She convinced my father to let her sing for the British delegates. My father, being very proud of his beautiful and talented daughter, agreed. I believe that while he could not see her behind the screen, your grandfather fell in love with her even then."

"That's a beautiful story. How ever did she convince her father to break her engagement?"

"She did not even try. She bribed her attendants and exchanged places with the woman sent to dance a *nautch* for your grandfather and his company that night. I remember waiting for her late into the night at the *zenana,* anxious to hear her daring tale of adventure, but she never returned. I learned later your grandfather smuggled her out of the city walls once he learned her identity, fearing she would be punished for what she'd done. He took her with him back to England." The maharani shook her head sadly. "For many years anyone who uttered her name was severely punished. But eventually, because of the Maratha threat, we signed our treaties with the English and all was forgiven—all except my sister. For my father, she was dead, an untouchable. She had broken the honor of her caste by marrying an Englishman, an untouchable himself. He would hear nothing of her spoken in his court. But Aisha was clever. She smuggled letters to me and I to her, so I learned of her happiness with her husband. And later, when I left Udaipur for my husband's kingdom, I was able to correspond freely. I learned of your mother's birth. Though it would always sadden her that she could not give your grandfather another child, she was very proud of your mother, especially her hair. She said it was yellow like the sun, a fitting color for a Rajput of the Sun Line."

"Was she happy with her choice?"

"Aisha never faltered in her love for your grandfather. She did complain about the coldness, dreaming of our warm mild winters. And she missed her family very much."

Nicole hesitated before asking her most important question. "But what about the sentiments in England toward Indians? Could she truly be happy there with so many prejudices against her?"

The maharani watched Nicole closely. She could see disapproval distinctly in her great aunt's face, but she continued nonetheless, "That is to say, did she feel unloved or lonely—she was so different from the English people—"

"She was a Rajput princess!" For the first time, the maharani's voice held a hard edge.

Nicole instantly regretted her clumsy curiosity. But the harm had already been done, so she met the maharani's challenging gaze and added, "Yes. I know. But perhaps the English did not treat her as well as she might have expected."

The maharani's face softened into a look of concern, as if understanding that it was herself Nicole spoke of, not her grandmother. She shook her head slowly. "I do not believe Aisha would care about such things. All she needed was her husband's love. She gave up her entire way of life for him, and she never regretted that choice. She said it was true love that called her—and one must always follow the call of true love or face the consequences." She watched Nicole carefully. "I myself married a man who was chosen for me. He was a good man and I have many children and much happiness from the union. But my sister's letters . . . they spoke of something else, something which I admit I have never known."

"True love." And as she said the words, Nicole knew it was the same emotion she felt for Holt.

Her aunt nodded. Then, staring at Nicole as if coming to some important decision, she said, "Aisha's granddaughter, I hope you will spend the rest of your stay here at the palace as my guest. It would give me much joy."

"Thank you. I would like that very much." Nicole's worries of offending the maharani lifted at the lady's invitation. "I want to know more about my grandmother—more about my heritage."

The maharani thought a moment, appearing to seek some hidden message in Nicole's words. Then she smiled and said, "Until you leave, Aisha's granddaughter, you shall live as your grandmother. You will stay here at the palace. You shall *be* a Rajput."

18

Holt followed the Suktawut guard down the marble corridors at a steady pace, refusing to break into a run even though the blood pounding through his veins drove him like the tomtoms at a *hankwa*. Marcus Marshall had arrived with Nicole's chaperone and luggage in tow. Her uncle was here to take her home.

Home. To England.

She was leaving him.

Turning down the last corridor with his escort, Holt tried to regroup his thoughts for his meeting with Marshall. He'd meant to speak to Nicole before her uncle's arrival, but his doubts about their future together had made him wait. Tomorrow always seemed soon enough to tackle their problems. Now his time had run out.

As his escort announced him, Holt waited before the apartments' arched entryway, thinking of how twisted things had become. As a soldier, during his years hunting and charting the wilds of India, he'd made dispassionate, *calculated* decisions that had very little to do with any emotion, much less fear. But with Nicole it seemed he'd forgotten all his training. When he'd seen a leopard charge her, a black cobra swaying inches from her hand, Nicole racing up the lighted hillside ready to jump into oblivion, each time he'd felt as if the curved blade of a scimitar had ripped through him. Agonizing emotions had choked him as he'd held her stiff and unconscious body the night she'd taken the *datura*. And now his fear that he would repeat the mistakes of his father, marry, sire a son, and send his family into exile, had stopped him from speaking of marriage to Nicole and admitting his love for her.

Holt raked his fingers through his hair. Dear God, what if she were with child? Life would be difficult for Nicole in India, but how much more difficult would it be if she went home to England as an unmarried woman expecting a baby? No, if she were pregnant, and damn him, he'd certainly done his best to get her so, he'd be forced to break his vow of a decade before, a promise he'd made at his mother's graveside. He would ask Nicole to marry him. There were worse things than repeating the mistakes of the past. But if she were not pregnant . . .

Holt cursed under his breath. He'd thought they had time to sort the thing out! To speak with Nicole of their choices. He'd had no idea she would ensconce herself on that damn island with the maharani. Yet, three days later, he still had not seen her. He'd sent messages. One, the first day. Three, the second—even more the third. Her responses were always similar to the first: *I miss you too, but you were right. I must do this.*

Blasted poor time to start taking his advice.

As he paced the inlaid tile floor waiting for Marshall, Holt again cursed the day he'd encouraged—no, urged— Nicole to visit the maharani at her island palace. He'd wanted Nicole to find her roots, not take root!

Holt stopped pacing, staring instead at the pattern of sunlight streaming through the lacy stone screens. If the truth be told, his desire to marry had little to do with a possible pregnancy—though a child would give him the excuse he needed for them to wed. He felt less than whole without her at his side. Three weeks he had slept, ate, even bathed with her beside him. They'd talked by the fire, exhausted themselves making love, fallen asleep in each other's arms. The memory of her, her laughter, tears, the taste of her warm skin under his lips, his fingers caressing her breasts—it was like a gnawing ache in his heart, constantly reminding him of his current deprivation. What would his life be like without her? Would his love melt into pleasant memories, or would the acid pain of losing Nicole grow worse?

And the most important question of all—if she weren't expecting his child, could he actually let her go?

At the call of his escort, Holt stepped into the apartments where Nicole's uncle waited. He barely crossed the threshold to the sumptuous chamber decorated with colored mosaics and detailed mirror work before Marcus Marshall accosted him.

"Where is she?"

They were the same gruff and urgent words he'd spoken when Holt had returned from the Gori Ganga without Nicole. This time Holt was able to reassure Marshall. Placing both hands on the older man's shoulders he said, "She's here in Udaipur, in good health and perfectly safe."

"Thank God!" Marshall released an audible sigh, reinforcing to Holt the man's deep concern for his niece. Holt frowned. He could just imagine what this English aristocrat would say if Holt asked for his niece's hand in marriage.

"You can't imagine how I've worried," Marshall said. Then giving Holt a good solid thump to the back, "And you, no doubt, are responsible for that good health, my boy. I'm not surprised. I'd been told you were the best tracker in the area. How can I ever repay you for what you've done? Name a price and it shall be yours."

Holt's lips twisted into an ironic grin. What would Marshall say when he knew Holt's true price? "A tempting offer, Mr. Marshall, but I won't hold you to it."

"My good fellow," Marshall insisted with the same stubbornness that had characterized him throughout their short acquaintance. "I think you take my offer too lightly. I know my nephew, the viscount. He would pay anything to the man who returned his sister safely to him."

"She isn't in England yet."

"What's that?"

"I said, all that can wait until she's safely home."

"That's just a matter of time, old chap. Under the circumstances, the hunt for the white tigress is off. Though I'm going home empty-handed, I've had my fill of this country and its infernal heat. The arrangements have all been made. We leave for Bombay at the end of the week. From there, we'll be taking a P & O steamer home. Six weeks later, the shores of mother England await." With a hint of a frown, as if he were thinking over Holt's enigmatic words, Marshall asked, "Where is the girl?"

"I can take you to meet the maharaja. He's waiting for us in the hall of the sun. From there we can make arrangements to see Ni—your niece."

"Why didn't she come meet me herself?"

"There's a slight problem." Holt turned and instructed the Suktawut. With the guard at the lead, Holt stepped down the hall, hoping Marshall would follow.

Marshall grabbed his arm and pulled Holt around to face him. "You said she was safe! What's happened to her that she couldn't be here to meet me immediately?"

"Nothing is wrong with your niece," Holt replied, again seeing the gentleman's concern. "She is at one of the island palaces, visiting with the Maharani of Jaisalmer," after a pause, "an apparent relation."

Marshall's face instantly lost its color. "Dear God! This is where that infernal grandmother of hers came from, isn't it? That's why the girl had you bring her here rather than Almora!" Marshall slammed his fist against his thigh. "How can you have been so stupid, man! I told you the girl had a wish to meet these Indians. How could you have let her trick you into bringing her here?"

"She didn't trick me into anything. I brought her here willingly."

"So she could fill her head with more fool notions about her ancestry? She must forget this nonsense about the Rajputs!"

"The only good thing that has happened to your niece on

this trip *has* been her chance to meet her relatives. You said it yourself—it's what she wants."

The unbecoming shade of crimson inching up Marshall's face threatened to erupt into unbridled fury. "You have no idea what harm you may have caused the girl," he whispered ominously.

Holt felt a stab of guilt. "On the contrary, sir. I have an excellent idea of all my wrongs against your niece. They do not, however, include bringing her to Udaipur."

Marshall met Holt's cool gaze with a venomous look that completely erased the camaraderie of moments ago. So much for his reward, Holt thought.

"Well, we'll just see about this." Sweeping past Holt, Marshall stepped up to the Suktawut escort. When the man remained frozen at attention, Marshall shouted to Holt, "By God, tell the damned heathen to lead the way!"

Holt watched Marshall's rigid back as the older man followed the guard down the marble corridor. He could hear Nicole's uncle mumbling under his breath, threatening to box Nicole's ears if "the chit" gave him any trouble returning to "good old English sod where she belongs." He muttered "Indians and Rajputs" as if they were the worst insults a man could think of.

A vision of Nicole the first time Holt had seen Marshall lay into her flashed through his mind. A young girl cowering before her uncle's anger, she'd been afraid to admit she'd gone off on her own without permission, nearly becoming leopard bait for her disobedience. Holt had called her "kid" after that, then *"bacchi"* as an endearment. But he didn't think of her as a child anymore.

What would the woman who had for the past three days gently but firmly refused Holt's demands to leave Jagmandir do? A curious smile crept across his lips. What indeed.

"I'll take you to her, Mr. Marshall," he said. "But I think you're in for a surprise."

* * *

Nicole stared at her reflection in the pool, relaxed and just a bit sleepy in the late morning's heat. By boat, the maharani had brought her to the "Gardens of the Maids," designed for the special use of the palace ladies. Nicole had spent the morning enjoying the beautiful black stone cenotaphs, monuments to Udaipur's past, and the profusion of fountains and ornamental pools. Now, drifting off to sleep under the shade of a mango tree, she dipped her fingers into the pool's lily-festooned water, causing a ripple to distort her image—the image of a Rajput princess.

Three days she had lived the life of her grandmother. Dressed in long flowing skirts and silk veils, her every step marked by the musical ring of her silver anklets, Nicole had at last found the answers she'd searched for. The satisfying thunk of her arrow finding its mark, her great aunt's admiring gaze as Nicole trained with a jeweled curved sword that had once belonged to her grandmother, the words of praise she'd received from the maharaja's daughters for her skill with her blade, all these had given her a sense of belonging she'd never found in England. Here, she was lauded for the very things she had been ridiculed for back home.

The most amazing experience of all had been the dancing. She'd never in her life finished a waltz or a quadrille without an embarrassed apology to her partner. Yet the Indian dances she'd learned came as naturally to her as breathing. With elegance and grace she'd executed the sensuous moves that told the stories of her ancestors and their gods. Nicole smiled. She couldn't wait to dance for Holt as her grandmother had done for her grandfather over sixty years ago. She hoped for the same effect—Holt would declare his undying love and ask her to be his wife.

Smiling at her fanciful thoughts, Nicole brushed her fingers across the moist petals of a lily. In Udaipur, she'd discovered a different Nicole, one who need not hide behind her trousers and a gun. She could be strong *and* womanly—like the ladies she'd come to know on this island. Veiled and jeweled, they wielded swords in the courtyard. With henna on their palms and perfumed skin, they pulled back the birch bow and loosed their arrows. *Johur,* the practice of descending into rock chambers to be consumed by fire while their men launched themselves into battles to the death, was their legacy. These warrior women trained in martial arts as well as wifely duties, seeing no contradiction between the two.

With Holt at her side, she could have the best of both worlds. She would not be forced to live the rest of her days in a *zenana,* unable to leave without full cover and an army of eunuchs. Nor would she spend her time in the frivolous pursuits of a lady of wealth in England, concerned only with gowns and jewels and the right offer of marriage. For once in her life, Nicole believed in the possibilities of her mixed heritage rather than its limitations.

"What are you thinking, Aisha's granddaughter?"

Nicole smiled at the reflection of the maharani in the pool, before turning around to greet her. "Oh, all sorts of things." She propped up on her elbows, squinting against the sun. "Do you know, about the age I fired my first gun, my grandmother was probably training with her sword?"

The maharani nodded. "The Rajput blood. It shows even then."

"I think I know why my grandmother was so happy in England. Why it never mattered to her if she were cut dead by society." Nicole sat forward, enthusiastic to share her discoveries with her great aunt. "She had all this to remember." She swung her hand around to the beautiful pools and fountains. "The palace, the lake and its floating manors. No one could hurt her by belittling her heritage. Their comments would seem ignorant and small minded. She *knew* how rich and marvelous her life as a Rajput was. She probably laughed at them all."

The maharani took Nicole's hand and placed her cool palm over it. "And now you also know."

"Yes." Nicole smiled. "Yes, I do." She shook her head thoughtfully. "To think I was actually frightened to come here to Udaipur. Frightened of what I might find." Her voice dropped slightly, as if hating to admit some failing. "Once, a man I trusted took advantage of me because I looked like a Rajput. I blamed my Indian blood for the harm he did me."

"But you found the strength to come here nonetheless."

"Yes." She thought of Holt. "With some help."

"From the gentleman who guided you here? The one who makes your eyes glow each time you speak his name?"

The maharani laughed at Nicole's startled reaction. Nicole joined in. "I didn't know it was so obvious."

The older lady sat down beside her at the pool. "He sends countless messages. It would not be difficult to believe he has a special interest, no?" At Nicole's nod, the maharani asked, "Interest that perhaps you share, Aisha's granddaughter?"

Nicole looked down to where her hand lay cradled within the maharani's. She recalled the child she and Holt had rescued. How its mother had cried tears of joy when she'd put the baby to her breast and the child had nursed. Holt had taken her hand then, lacing their fingers together, and they'd shared a silent moment of caring for the baby they'd taught to suckle. Nicole placed her free hand on her stomach where she suspected she carried their child.

"Yes, great aunt. I"—her throat swelled with the love she felt for Holt—"I share his . . . interest."

"Good." The maharani patted her hand then placed a folded piece of vellum within it. "Then perhaps this note you will answer more favorably than the others. The messenger grows tired of his frequent trips to find you."

Nicole laughed and opened the missive, not the least bit surprised. She had already received countless messages from Holt. She smiled, thinking how these letters made her feel more loved than ever. Maybe it was time to return to the palace and face one more challenge.

But when she read the contents, the pleasant smile left her face. The letter was from Holt, but it concerned her uncle.

He'd arrived at last from Almora. He was here to take her home.

Turning to the maharani, a desperate idea gathered in her head. "Your Highness—"

"Nicole"—the woman raised her hand in an elegant gesture of command—"we have already spoken of this. With you I will not abide this sorrowful formality."

Nicole smiled, warmed by the maharani's compliment to her. "I must ask a great favor of you, my great aunt."

"But of course."

"My uncle has come to fetch me home to England. I would like to meet him at Jagmandir, dressed as I am . . ."

"You need not ask. It would give me great pleasure for you to meet him as a Rajput."

The maharani stood and, after wishing her a fruitful meeting, turned away. Sighing, Nicole glanced back to her reflection in the pool, thinking of the impending confrontation with her uncle.

"What is it that you see in those waters, Aisha's granddaughter, that has you so puzzled?"

Nicole started at the maharani's voice, then caught sight of the lady's reflection in the water above hers. The older woman's expression looked kind and, at the same time, expectant of a response. Seeking an answer for her aunt, Nicole focused on the image of the young woman mirrored directly before her. Ebony curls peeked out from the covering of a long gold *chukkar* mantle. The eyes were large, almond shaped, the same shade as the veil. The lips full.

"I see my grandmother," she said at last.

Her great aunt's image shook its head. "I do not see Aisha."

Nicole fought back her disappointment. She looked closer. Three days of teaching her the traditions of Rajput women could not give her Aisha's bold spirit. And yet, Nicole sensed within her that same strength her aunt had spoken of when telling the tales of Nicole's grandmother.

"I see," continued the maharani, "a woman who *looks*

like my sister. But in her expression, I see something I do not recall ever witnessing on my sister's countenance. Yours is a face that has experienced fear—and conquered it. My sister led a sheltered life. She left her family's nest for the protection of a very wealthy British gentleman, a man whose influence and power protected her. I believe you have earned the courage I see reflected in the water; your spirit is not merely a legacy from my father." The maharani's expression turned thoughtful. "I wonder what stories you could tell, Aisha's granddaughter."

Holt caught his breath at the sight that awaited him when he walked into the receiving chamber at Jagmandir. More alluring than ever, Nicole sat atop a dais, as regal as a princess, as still as a golden statue in her shimmering finery. A velvet canopy supported by slim pillars framed her like the setting for a cherished jewel. Behind her the lacy gilt embellished with mirrored and brightly colored tiles added to the image of something priceless on display. Even the family emblem, a magnificent solar disk on a circular fan of black ostrich feathers, paled in the shadow of Nicole's beauty.

The metallic glitter of pure gold threads in the silk of her skirt and bodice caught the sun streaming through the carved latticework screens. The *chukkar* covering her soft black curls cascaded down the steps of the dais in a liquid pool of sunshine. Her skin seemed kissed by the sun's rays. Precious eyes, rimmed with kohl and glimmering with the heat of the smile beneath her diaphanous veil, shone brighter than the silks and jewels that adorned her.

Nicky's uncle stared about the chamber. His gaze flitted over his niece where she sat on a pillow no less magnificent than the maharaja's *gadis,* the velvet cushion that served as the royal throne. After scanning the room thoroughly, glaring at the eunuch guards with a hint of suspicion, the gentleman turned to Holt.

"Where is she? How much longer must I wait for the girl?"

Holt grinned as Nicole's musical laughter answered her uncle's demand.

"Uncle Marc, don't you recognize me?" She pulled back the veil to reveal her face.

The expression on Marshall's face would have been comical if not for the flash of anger that immediately followed. "Jumping Jupiter! Nicole?"

"Your eyesight isn't *that* poor, Uncle. Of course, it's me."

A color as rich as the ruby suspended from the gold circlet on Nicole's head crept up the old man's face. "Young lady, I am giving you half an hour—no, fifteen minutes—to get out of that getup and into *decent* clothes!"

The smile left Nicole's lips and her expression turned cool. Picking up the edge of the priceless gold *chukkar,* she looked at it thoughtfully before returning an unflinching gaze to her uncle. "Don't you care for the color gold?" She spoke in a low, well-modulated voice that complemented her royal attire. "Perhaps you think I look like a . . . what was that charming phrase you used at the commissioner's ball . . . a yellow dumpling?"

At that moment, Nicole appeared in complete control, while her uncle actually looked nonplussed by his niece. Holt felt a warm sense of pride spark inside him.

The older man's face went as smooth and cold as marble. "That little speech cost you a minute," he said in a voice like ice. "I suggest you hurry up and gather your clothes."

Holt stepped forward to protest, but Nicole held up her hand in a regal gesture befitting the maharani herself. "Mr. Atley, I would like to speak with my uncle alone."

The formal address stopped him more effectively than her hand. He noticed then that Marshall's words had not made a dent in Nicole's determined expression. He hesitated, unsure of this confident Nicole, who didn't appear to require his rescue. But then she smiled and added, "Please, Holt."

He nodded and gave her a small salute before turning to leave. Only at the scalloped arch at the entryway did he stop to add, "I'll be right outside . . . if you need me."

Nicole watched Holt leave the chamber with a tight ache in her heart. He was dressed in clothes she'd not seen before, a pristine white *anga* coat and white trousers, and his dark hair had been freshly cut so that it lay smoothly against his head rather than in its usual wayward curls. He looked more handsome than ever, so masculine. Her breath had caught in her throat when she'd seen him walk into the room behind the eunuch guards and she'd momentarily questioned her decision to stay at Jagmandir, away from him for three days and nights. From across the room, she'd wanted to reassure him, to smooth away his look of confusion. But she couldn't, not without alluding to the intimacy of their relationship in front of her uncle. *No, my love,* she thought, *you cannot help me this time.*

Turning her attention to her uncle's stony expression, Nicole sighed. This meeting was turning out just as difficult as she'd imagined.

"Young lady," he began in that awful voice that echoed years of, *you will obey me or else!* "I don't know what's gone on in my absence—I don't *want* to know—but from now on you will cease with these childish displays of fantasy—"

"Couldn't you force a simple, 'Nicole, are you well?' from your lips, Uncle Marc?"

Her uncle turned a deeper shade of crimson. "I will not have you speak to me in such a manner!"

Nicole shook her head sadly, surprised that he still had the power to hurt her so.

"Then perhaps," she said, "I will not speak to you at all."

Her uncle gave her a look of confusion. "What's happened to you, Nick?"

"Is what I'm wearing so important, Uncle Marc? More important than the fact that you've not seen me in a month and a half?"

"Don't you dare imply I don't care about you, girl! Not after the worry I've been through since you disappeared. I've already had a very thorough account of your health from Mr. Atley, thank you. It's your mental state I'm worried about after finding you dressed like a heathen."

"I'm wearing a gown similar to one worn by my grandmother."

"Your *heathen* grandmother."

Nicole sat straighter on her cushion, anger giving her the strength to challenge her uncle. "My grandmother was the Raj Kumari, a Rajput princess. For years, I've been curious about the woman whom I resemble a great deal. Naturally so, I might add. And for years *you,* my loving uncle, have played on my mother's fears about her mixed ancestry to prevent me from discovering anything about my grandmother." She watched her uncle closely, tried to let him see that she wished to understand, wanted to see the motives behind his actions. "Why, Uncle?" *Please, let me be wrong. Don't let it be simply shame or hate.* "Tell me why?"

"Haven't you caused enough trouble with your silly questions about your Indian blood? No decent man would even offer for you!"

Her lips pressed together in a bitter line. "I suggest they weren't so 'decent' then."

"Oh, I'll admit Lord Harrington turned out to be a bad egg. And I'm sorry my poor judgment put you in danger, Nick girl, more sorry than I can say. But can't you see your mother had the right of it? She never talked about her black blood. And with her fair looks and elegant manners, she was able to land herself a title! Dammit, Nick, that's what I want for you. To lead a normal life in England. Not to be shunned by your peers because you have a few drops of Indian blood!"

In a very quiet voice Nicole asked, "You've never quite forgiven my father for marrying Mother, have you?"

Her uncle seemed to think a moment, as if judging just how much to say. "He shamed us. And that's a fact," he said with his usual candidness. "He had the title. By God, he *knew* his responsibilities! Now I'm not saying I don't care for our darling Katherine. You know I do. But if he'd had a lick of sense—"

"And because he didn't, you've spent your life trying to undo his wrong. By wiping out every last vestige of my mother's 'flawed' ancestry."

He seemed stunned by her anger. Shaking his head, he said, "I'll never understand you, Nick. Your sisters, Charlotte and Annabella, they were sensible about the past."

"So it was *me* you had to work on. *I* was the one you had to train and watch and keep in line." Her voice choked just a bit, but she found the strength to continue, "That's why you've always shown so much interest in me. Not because I was special. Not because you loved me. Because I was the one who threatened to dredge up the past you feared *so much*."

"How dare you, girl! I loved you like my own. When your father died before you were born, I tried to take his place—"

Nicole shook her head, all the dreadful facts falling into place. "I remember exactly the day you started taking an interest in me. It was after the scene in the parlor. After Keane gave me the locket. The day I began asking about my grandmother." Trying to blink back tears, in a very low voice, she finished, "I wonder if you ever really loved me at all."

"By God." He looked about the room wildly, as if searching for something to throw. Nicole saw a shine to his eyes that confused her. It couldn't be tears? But then he seemed to rally a bit. "Until I fetch you home to your brother's side, I'm still responsible for you, girl," he said in a voice that almost vibrated with pent-up rage. "You just remember that, Nicole. I'll be waiting at the barge." He turned to leave and shouted over his shoulder, "You have ten minutes."

It wasn't until he reached the threshold that he stopped, as if about to turn and throw one final volley, but instead he remained facing the door, shaking his head. "Damn you, girl," he said in a voice choked suspiciously with emotion. "You're wrong. You're so wrong."

* * *

Marshall barreled past Holt, wiping tears from his eyes with the sleeve of his coat. Immediately, Holt turned to the receiving chamber, concern for Nicole ripping through him. But at the door, the maharani's eunuch guards blocked the entrance, their beefy arms crossed before them, scimitars gleaming at their side.

Apparently, their audience with Nicole had come to an end.

Holt searched for Marshall back at the quay where the maharaja's barge waited, anxious to discover if Nicky was well. As soon as he reached the older man's side, Marshall instructed him tartly to have the barge wait, adding "the chit would be joining them soon enough." Holt tried to relax, but his desire to speak alone with Nicole made him anxious.

"Blasted girl," Marshall said, boarding the maharaja's barge. "She doesn't know what's best for her, is all."

Holt reconciled himself to hearing Marshall's complaints about his niece, at least until Nicole arrived. Boarding as well, he sat beside Marshall on one of the long silk-covered benches.

"She acted happy as you please, sitting there dressed like some heathen Rajput."

Marshall spoke as if Holt were in total sympathy with his opinion of his niece's actions. Holt thought to set him straight. Maybe he could help Nicole by getting her uncle mad at him, letting the old man take out some of his anger on Holt instead of Nicole.

"Look, Mr. Marshall, you and I both know *why* Nicole came to India in the first place—"

"She tricked me, she did, making me believe she wanted the tigress as much as I."

"—and I can't see the harm of her meeting her family. A royal and prestigious family."

"No harm you say? I wonder if you'd keep that opinion if she got it in her head to stay here!"

Since that was exactly what he wanted Nicole to do, Holt asked, "Would that be so bad?"

The uncle's head jerked up and he stared at Holt in astonishment. His dark eyes narrowed and the bushy white brows furrowed together. "You tell me, Mr. Atley. What do you think would happen to my Nick if she stayed in this blasted country?" For a moment, Marshall acted as if the idea of teaching her a lesson by leaving her here appealed to him, then his face fell, and he grumbled, "Probably fall dead from some infernal disease before she turned two and twenty. Or get herself killed by some heathen. Damned girl would turn her back on everything she has in England! A loving family, a palatial home. A dowry that's sure to bring some buck to bay eventually."

Listening to Marshall recount each asset that awaited Nicole in Britain, Holt felt a tight knot form in his stomach. He wanted to shut Marshall up, wanted to stop the words from coming even as he forced himself to listen to them.

"By God, just three years ago these heathens slaughtered good English folk mercilessly. What about the massacre at Cawnpore? Two hundred women and children *butchered* after the garrison had been given safe passage." He shot Holt a steely look. "What's to prevent them from turning on us again?"

"India's part of the Crown now," Holt argued. "Soon to have its own laws and criminal code."

"Grand! And I suppose those things will cure our differences. Look around you, Mr. Atley." Marshall's arm swept across the primitive beauty of Jagmandir and the palace beyond. "This doesn't look too much like jolly old England, now does it? Will those laws keep her safe from malaria, cholera, not to mention any other number of vile jungle diseases she could contract here?"

Holt remained silent.

"But I suppose all that wilderness appeals to you Americans," Marshall added snidely.

"I grew up in Boston, Mr. Marshall. A more civilized town you'll not find anywhere."

"Then what ever made you come here? To this . . . this jungle world?"

Holt looked off into the green hills beyond the lake. "I was born in India. My father was a captain in the British cavalry. My mother came here with her father, a botanist from Boston."

Marshall's interest sparked. "And your mother? What kind of life did she have in this infernal country?"

Holt didn't even need to say the words that now blared through his conscience. It had been a hard life. His mother had often fallen ill from the heat. His father had told him there were times she had lain all day in bed with a cool cloth on her head. She had almost died in childbirth because of inadequate medical help. But it wasn't until their bungalow burned down, when Holt's safety had been put at risk, that she'd agreed to leave her husband's side for Boston. The doctors in Boston thought her years in India had made her susceptible to the illness that had eventually taken her life years later.

"It was a . . . difficult life." His dreams of a life with Nicole in India slipped away. "My father eventually sent us to Boston to live with my mother's family."

"A sensible thing that."

Holt looked out over the cool blue waters of the lake. "Yes. Very sensible."

"Wish my Nick would be sensible."

"She may have to be," Holt said under his breath. "She just may have to be."

19

Nicole sipped her Madeira, trying to mask the smell of curry with the wine's mellow aroma. In the noon heat, there seemed no escaping the odor emanating from the varied dishes of light curries served for *tiffen,* the midday meal. She took another fortifying drink of Madeira, wishing she'd pleaded a headache and forgone the maharaja's luncheon. She was not the least bit eager to witness the promised elephant fight to follow. If she hadn't been so anxious to see Holt, she would not have come.

Nicole leaned against the straight-back chair enjoying the breeze stirred by the servant's five-foot-long fans made of peacock feathers. Out beyond the balcony's balustrade, she could see the courtyard leading to the enormous stone corrals where the maharaja kept his elephants. A large crowd had gathered for the coming spectacle, but her attention remained focused on Holt rather than elephant duels. Two days ago, she'd capitulated to her uncle's order and left Jagmandir for the main palace. Since then, she'd not had a chance to speak to Holt alone, and he'd not sought her out as she'd hoped, a strange occurrence in itself given the numerous messages he'd sent to the island palace. Now, just a few days before her scheduled departure for Bombay, the first inklings of doubt started to penetrate her shield of confidence, and she worried he might actually let her return to England.

As another wave of nausea seized her, Nicole took a deep breath, hoping to ease her queasiness. A smile crossed her lips and she laced her fingers together, resting her hands on her lap. She'd heard her sisters complain too often about unsettled stomachs and the lethargy that had plagued Nicole the past week not to know what those symptoms heralded. Anxious to tell Holt, she nonetheless held back her news, still unsure of his feelings for her. A marriage should be freely entered into. She would never use her condition to coerce Holt into a lifelong commitment.

From the corner of her eyes, she peeked over to where he sat next to the maharaja's Minister of Affairs. Her uncle and the British Resident sat on either side of them. A Muslim, the minister entertained in the maharaja's stead as the Hindu raja's religion prevented him from sharing a meal with his untouchable English guests. Holt sported a Banya coat and white Moormen's trousers, looking cool and relaxed in his native apparel in contrast to the Englishmen who appeared half-baked in jackets and ties, swabbing their faces with linen handkerchiefs. Dressed in a tight-waisted muslin gown of lime green, Nicole longed for the loose silk skirt and bodice she'd worn in the *zenana*.

"What's the matter, dear? Don't you care for the fine curry?" asked Mrs. Tod.

Nicole wrinkled her nose, sliding her plate farther from her. "I'm not hungry, thank you."

Sitting beside Nicole in her ever-present black bombazine, Mrs. Tod examined her charge with unsettling zeal. To Nicole, the curvaceous, white-haired matron, who had outlived three husbands, made widowdom appear an art form. Although, judging from her uncle's new solicitous attitude toward the lady, Nicole guessed that in her absence her chaperone had made some progress in that quarter.

"You don't look well, Nicole. Perhaps this heat is too much for you? Shall we retire?"

Tempted, Nicole glanced over to Holt, trying to determine if torturing herself by staying would yield her an opportunity to speak with him.

"Oh, you mustn't miss the elephant duel!" said the Resident's daughter beside her as the servants removed the meal and offered fruit and *paan* to the guests. "It's ever so exciting to watch." The girl's pale blue eyes looked ready to pop out of her head in expectation.

The maharaja entered the balcony, cutting off Nicole's response. The ruler seemed young for his station, perhaps in his late twenties or early thirties, and he walked with feline grace. Elegantly dressed in a rose brocade coat, he wore a traditional jeweled sword at his side and his beard was parted at his chin and brushed back against his cheeks. In his turban, a reported eighty feet of starched linen, shone an emerald almost the size of Nicole's fist. But it wasn't his finery that caught her attention. Rather it was his startling gold eyes that drew Nicole. She smiled when their gazes met, having already spoken to this royal relative. The maharaja returned her greeting and Nicole again felt her connection to these people. Despite her uncle's dictum, she'd accomplished her goals here in Udaipur. All her goals but one, that was. Nicole watched Holt thoughtfully as the maharaja seated himself on his red cushion and signaled for the duel to begin.

Two enormous tuskers came into the courtyard, their *mahouts* seated at their necks. The drivers urged their individual elephants to fight before the crowd of spectators. Neither seemed inclined, but just the thought of the gigantic beasts drawing blood made Nicole uneasy and she held the scented handkerchief she'd brought for such an emergency up to her nose.

Beside her, the British Resident's daughter watched the proceedings with slack-jawed awe. Nicole looked farther down the table to where Holt sat casually turning the stem of his glass. When he caught her watching him, he lifted his glass in a silent toast. Nicole smiled and winked at him. He looked so surprised by her gesture she almost laughed. With a small salute, he gave her an admiring grin. Under Mrs. Tod's watchful eyes, they'd been limited to these small acknowledgments.

Men came out to the courtyard and began prodding the elephants with sticks, finally resorting to firecrackers to rouse the beasts into a mild butting match. But soon the tuskers lost interest. One *mahout* tried to engage his elephant by beating the animal. The driver's cruelty made Nicole's nausea worse. She stood, about to excuse herself, when the enraged elephant seized the driver off its back with its trunk. Nicole gasped as the elephant dashed the man to the ground and trumpeted a call of rage. Watching the animal pound the body with its tusks, Nicole felt her knees go weak.

The other elephant charged. Shouts from the crowd buzzed in Nicole's ears. The attacking elephant knelt on the downed driver, smashing the *mahout* into a bloodied mass. Darkness engulfed her. She was fainting. Grabbing up her muslin skirt, she stumbled, knocking her chair backwards to the stone floor. She could barely hear the shouted instructions from the tower balcony. Turning, she escaped from the hideous bloodshed in the courtyard to the palace interior.

Holt watched Mrs. Tod fall in a dramatic swoon to the floor as Nicole fled. Immediately, Marcus Marshall ran to the chaperone's side. "Are you all right, Lizzy?" He patted the woman's hand gently.

Catching Marshall's eye, Holt signaled that he would go after Nicole. He sighed with relief when Marshall gave a short nod of assent and returned his attention to Mrs. Tod. It didn't take Holt long to find her. Nicole stood just inside the palace hall, her head resting against the cool marble wall.

She looked elegant and untouchable in her English finery, the perfect picture of an aristocratic lady. Even dressed as a Rajput princess, she'd not seemed as distant as she did now. Holt had to remind himself that this was the woman he'd held in his arms and made love to night and day alike. He knew every delectable inch of her skin. The times he'd asked for more than what his touch could give him, for the secrets deep inside her, she'd shared even what was hidden in her soul.

Stepping quietly behind her, he placed his hands on her shoulders and turned her around. She wrapped her arms around his waist, fitting against him like a missing half. Of their own accord, Holt's hands threaded through the curls she'd pulled off her face with a ribbon. He didn't know if his heart pounded from desire ignited by the touch of her body against his or the prospect of having his questions answered and losing her.

"That was awful," she breathed against him. "How could anyone consider that . . . that . . . *brutality* entertainment?"

Too distracted by his worries, Holt didn't reply. After his talk with her uncle, he'd determined Nicole should go home. He couldn't even pledge to return with her to England and live with her there as man and wife. He was Steven Atley's son. Hadn't his father promised his mother, year after year, that he would join his family in Boston? But he'd never been able to leave his enchantress, India. What would prevent Holt from betraying Nicole in the same way?

There was only one thing that stopped Holt from telling Nicole his decision, one question he must ask before seeing her to the gates of Udaipur. If she carried his child, then—and only then—could he risk a future together. Yes, his mother had led a lonely and difficult life in Boston, but nothing could compare to the pain he would cause Nicole if he forced her into society expecting a child without the benefit of marriage. He'd already determined that. Nor would he let any child of his grow up without his name for protection. For his son or daughter, he would ask any price. Knowing Nicole as he did, Holt thought she would agree with his reasoning. She'd been too moved by the plight of the abandoned baby they'd found not to.

Nicole nuzzled against him. "Oh dear, I've missed this." She looked up and smiled. "I've missed *you*."

"I've missed you too, *bacchi*."

Her finely arched brows pressed together in a frown. "You do understand why I stayed with the maharani so long, don't you Holt? I didn't mean to hurt you; it was something I *had* to do. You do see that, don't you?"

"I understand, *bacchi.*" *More than you know.*

As naturally as if they'd been together a lifetime, Holt lowered his lips to Nicole's. He knew immediately that the blood racing through him, filling him, had nothing to do with his questions and a hell of a lot to do with the sweet taste of her mouth and the soft curves pressed against him. With his hand he caressed her cheek, enjoying the silky feel of her skin. He pulled away to see the sleepy look of desire that he knew would darken her gold eyes at his touch. God help him, but at that moment, he actually prayed he was as fertile as Nicole made him feel.

"You looked pretty pale back there," he probed, trying to get the information he needed before anyone interrupted them. "Are you feeling all right, *bacchi*?"

Nicole blushed, looking twice as kissable as ever. Holt leaned toward her tempting mouth before catching himself.

"I feel wonderful . . . except for . . . Well, I guess I just didn't care for the maharaja's little show, that's all."

There seemed no subtle way to ask. Yet, if he missed this opportunity, when could he find the chance to speak with her again? They weren't in the jungle anymore, and unlike her uncle, her chaperone was quite strict about the dictates of propriety. "Nicole, I need to ask you . . ." He watched her smile fade at his serious expression. Driven by his desperation to know the truth, he plunged ahead. "Are you carrying my child?"

Nicole felt herself blush, ready to nod and reveal her suspicions, but something in the tense way Holt held her, the way he looked at her, as if he were *afraid* of her answer, made her pause. "Why do you ask?"

Holt raised his brows in surprise. "I'd say that's pretty obvious."

Nicole fell speechless at his sharp tone, unable to understand the anger she heard in his voice.

"Look, I didn't mean that the way it sounded. It's just that . . . *bacchi,* if you're carrying my child, I think we should do something about it."

"Do?" Nicole's pulse beat at her temples. She pulled away from Holt, not wanting him to feel how her hands trembled. "What could we possibly *do?*"

"Get married. What else?"

A horrible suspicion dawned on her as she watched Holt. His expression revealed nothing, but his words, the cold, callous way he'd said, "What else?" frightened her.

"And if I'm not," she asked, her voice shaking. "If I haven't conceived. Would you marry me then?"

"Bacchi . . ." He reached for her.

Nicole stepped back, not letting him touch her. "Dear God, you wouldn't." Holt stood before her, not denying her accusation as her heart cried out for him to do. "You're sending me home." Nicole shook her head, as if trying to wake up from a nightmare. "I thought . . ." Choking back a sob, she turned to run, but Holt grabbed her arm, digging his fingers into her skin to hold her still.

"Dammit, we don't have time for this." His eyes looked as brittle as the glass tiles decorating the wall behind him. "Are you pregnant?" He pronounced each word slowly, distinctly, as if it were a death sentence.

Nicole fought back the horrible desire to cry. Clinging to the anger welling up inside her for strength, she swung her arm free of Holt's grasp. He was right. She'd be weak and silly to run away now. This was a fight she couldn't afford to run from.

Facing him, concentrating on answering him in a voice that revealed none of her pain, she said, "You are a fool, Holt Atley."

His beautiful green eyes darkened to the color of malachite. "That's a quick change of subject, isn't it?"

"If I told you I was with child, you would marry me," she

said, ignoring his sarcasm. "If you were lucky enough to escape that particular circumstance, are you saying that after all we've shared, all we've been through together, I mean *nothing* to you?"

"You mean everything to me, *ba*—"

"Don't. Oh God, don't." Nicole shook her head, unable to listen to the endearment. She'd been so sure of Holt's feelings. She'd thought they shared the kind of love that had brought together her grandfather and her grandmother against all odds. God in heaven, could she have been wrong?

Holt placed a hand on her shoulder, gently this time, as if apologizing for his painful grip before. But Nicole feared it was too late. Though she thought frantically, she could find nothing to stop the course of what was about to happen. He would marry her if she told him she was pregnant—yet she could never marry him for that reason alone. She wanted love, not a forced marriage to satisfy convention.

"Nicole, if you're expecting my child, I need to know."

"No." She stilled her features into a stoic mask. "No, I'm not."

For a moment, he actually looked surprised, as if he'd not expected her answer. But then his eyes narrowed with suspicion. "How can you be so sure? It's not been more than a week since—"

"I'm sure. A woman knows these things."

"Well, a man doesn't. So explain to me how the bloody hell you can be so sure!"

"I had my monthly," she lied. "Is there anything else you need to know?"

Holt watched her for a moment. Then, reluctantly, she thought, he removed his hand from her arm and stepped back, away from her. "No." He lifted his hands in an incomplete gesture, then dropped them. "I guess there isn't."

"Good. Because I have a few things *I'd* like to say." She took a deep breath, not wanting tears to mar her speech. "When I first came here, you accused me of wanting to destroy the white tigress, a heinous crime in your book. In fact, you spent a great deal of energy and time making sure I —or anyone else—didn't harm Enchantress. You made me understand that by hunting the tigress I would kill something unique and precious. Something beautiful that deserved to be saved and protected." She choked back a sob. "Don't you see? Don't you understand? You're doing the exact same thing! You're trying to destroy something beautiful."

He looked at her with an expression she could not quite understand, something between compassion and pain. "Perhaps," he said quietly, "I believe I'm still protecting something." He took one of her curls and wrapped it around his finger, then let it go. "Something much more unique and precious than Enchantress."

"Oh please," she said in a whisper. "At the very least, spare me that." Tears welled up in her eyes, but she blinked them back. "Spare me the speech that this is for my own good!" Nicole wiped her eyes, refusing to let tears slip down her cheeks. She raised her chin to Holt and willed herself to feel nothing. No pain. No hope. No love. Nothing.

But she could not.

"A long time ago"—she placed one hand on his face, forcing him to look at her—"at the commissioner's ball, I looked into your eyes." As she spoke, she stared into eyes as green as the hillsides, as lush as the forests, searching for her answer. "And I thought I saw something very special there."

Nicole waited—waited for him to admit his love. Waited.

Holt remained silent.

She let her hand fall. Slowly, she turned from him. This time Holt didn't try to stop her as she walked away. Shaking her head, as if she couldn't quite believe how their story had ended, she kept moving toward the balcony, away from Holt. She stopped. Looking over her shoulder, she said, "What I saw in your eyes . . . I guess I was wrong."

* * *

"Here, I found this in your trunk."

Nicole turned away from the palace servants transporting her trunks outside for the trip to Bombay and looked at her uncle, surprised by his appearance. Since their fight in the maharani's receiving chamber, they'd each kept their distance. Then she saw the shimmering gold silk as he handed it to her.

"My grandmother's veil?"

"Now don't go getting your dander up because I was pawing through your things. At the time . . ." The small quiver she heard in her uncle's voice stunned her. As she watched, her uncle cleared his throat and tried again. "At the time . . ." But his voice cracked just the same.

"Oh hell." He looked above her head, appearing engrossed by the latticework of the stone screens in the apartments. When he lowered his gaze, Nicole could see a deep sadness in his eyes. "I thought I'd lost you, Nick," he said finally in that gruff voice that she'd always thought meant he cared. "It helped to be around your things." Then, squaring his shoulder, "That's when I found that heathen thing."

Nicole pulled the precious silk through her hands, wanting desperately to hug her uncle. But she remembered too clearly their last conversation, the horrible conclusions she'd made about her uncle's interest in her. Though she wanted his love, she'd settle for his acceptance. Until he understood that, their relationship would remain distant.

"I've been wondering what happened to grandmother's veil." She began winding the silk tightly around her hand. "You took it from the trunk and kept it." She looked at her uncle. "Why? It didn't belong to you, Uncle Marc."

"I took it because, *that*"—he pointed to the silk as if it were a python—"got my steam up! I didn't even know you had heathen things about. I almost threw the damn thing in the river!"

Nicole felt like laughing . . . or crying. She was so mixed up she didn't know which anymore. To her uncle, this veil was merely "heathen." She looked about the Moor-

ish style apartments with growing nostalgia, trying to mem-
orize every detail. There was so much she was leaving behind here in India: her past, her family . . . Holt. With a
sigh, she carefully folded the silk veil, ready to pack it with
her belongings. As they always had, these small tokens of
her grandmother's past would help the hurt when it threatened to overwhelm her. But this time she'd have an even
greater legacy to help her through the rough times until the
day she could somehow return to India. She smiled, thinking of her child. She knew it would be difficult, but she
wanted this child desperately. It was the only thing of his
Holt couldn't take away.

After tucking the silk in her bag, Nicole faced her uncle.
"I kept the veil hidden from you, Uncle Marc, because I
didn't think you'd understand. And you don't. You never
have understood my need to know about my grandmother's
people." She looked at him sadly. "I don't believe you ever
will."

"An ignorant fool, am I?" Uncle Marc held out his hand.
"I suppose that's why you never mentioned this little treasure as well."

Cupped in his palm, he held her grandmother's gold
locket.

"My locket!" Nicole's hands shook as she picked up the
precious gold. For an instant, she forgot their differences
and hugged her uncle, kissing his cheek with joy. "Oh,
thank you." She kissed him again. "Thank you. You don't
know what this means to me." She opened the gold fastener
and looked at the miniature inside. "However did you find
it?"

The silence that followed made Nicole stop admiring the
locket and frown at her uncle. "What is it? What aren't you
telling me?"

"The news isn't pretty, Nick."

Nicole held the locket protectively to her chest. "What's
happened?"

"It's Drew. I'm afraid he was a thief as well as a kidnap-

per." Her uncle's lips pressed together in a tight line, and he
slammed his fist against his thigh. "Bloody hell, I still can't
believe I could have been so wrong about a man." He shook
his head. "When I think of how my poor judgment hurt you
Nick—"

"Don't." Nicole placed her hand on his arm. "Don't torture yourself like this, Uncle. What's done is done. Drew
had us all fooled." She gave him a sad smile. "He was very
good at deceiving people."

Her uncle clutched her hand on his arm and gave it a
tight squeeze. "Thank you for that, at least."

"Now, tell me what happened."

"They caught him inside the commissioner's home steal-
ing some jewels. It seems Mrs. Ratcliffe walked in on him
and he threatened her. Luckily, she shot the misbegotten
dog before he could harm her. I wish to God I'd gotten a
crack at him." Her uncle looked as if he'd missed the trophy
of a lifetime.

"They found this in his pocket." He held up Nicole's
hand with the locket centered in her palm. "From the picture, the commissioner suspected it was yours. As you probably know," he said dryly, "it's an excellent likeness."

Nicole stared down at the locket. So Drew was dead. Shot
in the midst of one of his many crimes. She thought of all
the pain he had caused her. Interestingly enough, she felt
nothing. No satisfaction at his passing, no ache for his betrayal. Holt's rejection overshadowed any hurt Drew may
have caused her.

"It appears the scare was too much for poor Mrs. Ratcliffe." Her uncle dropped her hand and touched his finger
to his head. "The commissioner himself told me she hasn't
been the same since. But he'll take care of her. He hasn't left
her side since the shooting. In fact, Ratcliffe has turned in
his commission. He's going back to England so the missus
can recuperate. He named your friend here, Mr. Atley, as
his replacement." Her uncle frowned slightly. "A curious
thing that." He shook his head. "I would have bet my best

mount those two hated each other, but the commissioner said something about misjudging him." For a moment her uncle's frown deepened the lines of his face, then he shrugged his shoulders and looked up as if he had puzzled it out. "Perhaps it was Mr. Atley's heroic rescue of you that made the commissioner change his mind." He grinned. "I told him about it myself as soon as I got your message. He wanted me to pass on his suggestion that Atley take his place. But it appears our Mr. Atley doesn't have a grain of ambition. He turned it down flat. He claims he's doing fine as a forest officer."

"Yes," Nicole said softly. "That's what he loves best."

Refusing to feel sorry for herself, Nicole shook off her brooding mood. She'd done all she could to convince Holt of their love. He'd still rejected her. Looking down at the locket, she felt a small seed of hope for her relationship with her uncle. "So, Uncle, I'm curious." She held up the locket, letting it swing from its gold chain in front of her uncle's face. "Why did you give me this? Why *didn't* you chuck the lot in a river? Or give them to Mother when we got home?"

In an uncharacteristic gesture of warmth, her uncle took both her hands in his larger ones. His dark brown eyes focused on hers. "I'm giving you the veil and locket so you can understand. Anything I've ever done, I've done not for myself, but because I cared for you. After your father died —a damned foolish death that could have been avoided if he weren't so pigheaded—"

He cut himself off and looked sheepishly at Nicole. She couldn't help but smile. Here again was the stubborn man she'd known all her life.

"Nick girl," he said gruffly. "I took care of your family like my own. But you've always been the special one. You reminded me of your father. You had so much spirit, so much heart, just like Nicholas. And I missed him so. It's not true, this nonsense about my wanting to wipe out everything Indian in the family!" When Nicole would interrupt, he held up his hand and continued. "Perhaps, I was wrong to treat you like the son I never had. Maybe I *was* too hard on you. I've thought about it a lot," he said softly, "and maybe, just maybe, I was even harder on you because your father never listened to me and you did. I don't know." He shook his head. "But I do admit I drove you to be the best. I . . . I couldn't seem to help myself. You were so *damn good,* Nick. Better than I ever was." He smiled in a way that for the first time showed Nicole how much joy he received from her accomplishments. "I just got carried away is all."

As Nicole held the locket, he wrapped his hands around hers, so that their hands encompassed the precious jewelry. "I'm giving you this, not because I want you to have it—I wish *you* would throw the thing in the river and forget all about your grandmother—but to show you I love you. I always have. And if you have to tell the whole world you're a damned heathen"—his hand tightened around hers—"I'll still love you. I'll think you're a fool for giving people the power to hurt you. But I'll love you just the same."

Nicole hugged her uncle as she'd wanted to do since he'd walked in the door, as she'd wanted to do all her life. "Thank you, Uncle Marc," she whispered in his ear. "I love you, too." Perhaps she'd lost Holt, but at least she had her uncle's love.

He squeezed the breath from her, then pushed her back to look at her. "You always had spunk, Nick. That's what I always liked about you." He patted her back roughly. "That and your eagle eyes. God, you've made me proud."

"I hope I'll continue to do just that." The queasy feeling in her stomach doubled as she thought of her uncle's reaction to her baby.

As if he'd read her mind, her uncle shook his head and sighed. "I have an awful feeling that when I get you back to England, you're going to be a great trial to me, girl." He placed his arm around her shoulders and turned her to the door. "Come on, Nick. Let's go home."

* * *

Nicole walked with the rest of the party down the crowded street to the Tripolia, the triple portals guarding the sacred enclosure to the palace. Beyond them etiquette permitted the visitors to mount their horses and carriages and continue to the "Gate of the Sun," where they would leave Udaipur. Until then they would walk on foot down the main street, followed by the *zenana* carriage conveying the maharani and her servants. On either side of them well-dressed natives shouted, *"Jy! Jy! Frengi ca Raj!"* wishing the English well. Nicole glanced at Holt beside her uncle, but looked quickly away when their eyes met.

At the Tripolia, the party came to a halt. For the first time since they'd begun their long walk from the palace, Nicole turned back to see its magnificent marble and granite walls. Its cupola-topped towers and enormous terrace ran parallel to Lake Pichola. The lake waters acted as a perfect mirror, reflecting the palace's majestic image.

Watching the shimmering picture in the water, Nicole thought of what her life would be like back in England. Unmarried and expecting a child was surely a formula for disaster. For an instant she wanted to run back through the streets and lose herself in the frescoed palace halls, but then she dismissed her fears. She'd never led a conventional life. She no longer craved the acceptance that had driven her to India in the first place. Perhaps with their newfound understanding, her uncle would find it within himself to help her provide for her child. Then there was her brother. Instinctively, she counted on his support as well until she could return to India. Though she didn't know when it would be possible, deep in her heart, she knew she must come back. No child of hers would grow up ignorant of their rich heritage as she had.

Inside the *zenana* carriage, Nicole hugged her great aunt, promising to write. Many of the women of the *zenana* had accompanied the maharani and all appeared sorry to see Nicole leave. Holding her great aunt, watching the sad faces of the women beneath their *purdah* veils, Nicole remembered happier times. They'd teased her mercilessly in the *zenana* about her age and unmarried status. It had taken Nicole some time to be comfortable with the ribald humor of the harem. Even more difficult to accept was her aunt, a woman of great dignity, as the interpreter for these suggestive remarks. But now she rejoiced in their past teasing as it permitted her to ask the one question she'd been unable to dismiss since Holt had rejected her.

At first, the maharani looked puzzled by Nicole's query. She questioned her attendants in *Mahari,* the dialect of the Rajputs, and the women laughed among themselves, then whispered their answers like naughty children. Her eyes shining with merriment, the Maharani asked, "You speak perhaps of the *Kamasutra?*"

Nicole blushed. "Yes. That's the book."

"Though I am reluctant to admit it, I am familiar with this book. My husband was very accommodating in satisfying my curiosity about such things. What is it you wish to know, Aisha's granddaughter?"

"It has rules?"

"Oh, yes. Many." She laughed and translated Nicole's question. Musical laughter filled the latticework enclosed cart.

In her mind Nicole saw Holt lowering her to the ground, hovering over her. He'd brushed the hair from her face and said gently: *Those rules don't apply to us.* As he'd spoken, the expression on his face had made her believe he loved her. It was almost as if, by telling her the rules did not apply to them, he was proclaiming his love.

"Those rules," Nicole asked. "Are there specific instances in which they no longer apply?"

The maharani's face softened. "I was once worried that I did not please my husband, that perhaps my education as a wife was less than complete. I wanted to know what I could learn from the *Kamasutra.* To ease my fears, my husband told me that I should not worry, that the rules do not apply to people who love truly, or so the sage Vatsyayana states."

She smiled. "He was a bit of a romantic, my husband." She looked thoughtfully at Nicole. "Remember the lesson of your grandmother and grandfather. No rules apply in true love."

One single tear slid down her cheek. Nicole brushed it away with her finger. "Thank you."

"Why so sad, Aisha's granddaughter? Was this not the answer you hoped for?"

Nicole shook her head, denying the tears in her eyes. "It's what I always believed. I'm just happy to know for certain, that's all."

Stepping outside the *zenana* carriage, Nicole searched for Holt. She found him standing apart from the others, his hands buried deep in his trouser pockets. He watched her with an unreadable expression as she walked toward him. Halting just within his reach, Nicole returned his gaze, trying to decide what had made Holt stop loving her.

Her uncle called to her to mount up. Nicky turned and walked to her pony. She swung her trousered leg over the saddle and looked for one final time at the man she loved so dearly.

Those rules don't apply to us, he'd said.

As she watched, Holt raised his arm, as if he meant to call her back with a wave. But then he stopped. Slowly, he lowered his hand and gave her a farewell salute. Nicole turned away before he could see her expression. Kicking her horse into a run, she headed for the city gates.

20

Padmini bowed before the stone image of the goddess. Clay lamps lit the temple walls as supplicants lay down their gifts of grain and incense purchased with *ghee* and copper money. Light-headed from nine days of fasting, Padmini prayed for strength as well as Nursoo's swift return. Incense filled the air in the stone and slate shrine and Padmini looked to where her offering of whole pulse lay piled in a small mound at the goddess's feet. A cobra slithered past an iron trident thrust into the dirt floor, moving toward a bowl of milk next to the grain offerings. As his assistant beat the drums at the entrance to the shrine, the *pujari,* the temple priest, waited for the supplicants to state their claims to the goddess.

"All that we were asked to do, we have done," Padmini's mother murmured to the goddess. "The girl speaks her *mantras.* She has fasted until I fear for her health. I have never lost faith, yet you do not listen to us. The groom has not returned. The girl's ill luck remains."

"You must be patient," said the priest.

"It is a new moon tonight, and yet we have heard nothing."

The *pujari's* expression darkened at this challenge to his influence. But before he answered, he appeared to give her mother's request some thought. "A stronger remedy is needed. The girl should continue the *mantras* and fasting as well as regular attendance at the temple. One rupee shall be delivered to the shrine at Pali. This shall appease the goddess."

Padmini's mother paid the *pujari* the cash offering, as well as flour and *ghee* for his services. Digging her fingers into Padmini's upper arm, she led her daughter out of the temple and down the small ridge toward the center of town. Padmini nearly tripped a number of times on the hem of her skirts, but her mother's merciless pace continued with the rhythm of her complaints against Padmini, a daughter who had brought her family nothing but hardship. As the sun set on the mountainside, not once did her mother lighten her tone or her grip.

For Padmini, seeing her house nestled against the hillside meant a release from her mother's poison tongue and a much-needed rest. With her vision blurred from hunger, she did not at first believe her eyes when she saw the beautiful white horse her brother Sagi tended just beyond the veranda. She blinked and looked again, almost stumbling off the stone causeway, but the apparition remained. The horse could belong to none other than the British sahib. Her pulse beating like the temple drums, she threw off her mother's hand and ran ahead to the raised path leading to the *ghar* house.

"You'd better pray to the goddess that the sahib knows your groom's whereabouts!" her mother shouted after her.

Padmini circled the veranda, entering through the rear. She staggered through the darkened room to the front reception chamber. Clutching her *purdah* veil, she waited at the doorway where she could not be seen, suddenly afraid of the plan she'd devised hurriedly before she reached the house. The voices inside sounded angry, difficult to understand. She tried to still her breathing so she could make out the words of the company inside.

"It shall be as I say, Nursoo. I am the girl's father. I decide who she will or will not marry."

"That decision was made long ago, when you allowed your daughter to keep my sister's necklace. The Nai and

Brahman were sent for. I have brought the sum you required from me. You must honor the *sagai* engagement!"

"But when the vows are broken—when the bridegroom defiles the bride before the wedding—he must be made to pay an adequate compensation."

"You imply—"

"I imply nothing! I say it outright. The girl has confessed to her foolishness. She says you seduced her of her innocence. For this you must pay. You have the six hundred rupees. What is one hundred more to one such as you?"

Silence followed her father's contemptuous words. Now was the time for her to reveal her father's game, to tell Nursoo that her family had little choice but to accept any offer given for a daughter who had already had the ill luck to be widowed. But despite her great desire to do so, Padmini's feet seemed planted as firmly as the great trees of the forest. She feared the contempt she would see on Nursoo's face when she told him the truth.

"I do not believe Padmini told this tale of seduction," Nursoo replied. The faith she heard in his voice made her ashamed of her own weakness and, despite her fears, she crossed the threshold. "More likely," his voice continued, "that her father has once again found himself in trouble with the moneylenders and gambles for what he has no right . . ."

Holt watched a girl dressed in colorful cottons step across the room to Nursoo's side as the Hindu's words trailed off. She kept her veil pulled over her head concealing her face like a monk's cowl. But Holt knew immediately by the gentle hand Nursoo placed at the girl's arm that this was Padmini, the girl they'd spent the last twenty minutes haggling over like fishwives.

"What you say is true," the girl said in soft Kumauni. The lilt to her voice made Holt smile for the youth and beauty it promised despite the concealing veil. "My father is no longer able to pay the interest on the money he owes."

"That's enough, Padmini." The girl's father grabbed her

arm and pulled her roughly away from Nursoo. Before Nursoo could counter the attack, Holt put a firm hand on his shoulder, knowing that a tug of war with the girl's father would not help his friend's cause.

"They try and trick you into marriage." Pulling away from her father's restraining arm, Padmini leaned toward Nursoo until her veil fell off her face. Almond-shaped eyes the color of obsidian seemed to plead with his friend. Looking at her perfect features, the high cheekbones heralding Mongolian ancestors, the full lips of her mouth marred only by their anxious turn, Holt knew immediately how Nursoo could have fallen in love at the mere sight of this girl. But the pallor of her skin, the perspiration on her brow despite the cool evening, worried Holt.

When her father tried to drag her from the room, the girl shouted, "They have hidden from you that I am a widow. Unclean. No man in the village will have me."

Her father turned her to him. "That you should dare to speak so!" With his open hand, he slapped his daughter's face, sending her to the ground. This time, Holt did not stop Nursoo as his friend pushed the father aside and knelt down to hold his betrothed. Holt stepped in front of the father, blocking his path to the couple before he could interfere.

"I never lied about the night we met," Holt heard Padmini whisper to Nursoo. "I *told* my mother how honorably you behaved, even though I was too much of a coward to admit how I implored you to break those vows."

"My love, do not—"

"My father will marry me to you at all costs. Who else would have me, a widow? And though my parents have hidden the truth from the village, I will never hesitate to speak it again." Holt watched her gasp for breath, as if she found it difficult to talk. With a warning glance to the father, Holt knelt down beside the girl. Her eyelids appeared heavy. Perspiration lined her upper lip. "Do not let him force you. I have never spoken of seduction. I have . . ."

She blinked rapidly; her fingers dug deeper into Nursoo's shoulder. "I have admitted to no—"

Her beautiful eyes rolled back and the girl fell limply against Nursoo.

"Sahib! Help me!"

Gently, both he and Nursoo laid her out on the ground. Pushing aside the heavy bracelets that covered her wrists, Holt checked her pulse. Her wrists were small, birdlike bones poking out from the skin of her hands. He could barely make out a pulse.

"She's very weak." He met Nursoo's worried gaze. Holt lifted up her thin arm for him to see. "At a guess, I'd say she's fainted from a lack of food."

The fury he saw in Nursoo's eyes frankly surprised Holt. Never had he seen his friend display anger so openly.

Turning on Padmini's father, he shouted, "She has been made to suffer for your foolish beliefs!"

The father looked worriedly at his daughter. "I know nothing other than that she visits the village priest with my wife. Is the girl dead?" he asked wringing his hands.

"No. Just fainted. She'll need some water," Holt ordered.

Padmini's father called for his wife. A woman whose veil could not hide her haggish posture or skin shriveled by years of working in the fields came into the room with two other women. After instructions from Padmini's father, the woman returned with a dampened cloth and a cup. The touch of the cool cloth woke Padmini from her stupor. Holt gave Nursoo an encouraging smile while she drank from the cup he held to her mouth. "She'll be all right with some food and rest."

After instructing the women on her care, Holt told Nursoo to carry Padmini to the room upstairs. Watching his friend's gentle care for his beloved, as if she were the greatest treasure in this world, Holt wondered again if he'd made a serious mistake by letting Nicky return to England without him. In the almost two months since her departure, he'd helped Nursoo to earn the money for Padmini's bride price.

The well had taken longer to finish than either had expected. During that time, India and her beautiful countryside had proven a poor substitute for Nicole's loving arms.

Forcing himself to focus on helping Nursoo, Holt banished his thoughts of Nicole when his friend returned. He could see Nursoo was close to losing control.

"You gambled correctly, old man. I want your daughter. My clan accepts widow-marriage."

"As do all low-class—"

"But you will settle for the six hundred you first coerced from me. I'll not give you an *anna* more."

For the first time, Padmini's father showed real fear. "But I need the money . . . the moneylenders threaten me daily."

Taking a kid-leather pouch from his coat, Holt threw the bag onto the floorboards in front of the father's feet. "There's over a hundred there."

Nursoo eyes widened. "Holt sahib, I will not allow—"

"An early wedding present." When Nursoo still protested, Holt said, "You're like a brother to me, Nursoo. Allow me this one pleasure." Then, glancing toward the stairs leading to the chamber above them he added so only Nursoo could hear, "If he doesn't get his money, he could take it out on the girl. She's not just weak from lack of food, Nursoo, there were bruises up and down her arms, and she'll have more come morning from that slap. Don't let her suffer anymore. Bend that pride of yours this once."

Faced with the possibility of danger to Padmini, Nursoo agreed immediately. "It will be as he says," he told the father. "But when I leave here with my bride, never will I hear from you again, old man. Never. Your problems are now yours alone."

Holt followed Nursoo to the door. At the threshold Nursoo turned back to Padmini's father. "The wedding ceremony will take place at my family's village. I will consult the astrologer for a speedy date."

* * *

Pacing outside the doors of her brother's study at Eldridge Manor, Nicole knew the exact moment her uncle told Keane about the baby. The rafters shook.

She should never have allowed Uncle Marc to speak with Keane first. Though it had only been three days since she had returned to Eldridge, the Salisbury estate where Nicole had been raised, she'd been perfectly ready to tell her brother about her condition. After all, if she could come through the gauntlet of Uncle Marc's anger and disappointment, she thought herself able enough to face her beloved brother's wrath. Though often absent during her years growing up at Eldridge, her brother had always been understanding. He'd been the only one to accept Nicky's desire to learn more about her Indian heritage. Of course an illegitimate child might test even Keane's composure.

"I know just the tack to take with Keane," her uncle had insisted. "I'm privy to a particular bit of information about your brother's past that will make your condition just a bit easier to swallow."

Nicole had found *that* difficult to believe. What could be more scandalous than a young lady of the aristocracy expecting a child without the benefit of matrimony?

The door slamming open startled Nicole from her thoughts. Keane Marshall, Viscount Eldridge, head of the ever-expanding Marshall household, stood indignantly at the threshold. Behind him hovered her uncle, his gray brows furrowed in concern.

"He didn't take it near as well as I'd hoped." Uncle Marc stared peevishly at Keane. "I thought I was the dunderhead when it came to you, Nick."

"Do shut *up,* Marcus." The tall and slim lord, his amber eyes blazing, his light brown hair devoid of white despite his forty-two years, looked angry enough to pull Nicole over his knee. The last time he'd done that Nicole had been eight. She remembered it distinctly as the first and last time he'd actually hit her. Disobeying her brother, she'd jumped a fence he'd said was too dangerous. When she'd fallen off her pony, Keane had been the first to make sure she was all right. Nicole remembered how angry she'd been with herself for recovering her breath and jumping to her feet, thereby proving to all she was in fine fettle—and giving Keane an excuse to give her a solid spanking.

Now, thirteen years later, her brother pointed in his study with the finality of the Grim Reaper. "Get in here, Katherine Nicole Marshall."

At the worst possible moment, Keane's wife, a beautiful redhead whose regal height had always made Nicole regret that she'd not inherited her father's stature, as her sister Charlotte had, appeared down the hall.

"Why in the world are you shouting at Nicky like that, darling?" Esmeralda hurried to Nicole's side, wrapping a protective arm around her. Nicky sighed, knowing her sister-in-law's intervention would only complicate matters. Nicole rolled her eyes upward in despair. Would it have been too much to hope that the motherly Esmeralda would be occupied elsewhere? Lord, where were her niece and two nephews when she needed them?

"This has nothing to do with you, Esmeralda!" Keane shouted.

The redhead's emerald eyes drifted from Nicole to Uncle Marc, as if waiting for someone to disagree.

"You can stop looking to them, wife, as if this were a vote in the House of Lords. They have got absolutely no say in this!"

"It's all right, Esme." Nicole brushed past her brother and uncle, into the study. "I can handle things now."

Her sister-in-law followed, apparently unconvinced. Giving her husband a stern expression of disapproval, she stood at the door. "When he starts calling me 'wife,' there's always trouble—"

"Esmeralda!"

Nicky gave her a nudge. "Please don't worry. I have Uncle Marc with me." When Esmeralda looked at her as if she were mad seeking protection from one tyrant against another, Nicole's gentle push out the door became insistent. "If he grabs for a sharp object, I'll be sure to call out."

Keane slammed the door as his wife's backside barely cleared the threshold. He turned and walked to his oak desk, glancing at the portrait over the fireplace as if seeking counsel there. The painting was of Philip, their deceased brother. Older than Keane, Philip would have inherited the family title if not for the sailing accident that had taken both his and their father's life. Though she'd been born after his death, she knew Keane had held a deep respect for his brother's judgment, and suspected that was why he had ordered the portrait hung in his study, where he conducted most of his business.

Nicole jumped at the sound of Keane's fist hitting the desk. She looked over to Uncle Marc where he leaned against the mantel. He looked worried. Very worried. But when her gaze returned to her brother standing behind his desk, his amber eyes shone with concern and not anger. "Ah, Nicky. Tell me it's not true."

"I cared very much for the father of my child, Keane," she answered softly. "I'm not sorry this happened."

She heard her uncle clear his throat loudly, as if to say this might be a poor tactic. But as Nicole watched, the hard lines of her brother's face eased a fraction. "Then it's true what Marcus told me. You weren't . . . forced?"

She shook her head, touched by her brother's concern under the circumstances.

"I was afraid perhaps . . . during your abduction, that is . . ." He seemed uncomfortable with the subject for a moment, then, all business once more, he said, "You could tell me, you know, if you were. I want to know the truth."

"I was quite a willing participant." Hoping he would understand, she added, "Keane, I loved him. I still do."

Keane closed his eyes, as if her words caused him pain. When he looked at her again, the fire had returned to his amber gaze. "Damn him for taking advantage of that."

Nicole walked to the armchair before her brother's enormous desk and sat down slowly. She used the expanse of wood as a barrier between them, as if needing the distance for protection. Thinking of all the things he could as the head of the family force her to do, Nicole watched Keane anxiously. Uncle Marc stepped away from the mantel to stand behind her chair, resting his arm across her shoulders in a show of support.

Keane glared at their uncle. "Sit down, Marcus. You're looking at me as if I'm going to clap Nicole in irons or have her whipped at the post!"

Uncle Marc stood his ground. "As I said before, I take full responsibility for what happened. You can't really blame the girl, Keane. The man rescued her from a grisly death. I'm sure she was grateful and he took advantage—"

"Actually, Uncle Marc"—Nicole stared down at her hands clasped on her lap—"the deed was done long before that."

"What?" This time it was her uncle who sounded angry. "Nicole! What in blazes—"

"Oh, for God's sake!" Keane shouted. "Does it really matter *when* it happened—"

"I just want to make it clear I acted out of my own volition." Nicole tried to explain.

"—this is not a tribunal on Nicky's morality," her brother continued, not listening to Nicole.

"You'd be the last one to point the finger if it were, Keane," her uncle rallied. "It's not like you've an unblemished record, after all."

For the first time in her life, she saw Keane lose his composure. A deep red flush, reminiscent of Uncle Marc's many fits of temper, crept up her brother's handsome face. She looked to her uncle, who now stood beside her, for an explanation.

"Are you going to tell her, Keane? Or shall I?" her uncle challenged. When her brother only glowered at him, he added, "It's only fair. Why should Nick think she's the only one with a weakness for the flesh?"

Keane laughed then, a harsh, grating laughter that didn't sound the least bit amused. "Weakness for the flesh, Marcus? That sounds a bit overdramatic even for you, dear uncle." Keane stared at Uncle Marc with a ferocity Nicole had thought he reserved for the bargaining table of one of the family's many enterprises. "All right, Marcus. You've made your point." He turned to look at Nicole with the same intense glare. Nicole sat up straighter in the armchair.

"You are a young lady in one *hell* of a lot of trouble. But I'm not here to condemn you for your actions. There was a time in my life that I acted without thinking of the consequences to my family name." Keane glanced angrily at her uncle. "When Marina was conceived, Esmeralda and I were not married. Through some careful paperwork, which Uncle Marc had a hand in, I was able to conceal that fact. By the time Marina was born, of course, we were legally wed, but the papers I have show a much earlier date."

"I could do the same for you, Nick," her uncle said promptly. "What do you think? Will the Atley fellow marry you? We could say you wed in India."

Nicole hated to shatter the expectant look on her uncle's face. She could see he wanted desperately to make everything all right for her. Truly she had never thought her uncle loved her as much as she did at this moment. But then she thought of Holt's cold proposal. *We should do something about it.*

She shook her head. "No. No, he won't marry me."

"The bastard." Uncle Marc punched his fist against his thigh.

Keane sighed, as if he'd hoped the answer would be that simple. "If I can, I would like to make arrangements for some suitable young man, perhaps someone already familiar with one of the Marshall enterprises—"

"No," Nicole said.

"The child needs a father," her uncle argued.

"I can't just marry anyone!"

"Be reasonable, Nick. Keane will find a decent fellow—"

"No!"

"I would think, Nicole," Keane said in an icy voice, "that having never had a father, you of all people would never deny your child the benefit of one."

Nicole vaulted to her feet. "Oh, unfair!"

Keane stood to her challenge. "I don't care dammit! I will not have you destroy yourself—"

"I've already thought of all that!" she yelled back. "I won't do it. And though I'm sure it's quite selfish of me, I . . ." She groped for the words, tears coming to her eyes. "I simply . . ." Meeting Keane's gaze, she pleaded, "Don't tell me to marry some stranger I've never met for the good of the baby. I can't. In my heart, I'll always be married to the father of my child."

"Nicky." Keane shook his head, leaning forward on his desk on both hands, as if defeated. "If you'd said anything but that."

Keane stared into the distance. Both her uncle and Nicole waited expectantly. He again shook his head, as if disbelieving of the entire situation, before looking up at Uncle Marc. "I would like you to leave us now, Marcus."

"But I thought—"

Stepping out from behind his desk, her brother stood to his full height. "I need to discuss some things with Nicole," he said, his voice that of a noble dictating orders with quiet authority. "Alone."

Uncle Marc's face fell in disappointment. He turned to Nicky. "I'll be outside if you need me girl. And don't you worry. Between your brother and I, we'll protect you." He gave her shoulder a pat. "I'll not let you down again, Nick."

Nicole watched her uncle exit the room. She couldn't speak, she felt so full of love for him. The relationship that had developed between them almost made up for everything that had happened to her in India. But when she turned back to her brother, she felt a wealth of sadness for the burden she had foisted on him.

With a sad smile, he said, "I can't help but feel that I've failed you miserably, scamp."

The use of her old childhood nickname made her throat grow tighter. She blinked back her tears. Maybe Uncle Marc and Keane weren't her father, but at last she knew for certain that these two men cared for her as if they were.

"I should have never let you go to India."

"But you of all people," she said, "know how much it meant for me to go there. You gave me Grandmother's locket. You smuggled all those books past Mother."

"Then I should have taken you myself, dammit. I could have protected you from what happened. I should never have allowed Marcus to take my responsibilities"—he slammed his fist on his desk, then shook his head—"as I *always* have."

Nicky could see he blamed himself. She didn't want her brother hurt. "Uncle Marc was very good to me."

Keane looked as if that were the last thing he'd expected her to say. "No. No, he wasn't. You see, I knew. I *knew!*" The lines of his face grew sharper, angrier. "Even as I let him spend more and more time with you after my marriage. Even as I let him take *my* place as your father while you grew up, I knew it was wrong. Oh, certainly I convinced myself it was for the best, that Uncle Marc would give you the attention you needed, attention I was having trouble providing for my own daughter and sons. But I knew it was wrong." His lips tightened. "Dammit, he treated you like a boy. You spent all your time isolated from any feminine influence, wearing trousers and hunting. I turned a blind eye on it all, telling myself it's what made you happy." He shook his head. "How would you ever know about the womanly things, to protect yourself from a man's passion?"

"Protect myself?" she asked, surprised by his logic. "And what twisted influence made Esmeralda susceptible to your wiles, Keane? No. You know that's not the way the thing works. When you love someone, really love someone, as Esme loves you—as I love my child's father—you *want* to give everything." She smiled, hoping her words eased his guilt. "No one could have protected me from that."

Nicole walked around her brother's oak desk to his side. She pulled him down to the carpet, making him sit beside her on the floor as she'd done often when she was a child. In a very soft voice, as if afraid to even confess the words out loud, she told him, "I did indeed feel quite sorry for myself when you turned your attentions away from me to your own children."

"Oh, scamp—"

"But I'm a mother now, or soon will be. And I think I understand. And I agree with your choice. You were right to put them first."

"No," he said stubbornly. "When Father died, and you were born, I swore I'd be both brother and father to you. I promised Mother you'd lack for nothing—"

"And as usual, you thought yourself quite invincible, capable of any task. But you're only *one* man." She took both his hands in hers. "You did as fine a job as you could. Keane, I learned a lot of things about myself in India. Including all those 'womanly things' you're so scared I may have missed under Uncle Marc's influence. So, you see, I'm quite whole now. It's my future we should be discussing, not my past."

Keane gave her hands a squeeze. "You're right, of course."

Nicole took a deep breath, worried that despite the closeness she felt with Keane, she was asking too much. "After my child is born," she said, "perhaps I will return to India. To him. For the time being, I wish to marry no one else, and"—she hesitated to burden him with this request—"and I don't want to go away for the birth. If I can't have my child in India with his or her father beside me, I want to stay here, at Eldridge, where I was born. With my family. You see," she said softly. "I don't really care to face this alone." Before he could interrupt, she added, "But I'm willing to go away, if you say I must, to save the family from scandal. But dearest brother—no matter what the consequences—I will never give up my child."

He shook his head. "I wouldn't ask it of you, Nicole."

"So. What do I do?" She waited anxiously for his decision.

Staring at her with those amber eyes that always looked so shocking in contrast to his tanned face and light hair, Nicole felt a little apprehensive. Her future lay in her brother's hands. She knew that no matter what she threatened, she would have to live with her brother's decision.

He released her hands and stroked her cheek. "You truly love this man and will have no other?" She nodded. "Well then." He sighed, rising to his feet as he pulled Nicole up with him. "We'll just have to think of some other solution."

"I have thought of a plan," she said tentatively, afraid to tell her brother of her preposterous idea. "I could," she said, "*pretend* to have married."

Keane stared at her in surprise. "Just tell everyone you actually wed the fellow?"

"Why not? Who could prove otherwise? He has little or no connections in this country. No title or money that would make anyone care if I were to take his name. I doubt he'd learn anything about it. He's in the hills of India in the north, as far away from civilization as possible."

Keane seemed to think a moment. "It might work," he said under his breath. He looked at her sternly. "Don't think for a minute it will be easy, Nicole."

She held her breath. "No. No, I don't believe it will be."

"There will be talk."

"I know that."

"*Lots* of it as long as no husband actually shows up—"

She lunged into her brother's waiting arms. "Oh Keane. Then you'll let me stay? You won't send me away?"

He hugged her warmly to him as he whispered, "It was never an option."

* * *

Holt scratched between the lemur's ears as he watched Nursoo, dressed in the traditional red coat and yellow loincloth for his wedding, smile at his bride as they exchanged garlands of flowers. Two months had passed since Nicole had left him. Holt had not anticipated the pain that would come with watching his friend happily wed Padmini, the woman he loved. But missing Nursoo's wedding had been out of the question. The marriage feast today marked one of many days of ceremonies to follow before Nursoo and his bride could drown the sacred jug together in the village stream. But the binding part of the ceremony, the steps taken around the sacred fire, had already taken place. Holt would leave his friend well and truly married.

As the women of the village led Padmini from her bridegroom, Nursoo managed to pull away from the revelers and walk over to Holt. He bowed in a deep *salaam.* Taking Jani off the perch of his shoulder, Holt returned the gesture, demonstrating that he shared his friend's deep respect. Each man watched the other silently for a moment before breaking into smiles and clasping each other in a warm embrace of farewell.

"You honor me and my family by staying for my marriage feast, Holt sahib. I know how anxious you are to begin your journey to Lucknow."

Holt placed Jani back on his shoulder, and the lemur curled around his neck. "Well, partner, do you think you can handle things while I'm gone? They're not much, but supervising two villages can be quite a job."

"Do not worry, sahib. I have learned from the best." Nursoo's smile faltered just a bit and his dark eyes grew somber. "How can I show you my thanks for what you have done for my family? The house," he turned to look over to the modest stone structure he would not have to share with anyone but his bride. "The money you gave Padmini's father—"

"I couldn't have my business manager impoverished!" Holt winked. "How would it look to the tenants?" When

Nursoo maintained his serious expression, Holt sighed. "We're a team now, Nursoo." Holt placed both hands on his friend's shoulders. "It's worth every rupee to me to know that things will be taken care of in my absence." Holt smiled. "Think you'll miss the *shikaree* business?"

Nursoo shook his head. "I shall enjoy managing my family's village and Baijnarn. And," he added with a glint in his eyes, "I believe I shall wish to stay closer to home from now on."

"Ah, yes. The alluring female you just married might change a man's views on endless wandering." Though he laughed with Nursoo, Holt experienced a sad emptiness when he thought of Nicole.

"There's one last thing I need you to take care of for me," he said after their laughter died away. He pulled the lemur from around his neck and gave her ear a last generous scratch before handing her to Nursoo. "Look out for her, will you?"

Nursoo placed the lemur gently on his shoulder. "Jani and I shall console each other at your loss."

"Thanks, Nursoo." Holt looked back to where he'd left his horse. "I'd best be going. It's a long trip to Lucknow."

Nursoo clapped his hand on Holt's shoulder, his expression one of deep concern. "The Khasiya believe it is inauspicious to visit these places of the dead you English are so fond of. But I understand that your customs are different. This is the way you worship your ancestors. Your father was a good man, Holt sahib. He did me a great kindness in my youth bringing us together. Be careful friend." Nursoo *salaamed* once more. "Do not let any spirits capture you at your father's grave."

"Actually, Nursoo"—Holt grinned—"I plan to dispel a few."

21

Standing before the enormous double oak doors of Eldridge Manor, Holt wondered if he'd made a terrible mistake.

In the four months since Nicole had said good-bye at the gates of Udaipur, it had taken half that time to discover he would rather live here with Nicky and raise a family than live anywhere else in the world without her. When he'd gone to his father's grave two months ago, he'd faced his fears for their marriage. He'd stood for hours at the grave side, comparing his life with his father's until he knew for certain he was not Steven Atley. He would never abandon a wife and child for adventure as his father had. But now looking at the doors of the palatial estate where Nicole lived, Holt wondered how things could ever work out between him and the aristocratic lady.

Funny how distance and time could blur a man's thinking and allow him to overlook the things he didn't want to accept. How could he have forgotten Nicky's background? He was a man of limited means. A position lecturing at one of the colleges would provide a comfortable living for someone used to camping out in the jungle, but their situation would be humble at best. The two villages he owned in India and the adjacent lands barely paid for themselves. Most of the revenues went to updating irrigation systems and providing a better standard of living for the natives who lived there. Staring up at the vine-covered eaves of the Tudor mansion, which could comfortably house the population of Baijnarn,

Holt had but one thought: *How the hell did I think I could take her from all this?*

He almost picked up his leather satchel and made his way to town on foot where he could hire a coach back to Oxfordshire. But instead, he forced himself to rap the heavy brass knocker and wait. He had come this far. He'd not turn back without at least speaking to Nicky.

One of the enormous oak doors inched open. A beautiful woman not much younger than his thirty-two years stared at him in surprise before consulting a watch pinned to the bodice of her elegant gown. She looked nothing like Nicole. Her hair was the color of the setting sun and her eyes were as green as the Udaipur emeralds. But Nicky had mentioned how different she was from her sisters, and this lady was most certainly a relative. Even though the woman gestured him in, Holt knew immediately from her elegant dress she was not a servant.

"Come in," she said, her educated voice confirming that she wasn't the hired help. "I'm afraid I've beaten Simms to the door again. He's certain to make a great fuss about it if he catches me. The man is such a ninny." Holt followed her through the door, a little taken aback by the lady's friendly manner. He'd always thought British nobility cold and standoffish.

"This way, please." At the end of the lavish entrance corridor, she looked both ways before turning back to Holt with a smile and leading him to a set of double doors. "You'll have to excuse my odd behavior, but the butler and I have this small misunderstanding about my 'usurping his duties' as he calls it. Last time he threatened to quit. Really, it's quite a challenge not to get caught. I must confess there's a certain thrill to it since Simms tends to be so dramatic about the whole thing."

Opening the doors to a salon, she froze. An elderly man dressed in a butler's uniform stood across the threshold on the other side.

"Your ladyship?" His watery blue eyes turned pointedly to Holt.

"Oh, Simms," she said giving Holt a conspiratorial wink. "I was just outside and ran into the Indian tutor Nicole's expecting. You do remember she said to be on the lookout for Mr. Singh around this time?"

Too stunned at the mention of the Indian tutor to correct his identity, Holt remained silent, trying to decipher the significance of this Mr. Singh. The butler's bland expression didn't change one fraction, but the redhead smiled as if she were enjoying herself a fair bit. "Would you please take Mr. Singh's hat and bag and let Nicole know her tutor has arrived?"

"Certainly, Lady Eldridge." With a sniff, and a quick turn on his heel that belied his apparent age, the butler quit the salon.

After the doors closed, a merry laugh escaped from behind her smile. "There now," she said, her green eyes sparking mischief. "I give the silly man ten minutes to find my husband and lodge a complaint." Motioning to the couch, she sat down in a tapestry armchair opposite. "Do make yourself comfortable."

Holt sat down on the couch, trying to decide whether to correct his identity before Nicole arrived. For all Holt knew, she wouldn't want to see him. His mistaken identity could be a stroke of fortune. He'd realized as soon as he'd handed the butler Professor Dawson's satchel, which Holt had borrowed as an overnight bag, that he could very well be mistaken for the expected instructor. In bold letters near the handle, the bag was stamped with the University's name and symbol. But why would Nicole need an Indian tutor? He'd thought she had made peace with her Rajput heritage and was ready now to settle down into the genteel life of a country heiress. Did India still interest her? *Why?*

"Nicole will be so pleased you've arrived." For a moment, she stared at Holt with a puzzled frown. "Although I must remark that you do not look a bit Indian, Mr. Singh." He was about to confess he wasn't, not prepared to out and out lie, when she continued, "But then to be quite honest I've met very few of your countrymen. Oh dear, I'm being terribly rude." She popped to her feet and offered her hand. Holt immediately rose and stretched his hand forward, meeting her halfway. "I'm the mistress of the house. Esmeralda Marshall, Viscount Eldridge's wife."

She shook his hand with a firm grip. "I'm so glad you've come," she said smiling warmly. "Nicole is absolutely desperate. She's had no luck at all finding someone fluent in *Mahari.* And she's so pressed for time."

The mention of the Rajput dialect surprised Holt. Nicole wished to learn *Mahari*? She was pressed for time?

"You are fluent in that dialect?" she asked worriedly. "I've not made a mistake have I?"

"I speak *Mahari,* yes," he said slowly. "But I'm better at *Kumauni.* "

She stared at him strangely for a moment. "Your accent? You're American?"

"My mother was American."

Lady Eldridge nodded, taking it for granted that his father had been Indian as Holt had intended her to. An absolutely incredible possibility was forming in his mind. Despite all the elegant wealth surrounding her, could Nicole be preparing to return to India? *To me?*

Sitting down in her chair, the lady gestured for Holt to do the same. "Well, I'm sure she'll want to learn anything you can teach her, *Mahari, Kumauni,* whatever. She seems compelled to learn everything she can before returning to India."

"Miss Marshall is planning a trip to India?"

Lady Eldridge looked startled, as if he'd said something wrong. "You mean *Mrs. Atley.* Nicole is quite married. In fact, my sister-in-law is returning to join her husband in India. I believe this was all explained in her letter of inquiry . . ."

Her words faded as Holt sat nonplussed on the couch. In

his head he could hear only the words "Mrs. Atley, Mrs. Atley," ringing over and over.

"You did receive Nicole's letter?" Holt looked up to where Lady Eldridge now stood in front of him, staring at him with an anxious expression. "You are the tutor she is expecting, aren't you?"

Holt rose to his feet, meeting Nicole's sister-in-law face to face. For the first time during their fantastical conversation, he permitted himself a wide grin. "I'm precisely the tutor . . . *Mrs. Atley* . . . has been waiting for." He gave the last name a mocking ring.

Just then, Simms opened the doors to the salon. Beside him was an Indian gentleman dressed in English clothing.

With an arch to his brow and a dry edge to his voice, Simms pronounced in a bored voice, "Mr. Arjun Singh, Madame." In his hand, the butler produced a silver salver with a delicate square of white centered on it. "This one has a card."

Esmeralda turned and stared at Holt. Her green eyes locked on his as her welcoming smile vanished. "Please show Mr. Singh to the blue room, Simms."

As soon as the door closed, her eyes narrowed and she crossed her arms before her. "All right. You've had your fun. Who *are* you?"

"The name's Holt Atley." Holt grinned as Lady Eldridge's disapproving features transformed into a look of utter astonishment. "Tell Nicole she doesn't need to go to India to find her husband. He's just arrived."

Nicole stood outside the salon doors, staring down at the pleated folds of her gown. Her sister-in-law had told her not to worry, that her condition hardly showed. But Nicole feared that the man familiar with every inch of her shape would know the instant she walked through the door that she had lied to him those many months ago. In her opinion, not only did she *look* five months pregnant, despite the gown's clever camouflage—she *felt* like she'd swallowed a pumpkin.

He'd be angry, she told herself. The fact that she was passing herself off as his wife was probably the least of her concerns. He'd asked her outright at the palace at Udaipur if she were carrying his child and she'd lied. He'd probably think it unforgivable that she'd withheld the truth about her condition, but Nicole knew she'd do it all over again given the circumstances. She wanted more than a commitment from Holt—she wanted love. Now, four months since they'd parted, she was faced with the possibility that he'd followed her to England because he did indeed care for her. Why else would he leave his beloved India? But would the fact she'd lied to him ruin that?

Taking a deep breath, Nicole opened the door and walked in to meet her fate. She saw him pacing in front of the mantel.

Hearing her entrance, Holt stopped, turning slowly to see her. Dressed in an elegant brown suit, he looked more beautiful than ever, so handsome and masculine, he took her breath away. He'd brushed his dark hair back off his face. His gold-green eyes mesmerized as always. As soon as their gazes met, a slow sensuous smile formed on his lips.

"Bacchi."

Before she could answer his soft call, his eyes drifted down her body and he frowned. A shiver of trepidation slipped through her and she folded her arms in front of herself trying to conceal the rounded stomach she hoped the furbelow skirts successfully hid. With a puzzled expression on his face, he stepped toward her.

"You look . . . different," he said.

I feel enormous. Nicole bit her lip to stop herself from blurting out her condition before he guessed. She followed him with her eyes as he approached. He stopped directly in front of her, so close she could smell the faint scent of sandalwood.

"You look . . ." He reached out with his hand and

placed a warm palm against her cheek. She knew there was a fullness to her face he'd never seen before. Holding her breath, she watched Holt stare at her, his dark brows knitted together as his clever eyes took in every curve, every line, seeming to miss nothing. Diverted by his watchful eyes, she started when she felt his hand press against her stomach where it bulged slightly with their child.

The babe kicked. Holt's eyes flew open.

"You're pregnant."

Nicole looked away, not wanting to see the anger and betrayal she'd heard in his voice.

"You lied to me, Nicole. Dear God, how could you lie about my child?" He lifted her chin, forcing her to look at him. "Why, dammit? Tell me why?"

Nicky twisted out of his reach, hating his anger. What hurt even more was the pain and disbelief she'd seen on his face. He sounded as if he had not thought her capable of such perfidy.

"Of course, I lied," she told him defensively. "What was I suppose to say? Marry me, Holt. I'm expecting your child? Do the proper thing!"

She walked away, trying to put some distance between them. He dogged her steps, refusing to allow her an easy escape.

"That's right! You were supposed to tell the truth! That I fathered a child!"

She turned to face him. "So that duty would force you to make amends for our passion?"

"So I could do my duty, yes!"

"And what about your commitment to me?" Tears filled her eyes. "Do you think it was enough for me that you love our child." A soft choking sound escaped her lips and she added in a low voice, "And not its mother?"

Holt stared at Nicole in shock. "Is that what you thought, *bacchi*?" Suddenly, he understood what might have motivated her to lie and he blamed himself for the pain he saw so clearly on her face. "Dear God, Nicky, I didn't ask you to marry just out of duty. I—"

The door banged open. Marcus Marshall barged in leading with his rifle. Lifting the weapon to his shoulder he aimed it straight for Holt.

"Uncle Marc!" Nicole stepped in front of Holt, but he immediately set her aside, giving her uncle a clear target. "Are you insane, Uncle? Put that down this minute," she shouted.

"We got him now, Nick," he said with relish. "The bird's not flying the coop this time!"

Mrs. Tod, devoid of her widow's weeds, swept into the room. The lady immediately sighted Marshall and honed in. On her heels followed Lady Eldridge accompanied by a tall, distinguished-looking gentleman.

"Marcus!" shouted Mrs. Tod. "What are you doing!"

Holt watched the very woman who had once fainted at the sight of blood grab Marshall's gun with the finesse of an experienced markswoman and uncock the rifle.

"We've flushed him out, Lizzy. Give me back my gun! I'll not lose him now."

Wiping away her tears, Nicole turned away and sat down on the settee. Gesturing to the group that now filled the room, she said, "Let me introduce my family." Her voice sounded so dispirited it made Holt want to take her in his arms and console her despite the watchful eyes of her family. "My uncle, you know. The woman beside him, whom you knew as my chaperone, has recently become my uncle's bride. May I introduce, Mrs. Elizabeth Marshall." The older woman leaned the rifle against the wall and stepped to her husband's side. She gave Holt a nod while Marcus scowled at him. "My sister-in-law, Lady Eldridge, you've already spoken with. The man beside her, who looks thoroughly bored with these proceedings, but is in actuality giving you a top-to-bottom inspection, is the viscount, my brother."

"To think I actually offered you a reward for saving Nick," shouted Marcus. "Saving her! Ha!"

"Keane, please." Lady Eldridge pulled at the viscount's elbow. "This circus has gone on long enough. Can't you see we're upsetting Nicky?"

Damn straight Nicole was upset, Holt thought. He himself had just about all he could stand of the palpable condemnation in the room. In a booming voice, so that no one would miss his words, he said to Nicole, "Did you happen to mention to these *fine* people who seem to want my hide mounted in their trophy room that I asked you to marry me already? Before you ever left India? That you turned me down *flat!*"

Nicole's jaw dropped open. "Turned you down?" Holt almost smiled as he saw some of her spirit return with her anger. Better to have her spitting mad at him than sitting on the couch looking like her whole world were crumbling apart. "Asked me to . . . ? As I recall"—she stood, facing Holt—"your exact words were 'we should *do* something' on the possibility that I *could* be pregnant."

"Well if everyone could clear the room," he said, keeping his eyes on Nicole alone, "maybe this time I'll get the damn proposal right!"

Total silence followed his words. Everyone watched the couple by the settee. Finally, the viscount took his wife by the arm and led her toward the door. He gestured for his uncle to proceed him. "Let's give him a chance, shall we?" He watched Holt carefully. Holt nodded his head, letting the viscount know he intended to set things straight with Nicole. Eldridge returned the gesture and stepped with his wife from the room.

When the doors closed behind them and only Nicole and he remained in the salon, Holt placed his hands on her shoulders and pulled her toward him. She hesitated a moment but his insistent tug brought her almost close enough to kiss, which he was very tempted to do. She looked absolutely precious to him, endearing with her new round shape.

He wanted to hold her and tell her how much he loved her. But the wary expression on her face told him to talk first.

"Why did you come here, Holt?"

"I came here to ask you to marry me. And I had absolutely no idea that you were expecting my child when I left India so I don't want to hear a word about 'duty' and 'not loving you.' There is no other reason in the world that would bring me here, Nicole."

Her gold eyes widened. A tremulous smile followed. "You l-love me?"

Holt brought them together with a step and tilted her face up to his with his hands. "It's not the same since you left, *bacchi*. I wake up in the morning and I turn to pull you to me—but I find myself hugging only cold sheets. I have no one to laugh with." He stroked away a tear that slipped down her cheek. "No one to cry with. No one to hope with." He smiled. "I've grown to despise cold sheets. I love you, *bacchi*."

Nicole shook her head, as if not quite convinced. "I always believed you did, but then, when you let me leave . . . I thought perhaps something I did made you . . . made you change your mind."

"Dear God, *bacchi*." He pulled her into his embrace and hugged her, hoping the tightness of his grip could take away the uncertainty he'd seen in her lovely eyes. "I don't think I could ever stop loving you."

"Not even knowing I lied about the baby?" he heard her whisper.

"No, Nicole." He led her to the couch and sat down beside her. "Though it makes me madder than a hornet that you did, I know why you lied to me. You wanted me to marry you out of love, not out of any sense of duty."

She nodded her head, sniffing back her tears.

"If I had told you how I really felt at the palace, that I loved you and *wanted* very much to marry you, none of this would have happened. I know that Nicky. Now, I need *you* to understand. I want to tell you why I let you walk away from me in Udaipur."

"All right," she said in a shaky voice.

"I told you a little about my family, but I failed to say the most important part. When my father sent my mother and me to Boston after our bungalow burned down, he intended to join us within a year, as soon as he could finish out his commission. But year after year, there was always one more project, one more thing he wanted to do before he quit India for good. My mother never lost hope that he would return to us. In the end, he never did."

"Oh, Holt. I'm so sorry."

"Nicky. I thought I was just like him." He clasped her hands in his. "I thought that if I married you and promised to join you in England, or even followed you here, I wouldn't keep my commitment. That like my father, I'd return to India, giving you only empty promises to come back."

"But—"

He held his finger across her mouth. "Let me finish. Please."

She nodded, biting her lip as if to hold back her words.

"You see how much I thought I could hurt you if I asked you to wed? I thought I would abandon you. In my mind, the only way I could justify risking that was if *not* marrying you could cause you even greater harm. Do you understand, *bacchi*? If you were pregnant, I had no choice. I would never allow you to be ostracized by society, to let my child grow up a bastard. At the very least, my father gave me the protection of his name." Cupping her face in his hands, he said, "I convinced myself if you were pregnant *then* I could marry you." He shook his head slowly. "It was an excuse to do what I wanted to do all along."

"Oh, darling." She hugged him and Holt wrapped his arms around her, relishing the feel of her softness against him, the child she carried pressed between them.

"Remember when I told you that you had to face your

past before you could be whole?" he whispered. "That you had to open the cage to your fears and meet them head on? Before I left India, I followed my own advice. I went to my father's grave in Lucknow. I"—he pulled away from her so he could see her eyes—"I talked to him, in a way I'd never spoken to him when he was alive. I ended up shouting how I hated him for leaving my mother and me. I stood there yelling, waiting for this dead man to ask for my forgiveness so I could finally banish the past. And after a while, I don't know how long really, I heard a voice inside me say that it wasn't my father I had to forgive. It was me. You see, *bacchi*, I could never forgive my father until I learned how to forgive myself. I had to forgive myself for wanting my father's love and acceptance so much that I ignored my mother, who offered it to me freely. I had to find the courage to forgive myself for spending a lifetime trying to mimic him. But most of all, I had to forgive myself for going off to Mexico to war when my mother needed me most."

"But you told me you didn't even know she was sick. How could you blame yourself for that? You're nothing like your father," she said fiercely.

"I know that now." He smiled, hearing in her voice the faith she had in him. Faith he had just recently acquired. "At his grave I realized for the first time that I had rejected everything that was important to him. I hated war. I considered hunting for sport a useless slaughter. And after you left, I knew India wasn't enough for me. I wanted a wife, a family. I wanted you, *bacchi*. I would never abandon you or our child. And the only reason I didn't realize it sooner was because I was still kicking myself for letting my mother die without me."

"Holt, darling." She reached for him, crying inside for the man who had banished himself to a lonely life without love as punishment for his mother's death.

"I'm telling you this so you understand why I let you go, *bacchi*. It was unforgivable what I did to you, both the first time we made love, when I told you to marry Harrington, and the last time, when I forced you to leave India without me. Can you ever forgive me?"

Nicole flung herself into his arms. "Of course, I can, silly. If you'd only told me this before."

"Then you'll have me? You'll marry me?"

Nicole pulled away watching him carefully. He looked so expectant, almost worried about her answer. She smiled. "Holt, I've just spent the last months preparing to come back to live in India and convince you of all the things you've just said!"

He kissed her, telling her with his mouth and his hands that their passion would only grow with time. When he pulled away, Holt put both his hands on her stomach and smiled as the baby moved beneath his palms.

"There's no need to go back to India," he said. "I'm making arrangements for a teaching position at Oxford. I have a friend there who will help—"

Nicole held her hand to his lips. She shook her head. "I'm not your mother, Holt. No more than you are your father. I won't perish like a Boston hothouse rose in the Indian forest. I have the blood of Rajput royalty." She held her chin up and then smiled. "I want to return to India . . . I want . . . I *need*, our child to know about its ancestry, not to grow up ignorant of it as I did. I want to go back."

"You mean it, *bacchi*?"

"Of course."

He frowned, watching her carefully. "It's hard to believe you would give up all this"—he looked around the elegantly furnished room—"and live in some bungalow in the wilds. Nicky, are you sure you know what you're doing? It doesn't make a lot of sense, leaving a secure life for the Indian jungle. Anyone would tell you—"

"I'm not just anyone. Holt, you're talking about convention. The rules by which others choose to live their lives." She smiled. "Don't you know? Why you told me yourself, my love." She wrapped her arms around his neck. "Those rules . . ." She watched Holt smile and lean down toward her.

  ". . . don't apply to us," they whispered together as they kissed.

Epilogue

The Kumaon Hills: 1863.

Nicole stared up the side of the hill, too exhausted to take another step. She sat down on the grass, refusing to budge unless Holt was willing to carry her as well as Damien on his sturdy shoulders. A little ahead, she watched her husband and their son, Damien Marcus Atley. With dark hair and green eyes, the toddler was a perfect reflection of his father, right down to the lemur, Jani, perched on his shoulders. She held her hand to her abdomen. Perhaps this one would be a girl.

Noticing that Nicole was no longer following directly behind him, Holt turned and smiled. "Come on, *bacchi.*"

"Come on, *Maji*!" Damien shouted with a wave from atop his father's shoulders, mimicking Holt in a way that always made Nicole smile.

"Gentlemen, I'm not moving one more inch."

Holt jogged down to Nicole, then lowered Damien to her side. "It's not far now. You want to see don't you?"

"But we hike up these hills every day and she hasn't come out once," Nicole complained.

"She's been in seclusion seven weeks. She's sure to come out any day now. Come now, *bacchi*. Remember? We're making sure that something unique . . ."

". . . and wonderful is preserved," she finished for him. "All right, all right." She stood, then looked up to the crest of the hill as if it were the Nana Devi of the Himalayas.

"What's the matter, *Ma*?" Damien placed a hand on her trousers. Even the ringtail lemur watched her with sympathetic eyes from her son's shoulder.

Holt pressed his palm to her stomach. "Are you feeling all right? Should we stop for today?"

From half-closed eyes, she could see the disappointment on both Holt's and Damien's faces at the thought of missing the important outing. Forcing herself forward, she said, "No. I wanted to marry a field biologist. I shall keep up with my end."

Holt smiled. "That's the spirit, *bacchi*."

Together the three climbed up the rolling hillside, until Holt told them all to stay quietly behind. Soon enough, he returned and they crept through the tall elephant grass to the bottom of a cliff. He raised his field glasses and smiled, then handed them to Nicole. Holding Damien still, Holt whispered in the boy's ear to remain silent. Nicole raised the glasses up to where Holt pointed.

At the top of the ridge she saw Enchantress with her new family. This was the first time she'd come out of seclusion since the birth of the cubs. Just last summer, she'd let her two-year-old tiger cubs go off on their own, and now, like Nicole, she was starting over. As the cubs frolicked, Nicole watched and waited. She spotted one, then two yellow cubs. When Enchantress moved to the side, Nicky saw what had brought such an enormous smile to her husband's lips.

There, cuddling next to his mother was one white tiger cub.

She dropped the glasses and looked at Holt. "Oh darling, she did it." She hugged Holt and he twirled her around, Damien dancing around them with Jani. Holt held her in his arms, and they both sat down on the grass. Damien nestled between them with Jani, and they shared the glasses back and forth, watching Enchantress and her family as they explained the significance of the new birth to their son. Their wait was over.

The white tigers lived on.

Author's Note
and Acknowledgments

Holt Atley was a good deal ahead of his time. It wasn't until the twentieth century that the first sportsmen gave up their rifles to become naturalists. Noted hunters in the 1930s bragged of "bagging" anywhere from one hundred tigers in their lifetime to over a thousand. The popular sport of *shikar,* as well as destruction of habitat, reduced the tiger population from forty thousand at the turn of the century to less than two thousand by the 1970s. Today, thanks to conservation efforts such as Project Tiger, the Indian tiger has made a dramatic comeback on reserves.

The white tiger, however, no longer exists outside captivity. The fate of this lovely and majestic creature lies in the hands of breeding programs. Mohini, nicknamed "Enchantress" by the staff of the National Zoological Park who retrieved her from India in 1960, was the first white tiger brought to the United States. Many white tigers today are descendants of her father, Mohan.

Three species of tiger are already extinct, the Caspian, Javan, and Balinese. Some say that the white tiger should be allowed to die out as well because it would be naturally extinct but for man's intervention. But I cannot help but believe, like Holt, that such a beautiful creature deserves to be nurtured. What a shame it would be if the white tiger joined the ranks of animals that we can show our children only through pictures.

* * *

Those of you who read my first book, *By My Heart Betrayed* (the story of Nicole's brother, Keane Marshall, Viscount Eldridge, and his wife, Esmeralda), will remember that Keane would not reveal his mysterious ancestry. Esmeralda guessed he was a Gypsy. She wasn't far off. Some theorists believe that the Rom, or Gypsy, originated from the Doms in India.

I would like to thank the many people who provided the information I needed to write *White Tiger:* the staff at the Arcadia Library, who brought the foothills of the Himalayas to me since I couldn't go there myself; my gun experts, Larry Martin, James Cohen, and the wonderful people at The Flintlock; David Lofgren at the Arboreta and Botanic Gardens; and Geeta Kakade, a fellow writer who shared not only her fascinating culture, but her time as well.

A very special thanks goes to Greg Lee for all his helpful information about tigers and for introducing me to Samson, a gorgeous white tiger. Greg, you and Marine World Africa USA, Vallejo, California, gave me the opportunity to see one of my characters in real life. Not many authors get that chance. A heartfelt "thank you!"

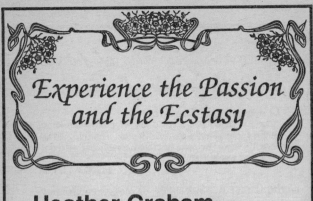

Experience the Passion and the Ecstasy

Heather Graham

☐ 20235-3 Sweet Savage Eden $3.95

☐ 11740-2 Devil's Mistress $4.95

Meagan McKinney

☐ 16412-5 No Choice But
                Surrender $4.99

☐ 20301-5 My Wicked
                Enchantress $4.99

☐ 20521-2 When Angels Fall $4.99